In a dodgy clu[ ] was hiding in plain sight.

The punk rock beat ricocheted roughshod through every cell in her body, and her heart rate accelerated to match its driving tempo. Drums pounded and electric guitars wailed in riffs so angry she could taste rebellion in her parched mouth. A kaleidoscope of purple-hued beams swirled around the club stage like warring light sabers. The mosh pit throbbed in time with the beat, and the crowd melded into a sweaty, pulsing amoeba which seeped into the bar area.

Noise crackled through her brain in quarter-time rhythm, crowding out everything else. Spilled beer coated the floor, adding a fresh, sticky layer of grime to ancient wood. The dance floor shook like an anarchist uprising, thundering vocals approaching primal screams. She needed this to forget.

As senior vice president of Kingsley Tech, she relished her anonymity here, far from the techies, investors, and sensibly dressed Londoners who populated the cybersecurity world. She'd spent the last year running from grief, circling the globe until her passport overflowed with stamps: Tokyo, Bengaluru, Seattle, Berlin. No matter—the loss always caught her.

The Unexpected Hostage

by

Allison McKenzie

The Unexpected Hostage

Cover Art by *Kristian Norris*

The Wild Rose Press, Inc.
PO Box 708
Adams Basin, NY 14410-0708
Visit us at www.thewildrosepress.com

Publishing History
First Edition, 2023
Trade Paperback ISBN 978-1-5092-4983-1
Digital ISBN 978-1-5092-4984-8

Published in the United States of America

Dedication

To all those who have suffered loss: may you find the strength to survive it and the courage to start again.

Chapter One

Summoned

In a dodgy club in North London, Tess Bennett was hiding in plain sight.

The punk rock beat ricocheted roughshod through every cell in her body, and her heart rate accelerated to match its driving tempo. Drums pounded and electric guitars wailed in riffs so angry she could taste rebellion in her parched mouth. A kaleidoscope of purple-hued beams swirled around the club stage like warring light sabers. The mosh pit throbbed in time with the beat, and the crowd melded into a sweaty, pulsing amoeba which seeped into the bar area.

Noise crackled through her brain in quarter-time rhythm, crowding out everything else. Spilled beer coated the floor, adding a fresh, sticky layer of grime to ancient wood. The dance floor shook like an anarchist uprising, thundering vocals approaching primal screams. She needed this to forget.

As senior vice president of Kingsley Tech, she relished her anonymity here, far from the techies, investors, and sensibly dressed Londoners who populated the cybersecurity world. She'd spent the last year running from grief, circling the globe until her passport overflowed with stamps: Tokyo, Bengaluru, Seattle, Berlin. No matter—the loss always caught her.

This club was the one place loud enough to block out her grief and shake her back to life.

Tomorrow marked one year. Somehow, she'd survived a full journey around the sun without her fiancé, Kyle. A car accident. *Instant.* Upon impact, the police had said, like those facts would console her. They didn't. Around her, the club-goers rocked and swayed like a wheat field bending in a windstorm. With their feet planted on the ground, they waved their arms back and forth. The crush of revelers failed to cure her loneliness.

Someone tossed a pitcher of water over the dance floor, splashing dancers alongside the stage. Frenzied howls erupted. Sweat dripped down her cheeks, and she pumped her hands in the air, pulsating with the crowd while the song bulldozed to a deafening climax. *Obliterate my every thought. Make this pain stop.*

Before the song ended in a crash of drums, Tess snaked her way to the bar. She squeezed into a small opening with her elbows to stake her spot in the queue. The barkeep's Mohawk spikes formed a line of neon-green swords, which were outnumbered by the metal piercings adorning his face. His tattooed arms strained his tight gray T-shirt, emblazoned *Torque.*

The barkeep ogled her Goth outfit. Tonight, she sported tight leather jeans with a lace-up corset layered over a sheer mesh top. A metal-studded dog collar and heavy rock-star makeup completed her ensemble. Except for her perfect pink nails, an aura of angst surrounded her. Here, she allowed herself to surrender to the darkness she carried every day, even wallow in it, without apology.

"Double vodka, right, bird?" he asked in a thick

Cockney accent.

The subwoofer thumped so loud it drowned out her own heartbeat. "Make it strong."

"What's your name, American Goth chick?"

"Jinx." Happy to abandon her corporate persona for the night, she embraced the freedom of nothing left to lose—no past, no future, just the present. She surveyed the swarming mosh pit while he poured her cocktail.

"Right. *Jinx*. You've been here before." His metal-laden eyebrows rose at her lie. After he slid her drink across the bar, he leaned toward her. "I know a guy who's got snow, ecstasy, anything you want. Interested?"

She drained her glass in one sip and, judging the vodka's curative powers lacking, slammed the glass onto the counter. A dizzying array of bad choices enticed her toward recklessness. No one at work would ever find out. In the morning, she would depart for Paris to spend the weekend with her best friend, Sophie.

"If you want, talk to Frankie, the bloke in the red leather jacket, by the door. Discreet." The barkeep polished a pint glass with a white, terry cloth towel.

She glanced over at the pock-faced man with a shaved head and wondered how many people he'd led straight to addiction, like innocent sheep to slaughter. While the devastation of losing Kyle eroded her sanity at times, she wanted to survive. Perhaps someday the grief would lift, although tonight she couldn't imagine a future free from the weight of loss. "No. Just make it a double, please."

"This one's on me." The bartender poured her third vodka tonic and winked. "You fancy partying, bird?

I'm off at two."

He couldn't be further from her type, and the odds she'd go home with a stranger ranged somewhere around one in three trillion. Still needing to numb her grief, she accepted the drink and downed it. Her phone vibrated against her hip, interrupting her train of thought. The familiar pulsing sequence meant one thing: work. "Give me a minute."

Digging into her leather pants pocket, she withdrew her slim satellite phone, grateful for the convenient interruption. The screen flashed the time, almost two in the morning, before displaying David Kingsley's text message.

—*Stuck in Berlin. Need u to lead Timberline security summit for me. Tilly booked u next BA flight to YVR. Potential $20-30 million in venture capital if u convince Bouchard to go with us for medical acquisition. Sorry to ruin your Paris weekend.*—

Without hesitation, she typed rapid-fire on her screen.

—*On my way.*—

The bartender had already placed another drink on the counter.

"Water, please." She pushed the fourth cocktail away. Jarred back to reality, she stretched taller in her combat boots, determined to claw back some equilibrium. The barkeep handed her a huge glass of water, and she gulped it, resolving to leave before temptation and bad judgment took over.

Another text alert appeared.

—*Eastern European security officials report a dramatic surge in attempted network attacks this week. Threat level elevated to orange.*—

Work would be slammed for a week, and this Canadian summit alone would burn three days. While she'd enjoy a Paris weekend with Sophie more, any distraction helped blunt the loss she couldn't bear: Kyle was dead.

"What do you say, Jinx?" The barkeep's neon-green Mohawk glowed in the dim light.

His words barely registered. Instead, she saw the rain-slicked road east of London, brakes screeching. Wooden guardrails breaking. Kyle's European sedan plunging over the high cliff, crashing into the water below. *Icy water, then nothing*. A sudden chill crept up her spine. She swallowed the lump in her throat and tucked an errant strand of hair behind her ear before meeting his overt stare. "Sorry, I've got a flight to catch."

Chapter Two

A Party Begins

The Timberline Ventures welcome party had already started by the time Tess's chauffeured sedan reached the final stretch of highway leading to the Cedarcliff retreat center, north of Vancouver. Harsh weather had delayed her flight from London, and her triple espresso wasn't working fast enough. Sitting in the back seat, her body cradled by the contoured, deep leather seats, she steeled herself for the meetings ahead. She hoped tonight's party and the weekend negotiations would engage her full attention, and, if not, at least offer an open bar.

After Kingsley Tech's new encryption technology skyrocketed in popularity last year, David often relied upon her to represent him at executive events around the globe. Canada marked the seventh country she visited this month, and she hadn't seen the condo she recently purchased in Seattle for weeks. Born into nomadism as a US State Department brat, she'd grown up in a series of embassy communities around the world. Now, a postmodern road warrior, she sped across continents, languages, and currencies with grace—comfortable everywhere, but belonging nowhere.

Memories of Kyle invaded her consciousness, but

she resisted getting sidetracked. She double-checked her jacket pocket, grazing her fingers over the fine-woven wool, reassured she transferred her security kit from her suitcase. A paranoid precaution, but one she required for every trip she took.

The Cedarcliff event venue came into view. Fishing through the conference packet a courier had hand delivered before her flight, she glanced at the identification badge and cursed. The organizers had given her David's. She threw it around her neck anyhow, annoyed she'd need to waste time getting it fixed. With one hand, she buttoned her Italian wool suit jacket and swept her hair off her face. Jet-lagged, she forced a smile and hoped her mouth's upturned corners suggested enough positivity to veil her sadness.

The sedan hurtled to a stop on the gravel road. Stepping out of the car into the crisp evening, she stole a few extra seconds outside to marvel at the moonlit mountains as a chilly wind nipped at her cheeks. Constellations burned like fire above her in the late autumn sky. She relished the fresh outdoor air and savored her last moments of freedom before jumping into the executive meet-and-greet.

George Bouchard, chairperson of Timberline Ventures, was the decision maker whose blessing she needed to secure more funding in David's absence. Schmooze or lose. Smoothing the wrinkles from her trim pantsuit, she counted the hours until she could trade the suit for fuzzy sweatpants. An inexplicable flash of foreboding washed over her, which she wrote off as fatigue. Determined to shake off her sleeping-pill haze, she straightened her shoulders and stretched her toes against the tips of her black suede boots. "Please let this be entertaining."

Tess followed the lights leading to the entrance of the wood-clad building, an architectural showcase of Northwestern flair. Floor-to-ceiling windows graced the spacious foyer, and she passed an imposing fountain built into an Asian sculpture cast in bronze. Streaming water gurgled down its smooth sides like a forest creek. The door opened, warm air flowed against her face, and peppy jazz piped through the speaker system, creating a festive vibe.

Cocktail glasses clinked and voices buzzed, reflecting the upbeat mood of the room. Groups of men in their thirties and forties led spirited conversations. Venture capitalists decked out in crisp suits and designer shirts mingled with engineering execs, who skewed younger and preferred uniforms of cashmere hoodies and expensive sneakers. She chose a glass of chardonnay from the bar and lifted it to sniff the bouquet of apples mixed with fresh-cut oak. With luck, the drink would wash away the remnants of last night's excesses and give her a clean slate. She shifted into work mode and prioritized which execs to chat up before she approached Bouchard.

The drinks flowed, and the chatter grew livelier in equal measure. Catering servers garbed in black offered salmon rillettes and beef satays on silver platters seeming to float above their hands. Executive perks. She accepted a shrimp canapé and savored the tangy mango sauce as it hit her tongue.

Her colleague Kavita Chakyar, dressed in a colorful orange and yellow sari, sauntered her way, and the women touched wine glasses.

"About time a vice president showed up. Cutting it

close, aren't you?" Over the rim of her glass, Kavita admonished her with a smirk.

"David's keynote in Berlin got delayed, so I raced across the pond to lead this." Despite having little patience for her underling's attitude, Tess suppressed her annoyance. As she scanned the perimeter of the room, she detected something missing. "Pretty light on security tonight, aren't they? No guards at the entry here."

"Now you mention it, you're right. Then again, this retreat building is remote, many kilometers from the main hotel. Besides, we're in Canada, and nothing happens here." Kavita sipped her drink.

"Right." Tess refocused on the meetings ahead. "Let's be clear about the stakes this weekend. If Bouchard approves our security strategy for this health care network he's acquiring, we could net substantial funding. You ready?"

"When am I not?" Kavita pursed her lips.

Tess stepped closer and lowered her voice. "Remember, it's not just this deal. If we expand our software market from banks into healthcare, our company could double or triple in size. Our stock could go public."

"I'm prepared, Tess, so get on with it."

"Since you're presenting our encryption technology to the investors first thing tomorrow, I convinced Riku to endorse your plan as the best one available. You're welcome." She leaned back, satisfied to have surprised Kavita. The tech industry touted Riku Yamashita as the father of cybersecurity and a pinnacle of integrity. Companies he endorsed often entered the stock market with stratospheric initial public offerings.

"Well done. I owe you one. How many millions are we talking?" Kavita's criticism abated several notches.

"Twenty to thirty. Enough to fund our expansion into the US." Restless, she bounced her foot, alert now her airport caffeine binge had kicked in.

Already perched on stilettos, Kavita straightened up even taller, and her gaze widened. "Wow, so that's why all the heavy hitters are here. Kieran Hughes from Timberline is attending, too. We'll see if the bloke codes as well as he used to play pro rugby. Hey, what's on your arm?"

The *Torque* ink stamp smudged Tess's pale wrist like a blurry tattoo. She adjusted her silk blouse cuff to cover it, the fabric cool against her skin. "Nothing."

Smiling through bared teeth, Kavita shook her head as she edged closer to Tess. "Millions at stake and you spent the night clubbing? Given you were too *busy* to prepare, David should have asked me to lead this."

"No time to bicker. I need to sync with Riku before I meet Bouchard." Biting her tongue, she chose to ignore Kavita's insubordination, for now.

As Tess stepped away to check her text messages, a *No Service* alert buzzed on her phone. The building's remote location meant they were stuck in a cellular dead zone. Searching the room, she found Riku strolling away from the bar, full glass in hand. She waved hello to catch his attention, and his face lit up with recognition. She bowed. "Riku-san, pleasure to see you."

He welcomed her by grasping her hand with both of his. "I understand you're David's acting CEO this weekend. He's lucky you're his number two."

Riku had invested years coaching Tess and David

on bolstering Kingsley Tech's rapid expansion, providing strategic industry insights and, when needed, infusions of cash to accelerate their growth. "Thanks. We'll develop a solid security strategy for George Bouchard, and he'll be able to complete his medical network acquisition. David hinted Timberline might offer us more funding." She offered him a sincere smile.

"Quite a coup for you to expand Kingsley Tech's realm from finance to include healthcare," Riku responded with a wink. "Bouchard's got more money than you think, but you'd better expect a serious grilling in tomorrow's exec review. If you nail it, you'll get his blessing and his funding."

Shit. Her attention sparked at his secret intel. A muscle in her cheek twitched, and she curled her fingernail tips into her palm to focus. Rather than spending her outbound flight working like usual, she had downed a hefty dose of sleeping pills to doze away the vodka at Torque. "I'm ready. Timberline will be our priority, and Bouchard's deal can proceed without delay. Kavita's engineering team streamlined the deployment process for our encryption tools, so we can move fast."

A flash of solemnity crossed Riku's face as he sipped whiskey from a crystal glass. "Kyle's encryption genius catapulted Kingsley Tech to lead the industry. His death was such a terrible loss."

"One year ago, today." Her mind fell blank, like a television flicking off, and she raised a hand to her neck to touch the gold Celtic amulet she never removed. Tension gripped her shoulders, and she took an ample sip of chardonnay. *Icy water, then nothing.*

Riku's smile faded, and with a deep sigh, he stepped closer and touched her shoulder. "I share your sorrow, but we must tackle urgent challenges. New terrorist groups are springing up all the time, and now we've got urgent threats in the financial sector."

The kind words about Kyle soothed her, and the fact Riku didn't dwell on it prevented her from plunging into a well of grief. Back on task, she cleared her throat and focused on work. "The cyber war never ends. Are you referring to the heightened activity in Eastern Europe?"

Riku folded his arms over his chest, and not a single wrinkle marred his crisp, white business shirt. "Indeed, but long-term, the actual threat is worse and far-reaching. Kingsley Tech possesses keys not to one castle, but many. Soon, the hacker world will discover its power and seek to conquer it. The more successful you become, the more your vulnerabilities increase."

Given Riku navigated by logic and not paranoia, she felt her uneasiness climbing several notches. Something malevolent brewed under the surface of this discussion. "What are you getting at?"

"Should one hacker obtain Kyle's original code and reverse engineer it, they could breach multiple banks, not just one. It wouldn't be one bank which falls. Entire financial systems could collapse in a moment, taking governments down with them." Riku regarded her over his wire-rimmed glasses.

The high stakes didn't scare her, and she remained resolute. "Remember, we've built ironclad contingency plans against hackers. Declan O'Leary obsesses over protecting our network perimeter. Kyle's technology would never fall into the wrong hands."

Riku tilted his head and shifted his weight from one foot to the other. "Well, Declan's a brilliant engineer, but not every attack can be fought with software code. Politics and allegiances matter more now, and breaches are growing harder to detect before extensive damage is done."

The party music grew decibels louder. Boisterous conversations and pockets of laughter reverberated through the room, but she ignored them. Various worst-case scenarios cycled through her mind, and she steered Riku away from the blasting speakers. "Be straight with me, Riku-san. Are we facing a specific, credible threat?"

Riku gave a tight-lipped nod and leaned his back against the nearby wall. He glanced both ways before speaking. "Dark web chatter escalated overnight. You, David, and I must meet somewhere secure Sunday. We can't discuss it here."

All the lights went out, and the music stopped. Multiple guests called out for someone to turn on the lights.

Audio and lighting mishaps weren't unusual at event venues. Given the high elevation and rugged mountains, she wondered if the wind had kicked up and knocked out a generator. Pursing her lips, she exhaled her aggravation. If the power outage proved to be a ridiculous leadership exercise, one which threw execs into a crisis, then used external consultants to evaluate their ability to resolve it, she'd be furious.

People began moving toward the lighted foyer and stumbled into each other along the way. Mumbles of confusion grew louder. The doors to the service kitchen clacked open, and a mass of silhouettes charged into the event space.

Gunshots blasted across the room. Tess's body startled, then clenched at the unmistakable popping sound. *No, no, no, not this.* As shrieks erupted and panic spread across the room, she spun to search for the gunfire's source. Chunks of the ceiling fell where the torrent of bullets hit, covering the guests in ghostly white rubble. Silver platters of savory mini-quiches and baked brie clattered to the marble floor in a quick series of crashes.

Her heart raced, and she grabbed Riku's arm and propelled him toward the green exit sign above the nearest door.

"Quiet! Hands up, no moving," one of the shadows shouted in a heavy accent.

The guttural voice sounded Slavic, perhaps Russian. Tess stopped abruptly, but her face tingled like she was falling from an airplane with wind whipping against her skin.

Several flashlights switched on in rapid succession and blinded sections of the room. The light above the bar reappeared, revealing a cluster of men wearing black military uniforms and toting large rifles.

As the Cedarcliff guests reeled from the shots, the apparent leader of the gunmen stepped forward, a clean-shaven, compact man with a hint of a port-wine stain peeking above his collar. He pointed a loaded assault rifle at individual guests in the room while he spoke. "Now, listen. We shoot anyone who moves. No phones. We've blocked all cellular signals. No help is coming."

Three words echoed through her brain: run, hide, fight. She scanned the room's exits for escape routes but found none. Nowhere to take cover, either. She had no move, not yet.

"No moving, everybody understand?" The leader surveyed the crowd, who held their hands up. He swung his rifle in a smooth, practiced arc, including all the guests in his target range. After several seconds, he lowered the rifle.

The remaining gunmen fanned out and encircled the group. They stood with their guns raised, ready to fire should anyone be foolish enough to disobey.

"I want David Kingsley. Now," the leader demanded.

The guests froze, not responding.

David. An electric shock jolted through her body, and her lungs mashed tight against her ribs. What did they think her CEO could give them?

The party guests regarded each other, frowning. "He's not here," an American man said.

"We haven't seen David," a Canadian man added.

The leader frowned and gestured one gunman aside, a lanky young man with a dark beard and almond-shaped brown eyes. "Dmitry, you said Kingsley arrived an hour ago," he said in hushed English.

"I hacked the hotel computer myself, Yuri. Checked in at six thirty," the young man replied.

"Where is he?" Yuri hissed.

Tess overheard their argument and remembered she'd used David's reservation to check into the hotel. With no time to waste, she'd left her bag at the front desk, then jumped back into the chauffeured car and drove straight to the retreat building, a couple of miles down the twisty mountain road. Unnerved, she couldn't stop her lower lip from quivering, and her palms grew damp. The realization struck her like a boulder: *I am David.*

Beside her, Riku stood mere inches away, and, like all the guests in the room, held his hands up, motionless. One hand still clutched his whiskey glass, and his forehead beaded with sweat.

Shock threatened to take her over, and she braced herself in defense. Weren't assault weapons banned here? Canada was supposed to be safe. In her peripheral vision, she glimpsed Riku's hand shaking.

Something crashed near her. The crystal tumbler in Riku's hand shattered, sending an explosion of glass shards across the slick marble tile. Three gunshots followed, and screams burst out across the room. Her legs buckled underneath her, and she slammed onto her kneecaps and face-planted with a thud on the ground.

Ears ringing from the gunfire, she crawled onto her hands and knees to check on Riku, who had fallen. Blood oozed across the front of his crisp white shirt in a spreading red stain. "He's been shot!" she cried.

When she bent over Riku to comfort him, her satellite phone bounced out of her pocket and landed in a puddle of blood. Something warm seeped onto her blouse, and her nose burned with the acrid smell of gunpowder.

The surrounding guests scattered away, forming an invisible perimeter to distance themselves from the bloody mess. "Sergey, *chto zhe ty sdelal?*" Several yards away, the leader, Yuri, yelled at the shooter, Sergey.

"*Eto byl neschastnyy sluchay,*" Sergey yelled back.

"*Slishkom pozdno, idiot.*" Beet-red splotches surfaced on Yuri's face, and he shook his fist.

Above the room, a massive glass chandelier creaked, then dropped from the ceiling and hit several guests as it plummeted to the ground. Mayhem ensued.

Ignoring the argument and the commotion, she scanned the guests around her for any possible aid, but no one moved. "We need help over here. *Now*."

Wetness brushed her torso, and seconds passed before she registered Riku's blood covered her blouse. She choked back nausea and tried not to faint. Her hands twinged with nerves poking like sharp needles lodged in her skin. She could not, would not, let her mentor die in front of her. Patience gone, she leapt to her feet. "Goddamn it. He's bleeding out. Help!" she shouted at the top of her lungs.

Across the room, an athletic man with short, dark blond hair stepped forward with his hands up. "I'm a doctor." Calm, yet imbued with command, he spoke with a hint of an English accent. Dressed in a refined charcoal suit with a rich, cobalt shirt that intensified his blue eyes, he gestured at the bleeding man on the ground.

Yuri paused his verbal assault of his trigger-happy shooter and faced the doctor. Scowling, he appeared to size up the blond man, who had raised his hands in surrender. "Whatever. He won't live." With a shrug, he lowered his gun, waved the doctor over to the fallen, bleeding man, then returned to his gunmen.

The doctor crossed the room with silent footsteps, quick and effortless. He dodged the overturned tables and the ceiling rubble littering the ground. Peeling off his suit jacket, he tossed it down before kneeling on the bloody floor next to Riku and across from her.

"His name is Riku-san. I'm Tess. He can't die.

17

Please don't let him die." Her words tumbled out in a rush, and she leaned back to give the doctor space to examine Riku's injuries. Agitated, her senses sharpened into hyperalert focus. Nothing else mattered now but Riku and whether this man could help.

He gave her a cursory nod and started work on Riku's torn-up chest. His expression revealed no shock at the carnage before him, and he maintained steady eye contact with Riku. "My name is Mark. First, slow your breathing down."

With visible effort, Riku managed to gurgle a response. "*Arigatō*. Yes."

"Slow breaths while I examine you." Mark ripped open Riku's bloody white shirt with a decisive tear and inserted his bare hands into the pool of blood. After he uncovered the ragged hole of the bullet's entry point, he checked Riku's pulse and frowned. "Weak and thready."

Rolling the man to one side, he appeared to search for an exit wound on his back, but Riku's shirt was clean. He leapt up and grabbed a pile of white napkins from the nearest bar table and packed the source of the hemorrhaging, leaning on his hands to exert steady pressure. "Keep breathing, nice and slow."

If the terrorists planned to kill them, Tess resolved to spend her last moments comforting Riku, not cowering in fear. After Riku's many years of mentorship, comfort fell far short of the one thing she wanted to offer him but couldn't—survival. His blood now soaked through the knees of her pants, but she emulated Mark's professional demeanor and spoke in a soothing tone. "Hang on, Riku. I'm right here, by your side."

Ignoring the one gunman hovering behind them, she focused on Mark's hands and how they worked in smooth, practiced patterns. Despite abandoning religion years ago, desperation prevailed, and she prayed this doctor could keep Riku alive long enough to get him to a hospital. At first, she took him for a Brit, but his direct formality suggested a dash of Germanic or Scandinavian roots instead. His eyes were sapphire, the deepest blue she'd ever seen, and his chiseled jaw remained tight and unmoving, set deep in concentration.

Despite the chaos, Mark didn't appear bothered by the loaded assault weapons near him, nor did he act intimidated by their assailants. He reversed his hands to put his left hand over his right, revealing a gnarled purple scar twisting across the entire back of his hand. As he attempted to curl his left fingers around the bloody napkins, he let out an involuntary groan of pain.

The marked break in his composure caught her attention. "How can I help you?"

"I need a big plastic bag," Without moving, Mark stayed focused on Riku's wound, but his scarred hand trembled. He kept pressure on the wound but lowered his chin down to his chest, took a deep breath, then adjusted his right hand to stabilize his left side.

Alerted by her sudden movement, the gunmen's weapons aimed in her direction in unison.

Her heart rattled, and she raised her hands above her head. "We need a bag. May I go to the bar to find one?"

The gunmen awaited Yuri's approval before lowering their guns and allowing her to proceed.

Debris covered the floor, and she sidestepped silver

platters and broken tiles to make her way to the bar counter. Glasses, limes, and booze lined the shelf. She opened drawers at random and rifled through their contents until she uncovered an empty ice sack. Tiptoeing back, she knelt and handed it to Mark.

"Thanks." With a table knife, he cut out a square from the bag as Riku gasped for air. Mark directed a glare at Yuri. "We need a hospital. He needs surgery."

"No." Striding toward them, Yuri traipsed over the red-stained marble floor.

Crouched low, Tess cringed as she watched the assassin tread through pools of Riku's blood as if they were rain puddles of no consequence.

"That wasn't a question." Anger flared in Mark's voice, and crimson flooded his cheeks. While keeping pressure on the wound with his right hand, he straightened his back, and his muscular shoulders strained against his dress shirt, now smeared dark red. Glowering, he spun to growl at Yuri. "He'll die if we don't get him to a hospital now."

"No." The silver cross around the gunman's neck glinted in the light.

Another gunman appeared with a first aid kit from the catering kitchen and handed it to Mark.

The box contained three gauze bandages, each smaller than a passport, laughably inadequate.

Mark fumed but dumped the gauze into the open crater of Riku's chest and gestured. "I need to pack this, so apply pressure with both your hands."

She nodded, but after studying the gory injury splitting open Riku's torso, she recoiled. Wincing, she gathered her courage and placed her hands on the warm wound. Blood seeped over her skin.

Riku moaned.

Nauseous, Tess trembled.

Mark tossed away the blood-sopped cloths, then added the plastic square along with more napkins. "I'll take over applying pressure now."

He slid his hands under hers, his fingers warm on hers for a moment, and released her from the task. Seconds ticked by, and while no miracle materialized, a world without Riku didn't compute, either. Torn apart by the scene unfolding before her, Tess grasped for any shred of hope. "Stay with us, Riku. Hang on."

"Marie. Tell my wife I love her." Sucking sounds emitted from his chest with each word he whispered. Blood saturated the fresh gauze in seconds.

Please don't let him die. She snuck a glance at Mark but couldn't voice the question. Watching the doctor for clues, she felt her hope sink when his mouth tightened into a straight line.

He gave a solemn, slight shake of his head.

"Riku, tell me about Marie." She strained to prevent her voice from wavering.

A faint smile appeared on Riku's pale lips, but his labored breathing grew irregular. "She is my sunlight." One gasp, then nothing. His face smoothed, no longer contorted with pain.

Mark bent forward and placed two fingers on Riku's neck. Shaking his head, he withdrew his hand and sat back on his heels. "I'm sorry. He's gone."

This can't be happening. Her world cracked open with a sonic boom, loud in her ears although the room remained hushed. Still holding her mentor's limp hand, she stiffened and felt a dull numbness set in. Too stunned to cry, she couldn't find any words at all, not even to thank this stranger for risking his life to intervene.

"Stay strong. We'll get through this." Mark leaned forward and touched her arm.

The firm command in his voice reassured her, despite the chaos which unfolded in every direction around them. A faint whiff of sandalwood drifted her way, evoking the peacefulness of a pine forest after a rainstorm. Disoriented from shock and denial, she glimpsed his scarred hand and slumped her shoulders.

"Enough. We divide you up. Men this side, women over there. Hands up, and no phones, or we shoot. No talking." Yuri lifted his gun and signaled to his subordinates.

Shell-shocked guests covered in white dust, seemingly ghostlike, shuffled to their designated lines in complete obedience. Several had suffered bloody cuts from the fallen glass chandelier.

One gunman guarded the few women standing together, and the men flocked to the large group opposite them.

Tess joined Kavita next to the two female caterers. Dust from the shot-up ceiling coated Kavita's once-vibrant sari, and her golden-brown forearms bled. In horror, she exchanged a glance with her colleague but didn't speak.

"Men, line up, side by side. Go." Yuri doled out more orders.

As the male executives shuffled into a neat row stretching the room's length, Yuri inspected each man. He patrolled the line of pressed shirts and trousers, studying each face and touching the men's hair. Lingering over the white men, he skipped the Asian and

Indian men and read every conference badge. With a grunt, he stomped a foot and screened the row a second time, examining every man through his narrowed gaze.

"Where is Kingsley? He checked in an hour ago. Everyone on your knees." Yuri whipped out his rifle and shot at the ceiling.

The guests covered their ears, and a few screamed and cowered.

Yuri glared. "Tell me fast, or we start shooting. Men, check the badges."

The room grew silent again.

The gunmen scurried around the room, searching each man.

Glancing down, her heart dropped. David's badge hung from her neck lanyard, brushing against her opened jacket. Holding her breath, she checked both directions to ensure no one was watching while she flipped the badge over, so David's name faced her chest. She needed to get rid of it, but it was too late to rip off the badge and risk unwanted attention.

Yuri charged toward the group of women. "Show me your badges." He checked off Kavita and the caterers before he stopped in front of her.

Hands loose by her sides, she willed them to stop shaking. When he flipped her badge over, the lanyard tugged hard against her bare neck, like a noose tightening.

"David Kingsley? Why are you wearing his badge?" Yuri's eyebrows squished together, and he tapped his fist against his lips.

"They gave me the wrong one."

The gunman loomed over her. "What is your name and company?"

Instead of replying, she shrank from the huge rifle in his hands, curving her back to withdraw her torso farther from his rifle's point.

"Name and company?"

Silent, she stood on the jagged edge of a cliff, losing ground by the second.

"Fine." Yuri lunged to the left and yanked Kavita to her feet. With one arm braced around her, he jutted the tip of his rifle under her chin, and his face reddened.

"Name and company now, or she dies."

Tears streamed down Kavita's cheeks, and her chin shook.

No, no, please no. A sob clogged her throat, but she choked it back and tried to inhale. "Tess Bennett, Kingsley Tech."

"Title?"

"Senior vice president."

Glowering, Yuri raised his right hand, swung hard, and pummeled her left cheekbone with his fist.

A thwack sounded, followed by a sting of metal slicing into her cheek. She cried out and slumped to the floor. Warm blood dripped down her face, nauseating her. Figuring he must have worn a ring, she compressed a hand firmly against her cheek to stop the bleeding, and her fresh blood mixed with Riku's on her fingers.

Gasps sprung up from around the room, and everyone stared.

Across the room, she spotted a man built like a World War II tank, a foot taller than the other men. Body poised, he stood with his fists clenched, ready to attack. The red-haired engineer who played rugby, Kieran Hughes. She caught his attention in time and shook her head, hoping to dissuade him from tackling the gunman near him. A pained frown crossed his features.

Hughes tilted his head to one side, but his fists remained tight as he scanned the room.

"Tell us where Kingsley is. Don't lie, or I'll hit you harder." Yuri surveyed her.

Blood trickled off the bottom of her jaw onto her throat, slid down her chest, and stained her ivory blouse. She wanted to throw up. "He's in Europe."

Beside her, Kavita covered her mouth, and tears leaked from between her fingers.

"I see." Yuri stood with his gun strap slung around his neck. He paced up and down the line of male guests one more time.

With her equilibrium thrown off-kilter, Tess struggled to stand. Queasy dizziness overcame her, and black spots distorted her vision. Her cheekbone throbbed.

From where he stood, Yuri addressed the crowd. "You will all remain inside this room. If you open any doors or windows before six hours, the motion will set off explosives we've planted, and you will die. Stay where you are." With a curt nod, Yuri faced her, with one side of his mouth curled in a snarl. "Since Kingsley isn't here, we'll take you."

Dmitry stepped forward and grabbed her by the right arm, shaking her off balance.

She wrenched herself away and stood tall with both hands braced on her hips. "Wait. Tell me what you want. What are you trying to find?" She needed to buy time and make sense of the attack. Her voice sounded like a feral growl, no longer recognizable as her own.

"Quiet. No questions."

Dmitry scampered over to Yuri's side and pointed to one of the other gunmen several yards away. *"Alexi ranen. Yemu nuzhna pomoshch,"* he said in a muffled voice.

Across the room, she spotted the gunman Dmitry pointed out. Blood flowed in multiple streams from his scalp and streaked his face. A jagged row of crystal glass shards stood impaled in his forehead and ear. She shuddered and shifted away.

"One more thing." Yuri signaled at Riku's shooter, who stood awaiting orders with his rifle cocked. He gestured across the room at Mark, who remained ramrod straight in the line of men near Riku's corpse, his shirt painted in a graffiti of bloodstains.

Folding his muscular arms across his chest, Mark glared at the gunmen.

"Sergey, take the doctor," Yuri said. "Dmitry, blindfold them both, and let's go."

Dmitry tied a scratchy blindfold around Tess's head, blocking her vision. A mix of terror and bile crept up her throat, and she gagged to keep it down. Hit with the bitter truth, she swallowed hard and acknowledged tonight might be her last.

Chapter Three

Taken

The night air hit Tess's nostrils as her captors led her blindfolded out of the Cedarcliff building. Heavy boots stomped behind her, and she assumed the other gunmen were escorting Mark. Careening, she missed dips in the rolling path. She calculated when morning would arrive in the United Kingdom. How much time would elapse before someone reported them missing, and when would David learn of the attack?

In the meantime, she sucked the cold, fresh air into her lungs. Her cheekbone ached, and she channeled her father for strength. A former US Marine who became a diplomatic security expert, Danger Dad taught her countless precautions throughout her childhood. Hypervigilant but teetering on paranoid, he required she study martial arts and master basic weaponry, even fencing.

Little good that would do her now. Unarmed, blindfolded, and faced with assault rifles, she had no option except cooperation, paired with a desperate search for escape options. She dug her fingernails into her palms.

The group stopped. Metal truck doors opened, and a gunman tied her wrists behind her back with thick rope. Hands lifted her into the vehicle and slid her onto the metal flatbed. Goddamn it. Their captors intended to transport them somewhere else. She wriggled around to find a wall to lean against, but the truck bounced, and a thud sounded near her. Faint sandalwood and spice permeated the air. The doors slammed shut with a metallic clunk. She kept her voice low. "Mark?"

"*Ja*, I'm here." Caution rippled through his voice.

"Eight o'clock, let's go." Outside, Yuri was shouting. "Dmitry, you drive. Sergey, take jeep."

The truck sagged from the weight of the gunmen entering the cab up front. Doors slammed and gravel shuffled. Moments later, the truck's engine roared to life, followed by a second vehicle. The jeep, she assumed. The truck lurched forward and raced over the unpaved road, tearing through the rugged terrain. To avoid the blindfold's scratchy fabric, she shut her eyes and groaned.

"Are you okay? If we keep our voices down, they won't hear us," Mark said.

"I'm fine, but we're in serious trouble now." In a breathless rush, her words poured out.

"Like we weren't before? I'd say not having a gun in my face is an improvement." Angry sarcasm strained Mark's voice.

"Once a kidnapper traps a victim in a vehicle, the victim's odds of surviving plummet. Now we're three times more likely to never return."

"*Helvete,*" Mark swore. "Hell. What now?"

"Our chance of survival drops every minute we're in here. When the truck slows, let's unlock the doors and jump out." She kicked at the metal floor with a suede boot.

"Bad plan. We can't run away if we're injured

jumping. Got anything better?"

The road transitioned from gravel back to smooth asphalt. She needed to find a way out, now. "Let's stand and find the door." Wobbling and blind, she and Mark searched the truck walls together, bumping hands. Empty floor, no windows. A heavy, impenetrable metal grate formed one wall. "Does the door latch?"

"No, it's a deadbolt lock," he said. "I lost my phone. Do you have yours?"

"Mine's gone too. Shit. Since we can't call for help, we'll need to escape from wherever we're held captive." Thwarted for the moment, she crouched to consider other options, desperate to chase any shred of hope.

"Why do they want David?"

"No idea. Last-minute switch. He asked me to cover for him since he was stuck in Berlin." Of all the times she'd covered for David, why did she end up with this one? To say she regretted answering his text message last night was a gross understatement. In a parallel universe which hadn't exploded in disaster, she'd be in Paris with her best friend Sophie now, enjoying French cuisine and abundant amounts of cabernet sauvignon. She imagined the buttery smell of fresh-baked croissants, but the truck bed's cold metal under her legs ruined the fantasy.

"How unfortunate you are the vice president."

"You wouldn't believe how unlucky." Dead fiancé? Check. A year of crushing grief? Check. And now, witnessing her mentor gunned down, and being taken hostage herself? Double check. A year so terrible, she almost dissolved into macabre laughter so she wouldn't cry instead. Given the kidnappers' arsenal, she'd prefer to be stuck with a US Navy Seal instead of a doctor but took comfort she wasn't alone. Statistically, two people kidnapped had a better chance of survival than one. "I'll bet they want us for ransom. David's wealthy, but plenty of richer targets exist elsewhere."

"Is David in legal trouble? Gambling, affairs, sketchy deals?"

"No way. He's an inventor, an engineer. Not someone who'd ever do anything illegal."

"Jealous competitors?"

"Sure, but CEOs slay each other with words, not guns." Bristling against being trapped, she slammed a fist onto the truck's metal floor. "I can't believe this is happening."

"I don't know if this helps you, but the gunman shot Riku by accident. Yuri was furious at the shooter for his mistake and called him an idiot."

"Christ. Riku died for nothing. Goddamn fuckwits." Ready to launch a tirade of expletives, she stopped herself. "Wait, how do you know?"

"I speak some Russian."

"I didn't peg you as Slavic."

"That's because I'm Norwegian. I spent three years on an international medical mission in Ukraine, near the Russian border."

"In the conflict zone?" She remembered Russia's annexation of Crimea, after rebels ousted President Viktor Yanukovych in Ukraine's 2014 revolution.

"Yes, I'm a trauma surgeon. We treated both Ukrainians and Russians. The languages share similarities."

"Stressful work."

He stifled a grim laugh. "Yeah, but not dangerous like medical consulting for Timberline's corporate board. Turns out this is a risky job."

"True." The cruel irony of his choice struck her as bad luck of epic proportion. "So, you're not practicing medicine?"

"No. Pro-Russian militants bombed our field hospital in Ukraine a few months ago. I injured my hand in the explosion, and I can't perform surgery until the nerves regenerate."

"You've survived two terrorist attacks in a year?" She dropped open her jaw and debated whether his luck was even worse than her own.

"Technically, only one. We haven't survived this one yet."

"Fair point." She monitored the truck's movement by the sound of the pavement. "Why'd they kidnap you? You're not in cybersecurity."

"No, but one of the gunmen is injured. I'm guessing they need me to provide medical care."

"Pretty unlucky night to be a doctor."

"Indeed."

"The gunmen are taking us north. Ocean's west, mountains east, Washington state south. They wouldn't dare cross the US border with hostages." Anxiety poured through her veins, and she struggled to wrest control of their predicament.

"We're not returning to Vancouver," he said.

The finality of his statement echoed her unspoken fear. "Afraid not." Her shirt stuck against her skin in sweaty clumps, and she shivered. Fatalism overtook her for a moment. "If I don't survive, please find my parents, Phil and Maggie Bennett. He's in Virginia, and she's in Boston. They're divorced. Tell them I love them."

"Stop it. We're not dead yet."

"Given they gunned down my mentor, I'm realistic. Had the gunshot been a few inches to the right, we wouldn't be having this conversation." The recent flashes of gunfire replayed in her mind, but she kept her voice even.

Mark paused before speaking again. "How about we aim to survive?"

"Sure, but let's be real. I was a US State Department brat, and I grew up in several scary places. Not everyone gets a fairy tale ending, even if they survive. Survival can be worse than being killed." A teenage memory resurfaced of when bandits shot her father during a carjacking on a remote highway outside Bogotá. Chronic pain from the gunshot injury, exacerbated by opioid addiction, plagued him ever since. Survival's consequences broke her family apart.

"True words. What's your plan?"

"We're going to defeat terrorists armed with assault weapons while blindfolded, bound, and unarmed. Escape. Get revenge for Riku's death. You with me so far?"

"Be reasonable," Mark responded with an annoyed grunt.

"I am. Escaping is our best chance for survival, period. Our odds are terrible, but not zero, so let's start there." The scratchy blindfold chafed against her raw cheekbone.

"Look, I'm scared, too."

The earnest vulnerability in his voice both surprised and touched her, and she lowered her guard a couple of notches. "Promise me one thing."

"Name it."

"I need to trust you. No matter how ugly this gets, tell me the truth." Defenses stripped, she needed reality, no matter how terrible, to fuel her aggression so she could keep fighting.

"I will. Please do the same for me."

"We need to prepare ourselves to fight." What remained of her lifeline continued to unravel, leaving precious few gossamer threads in her grasp. Until tonight, Tess believed the day Kyle died was the worst day of her life, a tragedy nothing could ever surpass. She was wrong.

The truck barreled down the highway, disappearing into the night.

****

On a rural road littered with bumps, the truck decelerated on a sharp turn, and their bodies jostled on the metal floor. Her heart pounded, and her palms grew damp in the darkness. Breathing in shallow gulps, she strained to inhale enough air. The truck's speed slowed to a crawl, and the engine idled a minute before turning off. Distant voices carried from the front cabin, three gunmen talking in muffled tones. The frosty night grew colder, and they were without coats. Two doors opened, followed by two slams and footsteps. A key jingled in the lock, and the truck's back doors sprawled open and bracing air flowed inside. She shivered.

"We move you now," said one of the gunmen. Sergey? Or Dmitry? A fourth voice piped up outside, one she couldn't identify. Rough hands dragged her across the metal floorboards, and her legs spilled over the back bumper.

"Stand," the voice commanded. The ground was soft and uneven, and a muddy field squished under her boots. A hand on her back propelled her forward.

Hoping Mark was close by, she obeyed, putting one foot in front of the other, her hands bound behind her.

"Walk. Step up. Again. Now step."

The male voice steered her ahead and she took a few more steps.

"Stop. Sergey, open the room," the voice said.

Tess entered a chilly structure not much warmer than the outdoors. A door slid on a rail, and a metal bar clanked. A hand rammed her toward the opening.

"Go."

Another hand shoved her into the room, tore off her blindfold, slammed the door shut, and clanked the metal bar down. A small cutout in the door, about eye height and covered by iron bars, allowed light to enter. She studied the room they passed through and noted the structure's size. A horse barn, perhaps? The solitary electric bulb hanging from the ceiling, reminiscent of interrogation rooms, sent a shudder through her.

Outside the cell, Yuri's voice boomed with a flood of words she didn't understand, and Tess assumed he was giving orders to his men until he broke into English.

"Doctor, you come with me," Yuri said.

The men left her alone and the cell fell quiet. Only an eerie silence remained. Minutes dragged by at the pace of hours.

Memories of gunfire replayed inside her head. She dug her fingernails deep into her palms to control her fear. Senses on overdrive, she paced around the small cell, testing every wall and crevice for a way out, but minutes later, she hadn't found any potential escape routes.

About forty-five minutes later, the collection of footsteps returned.

"Throw the doctor inside, too. This is the one stall with locks," Yuri said.

The door slid open with a loud clank. The two gunmen holding Mark threw him inside the cell. The heavy wooden door of their new prison slammed shut behind them, followed by the ominous metal bang of the thick bar locking the door. Their captors treaded away and left them alone.

She scanned him from head to toe for signs of distress. His blindfold was gone, but his hands remained bound in front of him. "Are you okay? Where'd they take you?"

"One gunman had severe lacerations and a concussion. No supplies or antiseptic. I used rusty tweezers to pluck about eighty shards of glass from his head, then I repaired the lacs with a sewing needle and fishing line. Primitive. Then they tied my hands again." A grimace crossed Mark's face.

"Was it the gunman clipped by the chandelier?"

Mark nodded.

"So, the thug gets to live." Wishing Riku had been lucky enough to survive, she found her hatred for the gunmen deepening. Bile rose in her throat.

"When terror strikes, nothing's fair. The guy's wound is susceptible to infection, and he could die of sepsis." He gave a grim nod and scanned the walls enclosing them.

Together, she and Mark surveyed the room, about

ten square feet, with one wall stacked high with hay. The one light bulb remained off, leaving the room dim. Wood planks lined the floor, and drywall covered the smooth walls. A huge green plastic bin stood in one corner.

Mark shuffled over and wrangled the top open with his tied hands working as a lever. Once he lifted the lid several inches, she anchored her shoulder under it so they could peek inside. The smell of grain wafted through the room, probably livestock feed.

"We're in a barn, a farm in the countryside." He faced the door to inspect the lock.

About six feet tall, Mark carried himself with confidence, and his every motion exuded athleticism and strength. In the tight space, she registered his movements and her body hummed due to his presence. Flustered, she chastised herself for the distraction and focused on finding an escape route. Footsteps approached, and she tightened her muscles.

Mark swiveled to face her. "Whatever happens, stay calm," he whispered.

The door burst open, and Yuri, the gunman who fractured her cheek, stood alone. With a menacing squint, he analyzed them from top to bottom before yanking a large hunting knife from his holster and holding it high above his head. The razor-sharp blade gleamed in the dingy light.

"Face wall." Yuri growled in English and pointed.

She gasped but obeyed his order. Out of the corner of her eye, she glimpsed Mark beside her, his jaw clenched tight. Sweat coated her face with a sticky sheen. *So, this is how my end begins. Please don't let it be torture.* At least Mark was with her, so she wouldn't die alone. Panic buzzed loud in her head, followed by a vision of the afterlife. As a young girl, she attended church, and remembered sermons promising eternity in heaven, complete with angels in white, lounging on fluffy clouds. After tonight's brutality, she doubted such a place existed and questioned what kind of god would permit this bloodshed.

Yuri grabbed her tied hands, yanked them up, and sliced off the rope binding her with one swift cut. He did the same with the rope confining Mark's wrists. Without a word, he left.

Dmitry appeared a second later and threw two bottles of water into the cell. The door shut again, locking them in for the night.

After both men disappeared, she stared at Mark and opened her lips, but words failed her. Uncertain the danger had abated, she felt her heart race ahead without her.

"He didn't kill us. Wow." Mark dropped his chin toward his chest and relaxed his rigid posture.

"I thought…" As the knots confining her shoulders unwound, she found her breath again.

"I know what you thought because I did, too. Hey, what's wrong?" He stepped closer and narrowed his gaze.

"I'm fine." Her voice tight, she backed away in self-consciousness.

Scanning both sides of her face, he frowned. "You're injured, and your cheek is a mess."

"I'm fine." Despite his blunt, direct assessment of her injury, she refused to admit an ounce of fragility.

"Don't argue with me and let me examine the wound. Come here where I can see it."

Weak light filtered into their cell through the metal bars, and reluctantly, Tess shuffled a few steps forward.

"I need to clean off the blood to see better. Lean back." Mark tilted her beaten cheek to one side, before bending over to grab one of the water bottles. He opened it with his right hand, then poured a stream of water over the wound.

The tepid water stung as it splashed her laceration. Staring straight ahead, she gazed at Mark's open collar and observed the smooth golden skin at the top of his chest where it curved upwards toward his neck.

Focused on her injury, he used his shirt cuff to dab away excess water and made quick, gentle pats to remove bloody debris. He inspected her swelling cheek from all angles and palpated her cheekbone.

Determined not to wince out loud, she bit her lip.

"The bone is cracked, and it's going to bruise and swell. I'd recommend you get stitches right away. Might hurt a couple of weeks. If…" He paused, then exhaled. "*When* we escape, a plastic surgeon should evaluate your wound." Diagnosis complete, he stepped back and regarded her again.

"Could've been worse." She ignored her throbbing pain and resolved not to waste energy complaining. Feeling exposed under his steady clinical gaze, she blew her hair off her face.

"Water." He pointed at the water bottles resting on the wood floor. "They brought us water. The rule of threes."

"I don't follow." Trying to collect her ragged nerves, she smoothed her hands over her thighs.

"You can survive three minutes without air. Three days without water. Three weeks without food. Three months without hope. We've got water, which means we can ride out at least three days here."

"That's positive news?" While she was grateful for the water and Mark's optimism, neither guaranteed their freedom. The room lacked enough oxygen, and every moment in her life reduced to the current one. All the friendships, graduations, and promotions shaping her past fell away, and her entire world shrank to a four-wall prison. "We need a solid plan, fast."

"Take a seat." Mark gestured to a couple of hay bales on the center of the floor.

Gathering her black wool suit jacket tighter around her chest, she chose one of the bales and sat. Hay poked through her pants in random places, which made for uncomfortable sitting. Her heartbeat sped in rhythmic pulses and pounded her cheekbone every second. She craved painkillers. Running a hand over a bulge in her pocket, she perked up. "My kit. I have tools to help us."

She stood and peered out the barred window to confirm no one was approaching. Opening her jacket, she unzipped a discreet interior compartment and retrieved a couple of items. In her palm, she displayed them. "Here. I've got a full container of military-grade pepper spray and a brand-new pocketknife."

"You know how to use them?" Mark did a double take.

"Given I often travel alone, I like to be prepared." When Tess hit adolescence, her father scared her with countless cautionary tales, most involving predatory men. While she became more paranoid than most people, the upside was she anticipated the unexpected, without fail. "You never regret being ready."

"Sure, but no one expects a terrorist attack." Mark

scowled, then kicked at a spider scurrying across the floor.

"You've never met my father. Let's search this room again." She tugged at the heavy wooden door. Certain their captors locked it, she tested to measure how much it could budge but found no movement. She knocked on the wall in several places, listening for wooden studs, but couldn't locate any. "Busting down the door won't work. Cutting out the drywall would eat lots of time, and we don't know what's on the other side."

"What about your weapons?"

She plopped on the hay bale to think. "My pepper spray canister has a twenty-foot range, but I prefer to use it at close range. Easier to hit the target and obtain maximum potency."

"I'll take your word for it."

She lowered her voice. "Since these guys are armed, the pepper spray gives us one chance to escape. At best, we'll gain seconds. If we're lucky, and only one gunman guards us, we could take him by surprise. You hold the pocketknife for backup, and I spray the canister to disable him, grab the gun, and lock him up so we can run for it."

Mark held his hand up, and his eyebrows rose. "Whoa. Let's think about this and try something less confrontational, like negotiating."

"Right. By surprising them and attacking first, we escape and avoid confrontation." Her forehead furrowed, and her muscles stiffened.

"But if something goes wrong with your plan, we die."

"Given they could kill us any second, escaping is

our best chance of survival." Fear of dying fueled her determination, and she clenched her jaw. She rose from the hay bale and paced the floor back and forth, hoping inspiration would offer up a clever solution. The persistent smell of cow manure, while faint, annoyed her.

Haunted by the shiny glint of Yuri's hunting knife, she avoided letting her mind play out worst-case scenarios. Instead, she channeled her father, wondering how he'd handle this situation while unarmed.

Run, hide, fight. The first two options weren't possible, which left fighting. Arms crossed, she gathered her courage and shifted her mindset to survival. *Whatever it takes.*

Chapter Four

Trapped

Early morning light filtered through the cell's iron bars, and pungent earthiness infused the damp air. Disoriented by the hard, solid wood floor, Tess curled her aching body into a ball. Her gluey eyelids stuck together and resisted opening. She registered pain but couldn't decide if it was the mother of all hangovers or a full-on blackout. Doctors had long warned her cavalier use of sleeping pills could induce neurological lapses, but the risks never deterred her. An oversized ant crawled across the barn floor, and dry straw crackled under her as she shooed the insect away. The unmistakable smell of dried hay meant last night's horror was real, and she groaned. She had to escape.

Across the room, Mark stretched his muscular arms above his head and rotated his broad shoulders. Overnight, blond stubble emerged on his cheeks and the chiseled angle of his chin, and she was irked to find him so attractive.

"Morning. We survived the night," he said.

Groggy with sleep, Mark's accent was thicker than she remembered. "We have to escape this cell." Dizziness swirled in her head, and she grasped the wall to keep her balance until she was steady on her feet. The locked door failed to budge, and she stretched tall on her tiptoes to peek out the barred window, frustrated the view offered little help. Footsteps sounded, and when the cell's wooden door banged open, she jumped.

"Bathroom break." Dressed in black fatigues, Sergey stood with his gun slung over one shoulder. He gestured for her to go first.

As she stepped forward, she felt Riku's killer grab her left arm, and the revulsion made her want to spit. He led her out of the cell and relocked the door before hauling her down a short hallway and pointing at a small door at the back of the barn.

Although the tiny bathroom was grungy, she appreciated the break. Obsessed with escaping, she searched every inch of the walls and floors. No window, no air vent, no cabinets—just an old toilet, a filthy sink, and a cracked mirror. She longed for a toothbrush. The faucet handle squeaked, and rust-color water drained out before turning clear. An ancient chunk of soap, veined with dirty black lines, and far from sterile, rested on the basin. Frowning, she washed her blood-stained hands and splashed handfuls of freezing water on her face. The mirror revealed a splotch of purple encircling her lacerated cheekbone, and one eye had swollen half-shut. With gentle dabs, she cleaned the wound using the questionable soap. Acknowledging no escape was possible from the room, she shook the water off her hands and marched out.

In the hallway, Sergey waited to escort her back to the cell. He gestured at Mark, who rose to his feet and exited into the hallway.

As the two men walked, another gunman with a maze of scrapes and stitches across his forehead appeared and signaled at the first. "*Ya prinesu zaklyuchennym zavtrak.*"

"*Khorosho, Alexi.*" Sergey saluted him.

After Mark finished, the gunman deposited him back in the cell and locked the door.

"What did they say?" She detected interest in his expression.

He stepped closer. "Our captors are getting breakfast for us. The guy I sewed up last night is Alexi. I'll keep listening to figure out their plan," he whispered.

Her stomach growled in anticipation of food and water. The slightest motion sent pulses of pain into her cheek, and little by little, she eased herself onto a hay bale to wait.

The new gunman, Alexi, appeared a few minutes later. The cell door slid open, and he leaned inside to hand them a sizeable brown paper bag along with water bottles.

A maze of cuts and stitches marred his scalp, which resembled raw hamburger. Stomach turning, she averted her gaze.

He slid the door shut, relocked it, and left.

She opened the bag and found a package of brown bread labeled in English and French. Its expiration date passed three days ago. Rifling around, she uncovered a pack of sliced cheddar cheese and two bruised red apples. "Well, at least they don't intend to starve us."

After moving one block of hay to serve as a rough table, she and Mark split up the food. Sitting on their respective hay bales, they ate without discussion. Famished, she tore off hunks of the bread and layered cheese slices on top. The bread tasted like cardboard, and the apple mushed against her teeth, but she was grateful for the energy. "They can't keep us in this barn forever, no matter how remote this is. The other guests must have escaped Cedarcliff and called the police by now." At least, she hoped they had.

"They won't have much to go on, though. No one saw the truck, including us."

"Right. No one will find us here, so we need to escape, fast." Reconsidering their options for the thousandth time made no difference, and promising solutions eluded her. Digging her pocketknife out of her hidden jacket compartment, she handed it to Mark. "Here, take this. For later."

Scowling, he shot a glare at the knife before plucking it from her palm. "I'm not convinced we should do this." He fidgeted before pocketing it.

"No other option." She patted her jacket pocket to confirm her pepper spray canister was still at hand. "Last night, Riku warned me Kingsley Tech might be in danger."

"Did he say why?" Mark leaned his back against the wall.

"A new enemy motivated by politics and allegiance has emerged, and robbing banks for money is only one part of their modus operandi. He wanted to meet with David and me Sunday in a secure location."

"Any chance Riku was playing for the other side?"

"Of course not," she responded with an indignant glare. "He's on our board. If any threat existed, he would alert us right away."

"Sounds like you trusted Riku." The hint of a question remained in his voice.

"Implicitly. He's mentored me for years, and David longer."

"You must have something they need, or else we wouldn't have survived the night. Any ideas what they want?"

Before she could answer, the exterior barn door opened, and footsteps approached.

The cell door slid open without warning, and Sergey and Alexi appeared.

"You come with us." Sergey pointed at her.

Anxiety crushed her like an anvil. Taking a deep breath, she straightened her posture and offered a silent prayer the criminals wouldn't torture her. The gunmen took her by the arms and guided her out into the daylight. Unable to block the light, she squinted and tilted her face toward the ground. They crossed a small agricultural compound and passed a covered area which sheltered feed troughs behind the barn. Puddles of mud dotted the barnyard, and her boots made squishing sounds with every step. The rank smell of cow manure assailed her nostrils.

A ramshackle shed made of industrial aluminum siding stood a short distance away. Trees lined the rest of the property, which contained acres filled with open pasture. Angus cows grazed in the nearby grass, oblivious to the nearby criminal activity. To the south, a dense forest of trees swelled onto an imposing hill.

The captors directed her toward the metal shed across the barnyard and jostled her through the doorway. Parked inside sat several ancient tractors and random farm equipment, all covered in dust and cobwebs.

Inside, Yuri waited in the corner, his black military boots shining under a battered wooden table.

The captors deposited her in a ratty wood chair

opposite him and assumed their posts by the entrance, guns cocked and ready.

Yuri shouted a command at the two gunmen, who exited the room and shut the door behind them.

The man regarded her like an annoying stray dog he wanted to kick. She doubted he even remembered hitting her last night. The rigid, unforgiving wood of the chair dug into her back, compounding her discomfort. Every breath of motor oil residue and cigarette smoke irritated her lungs, and gruesome images of Riku's senseless death replayed in her mind. She swallowed and reminded herself to breathe. Bereft of freedom, or even fresh air, refraining from lashing out required considerable energy.

"So, you're representing David Kingsley." He leaned back in his chair and stared.

The interrogation had commenced. Adopting a neutral, impenetrable expression, she remained silent and stared straight ahead.

"Full name," he commanded.

"Tess Madeleine Bennett." Burying her hesitation, she sped to plant seeds of negotiation in hopes of avoiding a one-way grilling. "You need something, and I want to understand what it is."

The gunman tilted his head and squinted. "I ask the questions."

To reduce her anxiety, she reframed him in her imagination to be an important but aggravating client needing appeasement. "Let's discuss what you need and how I can help," she said, using a firm, but non-threatening voice.

"Citizenship?" After an eye roll, he resumed his rapid-fire questioning.

"American. And you?" She noticed the port-wine stain above his collar darken.

"Any other residency?" He raised an eyebrow.

"Permanent resident card in the UK." During her childhood, Tess's father often shared anecdotes about his work at the family dinner table and dispensed gems of advice should one find oneself in an unsavory position. For example, while being interrogated, say as little as possible, and be honest until conditions demand a lie.

"Why did you come to Cedarcliff?"

"David asked me to take his place yesterday." Determined to assert control over her reactions no matter what, she clenched her fists and willed herself to be patient. His searing gaze felt like a laser burning her skin, and she looked away.

"How long have you worked with Kingsley?" He emitted a phlegm-laden cough and stared.

"Ten years."

"Were you romantic with him?"

"No." Her ethical hackles prickled at his weird question. She'd sooner resign her job than sleep with her boss. Where was he going with this?

"Do you know the engineering project codenamed Firefly?"

Firefly was the core of Kingsley Tech's prized encryption software and the crown jewel of Kyle's professional legacy. The gunmen were after money, but why and for whom? To buy herself more time, she stalled and tapped her fingers against the seat of her chair. "Firefly? Yes."

"What about Rapadon?"

"Never heard of it." She studied her interrogator,

and the hostility in his expression made her shudder.

"You have a problem." He stopped stabbing the table with his cheap pen, and his mouth locked into a horizontal line, like soldiers standing at attention, awaiting inspection.

The word *problem* crackled through her body, and her face flushed warm as she shifted her weight in the wooden chair. Suddenly overheated, her body temperature spiked and felt out of sync with her freezing hands and feet.

Across the table, Yuri coughed, then hacked until he spat into a dirty handkerchief, which he threw on the table.

Fresh red blood and gobs of mucus stained the cloth. Disgusted, she wrinkled her nose and curved her body away.

He cleared his throat. "We need fifty million pounds sterling and the original source code from the Firefly and Rapadon projects."

Tiny beads of sweat coated her forehead, but she resisted the urge to wipe them away. Refusing to panic, she attempted to engage him with questions. "If you want money, why not attack a multinational tech company? PeopleClick is booming by the billions. Kingsley Tech is a small company."

"What makes you think we haven't taken over PeopleClick?"

"You're bluffing." Judging his insinuation ridiculous, she stifled a laugh. To her surprise, he laughed out loud and slapped his hand on the wooden table. An ugly smile spread across his thin lips.

"You geeks are fools with too much money. Nothing is private." He rotated his mobile phone to display its screen.

She recognized a recent social media post she made. The photo depicted her smiling with her best friend, Sophie, in front of a London art museum. A whole new wave of fury raged inside her, but she clamped her lips together so she wouldn't yell. To protect Sophie's professional need to remain under the radar, she'd locked the picture so no one else could view it, and she secured her account with the highest privacy settings. At least, so she thought.

"Again, you will give me the code and money."

Tess shifted in her seat and her entire back itched. "I don't have it." Whatever mirth he expressed earlier was replaced with a cold, calculating stare, and she sensed an inevitable impasse approaching.

"You're Kingsley's vice president. You'll find a way." He shrugged.

"How the hell do you expect me to dig up code here? I'm locked in a cell in the middle of goddamned nowhere." Despite her best intention to be cooperative, she couldn't contain her anger and made a fist, fuming.

"Don't lie to me. You must have high-level permissions to access anything."

After a quick pause to strategize, she opted to play to the gunman's presumed expertise. "Standard security protocol prohibits granting unnecessary access to the system. Given I don't work on source code, I don't need to access it." In truth, David possessed permissions to all their network servers, but she refrained from revealing the detail.

"Who's in charge of the engineers? I want his name." Yuri pounded his fists, and the ancient table shook.

Tess bit her lip and kept silent. She wasn't about to rat out her colleague, Declan O'Leary, who also had been one of Kyle's best friends.

"Fine."

Maliciousness filled his voice. Before she knew it, he had scrambled around the table and snatched her left hand. He wrenched her wrist at such a torqued angle that she gasped, both from shock and pain.

With his other hand, he whipped out his hunting knife from his belt sheath, and its sharp tip gleamed in the dull morning light. "Last chance, or I cut off one of your fingers." He dragged her hand toward the table.

Jesus Christ, no. I can't do this. She observed the odd sensation of floating above her body, watching herself, and wondered if this was what people experienced right before dying. "Please don't hurt me." Voice cracking, she parted her parched lips, which were stuck together and dry like raw cotton. Heart pounding, she worried her ribs might break.

"I'm waiting." With his rough hands, the gunman yanked one of her fingers from her clenched fist and straightened it out on the table. Lifting his arm, he positioned the knife over her left ring finger.

"Stop! It's Declan O'Leary." Ashamed about breaking under pressure so soon, she emitted a raspy whisper. The sick irony of the finger he'd chosen made her want to cry. If Kyle hadn't died, she'd be wearing a wedding band on that finger now.

With one swift motion, Yuri swung his arm and slammed the blade down.

She shrieked. Unable to detect any feeling in her hand, a wave of bile surged in her throat, and she compelled herself to glance down. The knife stood upright, impaled in the decaying soft wood of the table. Splinters clung to the blade's tip, a hair's width from her finger.

"You might be more useful than you realize." A smile curled onto Yuri's mouth.

Face frozen, Tess stopped holding her breath, and her lungs deflated like a popped balloon and didn't refill until she remembered to breathe. Drenched in sweat, she felt her blouse clinging to her torso in clammy patches. Terror morphed into anger, and she glared. "Why are you doing this?"

"Do you know what it's like to have your village destroyed by enemy militants? To watch your mother killed in front of you, your house burned, and neighborhood children murdered in the street?" Yuri pounded his fists on the table, and his face reddened like a rotten tomato about to burst. He grabbed her throat. "Do you?"

Trapped like a caged animal headed for slaughter, she gasped, her pulse pounding in her neck against his grimy hand. "No." All she could muster was a rasp.

"Rich American. You don't know sacrifice. Try surviving on rotten fish for months. Now I kill for money. That's why."

Was he trying to elicit sympathy? If indeed he was on a ledge, she'd coax him away. "I'm sorry you suffered, but why do you want our code?" She inflected genuine empathy in her voice in hopes of keeping him talking.

"I give you nothing."

The waistband of her wool pants itched against her lower back, and the irritation canceled out the comforting warmth they provided against the wintry, raw morning. "Why would David roll over and hand you our intellectual property?" She glimpsed a flash of his knife as he flew around the table, and suddenly, the angled tip of the blade pressed tight against her throat. The pressure compressed her carotid artery, and her thudding heartbeat reverberated through her head. She doubted she'd escape his wrath this time, and wondered if his reeking, smoky breath would be her last conscious sensation.

Yuri leaned over and placed his mouth near her ear. "Because if Kingsley doesn't give us the code and money in the next twenty-four hours, I'll kill you myself. Slowly," he hissed.

Incapable of processing the threat, her mind went blank. Static buzzed in her head until it became deafening, like she was tumbling off a cliff and crashing to the ground, where vultures circled, ready to gnash apart her bones and flesh. She shook her head to rid herself of the macabre images, but her synapses had tangled into gobs of slush.

Keep breathing. Inhale four seconds, hold four seconds, then exhale four seconds. Grateful she had learned combat tactical breathing, courtesy of her dad, she overcame the vertigo, and her vision cleared. The knife hadn't punctured her neck's skin, and she pushed her feet hard against the floor to steady herself. She was alive, for now.

"I kill people, and you're my paycheck for this week. Do you understand me, Ms. Bennett?" Yuri continued, his voice louder than before.

"Yes." Jaw set, she faced Yuri, petrified by the complete lack of humanity in his expression. The top of her scalp tingled like pins and needles poking her.

53

Somehow, her brain and body felt split off from each other, no longer linked.

The two gunmen reappeared and stood guard nearby.

She heard one click behind her, then another, and groaned inwardly. They'd switched off the safety latches on their rifles, which meant if she bolted for the door, she wouldn't survive. Nothing in the embassy crisis training sessions of her youth prepared her for the actual sensation of death being so near. A binary choice remained—cooperate or die.

"My boss needs this money and code, fast. If you fail, I fail. You and more people will die, so think hard about how you'll get Rapadon for me."

"I told you, I don't know what Rapadon is." She tensed as if suddenly walking on a tightrope without a safety net. Layers of old sweat and stale smoke wafted from Yuri's clothes, and she suppressed the urge to gag. Her stomach roiled, and she avoided inhaling any of his unwashed male odor.

"You'd better figure it out. Time's ticking." Extending a grubby hand, he touched a curl loose on her cheek and tucked it behind her ear. He paced back to the other side of the table, returned to his chair, and resumed glaring. "You keep thinking, Ms. Bennett. I'll be here, sharpening my knife. Sergey and Alexi, take her back to the cell."

The gunmen, evil twins of malice, grabbed her by the arms, rougher this time, and carried her like a statue. Unwilling to make their job any easier, she dragged her feet, but the resulting pain in her arms forced her to keep walking. They propelled her through the shed's aluminum doors and across the yard to the barn. Once inside, they slid open the cell at the end of the hall, tossed her inside, and locked the bar across the gate.

Finally, they left.

Releasing a relieved breath, she scanned for Mark in the barren space, but he was gone. Determined not to panic, she paced back and forth in the cell. By her accounting, the expiration date Yuri had just stamped on her forehead was at least five decades premature. As the dire situation sank in, she slumped, her resilience faltering. Intent on expending her fury, she kicked a hay bale, and the fear she'd contained last night overflowed like a river. She slammed a hand against the wall and burst into gasping sobs.

Her father's voice bellowed inside her head: *Damn it, you're a Bennett. Pull yourself together.*

Determined to cry out all her fear, in hopes her courage would rebound, she allowed herself two minutes. Tears streamed down her bruised face, and her limited respite passed in a blink. Enough weakness—time to woman up and fight.

Using her shirt cuffs to dry her face, she took care not to jostle her injured cheek. Questions crowded her mind, and she leaned against the wall, trying to calm herself. What did these men want with Kingsley Tech's code?

Her dad's war tales from decades of protecting US diplomats rushed through her head. Analyzing his misadventures, the consistent thread weaving all her father's anecdotes together emerged: survival. Last night's chaos had blurred her focus, but now her mission crystallized in an instant—escape. Nothing else mattered, and answers could wait.

The outside barn door opened, shining slivers of daylight into the cell, and footsteps approached. Nerves jangling, she formed fists to protect herself.

When the door slid open, Mark entered.

Dmitry slammed the door shut and locked them back inside before turning and leaving the barn.

Once they were alone again, she checked Mark for any obvious injuries. "Are you hurt?"

"No." He studied her carefully. "Did they harm you?" he asked in a low voice.

"Yuri threatened to cut off a finger. If they don't obtain Kingsley's source code in twenty-four hours, he's going to kill me." Despite the defiance she projected, she couldn't stop her lower lip from trembling. A lump formed in her throat, but she choked it back down. Body taut, she stood tall and kept her back straight.

"Christ. We'll find a way out, somehow." Frowning, he shook his head and placed a hand on her shoulder.

"I'm fine. I'll survive this." She crossed her arms and fixed her gaze on the floor, but inside, her mind spun in dizzying circles. His hand, still warm on her shoulder, comforted her in the drafty barn. "I'm fine."

"Tess."

Gentle but firm, his hand remained, radiating heat through her blouse, and she didn't ask him to move. Dropping her gaze to the golden curve of his neck, she fantasized they could disappear from this nightmare.

"*Helvete.* We're hostages, and you're injured. You're supposed to be scared. I'm scared."

Mark's Nordic accent and baritone voice offered soothing balm for the terror she suffered this morning.

Concentration wavering, she shoved away conflicting fears and desires to regain her composure and focus. "We don't have time to be afraid."

"I wouldn't think any less of you if you were. You handled the attack last night better than most of the men, despite Yuri beating you." Mark removed his hand.

Unsure how to acknowledge the compliment, she glanced at the floor. Her father had raised her like a boy and taught her to respond to danger with toughness and grit. The only time he ever acknowledged her femininity was to preface lecturing her about the need to master extra self-defense techniques to avoid getting assaulted. She shook the thought away and wondered where Mark had been so long. "Where'd they take you?"

"One of our kidnappers, Dmitry, led me to a small cottage near here. The old man who owns this farm, Anderson Campbell, was taken hostage, too. He's ill, and Yuri ordered me to treat him."

"What was wrong?"

"Massive diabetic foot ulcer, stage four. Impressive. When I cut away the infected tissue, our young captor, Dmitry, ran out of the room and threw up. It's not every day you come across a squeamish terrorist."

His deadpan humor evoked an amused groan. "Ironic, but also helpful. We'll leverage his weakness to our advantage." She jumped her thoughts to how they could exploit the gunman to aid their escape.

"*Ja,* strange Yuri would bother to care for anyone, but I was glad to treat the farmer." He swept a hand through his tousled hair and sat on a hay bale.

"You sure we're talking about the same guy? The psychopath threatened to cut off my finger, and he plans to kill me." The sensory memory of Yuri's grimy hand splaying her fingers on the wood table felt like a burn imprinted on her skin. She wiggled her fingers, never more grateful all ten remained intact.

"He wears a silver cross. Maybe he's religious."

"Right, the devil incarnate. Bastard." She kicked a hay bale and folded her arms. She'd never forgive Yuri for threatening her.

"Anyhow, while Dmitry was vomiting outside, the farmer, Anderson, told me we're about three hours from Vancouver, north of Lillooet, and south of Pavilion. And the best part—a highway runs about twenty kilometers west of here." Mark kept his voice low.

Her hope swung like a pendulum, rising from defeated to hopeful, then plummeting to despair again in rapid cycles. "If we can escape, we could run to find it and get help. That's about twelve miles, so it's doable."

"Right. Even better, the farmer explained how we might escape this cell. This room was an add-on to the barn. The original wall had a small grain door, which connected to a feed chute that runs outside. If we can find a loose wall board in there, we've got a chance."

Her optimism surged, and she leapt up to gesture toward the wall. "About time we got a break. Let's carve the drywall away using my knife. I'll search this half, and you take the other." When Mark hesitated to respond, she detected a flicker of doubt in his expression. "What is it?"

Rocking back and forth on his heels, he thumbed at his ear. "I suspect the farmer suffers from dementia. He might be mistaken."

The optimism she felt seconds ago dropped like a boulder, and she tightened her jaw. Lips pressed together, she stared at the ceiling. "Doesn't matter. This tip's all we've got, so let's move."

"Fine, but first, take this acetaminophen I found in the farmer's cottage. It will help your cheek." He presented a small handful of white capsules and deposited two onto her palm.

"Thanks. Let's get going." Without water, the dry pills stuck in her throat, but she choked them down. Inch by inch, she brushed her hands over the wall and scanned for bumps or cracks, tapping to listen for hollow spots. "If we find this chute, we can escape after nightfall."

"Yes, but, if we're caught…" He ambled opposite her and scoured the flat wall's surface.

The sentence hung between them, unfinished. Wishing to project bravery, she convinced herself she possessed the courage to fight through to the end. Not surviving wasn't an option, and defiance fueled her determination. She set her hands on her hips. "I refuse to die here, period."

Before either of them could say more, the exterior barn door clattered, then groaned open. Their captors returned, carrying rifles in their hands.

Losing Kyle and Riku made her want to kick the wall. Feeling cursed, she clenched her eyes shut. Neither Kyle nor Riku had a chance to survive, but she did, and she resolved not to waste it. Whatever it took, she vowed to escape this hellhole, even if she died trying.

Chapter Five

Captivity

Their captors hovered in the barn near them most of the day, entering and exiting every few minutes, which thwarted their search for weak spots in the drywall.

Time sped up and slowed down at ragged intervals. Each minute in their cell passed like a slow drip of molasses, and time stretched to impossible lengths. Arms crossed, Tess leaned against the wall and tapped a foot as her impatience grew. Her skin itched from the scratchy hay, and she couldn't control her agitation. She drifted her gaze to Mark, who was exercising on the barn floor.

He'd taken his bloody dress shirt off and formed it into a padded cushion, which he slid under his scarred left hand. Undaunted, he proceeded to whip out countless push-ups and sit-ups. After several sets, he repeated the series, keeping his back straight as a wooden plank. His arms curved in symmetry to his broad shoulders, and he executed each push-up in perfect rhythm, as if timed to imaginary music. Defined pectorals stretched his white T-shirt.

Catching herself daydreaming, Tess couldn't focus on anything else in their sparse cell. Watching Mark exercise, she noticed his expression remained placid, almost meditative, and the dusting of blond stubble on his jaw only enhanced his rugged allure. A surge of warmth crossed her pelvis, an inconvenient reminder of the persistent celibacy she'd endured for a year. Flustered, she steered her thoughts to platonic territory but failed. She imagined a tropical sea, where they swam naked and floated atop gentle, turquoise waves, watching as palm trees swayed under the golden sky.

A door slammed.

She heard footsteps pad away, along with voices speaking what she assumed was Russian. Startled back to attention, she pressed a hand against her cheeks, which were hot with embarrassment, and she chided herself for indulging in whimsy. If Mark had noticed her wandering gaze, she'd be mortified.

Without warning, he abandoned his current set of push-ups. Glowing from exertion, he dabbed at the semi-circle of sweat glistening on his chest. He stood and walked to the cell door, then cupped one hand around his ear a few seconds. "They said they're going to fetch lunch."

"Glad those bastards finally left. Let's find this chute." Relieved to focus on something productive, Tess rose and debated where to start.

"I'm ready." He mopped his forehead with his bloodied dress shirt, then slipped it on, leaving it unbuttoned. On his feet, he muscled the grain bin aside and managed to avoid making any noise. Skating his hands across the wall, he searched for loose boards. "Nothing here. Let's start on opposite sides and meet in the center."

"Sure." Using her hands, she drew circles to detect any irregularities but found the wall's construction solid. Crouching on the floor, she scanned the wall from the baseboard all the way up toward the ceiling. "Nothing."

"Let's move this hay," Mark said.

They stored away the remaining hay bales before continuing to search.

Growing tense with anticipation, Tess kneeled to examine another space where the wall met the floor. One foot up, she detected a tiny ripple in the drywall. "Come feel this. Can you chisel this out?"

Nodding, Mark grabbed her pocketknife and got to work. "Will you keep watch?"

"Of course." Perched on a hay bale, she spied out the barred window. Observing his progress carving the drywall from the ripple, she wedged a block of hay in front of him to hide the growing hole from view, should their captors return.

"One board's bigger than the others. Hope this is it." He chose the knife's widest blade and cut around the swell in straight, surgical lines. "Quality knife. Sharp blade helps."

"Never used it before. My fiancé gave it to me as a good luck travel charm." She watched as he finished outlining the swollen board.

Pausing to wipe sweat off his forehead, he turned and offered her a small smile. "Well, lucky for us, you carried it on this trip. When's your wedding?"

Icy water, then nothing. In a split second, grief managed to find her, even in this remote barn. A gasping sound escaped her throat, and tears dampened her cheeks before she could swipe them away. Attempts to outrun Kyle's loss by crisscrossing the globe had failed. Numbing her pain with vodka and copious amounts of denial also proved useless.

"Tess?" Mark edged closer. "What's wrong?"

"No wedding. Kyle was killed a year ago yesterday." She dug a fingernail deep into her hand, intent on creating enough physical discomfort to offset her emotional pain. Despite attempting to keep her voice measured and even, it still broke.

The pocketknife Mark held clattered to the floor, and he squatted to pick it up. "Killed? What happened?"

The empathy in his voice soothed her, but she avoided meeting his gaze for fear she'd cry even harder. Instead, she fixated on a point far beyond the barn. "Kyle and I met at Kingsley Tech. He was a software engineer, an encryption genius, and he wrote the code these criminals want to steal. Right before our wedding in London, his car smashed through a guardrail and went over a cliff into icy water. The police said he died on impact." Her voice sounded far away, like an identical understudy was narrating her tragedy's arc from backstage.

Tess extracted the gold chain around her neck and fingered the pendant, an elaborate Celtic knot. "Kyle was wearing this when he died. The police suspected a second car was involved, but they never found any witnesses. Even if they did, it doesn't matter. He's gone."

Mark plopped onto the hay bale in front of the uncovered hole on the wall. He leaned over and rested a hand on top of hers. "I'm sorry. Trust me...the grief will heal, given time."

The sympathetic gesture caught her off balance, and her tangled emotions of loss and anger leaked out before she could contain them. Cheeks wet with fresh tears, she turned to face him. "When they retrieved Kyle's body from the water, he was mangled beyond recognition. Seeing him destroyed like that…broke me." The memory of identifying Kyle's body in a London morgue, laid flat on a metal coroner's table, tightened her throat like a vise. Given the severe nature of his injuries, Kyle's parents opted for cremation, then buried his ashes in a cemetery near Sevenoaks, outside London.

"Death is hell. I know firsthand." He squeezed her hand before moving away.

"How could you understand?" Drowning in a pool of her own self-pity, she couldn't stop herself from lashing out. "I lost *everything*."

"Because I lost the two people I loved most. Life has never been the same, and it took me three years to accept they were gone." He stepped back and pressed a fist to his lips as he shifted his gaze to the barn floor.

His admission and the painful edge to his voice gave her pause, and she softened her indignant tone. "*Three* years? I can't imagine bearing this grief so long. What happened?"

"My wife, Maya, died in childbirth. Pre-eclampsia. My son, Nils, died minutes after he was born. I was shattered." Shoulders slumped, he frowned and raised a hand to his chest.

At once, Tess recognized her own grief, and the mood in the cell darkened like a cloud had obscured the sun. She understood the sudden shock of a life stolen without warning. While not the first person in history to have lost an intimate partner, she long believed her loss hurt the most. Her empathy swelled, but she lacked the words to express how well she understood his pain. "I'm so sorry," she said softly and clasped her hands in front of her.

"I miss them, and the life our family would've had together. The reality still crushes me sometimes." He shifted his gaze toward the ceiling. "I couldn't stand working at the hospital where they died, so I left and joined a humanitarian organization that provides medical care in war zones. I accepted a trauma surgery mission in Ukraine, right in the middle of the Crimean conflict. The loneliness followed me, but since I didn't have time to pity myself, things got better."

Knowing intimately how Kyle's death gutted her, she couldn't imagine enduring two serious losses at once. She stole a glance at Mark's hands, which lay resting on the front edge of the hay bale. No ring. "Did you ever, well, move on?"

"Jeg har ikke bitt i gresset ennå." He shook his head with a sad smile.

"Sorry?" She had no idea what he said.

"Ah. I meant, not yet, but I'm not eating grass."

"Eating grass?" She wondered if he was referring to smoking marijuana, or perhaps edibles.

"I haven't given up on life yet." Wearing a lopsided grin, he ran a hand through his hair.

They sat for a moment in the stillness.

He stood and returned to carving the wall. A few minutes later, he leaned his weight against the wood plank he'd outlined and pounded it twice with his fist. "Hey, this board's loosening, but I can't tell what's behind it." He wiggled the blade's tip and popped off a rectangular chunk of drywall. He brushed aside the dust, and underneath, exposed inches of dry rot next to a stud.

Noticing the hole expanded to expose the old wood, Tess placed another bale of hay at a strategic angle to hide his handiwork.

"I'm going to break it down." From the opposite side of the cell, he accelerated a few steps before pummeling the wall with an explosive kick. Wood splintered, and a tinny, metal sound rang out.

"We've got something." She removed scraps of plaster from the caved-in wall. Crouching beside him, she studied the open space. A burst of brisk air flowed inside the cell. She squinted, hoping her focus might change the view. "Wow, the space is…"

"Tiny. I'll never fit inside. Can you?"

Skeptically, she surveyed the narrow opening. The exposed chute was a literal hole in the wall and not at all the spacious escape route she imagined. After examining it in silence, she stood and stared into the dark hole. "It's tight, but I'll try."

"Good." He handed back her knife and pointed to the drywall mess on the floor. "We'd better clean this up before they return."

Together, they arranged the hay bales to hide their escape route.

"Let's wait until after dark before I try to go through. Best chance of avoiding capture." She rubbed white dust off her hands.

"Hopefully, this chute dumps outside our captors' view."

"Right. I'll sneak back inside to release you. We need a Plan B, though. If they enter while I'm circling back, use the knife and escape out the front door."

"You mean kill the gunmen?" He started pacing

back and forth across the cell and used both hands to rub his forehead.

"Well, they're going to kill me. Any other ideas?" Given a choice to kill, or be killed, preserving their kidnappers' lives wasn't a priority. She assumed what her plan required of him was obvious, but his face formed an awkward question mark.

"Give me time. Once we're out, we'll search for the road—"

"No. They'll find us on the road, and we need woods for cover." Growing anxiety swept away her patience.

"Fine. We'll aim for the woods, then we can head for the highway. Might make it before dawn."

"Let's escape around ten. Gives us at least eight hours of darkness to travel." The prospect of freedom energized her, and she longed to run under a boundless sky, free from their cell.

"The woods appear quite rugged. Long night of trekking ahead of us, should we make it outside. Better rest now." He stretched his arms high above his shoulders before sitting on the floor and straightening his legs.

The afternoon crawled by. Around sunset, the outside door yawned open, and two gunmen approached their cell carrying a small box.

All evidence of their plan hidden away, Tess and Mark each retreated to their respective sides of the cell.

"Dinner." The metal bar clanged as Alexi, the gunman sporting stitches on his head from the fallen chandelier, slid the door open. He placed a box of sandwiches and water bottles on a bale of hay. "Bathroom?"

They both nodded.

The other gunman, Sergey, gestured at Tess to go first, and he followed her out of the cell. Holding his rifle in one hand, he used his other hand to pinch her left buttock, hard.

Unamused, she swatted his hand away. "Stop it."

"*Goryachaya zhenshchina, ya by khotel razdet' yeye.*" Sergey threw his head back and laughed, making obscene sounds.

"*Ne seychas. Vy poluchite svoyu ochered', chtoby poveselit'sya s ney.*" Alexi pointed at her and broke into laughter.

She turned and stared at Alexi, who had addressed Sergey as if disciplining a small child. Unsettled, she glanced over her shoulder and caught the look of disgust etched on Mark's face.

"Keep your hands off her," Mark shouted, and he jumped to his feet.

Both gunmen paused to gawk at his outburst.

"What's wrong with you? Sit, doctor." Sergey steered Tess toward the bathroom.

Although she assumed Sergey said something raunchy, Tess discounted the comments and ignored the scuffle behind her. Once in the bathroom, she locked the door, used the toilet, and scrubbed her hands using dingy soap under the frigid running water. The mirror reflected her cheekbone, which had darkened to violet since morning. She shook water from her hands and exited the bathroom, careful to avoid eye contact with Sergey as she trod back to the cell.

After their captors departed, she bit into one of the sandwiches, but it tasted like cardboard. Anxiety stole her appetite, and she grew somber while contemplating the peril awaiting them. Unable to make herself eat, she set her sandwich on the hay bale. "Escaping alive isn't a certainty, and we could die tonight."

"You're not having doubts, are you?"

"No, but I can't sugarcoat the risks we each face." When she registered the concern imprinted in Mark's expression, she softened her voice. Facing danger's onslaught, everything fell away, unimportant, leaving nothing precious but life itself. "Thank you for trying to save Riku last night. You risked your life by stepping forward, and I can't help thinking if you'd stayed silent, you wouldn't be in this mess."

Mark clasped his hands together. "I'm a doctor, which means I'm bound to honor my Hippocratic Oath to heal. 'If it is given to me to save a life, all thanks.' I'm sorry I couldn't save your friend."

"You gave your best. And don't worry about me, because I refuse to die at the hands of these pigs."

"I've got your back."

She gazed at him while trying to decipher his mood, which exhibited determination, fear, and an unexpected green sprout of curiosity. Daylight faded hours ago, and minutes ticked by in slow motion while she waited for night's dark cover. As the evening grew still, only a steady, bitter wind sounded beyond the barn. Nighttime arrived, signaling it was time to go. She delayed until fifteen minutes of quiet had passed to ensure their captors were far from the barn.

Mark shoved the hay bales away from the carved hole in the wall, exposing the narrow chute. He stood watch by the metal bars above the cell door and scanned for their captors. "All clear."

Tess brushed her hair back from her bruised cheek,

took a couple deep breaths, and stretched her arms up high to lengthen her body. Remembering her pocketknife, she extracted it from her jacket and held it in her palm. "Here. In case you need it."

He stepped forward and pocketed the knife. "I'll give you a hand."

She crouched and stared into the dark, square hole to plan her descent. "On my back, feet first, so I land upright." On the floor, she lay down, knees bent, and stuck her feet into the opening, heels pointed to the bottom. Scooting her hips into the opening in the wall, she angled her feet to gain more space. "Give me a lift."

"Ready?" Mark knelt on the ground behind her and slid his forearms under her back to lift her to the chute's opening.

Tingling electric energy ran through her body from the touch of his warm hands as they guided her torso into the opening. "Now, shoulders."

He eased her body through the opening of the feed chute.

"I'm stuck. I need to twist." Her mouth grew dry, and her shoulders wouldn't budge. *Focus.* In the claustrophobic, tight space, she lay flat and crammed her arms over her chest to squeeze her body into a narrow log, tilting at a slight diagonal to compress even more. Bit by agonizing bit, she scooched inches at a time and eked her way through the tube. Complete darkness filled the chute, and she fended off panic by taking slow, steady breaths to keep her rib cage compact.

"Everything okay?"

His voice sounded muffled. "Yes." A blockage near her feet slowed her progress, and she stretched her toes to tap at something. "I've got fresh air, and there's something rubbery at the bottom. A flap." One more slide, and her feet popped through the bottom's opening. Frigid air swirled around her ankles. She exhaled to empty her lungs of air before she resumed scooting downwards. With morbid amusement, she rebirthed her grown body in the breech position, feet first, out the grain chute. Hopefully, she wouldn't be reincarnated as a cow in her next life.

After one last slide, the flap swung and whacked her face. She tumbled into a heap on soft earth smelling of grass, mud, and grain. Disoriented, she paused to allow her vision to adjust to the darkness, and the sound of heavy panting nearby alarmed her. Given she had zero cover, she chose to play dead on the ground, leaving her injured cheek exposed to the raw air.

A huge black shape loomed above, then meandered closer.

For God's sake, now what? Earthy warm breath blew in her face, and something scratchy and wet licked her cheek. A distinct bovine "moo" sounded. She wanted to laugh out loud. The cow mistook her for dinner, given she reeked of grain. She waved the cow away with a muddy hand and ascended from the ground.

Hugging the edge of the barn, Tess scanned the clearing for places to take cover, if needed. A stack of hay bales towered next to two water troughs. Keeping close to the wall, she sidestepped until she rounded the corner. Across from the gate, she recognized the shed where Yuri interrogated her. A trailer stood in the distance, and bright lights glowed through the windows farthest from the barn. In the quiet night, all she could hear was the muted sound of farm animals. Time to make her move.

Crouched low, Tess crept toward the front of the barn. After she cast a glance to confirm she wasn't being followed, she studied the entrance. The sliding doors were joined by a metal bar latched above adjoining handles. Praying the bar wouldn't squeak, she lifted it and slid the door an inch to the right. Once she opened the door several inches, she squeezed through the narrow opening, then slid it back and left the bar open, so the door appeared shut from the outside.

She tiptoed across the barn to the cell. The prospect of freedom sent her hope skyrocketing, and joyful tears sprang to her eyes. For a precious moment, she relaxed her body, the first time since last night's gunfire, and she beamed. "I made it."

"Great. I'm ready to go." Mark was waiting with his hands wrapped around the bars above the thick wooden door.

In the dim light, she fumbled to unlock the metal bar and slide the door open. Out of nowhere, the sharp point of a knife clamped against her throat. She gasped.

"Don't move," a voice hissed.

A vodka-tinged breath exhaled near her ear, and a rough hand seized her left arm.

Her earlier daydream of a sun-drenched beach crashed into pieces. Trigger-happy Sergey was behind her. All hope she harbored of escaping unharmed vanished. Afraid to breathe, lest the knife nick her throat, she avoided inhaling. Damn it, how did she not hear the door slide open behind her? Worse, Sergey was touching her.

"Trying to run away, bitch? I don't like women

who misbehave."

Her stomach quivered in revulsion as he panted, warming the sharp point of the blade against her neck. Sergey's breath reeked of onions, meat, and stale cigarette smoke, and she scrunched up her nose to block the smell. Her hands trembled, and she willed herself silent. His earlier comments dismayed her, and her body tensed, rigid as a stone. Given Mark was still locked up, she was unsure what to do next. Her lungs tightened, as if the barn had collapsed and crushed out her breath. Fighting to control her panic, she breathed in four counts, paused, then exhaled in four counts.

Behind her, she heard Dmitry join Sergey and say something in Russian.

Sergey gave a crude laugh, accompanied by a hip thrust against her back.

To escape his grip, she jolted forward and recoiled from him. Sergey's tone of voice left no doubt what unique danger she faced as a woman, and she couldn't stop her hands from quaking. She wriggled and attempted to shake off his body, which was still plastered against her back like filthy mud.

"Let her go!" Mark rattled the metal bars of the window.

"*Yesli ty ub'yesh' yeye, my ne poluchim deneg. Yuri porezhet tebya na melkiye kusochki. On ubival lyudey za men'sheye.*" Dimitri shook a fist and shouted a long string of words.

"*Eto slukh KGB, ne boleye togo.*"

Listening to the men argue, she rotated slowly to watch them. She concluded whatever Dimitri yelled in his angry diatribe, it didn't rebuff Sergey, who stood wearing a smirk.

"*Yuri tochit nozhi kazhdyy den. Ne zli yego.*"
Dmitry pointed a finger at Sergey.

Judging from Dmitry's tone of voice, Tess guessed
he had issued Sergey a warning. From behind, Sergey
locked his calloused grip around her arm like a vise so
tight, it cut off her hand's circulation. Somehow the
door slid open.

Sergey wound up his fist and walloped her back.

The force jettisoned her across the cell, and she
landed with her face buried in the hay and gasped for
air.

"Don't run away again. We guard you all night
tonight." Sergey grunted, then locked the door before
he lumbered out of the barn.

Inside the cell, she groaned from the impact of the
hit and curled into a ball on the floor.

Mark rushed over. "Are you hurt?"

The savage hit knocked the air out of her, and she
gasped several times to refill her lungs. Grimacing, she
used her hands to ease herself into a sitting position.
Scratchy hay prickled her face, and she swept it away.
"Damn it, I was so close and almost made it. I didn't
see anyone in the barnyard." She studied Mark's frown
and glimpsed his clenched fists. "What were they
talking about?"

He avoided meeting her gaze. "Ugly things. Sergey
wants to, uh, do bad things, but Dmitry said if you die,
they don't get paid. If Sergey ruins the ransom deal,
Yuri will kill him with sharp knives. Sergey doesn't
believe it, but Dmitry's damn scared of Yuri."

"Figures. We need a new plan." She didn't need to
guess what things Mark avoided translating and
wouldn't say out loud.

"Don't apologize. We'll find another way, but we need to get you out of here fast." He studied her again. "You took a brutal hit. Let me check your back."

Too crestfallen to protest, Tess relented. Her once-ivory silk top was untucked, and she reached an arm to lift its back.

Mark stopped her. "Don't twist. I'll lift it for you."

His hands were warm and confident. Embers of attraction sprang up underneath the surface of her pain. He placed one hand on her back to hold her blouse up, and with the other, he palpated the area where Sergey had pummeled her. When his hand grazed her bare skin to examine her injury, sparks of unexpected pleasure assuaged the raw ache. Inadvertently, she leaned into his hand a couple inches. For a moment, she imagined him slipping his arms around her, holding her. No one had held her since Kyle died, and her yearning for comfort overwhelmed her at the worst possible time.

He placed his ear against her back. "I need to hear your lungs. Breathe, please. Again."

She complied. He discovered the target of Sergey's punch, eliciting her painful wince.

"This spot will be tender, but he didn't break your ribs. No aeration indicating damage to the lung. Slow your breathing, if you can." He dropped the bottom of her blouse over her bare skin and stood, then extended a hand to help her to her feet.

"Thanks." The physical pain she could ignore, but her hypersensitivity to Mark standing so close, paired with the warmth radiating off his body, confounded her. She careened between anger at their failed escape, her pain, and ill-timed, yet irresistible, desire. She stretched tall and stumbled to a hay bale, clutching her rib cage in self-protection.

Mark crouched on his knees beside her. "We've got to get you out of here fast. Dmitry convinced Sergey not to, uh, harm you now, but they're coming back to guard us tonight. We've got a few minutes alone now." He lowered his voice to an urgent whisper.

The mention of Sergey's intentions chilled her blood. Her dad's worst fear, and her own, too, lurked outside the barn, mere yards away. "We need to be more aggressive. I've got my pepper spray in my jacket, and you have my knife."

"What next?"

"They've let us out for bathroom breaks before. We could ask for one later tonight and strike then." A new plan formed inside her mind, and she focused on the ceiling to concentrate.

"They plan to guard us in shifts, so if we're lucky, we'll have one gunman to fight, instead of two," Mark said.

"I'd prefer we face Dmitry rather than Sergey. Sick bastard."

"Agreed. Also, Dmitry vomited today, which means he'll be dehydrated and weaker."

Discomfort furrowed her brow, and when she tried to arch her back, she flinched. "Doubt we'll get a choice. All we need is enough time to hike those twenty kilometers to the highway."

"Let me make sure they're gone." He checked the barred window, then jumped off the hay bale. Before turning in her direction, he brushed away random pieces of straw from his pants. "Then what?"

She hoisted herself up and paced the cell, taking a few steps forward, and then backward, like rehearsing a dance. "They'll be armed, and if just one of them comes…" She paused to test the heavy wooden door. "I'll say I'm sick and demand a bathroom break. When one of them opens the door, I'll spray him. You grab him, throw him into the cell, then take away his weapons and phone. We get out, lock him inside, and run."

"Well, it buys us time to escape, if our captor isn't discovered missing right away."

"Sure, best case. If two of them come, you've got my knife. You're a surgeon and know how to disable someone, if needed."

He opened his mouth to speak but fell silent.

At once, she stopped, and her concern escalated. They couldn't afford an ounce of doubt; any hesitation could prove fatal. She grabbed his shoulder. "You must be prepared to use deadly force. You understand that, right?"

"I hate this. I've spent my life healing people."

"I know, but here we are, and if we don't fight, we die." She recognized the resentment running through his voice, but doubt wasn't an emotion she could tolerate right now. She needed to be certain he could take lethal action if necessary, or else their plan would fail. "Mark, you need to commit 100 percent. Any doubt could kill us. Are you ready?"

"We're out of options."

"You didn't answer my question. Practice with me. Let's master this sequence so we're both ready."

Together they mapped out where each of them would stand, with weapons ready, which hand signals to use, and how to maneuver to trap their captor. They pantomimed the ambush and rehearsed every footstep to memorize the cell's space, as well as mapping the sequence of each motion for the first critical seconds.

"Can you move the hay bales away from the door, so we have more space?" While she waited, she inspected her pepper spray canister, double-checking it remained loaded and functional.

"I hear someone." He grabbed her arm and raised a finger to his lips. They stopped practicing and waited to see which captor appeared. He leapt onto a hay bale by the door and peeked out the bars. "Ah, we're in luck. Dmitry."

"You ready?" Dress rehearsal was over, and she tightened her jaw. To squash her own doubts, she imagined her fears as innocuous objects she could store in tidy, sealed boxes in her mind's attic and ignore forever.

"No choice, right?"

"Here we go. Give it your all." Luck wouldn't be enough to save them, and she didn't believe in miracles. Survival depended on their courage alone, and she hoped they didn't run short.

Chapter Six

Barn Battle

Perched on her tiptoes on top of a hay bale, Tess peered out their cell window and spied Dmitry entering the barn. Inside, she worked up her courage.

He carried the battered wooden chair from Yuri's interrogation shed and a newspaper, blanket, and bottle of water. He placed the chair on the floor in plain view, about four yards away, and took a seat. Every time he shifted, the chair creaked from his weight. Engrossed in his reading, he flipped the crinkled pages, which rustled like falling leaves.

"Does he have a rifle?" Mark asked in a faint whisper.

"Yes, on the floor beside him, but he could have a gun in his pocket. He's reading now," she whispered. Adrenaline pumping, she hopped from the hay bale, ready to set their plan in motion. On impulse, she grabbed Mark's hand and squeezed it. "Let's go. Good luck." Standing tall, she took a deep breath and crossed her fingers, hoping she'd trick Dmitry on the first try. "Excuse me. I need to go to the bathroom."

"No." Dmitry didn't glance up from his newspaper.

She scowled at Mark to express her frustration. "I'm going to be sick, and I need a toilet, bad. Please." This time, she injected more panic into her request.

"She's sick. Get her out of here," Mark said.

He spoke in an annoyed, gruff voice, as if she were an unpleasant panhandler on a dodgy street. Grateful for his convincing backup, Tess hoped the ruse worked.

Wearing a smirk, Dmitry rose and dropped his newspaper. He stretched to view their cell, then shuffled across the room.

"Hurry, I gotta go really badly." Behind their cell's door, she stood in the formation they'd practiced, with Mark across from her. Her feet inches apart, she tensed her leg muscles like a lion ready to pounce. She gripped the canister and poised her trigger finger on the spray valve. Feigning illness, she bent over and held her stomach, all while emitting a loud moan.

"Only woman leaves the cell," Dmitry said through the door. The cell door's metal bar clanked as he unlatched it. The door slid open, and he poked his head inside the cell.

At close range, Tess shot pepper spray into Dmitry's face, and she made certain to coat both his eyes with plenty of the noxious liquid.

Blinded, the man wailed and stumbled.

Mark flung Dmitry into the cell, where he landed with a thump. Using one foot to keep Dmitry from escaping, Mark searched the gunman's pants for a handgun but found nothing.

Wasting no time, Tess grabbed Mark's hand, backed them out of the cell, and slid the door shut. She pulled on the lock to double-check it was secure while ignoring Dmitry's furious shouts. Looking behind her, she regretted not gagging him but couldn't risk taking the time to silence him. Following Mark, she raced down the barn's dark hallway and swerved toward the exit.

Suddenly, the barn door burst open.

She felt a gust of cold air.

Sergey barged inside and almost collided with them. He yelled something unintelligible and clenched his stubby fingers into fists. With a barrage of wild swings, he walloped Mark repeatedly and landed several punches square on his chest.

Mark crumpled to the ground and groaned, then fell quiet and motionless.

Fearing Mark had lost consciousness, Tess blasted Sergey's back with her fists to distract him, but her jabs failed to slow the beefy-fisted gunman. Frantic to reach Mark, she struggled to dodge around Sergey, but his body was like an immobile brick wall, blocking her passage.

"I don't care what Yuri says. I take what I want." Sergey lurched over to Tess.

He snapped her arm behind her back using such force that her shoulder joints seized in protest. Stunned for a moment, she wrestled herself away and assumed a fighting stance, grateful the muscle memory from her training decades ago kicked in. The warm gold of Kyle's Celtic knot amulet heated her chest's skin and channeled power into her bloodstream. Anything superfluous dropped away, and the clarity enabled her to focus on one goal: fight strong.

In a flash, Sergey whipped a knife out of his holster and placed the gleaming tip against her neck. "Do you hear me now?" He shook her again.

"Yes, I do," she said in a loud, clear voice. Alone now, she experienced her courage rushing in, and new energy fortified her. Lengthening her body, she stood tall with her feet grounded on the solid barn floor, and she held her chin high. Hands clenched, she ignored Sergey's pungent body odor. Adrenaline surged through her body like wildfire. Raging with raw aggression, she swung with all her strength.

Grunting, Sergey punched her upper right shoulder. The impact knocked her flat, but she crawled onto all fours and kept her gaze trained on him.

Still holding his knife in one hand, he used his other hand to unbuckle his belt. His black military pants dropped around his ankles, and the heavy buckle made a dull, metallic thud on the barn floor.

Her stomach churned, and she tried to unsee his naked legs. "Don't you dare touch me, you rodent." She growled and crawled on her hands and knees, but her shoulder contorted in pain, and she dropped back to the ground. Uncertain whether Mark was conscious, she shouted his name in hopes he'd hear her.

"I'll kill you," Sergey snarled.

Across the room from her, Mark writhed on the barn floor and attempted to get up but fell, clutching his rib cage. "Leave her alone," he yelled.

"Shut up," Sergey hissed and waved his knife.

With no pathway to escape, her only choice was to fight. Ignoring the crushing throb in her shoulder, Tess summoned her strength and jumped to her feet. Woozy from the exertion, she raced to assess her options.

Sergey's gleaming knife pointed in her direction, but he held no gun. The captor stood a few inches taller than she, but he was stout and sported a hairy potbelly that jiggled and spilled over the top of his white briefs. Revulsion overcame her logic, and she lost her focus for a moment.

He lunged and grasped for her blouse. With his hands grabbing her shoulders, he shoved her against the wall.

Revolted, she spat on the ground. She ducked low under his armpit and twisted out from under him, then snapped tall again. However, she only traveled a couple of steps before he grabbed her and whipped her body around to face him.

Roaring, he wound up his fist to hit her again.

Without hesitation, she shoved her hands into his face and dug her fingernails into his eyes.

He howled and dropped his knife, swatting his hands in the air. Lines of blood streaked his cheeks from where her fingernails punctured his skin, and he swiped at his face to rub it away.

"Dmitry, help!" he shouted.

Meanwhile, Tess gathered her strength and kneed him in the crotch. *All those years of soccer paid off.* The blow didn't knock him unconscious, but it disabled him enough to buy herself critical seconds. She raced over, squatted by Mark's side, and shook his shoulder. "Get up." Focused on rousing Mark, she couldn't see behind her but felt her ankle yanked. Losing her balance, she stumbled and tripped before landing on the floor.

Somehow, Mark found his way to his feet, and he charged Sergey like a bull. Taking the gunman by surprise, he tackled him to the floor.

Free from Sergey's grasp, Tess managed to stand and catch her breath.

In front of her, the two men rolled over each other on the floor twice, then again, intertwined in a macabre *pas de deux*. If anything, the blinded gunman renewed his savage assault of Mark, striking wildly and landing his fist with loud smacks.

Sergey kept grasping at the right side of his military fatigue pants, loose around his ankles.

A gun handle extended from one of the cargo pockets.

Mark slammed a round of punches at Sergey, which prevented him from retrieving his weapon. "Run, Tess! Go!" he shouted.

Dazed, she sucked in a breath and felt her beaten shoulder pound in time with her heartbeat. A soft clunk sounded near her, and when she turned, she spotted Sergey's gun on the floor, partly covered by his pants. Instinct made her back away from the men dueling on the floor, and she sidestepped to avoid their flailing arms and legs. Biting her lip, she debated whether she could reach the gun but decided against it. The only gamble was whether Mark could endure a few more seconds.

Fueled by fury, she scrambled past piles of buckets, feed bags, and brooms. She bulldozed useless farm equipment out of her path. Around the corner, she glimpsed a formidable stick hanging on the wall. *Yes.* She grabbed it and sprinted back across the room, trying to figure out how best to intervene.

Sergey had rolled on top of Mark and straddled him so he couldn't move. Like a sadistic machine, he pummeled Mark's chest.

Yelling, Mark thrust his arms upward to block the hits, and he shoved his attacker's chin up and away. His scarred left hand spasmed and dropped to his side, leaving him one arm to fight. Just then, he took a strike on his lower rib cage. A bone cracked, and Mark howled.

Sergey found the gun extending from his cargo pocket and clicked the safety off.

Watching Sergey taunt Mark, Tess wagered the gunman hadn't spotted her standing behind them. However, Mark must have seen her, because he covered his head and bolted to his right, bucking Sergey off-balance.

The four steel tines of the pitchfork in Tess's hands glinted in the light, and she tightened her grip on the handle. With her entire weight behind the pitchfork, she thrust it deep into Sergey's back. The tines punctured first flesh, then muscle, and, with a final, bloody squish, organs. The sickening sound made her gasp, and her breath came in irregular bursts.

Wretched gagging sounds emitted from Sergey before he slumped over with a thud. His gun slipped out of his hand and dropped onto the floor. Blood flowed from his back and abdomen and pooled into a garish Rorschach pattern. His black pants lay twisted around his ankles, exposing his hairy legs.

Her heart thumped like a tom-tom, and every beat pounded inside her skull. She stared at the pitchfork, which remained lodged in Sergey's back.

Mark rolled away from the body and struggled to his feet while clutching his rib cage. He leaned over and placed two fingers on the gunman's neck. "He's gone. You skewered him."

Bountiful amounts of blood seeped onto the floor. As the red stain spread, she backed away and covered her mouth. The barn surroundings reappeared in her field of vision. "What have I done?"

"You saved my life." Mark grabbed her and wound

an arm around her.

A sob escaped her throat, and she peeked around his broad shoulder to stare at the corpse on the floor, fixating on the shiny steel tines. Electric shocks stung throughout her body, and lines deepened on her forehead. Numb with disbelief, she felt tingling in her cheeks.

"We need to go. Now, before Dmitry makes trouble." He shook her arm to get her attention.

Spotting the gun on the floor, she rushed to pick it up and clicked the safety on. Wanting nothing from the gunman to touch her, she held it out. "I can shoot, but I don't want to carry it."

Mark nodded and slipped the weapon into the waistband of his trousers.

She stepped forward, her legs lurching, and she welcomed his hand on her back to guide her to the barn's front door, which Sergey had left cracked open. A battered barn jacket hung on a hook next to the door.

"Cold night. You'll need it." He snatched it from the hook and placed it in her hands.

She slipped on the jacket, three sizes too big, and the excess cloth swallowed her slight frame. Muffled but agitated voices buzzed somewhere beyond the barnyard. A door slammed and startled her, but she shook off her fear and mobilized.

Outside the barn, the smell of manure hit her, but no cows were milling around. She signaled Mark to follow her and retraced the path she'd taken earlier that night. Spooked by a sudden burst of paranoia, she broke into a run. Heading behind a cluster of oak trees which lined the pasture, she aimed their trajectory far from the trailer, where she assumed Yuri and his gunmen were camped out. The earth beneath her feet was solid but damp. Wet autumn leaves lined the ground and hid the sound of their footsteps.

She knew they weren't running fast enough. Once their captors found Sergey and Dmitry, they'd hunt them without mercy. Her adrenaline switched from fight to flight, and she accelerated her pace. Heat flushed her face, but her hands grew cold. After gesturing at Mark to hurry, she remembered his cracked ribs and regretted pressuring him.

He was trailing well behind.

When she heard him wheezing, she stopped to wait.

Out of breath when he reached her, he coughed and huffed several times. Without speaking, he pointed out Anderson Campbell's darkened cottage across a small clearing.

Using the farmer's house as a landmark, Tess steered them south past it, then led them up a tree-lined hill into a dark clump of woods. Once under the thick cover of trees, fallen branches and debris blocked their path, forcing her to slow. Determined, she kept slogging through the terrain.

Mark followed her, this time only a few steps behind.

In a silent, trance-like state, she attempted to erase ghastly images of Sergey. She also prayed Mark could keep moving long enough for them to find a safe place to hide.

They had no choice but to keep hiking through the woods.

Chapter Seven

In the Woods

In the dark woods, Tess trekked, leading them for over thirty minutes without stopping. The earth absorbed their footsteps, and as they distanced themselves from the farm, sounds of livestock faded. Clusters of cumulus clouds sped across the sky, allowing intervals of moonlight to light their way through endless hills, which swelled and receded. Tess kept the lead and pressed forward at a rapid but sustainable pace. She dodged tree branches and autumnal debris underfoot and took care to skirt open clearings which might expose their location.

Hoping they'd eluded their captors, Tess enjoyed a moment of optimism, until she realized how far Mark lagged. Breathing hard, she stopped to rest and leaned over her knees to wait.

When he finally appeared, weariness lined his face, and he wheezed every few breaths.

"Hey, you don't sound good." She reached out to touch his arm, and her forehead creased as she studied him.

"Pain is weakness leaving the body." Grunting, Mark bent over and mumbled something unintelligible.

"No need to act tough for me. The bastard pummeled you."

"I've got one or two broken ribs, and my left lung is bruised, possibly aspirating. *Helvete*." He leaned his head back and stared into the dark sky.

Given her cracked cheekbone and battered shoulder, she had to admit her resiliency was flagging. She bit her lower lip and ignored her exhausted legs. When they fled, she only thought to run, and everything else dropped away. As reality set in, she worried the combination of their injuries, fatigue, and lack of shelter from the cold jeopardized their chances of reaching the highway alive. Lacking a magic wand to transport them home, she prayed grit alone could power them through this trek.

Grateful for the brief respite, she shook her legs out and stretched her arms. Loud Technicolor static buzzed inside her brain, and a thousand emotions, all indecipherable, churned in tandem. For now, she and Mark had survived, and a quiet sigh slipped past her lips.

Restless, nervous energy burned through her, and she shifted her weight from one foot to the other. They couldn't afford to stop for long, but she forced herself to give Mark a reasonable break. "Can you keep going?"

"Not gonna quit now." He straightened his spine and coughed. "What about you?"

"Never." Still wired from their escape, she inhaled, but her emotions swerved between terror and elation. If her luck hadn't been so terrible, she'd laugh. Enduring a terrorist attack and running for her life was the perfect way to cap off the soul-sucking year she'd spent grieving Kyle's death. Work and nonstop travel failed to heal her loss, and avoiding romantic connection only amplified her loneliness. The raw truth Mark spoke resonated deep in her bones. *Wherever you go, loneliness follows you.*

She watched as he shuffled around the hidden grove of trees where they'd stopped. In these dark hours, Mark had raised her spirits after their ordeal, and inspired sprouts of hope the wretched situation didn't warrant. Unable to discern whether it was primal instinct or lust which drove her, she abandoned caution.

Acting on pure impulse, she stepped closer and placed her hands on top of his shoulders, where they curved in a smooth line to his neck. In the frigid air, she felt him radiating warmth and grasped his shirt. Using her hands to span his solid broad shoulders, she slid them over the inverted triangle of his torso as it tapered to his waist in chiseled lines. For a transitory moment, she found safety and clutched him tight.

In response, he wound his arms around her and stroked the back of her head.

"Thank you," she whispered. His warm hands enclosed the gentle arc of her aching back, and long-dormant parts of her began to thaw. Relishing the peaceful moment, she unwound several degrees.

"You're the one I want to thank. Sergey would have killed me." He patted her back.

"We saved each other." The enormity of the sacrifice he had offered took her breath away.

He kept his arms tight around her.

The momentary solace allowed her a sliver of time to absorb what they'd just endured. "Sergey would have …" She couldn't utter the word out loud. Instead, she covered her mouth and gasped in uneven bursts as visions of alternate, horrific outcomes for each of them flashed through her mind. Resting her head against his chest, she clenched her eyes shut, determined not to cry.

"Sh. *Vi kommer til å overleve.*" Mark pulled her closer and rested his chin atop her head. "We're going to survive. You've been so strong."

"I wanted to stop Sergey, not kill him." Recalling the feeling of thrusting her weight behind the pitchfork as she plunged it into the gunman disturbed her. Nor could she erase the gruesome sound of metal puncturing flesh, which kept replaying in her mind. She broke away from Mark and searched her hands for telltale bloodstains, like Lady Macbeth. Despite careful examination, she found her skin remained milky white.

"Listen. You acted in self-defense, and you did what was necessary to survive." Using his fingertips, Mark lifted her chin and gazed at her. "He was an assassin. Don't waste a moment feeling guilty. If you hadn't acted, we'd both be dead."

The horrific event was too recent to apply any objectivity. Meanwhile, visions of Yuri sprang to her mind, turning her blood cold. If Yuri caught them, he'd exact sadistic revenge for Sergey's death. The fear threatened to immobilize her, and she yearned to run to regain control. "I'm afraid Yuri will stalk us like prey. We'd better go."

"Agreed. Let's find the highway before daylight."

Glad Mark didn't need any extra encouragement, she led their trek through the dark woods. Endless obstacles slowed their progress. When the clouds cleared, the moon shone in filtered slivers and bounced off the dew-soaked pine needles lining the forest floor. She pressed a hand to where her shoulder cramped from Sergey's beating and trudged ahead, dragging her legs like cement blocks. After plodding another forty-five minutes, she struggled with every step. Mutual fatigue demanded she and Mark slow their pace to a crawl, but she hoped they'd traveled far enough to elude their captors.

"Let's find shelter and stop awhile. Rest a couple of minutes." Chest heaving, Mark wheezed again and curled his left hand against his side.

"I need a break, too." She let out an exhausted sigh. Luxurious images of London tantalized her, and she reminisced about the five-star hotel near Covent Garden, where she'd last stayed. Crisp white linens and a goose-down duvet had lined her heavenly cocoon of a bed, and piles of fluffy, cloud-like pillows graced the plush headboard. She longed for safety, followed by food, water, and a hot bath. Lacking all those things, she shivered. In the darkness, the woods grew ominous. The temperature dipped further, and the brisk air cooled her aching lungs.

As Mark hiked behind her, she traversed a dense patch and scanned for a hollow of foliage suitable for a hideout. She pointed at a heavily wooded section. "See the pile of logs over there? If we collect a few downed tree branches, we can prop them up and build a small fort."

"Good. Let's search for branches."

Together, she and Mark plucked sturdy branches from the ground. In minutes, she stacked a mix of cedar and spruce branches to form a makeshift shelter against three fallen logs.

Mark brushed away the rocks and pebbles, then scattered handfuls of pine needles to soften the ground.

Tess piled on more fir branches to create a thicker

cover. The hideout wouldn't be warm, but it would suffice. Behind the logs in the shelter, Tess yawned and eased herself to the ground. Running in dress boots through the rugged terrain had left her feet blistered and raw. The constant throbbing in her shoulder and back from Sergey's blows drained the last of her energy.

Mark foraged for more branches to shield them, then crawled on his hands and knees into the shelter and sat. He withdrew Sergey's handgun from his waistband and placed it on a nearby log. Digging into his pocket, he extracted a handful of white capsules. "These are the last of the painkillers. Want some?"

"Please. The brute clobbered my shoulder." She selected two capsules from his open palm and popped them in her mouth. The pills lodged in her dry throat, but she choked them down without water. Still wearing the oversized barn coat Mark found, she scavenged through the pockets. One contained a broken pen and loose birdseed. Moving to the other side, she grazed her fingers over a sizable glass bottle and held it up in the moonlight to read the label. "What luck. Tennessee whiskey, half full."

"Yes!" Mark pumped a fist. "Better than half empty. Farmer Campbell swore he didn't drink hard stuff, but luckily, he lied."

"Drink?" She gestured toward the bottle and observed his face relax in profound relief.

"God, yes. You go first."

Tess took a hefty drink and savored the peaty liquid. Cold, achy, and sore, she appreciated the immediate salve and warmth the alcohol offered. She handed him the bottle. "Ahh. I've never been so grateful for whiskey."

"*Skål*, to Farmer Campbell." He raised the bottle in a toast. Pressing the bottle to his lips, he took a long sip, then another. "Best shot of whiskey, ever."

Taking turns, she and Mark quickly drained the bottle.

The whiskey warmed her throat and coaxed away her inhibitions. "Tonight, I figured out I want to live."

"Well, survival *is* the strongest human instinct, followed closely by desire and fear." Seated on the ground, Mark wrapped his arms around his bent knees.

The word *desire* piqued her interest, but she needed to release the weight she'd carried all year before acknowledging it. "The point is this—survival isn't enough. All I've been doing since Kyle died is surviving, but I want to live and experience things. I'm done with slogging through every day." The nights she spent seeking sensory overload in London clubs failed to revive her spirits and only left her exhausted. Even her escapist adventure the night before Cedarcliff offered no solace. For an entire year, she failed to break through her grief and find joy again. Now, she hungered to restore the life force in her veins.

"Hmm. When we encounter death, it warns us we don't live forever. After living in a war zone for three years, I know the only thing we can count on is the present." He shifted his position on the uneven ground and smoothed a pile of pine needles. "Buddhists talk about it all the time. We can't change the past or control the future, which leaves us—"

"Now." After finishing his sentence, she gazed in his direction for a moment and then glanced away, self-conscious.

"Right."

The lilt of his soft baritone soothed her. Amidst their harrowing escape, she sensed something brewing under the surface, something so unexpected and out of context given the attack that she couldn't process it. Peeling off the farmer's coat, she rotated it to form a blanket. Careful to coddle her shoulder, she settled onto the bed of pine needles, then groaned. "I can't move anymore."

The earthy smell of autumn leaves filled the air, and the icy edge of the night cooled her bruised cheek. The trek had decimated her physical reserves, but she remained wired, almost delirious. The temperature dropped toward freezing, and goose bumps covered her skin. She trembled and crossed her arms as a deep chill settled into her body.

Mark lay next to her, neither touching nor speaking.

He rotated to lie on his side, and leaves crunched as he rolled over them. "Your teeth are chattering." After breaking the silence, he slid his right arm over her and pressed the length of his body against her back. Throwing the old barn coat over them, he created an insulated tent of warm air over the top half of their bodies. "Better."

Despite the bristly pine needles and the uneven forest floor beneath her, Tess relaxed her tense body against the ground. Calmed by the warmth of Mark's body, she gave in to fatigue as he murmured a few unintelligible Norwegian words and fell quiet. Seeking more heat, she stretched a hand to reach his hip bone, which rested square against her own.

The night grew still, and a gentle wind rustled dry leaves. An owl hooted at occasional intervals. Behind her, Mark's chest rose and fell in a slow, rhythmic cycle. Bone-tired, she listened to him breathe. Too wired and frightened to fall asleep, she stared at the swaying shadows of tree limbs and prayed she'd live another day.

****

Swishing tree branches awakened her. She opened one bleary eye to confirm darkness still hid their location. Mark had wrapped his muscular arm tight around her waist, and warmth spread through her back. Like a broken mosaic, disordered images from the past two days appeared in her memory without warning but didn't make any sense. Eager to wish their ordeal away and return home, she burrowed closer to Mark's chest. She visualized packing away all the painful memories into tidy boxes in her mind's attic, then locking the door in hopes they'd disappear forever. Later, she could reconcile all she'd seen and, worse, what she'd done.

Mark stirred, and his left arm tightened around her waist.

They'd stayed spooned together since falling asleep, and their proximity revived a sublime, intimate comfort she sorely missed. Although they were fugitives struggling to survive, she let her mind run wild for a few moments. Smelling the remnant wisps of his cologne, a heady mix of sandalwood and amber, she felt her restraint slip away.

She scolded herself for daydreaming and decided he'd kept her warm to protect her from becoming hypothermic, an obstacle that would jeopardize their escape. And their earlier embrace? She wrote off his expression of gratitude as an anomaly and nothing more.

He repositioned his body a few inches, and his top leg curled over hers.

"Mark, are you awake?" she whispered.

He jerked and moved his leg away. "Now I am. Everything all right?"

Groggy, his raspy voice held a note of concern, but she hadn't meant to startle him. "Yes, but we'll need to start running again soon."

"Not for a couple of minutes at least," he mumbled into her back.

Soaking up their shared warmth, she rolled over to face him and tucked her head against his chest. "Thanks for keeping me warm. How are you doing?"

"Other than hiding out from terrorists and sleeping in the woods? Achy."

"Pretty well, then."

"I'm alive and didn't wake up alone, so I'd say yes." Stretching his arms, he yawned.

She smiled in the dark. "Thanks to you, I'm alive, too."

The clouds above shifted, and moonlight beams shone through the fir tree branches into their fort. Mark nestled closer with a sleepy smile, and the lengths of their bodies pressed together. The sounds of the forest grew quiet, and something unspoken, yet palpable, passed between them.

His blue-eyed gaze entranced her, magical like perfect, round-cut sapphires. She couldn't help but notice an unmistakable firmness against her lower hip and wondered if perhaps he wasn't so exhausted, after all. Unable to resist, she touched the golden stubble on his cheek. "What should we do?"

He didn't answer for several seconds. "I want to

kiss you."

A hint of confession mixed with desire infused his voice. Without waiting for an answer, he cupped her face with his hands and kissed her lips tentatively. The sudden, intimate gesture ignited a long-dormant flame inside her, one she'd assumed was forever extinguished. His second-day stubble tickled her cheeks, and she tasted salt. Melting, she sought his lips again and caressed his cheek in a tender motion.

He returned the kiss and stroked her body gently, forging a pathway of heat running across her neck, where his lips touched her skin in soft kisses.

The restless desire which had drifted through her like a passing cloud became an urgent need.

He kneaded her hips in firm circles with his hands, then lifted a fingertip to trace each of her breasts. After opening her blood-stained ivory blouse, he lingered to massage her torso before grazing his lips over her skin.

Pleasure roused her, and she unbuttoned the top few buttons of his shirt to rest her fingertips on his chest. Avoiding his injured ribs, she traced invisible lines down his pecs.

Mark tugged the remaining buttons of his shirt open, and the white pearl disks tumbled into the pine needles. He unclasped her lace bra, and when their bare skin met for the first time, he exhaled hard.

A critical question interrupted her intoxicated, dream-like state, and she stopped. "Wait. I don't even know your full name."

Transferring his attention from her bare breast to meet her gaze, he laughed softly before replying. "Dr. Markus Henriksen Nygaard."

"Tess Madeleine Bennett," she replied in kind.

"Pleased to meet you, Ms. Bennett. May I continue?"

"Yes, please." Wanting more, she groaned with pleasure.

His hand skated farther down her chest, over her stomach's flat, narrow field, and unzipped the top of her wool trousers to reveal silken underwear.

She sensed her breath quickening as he caressed her in attentive, firm strokes. Heat spread across her cheeks, and desire hummed through every cell in her body. She couldn't deny it—she wanted him badly. The world had tilted off its axis since the moment gunfire erupted at Cedarcliff. Time traveled in a strange cadence, where the uncertainty of any future meant only the present mattered. No rules or inhibitions remained, and she only cared about survival and desire. Whatever caution once dictated her past life disappeared. "I want you," she blurted out loud. "We could die tomorrow and—"

"I want you, too. I just…" His voice drifted off before he finished his sentence.

She detected uncertainty in his reply and panicked he might reject her. Feeling exposed, she held her breath and waited to hear what he'd say.

He sighed before speaking again. "I haven't done this in a long time."

"It has been a long time for me, too." She thought she might be able to breathe again. "I need to know I'm alive and not broken, and there's life beyond the death and hell we escaped. I need to feel something."

"Me, too. I know exactly what you mean. Lucky for us, I think I remember what to do."

The canopy of trees blanketed them in safety and

served as a shield from the chilly wind. With Mark's hands against her, she relaxed into his touch and forgot everything else. The forest air smelled of conifer and pine, and the fresh, soft moss coated the damp earth beneath them. The occasional bit of dry leaves crackled and crumbled as she fumbled for him and peeled open only the interfering layers of clothes.

When their bare skin touched together and his readiness pressed against her hip, she couldn't wait any longer. "Yes," she whispered.

"Move with me," he murmured, stroking her back.

Tess clasped him with firm but careful hands, avoiding his injuries and proceeding with slow, gentle motions. Tess marveled at how well their bodies fit together like they'd been separate puzzle pieces designed to connect. Each curve lined up against a corresponding, opposite curve. Savoring every sensation, she roamed her hands over his body while they remained sealed together. Still gripped by the fear of dying, she nearly cried from the gift of connection and safety. Consciously, she held nothing back, in case this truly was her last night alive.

Afterward, encircled in his arms, she floated in the surreal afterglow, both stunned and relieved to experience desire again. The lonely desperation she endured just two nights ago at Torque seemed a lifetime away. Tonight, she no longer recognized any aspect of her life, and the unexpected return of intimacy both energized and mystified her. The air grew chillier, and she leaned over to kiss him again before wrestling back into her clothes.

"We're alive," she whispered, "though I can hardly believe it. Thank you."

"I needed this, too. Whatever happens, we'll survive." After pulling up his trousers, he pointed to the sky. "Look up—it's the constellation of Orion the Hunter." With a finger, he outlined the three bright, shining stars which demarcated the hunter's belt.

The sky softened from charcoal to ash as she searched for other constellations. Leaving their temporary shelter was the last thing she wanted to do, but sunrise would arrive soon and risk exposing them. "We should move before daybreak."

When she started running again, she forgot her blistered feet and battered shoulder. The threat of Yuri finding them kept her charging through the woods. Unlike the trek a few hours ago, new optimism energized her, as if every step brought them closer to freedom. If these proved to be her last hours, she was satisfied she'd spent them well.

Tess was no longer alone, but the unfortunate reality remained—their chances of surviving the day were almost zero. Fresh panic lodged in her heart, and she pushed herself to run faster.

Chapter Eight

Wilderness Trek

The sun had yet to rise over the woods in western British Columbia, and a thick fog filled the sky. Tess glanced at the cloud layers and noted they had shifted from charcoal to dull gunmetal-gray. Depending on the foliage, the variable terrain forced them to alternate between a brisk run and a slow plod. As she and Mark raced to beat the sunrise lurking in the east, they settled into a comfortable pace. Once daylight broke, they'd gain better visibility, but at the cost of losing their cover—a poor trade. At the first open clearing, Tess slowed to a stop, reluctant to leave the protective camouflage of the forest. "How far do you think we've come?" Disoriented by the woods and overcome by exhaustion, she lost all distance perception.

"Climbing hills and breaking through so much foliage slowed us down. I'd guess around ten kilometers last night and three so far this morning." Mark raised a hand to cradle his left rib cage.

"If we're going the right direction, we've got seven kilometers left, correct?" Remembering kilometers were shorter than miles, she perked up, relieved they might find civilization sooner.

"We're heading west like the farmer advised, but maybe we went off course in the dark." Mark gestured toward the lighter side of the horizon, still smothered in clouds. "The sun's east. If we orient ourselves to it, west is this direction." He spun and adjusted their trajectory a few degrees. "Let's go."

Tess stepped into the lead. Not a single tree interrupted the open field. Given the landscape offered no place to hide for about two hundred yards, she rushed ahead, determined to find more cover. A sputtering wheeze sounded behind her, and she pivoted to check for Mark. "Are you in pain? We can rest if you need to."

"*Helvete.* I'll keep up, damn it. We must keep going." He kicked a rock on the ground and cursed while clutching his side.

"You don't look so good. We need to get you to a hospital." The pallor on his face worried her, and she walked over and placed a hand on his arm.

He yanked his arm away. "I said I'd be fine," he snapped. "Why the hell haven't they found us? They're armed and outnumber us, and they've got a truck. What if we're falling into their trap?" Sweat coated his cheeks, and he pinched his lips together.

Not sure what to make of this sudden mood swing, Tess stopped in her tracks. "We've made it this far, and they can't kill me—they need me alive until the ransom deadline."

"So, if they find us, you think they'll just let us go?"

The irritable edge to his voice burned with sarcasm. Offended by his aggressive tone, Tess blinked several times and tightened her spine. "Of course not."

"What if they're not asking ransom for me? Have you considered they have no reason to keep me alive?

Have you?" He raised his voice and narrowed his gaze.

"I'm scared as hell, too, but let's not waste time arguing." Along with his antagonism, she detected a frantic tone to his speech. His sudden anger stung her like a hornet, and a pit formed in her stomach. She couldn't believe they'd slept together mere hours ago. The sweet afterglow drained away, replaced by something unstable. Uncertain whether she should soothe his anxiety or confront his attitude, she stood motionless.

Growling and muttering, Mark tromped over to a tall maple tree. He kicked the dirt at the tree's base, swiped a sizeable rock from the ground, and hurled it at a nearby cedar tree. The stone ricocheted and tumbled into neighboring bushes. Hands on his hips, he stomped on a pile of dead branches while pacing and cursing.

Dumbfounded at the strange break in his demeanor, Tess remained at the clearing's edge, a safe distance from his outburst. This couldn't be the same man who woke up beside her, and she grew more alarmed every second. Had she truly misjudged his character so greatly? Nothing made sense, and she decided to count to ten before taking slow, tentative steps toward him. "Are you done?" She used a measured, non-threatening voice, hoping not to startle him.

Mark reeled to face her. "Yes."

"Let's head for the road." Tess took charge and waved for him to follow. Trying to read his mood, she saw his stern expression soften several degrees, like a toppled sandcastle dissolving back into the sea. For a moment, he seemed on the verge of crying. While the uncomfortable silence unsettled her, she kept forging forward. Dependent on each other to survive, she couldn't afford to add personal conflict to an already staggering list of obstacles.

As she swatted away bushes and tall grass blocking their way, she tried to empathize with his terror, anger, or whatever set him off. No doubt, they faced grave danger, but his outburst hinted at something lurking below the surface that she couldn't identify. Given her own meltdown yesterday, she considered whether he was overdue to let off some steam, especially after how calmly he handled the Cedarcliff attack.

The terrain became more forest-like, and the trees grew thicker, offering them much-needed cover. As the minutes passed, Tess stole quick glances at Mark and judged his outburst was over. She longed for water, anything to quench her thirst and relieve her dry mouth. Without stopping, she plodded ahead for another hour, but eventually, she needed to relieve herself and ducked behind a clump of trees. "I need a minute—bio break. Be right back."

When she returned, rustling sounded nearby, but its source wasn't visible. Twenty yards ahead, she spotted Mark's blue shirt, yet hesitated to shout and reveal their location. The noise persisted. She peeked over her shoulder, and nothing appeared. The wind had calmed, and the tree branches remained still. She hiked several more steps but stopped when another tree branch broke. Could Yuri and his men have found them?

"You coming?" Mark called.

He waited about ten yards beyond where she stood. So much for keeping quiet. "Something's in the bushes, but I can't see it." Rotating a full circle, she rechecked the foliage for any movement.

"Let's move closer to the trees—more cover, if we need it." He shifted his trajectory to align with the thickly wooded ridgeline ahead.

Concerned about noise and Mark's state of mind, she checked their surroundings for threats. He seemed to have reverted to his usual demeanor, and she questioned whether she'd overreacted to his outburst. "Look." Tess gestured several yards ahead toward a broken line of railway ties. "An old railroad. We're getting closer to civilization."

The rustling sound repeated. Whipping around, she searched in every direction but detected nothing. A cluster of evergreen trees swayed in gentle arcs from the western wind, and the scent of fragrant fir branches filled the breeze.

Continuing to hike through the dense woodland, Mark trudged a few yards ahead and kept one hand on his left rib cage.

The crackle of leaves sounded behind her, and she turned to find herself face-to-face with a black bear the size of a two-seater car.

The animal lurked closer.

Calling out for Mark, she couldn't keep panic from rising in her voice and backed away one step at a time, careful not to provoke the wild animal. Play dead, or make noise? Not knowing which approach to take with this bear species, she cursed under her breath.

The bear roared and stood on its back legs, reaching its full height, high above her.

"Go away!" Instinct trumped memory, and she screamed.

The black bear plunked onto all fours but approached again to nudge her legs.

She stared at its shiny fur coat and pointy ears, but when the bear's nose sniffed her with interest, she froze.

The bear headed in the opposite direction but spun without warning and charged.

In an instant, she broke away and sprinted. Despite its furry bulk, the bear lumbered lightning-fast and swiped at her right leg, missing it by inches.

Finally, it scurried away, and its woolly mass disappeared into a thicket of trees and crashed through the bushes.

"Shit, the damn thing almost attacked me." Breathless from the near miss, Tess pressed her hands against her knees and attempted to calm herself.

Mark hustled back to rejoin her. "Lucky…break." Out of breath, he wheezed between each word, and his chest rose and fell.

"Lucky? You're kidding, right?" His words hit her like a lit match sparking dry, brittle kindling. *Snap.*

"I meant, you're lucky it ran away. Bear attacks are often fatal. I've never treated one."

She gawked. His expression remained flat, like a worn stone, and something imploded inside her. How could he be so emotionless? "Well, sorry I deprived you the chance to see one up close. I'm sick of being hunted and want out of this fucking forest." She lashed out with uncharacteristic sarcasm.

"I was supposed to be safe at this goddamned job, and here we are, stuck in these shitty woods. *Helvete.*" He kicked a rock, sending it scuttling over the ground. He grabbed clumps of his own hair while glaring mutely at the sky.

Despite their grumpy, silent détente, she managed

107

to lead them forward for another ten minutes. Mark's pace slowed, but suspecting the extent of his pain, Tess resisted pushing him any harder. Growing paranoid, she feared their captors were gaining and kept checking over her shoulder. The longer they slogged through the forest, wounded and hungry, the more her spirits deflated. The afterglow she'd experienced earlier had dissipated like steam into the air. At this point, she figured she'd hallucinated their entire sexy interlude.

A gunshot rang out and shattered the silence of the forest.

By instinct, Tess spun to search for the shot's origin but saw nothing. A moot point, she reasoned, given the gunfire proved they were no longer alone. "It must be Alexi or Yuri. Run!"

With no option other than to delve deeper into the woods, she accelerated and hoped Mark could pick up his pace. The bushes grew denser, forcing them to trek single file to squeeze through tricky passages. The path ahead narrowed, and she gestured for Mark to lead the next section.

He reached for Sergey's handgun, still tucked in the waistband of his trousers but didn't withdraw it.

Alternating positions, Tess slipped in front of Mark and swatted her way through bushes and blackberry brambles, unable to see her feet. She beat out her exasperation on the branches by fighting every vine clogging her path like a mortal enemy.

When she stepped forward, the ground disappeared beneath her, and she plummeted into the steep ravine. Prickly bushes with thorns attacked her body from all sides before she landed with a thud. Something sharp punctured her leg. She screamed as warm liquid gushed over her ankle. Afraid to brave looking at the injury, she bit her lip until she tasted blood.

"What happened? Are you hurt?" Mark shouted from the ravine's ledge.

"Yes, I hurt my leg. Bad." Cursing, she sputtered in short bursts with ragged breaths. She glanced up the hillside, stunned to see how far she'd fallen.

"Hang on. Let me get to you." Mark plowed through the bush. Using a broken cedar branch like a machete, he swept away spiky vines to make his way down the slope. Red lines of fresh blood crossed his hands and multiplied as the brambles grew denser. The steep ravine offered few footholds, and he used his hands to brace himself but careened the last drop. Landing with a clonk, he scrambled over the ground.

"Shit, get this thing out of my leg." Flat on the ground with her ankle twisted at an unnatural angle, she gasped for air. Shielding her eyes, she peeked through her fingers and stole a glance at the wound. A jagged tree branch impaled the width of her lower leg, leaving her bone visible, and blood flowed freely. Dizziness seized her, and she hyperventilated.

Mark knelt on a flat patch of dirt. "First, slow your breathing. Take slow, deep breaths. I need to move you to solid ground."

"Fine." The pain made her groan, but she managed a nod while noticing his earlier robotic mood had disappeared, and he'd clicked into doctor mode, precisely what she needed. She struggled to extricate her torso from the tangled mess of bushes, and a blackberry vine covered in thorns caught on her bloody shirt and lodged against her chest. Without thinking, she yanked it away, puncturing her palm in multiple spots. Several thorns remained stuck in her décolleté, and tears slid from the corners of her eyes. "Damn it."

Sweat drenched Mark's face, and he lost his balance as he lifted her out of the brambles. Extracting her from the scrub brush and moving to a flat grove took multiple awkward attempts. With quick, light motions, he palpated her lower leg around the bleeding punctures and scrutinized the entry and exit points of the tree branch. "I need to extract this carefully. The stake could sever your artery, so please don't move. Sorry, Tess, but this will hurt."

"Just get it out. Fast." Mad with pain, she tensed her body in self-protection and focused on keeping still at all costs. The expectation of more agony overwhelmed her with nausea, and she broke into a cold sweat.

"Take a big, deep breath. Ready?"

Worried their captors might lurk nearby, she covered her mouth to muffle the sound if she screamed and gave Mark a thumbs-up. She watched as he inspected both sides of the wound and placed his hands in position to remove the branch.

"On three. One, two…" In one twist, he extracted the thick, spiky branch.

Tess cried out into her hands. She rolled on her side to vomit but produced nothing but dry heaves, given her empty stomach. Clammy sweat coated her face, and her blood dripped off the ragged branch in Mark's hand and fell to the ground. She groaned. "Damn it. You said on the count of three. Christ."

"Sorry, but you experience less pain if you're not quite expecting it."

"Whatever. Still hurt like hell. Now, help me get

up."

"You've got grit, Tess Bennett, but don't move until I stop the bleeding." He ripped neat strips off the bottom of his shirt to create a primitive dressing, winding fabric around the injury and tying a series of knots.

"My leg's going to be okay, right?" As she waited too long for a reply, she swore her thudding heart might break her ribs. The grim cast of his expression discouraged her. "Please say something."

"You've got multiple, deep puncture wounds, and you need a hospital." Avoiding eye contact, he drew his eyebrows together and studied her injury before tightening the cloth strips.

What Mark didn't say out loud worried her more. The harsh reality was she wouldn't see the inside of a hospital unless someone rescued them before Yuri's men reappeared. The vital need for rescue spurred her to ignore her pain, which bordered on unbearable. "We need to go. We need a new plan. Any plan."

A wheeze sent Mark into a coughing fit. Clutching at his rib cage, he extended a hand to help her. "Lean on my left side, and don't put any weight on your injured leg, period. I'll find you a walking stick to help you balance."

"Thanks." Pressing up with her left leg, she wobbled to stand. Sweat trickled from her forehead, and dizziness kept her stomach swirling in protest, neither of which would help her find safety faster. Despite her stoic intention to conceal her pain, she shored herself against a tree to rest, huffing and puffing.

He searched the clearing and picked up a tree branch just over a yard long, which he carried over and placed in her hand. "Not ergonomic, but this will help you balance."

Assessing the branch's weight, she judged it light enough to maneuver. Tess planted the stick on the ground and took one tentative step, and her uninjured leg trembled. "I'll be slow, but I'll manage." Without complaint, she limped ahead, but each step required laborious effort.

"Keep heading west. The highway must be close."

Mark wrapped a steady arm around her shoulders to help her stay balanced. The pain alone revealed more than she wanted to know, and she avoided viewing the injury. Hot tears coated her cheeks, but she concentrated her waning energy on traversing the woods. Back in the cell, the plan to find the highway seemed straightforward. Escape, run, and get help—a simple plan. The reality proved infinitely more difficult than she anticipated.

The terrain leveled out, and she and Mark curved around a group of trees into another wooded patch. Realizing any tree or thicket could be hiding their captors, she grew more paranoid with every step. She peeked over her shoulder at the clearing they'd left, and she felt her heartbeat pounding inside her head.

A familiar figure carrying a raised handgun raced in their direction.

"Damn it. Alexi's gaining on us." Her injury limited how far and fast she could cover the rugged terrain, and given she was falling behind Mark's pace, she feared she might need to be carried.

"Go faster." Breathless and wheezing, Mark leveraged his arm to help drag her along.

"Crap." Hissing, she summoned more adrenaline to

power her body forward. Images of Sergey fueled enough anger to keep pushing ahead, but the burst of energy quickly drained away.

A gunshot rang out, and the bullet torpedoed a nearby tree and shattered its bark. Any remaining safety they had was vanishing. Another gunshot sounded, but this one wasn't as loud.

"Goddamn it." Mark grimaced and extracted Sergey's gun from his waistband. "We're getting shot at from multiple directions."

Observing his awkward weapon handling and perplexed frown, Tess recognized his discomfort holding the gun. She leaned over and clicked off the gun's safety in one decisive motion. "The international signal for help. A burst of three sounds in any form of noise. Five seconds between each shot. Do it."

"Nothing to lose." Pointing the gun toward the sky, Mark pulled the trigger and flinched when the first shot rang out. After five seconds, another shot. Five more seconds, then the third shot.

Each blast sounded like a bomb exploding across the sky compared to the forest's silence. With luck, someone, anyone, would rescue them.

Far across the clearing, Alexi approached within a couple of hundred yards of closing the gap on them.

Time ran out. Recalling the active-shooter safety drills her father taught her, she prioritized their remaining options: run, hide, or fight. "I can't run faster, so we need to hide. We've got to avoid a firefight at all costs." Meanwhile, she prayed more ammo remained in the bullet chamber, or else they'd have no way to defend themselves.

Mark pointed at a thick tree grove and guided her

to the densest section, where they both took cover.

The wind carried the faint sound of voices coming from the opposite direction, and Tess panicked. Was Yuri in the woods, too? If all three gunmen surrounded them, no escape path remained. Given her crucified leg, she couldn't go much farther. As the voices grew louder, the green walls of the forest seemed to shrink around her and block the gray sky.

"Hey, we heard your three shots. Does somebody need help? We're two hunters, and I can't see where you are. Give us a shout, eh?" The voices got louder.

"They're Canadian." The telltale "eh" sound sent her hopes soaring, and she beamed as she and Mark crouched in the tree thicket, listening.

"Yeah, but Alexi will shoot them if they get any closer." He held a fist at his mouth and wheezed.

"I'll warn them." Behind a tree deep in the thicketed grove, Tess perched on her uninjured leg. "Be careful. There's a sniper out here. Take cover," she called out at the top of her lungs. Immediately, she ducked to the ground and grabbed Mark's arm to tug him down, then covered her head to avoid stray gunfire once flat on the ground.

"We hear you. We're on the lookout," one of the hunters shouted back.

Tess surmised the Canadian men must be near their hiding spot and prayed Alexi hadn't spotted them yet. She lifted her head a couple of inches above the muddy ground to search the clearing.

Alexi dashed into her view but stopped with his rifle in the air. He rotated a full circle and appeared to search the trees.

"Give me the gun," she whispered to Mark.

Mark's lips formed the shape of a question, but he handed over Sergey's handgun.

Without hesitation, Tess clicked the safety off and crawled forward through the underbrush, scratching her stomach and elbows. With the gun in one hand, she nestled into the dirt and double-checked to ensure the thicket obscured their location. Although she hadn't fired a gun in years, she felt the muscle memory of shooting reactivate, a benefit earned from a decade of target practice with her dad.

Another gunshot rang out in the woods.

"Stand down and disarm at once." Unseen, one of the hunters roared into the woods, and the sound echoed across the treetops.

"You, the man in black. Drop. Your. Gun." A different voice shouted this time, the other hunter.

"*Nyet,*" the gunman shouted and marched forward with his rifle on his shoulder.

From her vantage point on the ground, Tess spotted the hunters, dressed in camouflage, approaching Alexi from behind a group of trees with their rifles cocked.

The gunman stood alone in the clearing and spun.

"I said, stand down and drop your gun," the Canadian man with the booming voice repeated.

"Stop, or I shoot you." Alexi's Russian accent rang through the air as he raised his gun.

Tess leaned on her elbows, the gun still in her hand, and tracked Alexi's movements in the clearing. Through a tiny opening in the bushes, she evaluated the best angle to target him.

"What next?" Mark asked.

"Keep your head down. I've got a clear shot." She closed a hand around the gun's familiar metallic curves, and her training, while rusty, took over. Ignoring her racing pulse, she shut out everything but Alexi's movements.

A couple of seconds later, Alexi stopped wandering. He lifted his rifle and pointed it toward the hunters.

Forced to make a split-second decision, she didn't hesitate. *I will not let these hunters die.* Hands steady, Tess aimed straight at Alexi's rifle, which projected from his right hand. With laser-like focus, she centered the target in range, held her breath, and fired.

The peace of the primordial woods cracked open, and a shower of gunfire blasted across the trees. The next few seconds rushed past in a blur. Tess hit the target, and the bullet exploded Alexi's gun out of his hands.

Barely a second later, the hunters returned fire.

The acrid smell of gunpowder filled the air, and clouds of dirt obscured any visibility. The scuffle of running feet pounded the earth. She and Mark kept flat on the ground in the bushes, hidden from the crossfire. The pulsing pain in her wounded leg took her breath away, and she gritted her teeth to avoid moaning.

"Is he down?" Mark cradled his torso and muffled a wheezing cough.

"Think so, not sure." Tess spied through the thicket to see if Alexi was alone and prayed Yuri and Dmitry weren't lurking nearby.

Below the ridge of foliage, Tess's position afforded her the best view of the scene unfolding. When the dust settled, two figures in camouflage emerged and raced over to Alexi, who was covered in blood and remained motionless in a crumpled heap. One of their shots had hit him, and fragments of a broken rifle peppered the ground around the sniper.

"Jesus, bro." Gagging, the younger hunter covered his mouth and recoiled.

"Shit. Think the guy's alive, Derek?" The older hunter, built like a retired football player, stood staring at the fallen sniper. He pulled a mobile phone out of his hunting vest pocket.

"You shot him square in the chest, Bob. Nobody could survive that." Derek, a younger version of the first hunter, shook his head.

Tess continued to eavesdrop while Mark helped her rise from their hideout in the bushes. Clinging to the tree branch for balance, she managed a couple of leaden steps at a time to follow him toward the hunters.

Bob entered three digits on his phone screen and stood, tapping his foot. After a few seconds, he kicked the field with his muddy boot and replaced his phone in his pocket. "Dang it. No reception. What the hell was he shooting at us for?"

"Sniper in a provincial hunting reserve? You got me." Derek leaned over the corpse and ran his hands along the man's sides. He pulled out two switchblades, a baton, and a handgun holstered in an ankle strap. He let out a long whistle. "This guy was armed up the wazoo, but not for hunting. Whadaya make of him?"

"He's an assassin." Mark scuttled over to Bob and Derek and pointed at Alexi's corpse, which lay flat on the muddy ground, stained with blood.

"The bastard shot at us without cause. We had to defend ourselves." Bob's voice shook.

"Are you both unharmed? I'm a doctor," Mark said.

"Yeah, but that guy's not going anywhere." Derek stood with his rifle pointed at the ground.

Mark approached Alexi, reached over, and placed two fingers against the sniper's blood-spattered neck. "He's dead." Without further investigation, he stepped away from the crumpled body.

"Thank God." About to collapse, Tess let out a huge sigh and sagged against the nearest tree to support herself. A sob caught in her throat, and an incredible sense of lightness settled over her, like a two-ton boulder had lifted away from her body.

Bob and Derek exchanged glances, and their nearly identical faces wore lopsided frowns of guilt mixed with relief.

"Weirdest thing. The guy's gun exploded right out of his hands, just when I thought he was gonna shoot us dead," Bob said.

"Doctor, you're one helluva great shot, shooting his gun out of his hands like that." Derek turned to Mark to shake his hand.

"I can't claim the credit. Tess is the one who saved you." Mark gestured behind him.

Having overheard the conversation, she bristled at the hunter's assumption a man fired the saving shot and limped over to join the men. "The sniper was aiming right at you, so I took my shot at his gun before he could pull the trigger."

"Well, your shot saved our lives, ma'am. Thank you." Bob's eyebrows flew up, and he did a double take. He shook Tess's hand and squinted. "Good Lord, what kind of trouble are you folks in?"

Tess only could imagine how wrecked she and Mark must appear. Judging from the sting of countless lacerations suffered during her ravine fall, she figured she was literally a bloody mess, and her leg stood at an unnatural angle. Her ripped, stained ivory blouse stuck out from under the barn coat.

Mark hadn't fared any better. Huge bruises in multiple shades splotched across his skin, and blood stains ruined his blue shirt.

Derek stepped closer and inspected their faces. "Holy crap, you must be those people kidnapped from Cedarcliff. Your photos were on the TV news, and all of British Columbia is searching for you two."

"Yes, I'm Tess Bennett. We were taken hostage but escaped into the woods. How far is the highway?" Impatient to leave, she wasted no time grilling them.

"I'm Mark Nygaard, and we need a hospital. Do you have a car?"

"Yeah, a kilometer away. We gotta hike there to get cell reception to call 9-1-1." Bob blinked before taking a last glance at Alexi.

She followed Bob's gaze to the residual gore on the ground around Alexi's corpse. His cheeks paled under his reddish beard, and he registered a mix of shock and disgust.

"Thanks for the help. Glad you two weren't hurt." Mark coughed, emitting a wheezing sound.

"My brother and me, we know these woods like the back of our hands. We're not gonna let a damn sniper gun us down in our backyard," Bob said.

"Let's leave the sniper here and get you folks to safety. Tess, we'll help you hike out of here." Derek extended his arm, gesturing for her to hold on.

"I can manage." Determined to leave the woods by her own power, she clenched her jaw tight and

119

concentrated on bearing her pain. Defenses on high alert, she feared Yuri and Dmitry could ambush them any second. The open clearing where they stood left their group exposed like sitting ducks. "Let's go."

"Damn it, Tess. You're wounded and bleeding. Let us help you," Mark said.

She pretended not to see his stern frown or hear the exasperation in his voice. Despite protesting, she ended up sandwiched between Mark and Derek and wound an arm around each of them to support herself while taking small, deliberate steps with her good leg. Traversing the steep incline aggravated the leg wound, and her initial relief of being rescued faded as the pain intensified.

Careful not to slide down the steep sections, the motley crew of four made their way out of the woods in a jumbled mass, and the terrain shifted to a hilly meadow.

"*Se, jeg fortalte deg at vi ville overleve.* I told you we'd survive," Mark whispered in her ear and squeezed her shoulder.

His soft breath warmed her cheek, and she managed a faint smile before channeling all her energy into moving forward. The majestic British Columbia mountains sprang up from nowhere, touching the sky, and she hadn't noticed them since the night she arrived at Cedarcliff. After crossing a small meadow, she spotted a battered, four-seater pickup truck parked alongside an empty dirt road lined with cedar trees.

Clicking the back of his truck open, Bob reached into a box on the flatbed and handed them water bottles.

Derek helped her into the truck's back seat and wrapped a wooly blanket around her shoulders.

Once seated, she gulped her entire bottle of water

and glanced at her leg. A red spot spread in a circle several inches in diameter on the thin bandaging. Whatever the cause, it wasn't a good sign.

Mark slid into the back seat beside her and elevated her right leg on his lap to inspect the makeshift dressing he had applied at the ravine. "You've got resurgent bleeding, and I need to tighten these." After applying pressure directly to stop the bleeding, he untied the bandages, then retied them tighter.

The strip of shirt cloth above her ankle constricted several notches, and she winced. Instead of increasing her comfort, the leg's sensation trickled away and became numb. Nerves sparked at random intervals, stinging her like a hundred knife tips puncturing skin. Energy reserves spent, she leaned her head against the dusty vinyl headrest and prayed for cell reception.

Outside her door, Bob stood with his phone in hand and punched in three digits on the keypad. "9-1-1? Yeah, we found the Cedarcliff hostages out here in the hunting preserve. We need an ambulance ASAP." He raised a thumb and nodded at Tess.

While waiting, she drifted off toward delirium but jerked her head up several times to stay awake. When the sound of tires grinding over gravel grew louder, she felt relief pour through her veins. Never had Tess heard a more welcome noise.

A Royal Canadian Mounted Police SUV screeched to a stop and parked next to Bob's truck. Two uniformed officers jumped out, and the older-looking man with a gray crew cut waved at the two brothers. The senior officer approached the truck where Mark leaned against the open door, just outside where she sat inside the cab.

"Folks, I'm Sergeant Hal Morrison. You two were damn lucky to survive this."

"I'm Tess Bennett. Glad to be alive." She rallied long enough to nod. Too exhausted to say more, she listened to the men's conversation outside the cab.

"And you must be Dr. Nygaard." Morrison tipped his hat at Mark.

"Yes. We need the nearest hospital." Mark stood with his hands on his hips. "Fast."

When Tess noticed all the color had drained from Mark's face, she forced herself to stay alert. The pale pallor of his skin alarmed her.

"We'll take you to Vancouver General, a couple of hours south. I'll escort you, and Sergeant Peters here will meet the coroner to recover the suspect," Sergeant Morrison said.

A faint siren wailed in the distance, and Mark held up a hand. "Wait. You must send someone to Anderson Campbell's farm, where we were held captive. The gunmen took him hostage, and he needs hospitalization if he's going to avoid having his foot amputated."

"You're telling me the suspects took over Campbell's farm?" Morrison dropped his mouth open, whipped off his sunglasses, and squinted at Mark.

"They imprisoned us in the barn, but we escaped into the woods. Two of the kidnappers are still searching for us," Mark said.

"I've known Campbell since I first moved to BC. Did they hurt him?" Morrison's forehead wrinkled, and he extracted his phone from his pocket.

"No, but he's got a septic infection and needs immediate care. He told me how to escape the barn, which saved our lives, and I'm grateful he helped us."

Morrison nodded. "Gem of a guy, though he sure loves his whiskey. If you'll excuse me, I'll send a unit over to help him ASAP." He stepped away and leaned an arm against Tess's side of the truck.

Tess overheard Morrison call the Vancouver RCMP office and order an emergency response team to the Campbell farm. Awake again, she leaned her head out the door. "Sergeant? You'd better warn them the armed suspects could still be at the farm."

"Affirmative." Morrison gave her a thumbs-up and nodded.

Peering out the dusty truck window, she saw the ambulance truck arrive and pull up alongside the RCMP SUV. The tension in her body released.

Outside, Mark staggered to the ambulance and slumped limply against it.

Before Tess could shout for help, one EMT rushed to catch him and quickly strapped an oxygen mask over his nose.

After the EMTs got her loaded into the two-stretcher cab compartment and set up a line containing IV painkillers, she waited for the pain relief to kick in. She heard Mark groaning in the stretcher next to her and reached over to squeeze his hand. Glimpsing his smile under his oxygen mask, she leaned her head back and closed her eyes.

When she realized she hadn't thought of Kyle since yesterday afternoon, she suffered pangs of guilt. Still holding Mark's hand, she lifted her other hand to touch the Celtic amulet around her neck but found only her bare, scraped skin. The necklace was gone. She patted her neck several times, then checked for it inside her blouse, as well as in the oversized barn coat. Nothing.

Stifling a sob, she bit her lip. Was losing Kyle's amulet her punishment for having sex with Mark? If there was an afterlife, would Kyle know she had slept with Mark?

Hurtling over the twisting road, the ambulance headed south on the Sea-to-Sky Highway to Vancouver. Towering rock walls formed the road's eastern side. To the west, snow-capped mountains rose from the Pacific Ocean and reached toward the sky.

Hazy from the painkiller, she perceived the view as a dreamy mirage. By all measures, she should feel more relief. Returning to civilization assured her physical safety, but the fresh, raw emotional trauma retained its grip. Inside her head, she still perched on a wobbling, craggy precipice atop a cliff that could collapse at any moment. After countless dark moments since Friday night, she expected the mere act of rescue to fix everything—injuries, shock, and trauma. Despite the blasting heat inside the ambulance, she shivered as her body turned cold from the fear haunting her. *Yuri and Dmitry are still out there.*

Chapter Nine

Aftermath

A couple of days later, Tess leaned on her crutches in her living room and gazed at Seattle's Lake Union in the first light of dawn. The colorful collection of yachts, speedboats, and kayaks docked around the lake stood out in contrast to the dull, gray sky. Soft drizzle filled the air. The scene reminded her of September's golden days when she moved into her condo, which now seemed like several lifetimes ago. Since she returned home, these signs of everyday life comforted her and proved she had survived and wasn't trapped or suspended in time.

The attack in Canada was over, and the police completed their gritty accounting of witness interviews, physical evidence, and bullet casings. Out of respect for Riku's death, Timberline Ventures hadn't rescheduled the cybersecurity summit, and all new business remained on hold. Mystified the earth could keep turning on the same axis, Tess couldn't understand how the snow-capped Canadian mountains stood untouched as if nothing nefarious had happened. Despite the bright daylight, a persistent chill remained lodged under the surface of her skin. Fear had burrowed deep in her consciousness, making her uneasy. Her life had divided into two halves—one before the attack, and this other one, a present filled with nothing but uncertainty.

At first, all she remembered were sounds, which replayed in her mind: the gurgling bronze fountain in Cedarcliff's foyer, Riku's crystal whiskey glass shattering, then gunfire. She recalled Mark's soothing voice assuring her they'd survive. Other sensory memories jarred her at strange moments without warning, like the metallic smell of blood and the taste of the farmer's whiskey burning her throat. Buried deeper were the forest scents of fresh, wet pine trees and Mark's sandalwood cologne. Sometimes she couldn't remember anything except the hospital's antiseptic odor and the buzz of morphine coursing through her body after surgery.

Her days in the hospital remained a blur. A vague recollection of arriving at Vancouver General surfaced. Overnight, she and Mark became accidental celebrities, dubbed the "Cedarcliff Hostages" by Canadian media. Terrorist attacks and high-profile kidnappings were unheard of in British Columbia, and the hospital staff had hummed with curiosity around them. The hospital lights blinded her with brightness, and she wanted to run away but couldn't flee due to her injuries.

When she had fallen into the ravine and impaled her leg on a tree branch, she was left with two gaping wounds. Her leg had swollen to a shocking size at the hospital, and she had lost all nerve sensation. An argument ensued near her, filled with loud voices and words like *severe* and *emergency*. Groggy from painkillers, she couldn't focus on anything except Mark's worried gaze, although he reassured her everything would be fine. Unable to recall any details, Tess experienced flashes of random, disturbing moments she couldn't connect.

The day after surgery, her nurse shared Mark refused treatment for his broken ribs and injured lung until he was satisfied with her doctor's surgical plan. Another nurse confided Mark spent hours by her bedside while she recovered post-operatively. After the police ran tests on it, her bloody satellite phone arrived in a plastic evidence bag. A nurse cleaned it before returning it to Tess, mercifully sparing her the sight of Riku's blood.

The first dressing change after her surgery proved a rude shock and revealed two raw incisions carved into her lower calf, both red and angry. During the same surgery, a plastic surgeon sewed together the broken skin over her cheekbone with a thin, neat line of stitches designed to minimize scarring. She hoped it worked. Not for vanity but to avoid reminders of Yuri whenever she passed a mirror for the rest of her life.

A reminder beeped on her phone, announcing her next painkiller dose was due. She swallowed a white capsule with water and eased herself back onto the couch with a fresh ice bag. Wide-awake and restless, she got the random idea to call Kavita Chakyar.

"Tess, my goodness. How are you holding up?" Kavita answered on the fifth ring, breathless.

"Pretty sore and bruised, and I needed surgery on my leg. How are you?" While Kavita's voice tended to trigger her annoyance, today, Tess curved her mouth into an awkward smile of relief.

"Stitches for cuts on my arms. Lots of bandages, but I'll heal. They wouldn't tell us what happened to you."

"I'd rather not recount it." She hadn't considered

yet how much to share of her ordeal.

"We read they found Dr. Nygaard with you. Quite a handsome bloke—hope you got his number."

In a flash, she was back in the woods, pressing her body against Mark's and smelling the damp, earthy forest. "Now you mention it, I didn't. I'm just glad to be home." Given her liaison with him, she felt uneasy not having his contact information. She regretted the omission and found her complete lack of command over the past few days disturbing.

"Speaking of men, I got a date with Kieran Hughes."

"Well done." Shocked Kavita had shared something personal, Tess found her buoyancy mystifying, given what they'd endured. "I never figured you to be one for the rugby type."

"Did you see his muscles?"

"Didn't notice, I'm afraid." Tess puzzled over why Kavita was behaving more chatty and friendly than ever before, practically purring into the phone.

"Ah, well. Anyhow, I'm sorry I was such a bitch before the attack."

"Thanks." Before Cedarcliff, Tess would have relished Kavita's apology, but considering the deadly attack, their past animosity now seemed petty. "Hey, I know you were sore about not getting my vice president job, but Kingsley Tech needs our focus now, and I hope we can put aside our differences."

"Fair enough. You've had terrible luck and have been so, well, *out of control* lately, which is rather unlike you."

Three whole seconds separated Kavita's apology from a fresh jab, and Tess blamed the painkillers for tricking her into believing collegiality was possible. She snickered at her underling's frenemy-like qualities. Should anyone discover how nearly she'd careened off the rails at Torque, she expected Kavita would use it against her with glee.

Over the phone line, an airport announcement blared, along with the clink of glasses and muffled voices. "Not to worry. I just had a bad week. Where are you right now?" Tess faked nonchalance.

"The executive club at Heathrow. Just landed. I planned to visit my parents in Mumbai, but David needed me in London to oversee our emergency procedures. He's calling a tech review soon, but I'm not sure when. Declan's analyzing the Firefly code, and I'll review our network perimeter to reinforce our lockdown the second I arrive."

No way in hell would Tess allow an investigation of Kyle's code without her being present. "Tell David I'll be there." Tess furrowed her brow. She needed to get back to work, fast.

"Forget it. David's torn up about sending you to Cedarcliff in his place. I called him about the attack, and it's like the bloke came completely unglued. He said you can't return until you're 110 percent healed."

"No one really expects a terrorist attack." At best, Tess's healing had barely started, and her complete recovery might stretch weeks. Cobwebs clogged her brain, and she couldn't focus for more than short blocks of time.

"The Metropolitan Police believe David is still in danger, so he's quite stressed out," Kavita said. "Don't worry about a thing, though. I can cover your work."

"No need. I've got this. A couple of days more and

I'll be fine." Not to be discounted, Tess rallied to defend her turf and projected wellness in wild excess of reality. A shameless self-promoter, Kavita never missed an opportunity to snatch bits of Tess's job for her own benefit.

"If you say so, but you'd better rest up." Kavita signed off.

Tess gazed out her windows at Lake Union. London seemed impossibly far away, like a distant planet requiring too much effort to visit. Minutes became elastic, stretching to endless lengths ahead of her, then snapping back to mere seconds. Fretting about work, she downed another cup of espresso, bitter in her mouth, to chase away her painkiller-induced fog.

She turned her mind to the Rapadon mystery and considered that the terrorists might not know what the Rapadon program was, either. Intuition told her everyone was missing something, and she stretched her mind to figure out what eluded them. Caffeine hit her bloodstream, but the soft autumn drizzle enveloping Seattle failed to soothe her restlessness.

Chilled, she flicked on her gas fireplace and paused to reminisce over Kyle's photograph on the mantel. One of her most cherished memories, she had snapped his photo the day they got engaged at Walworth Cove. Standing on the sandy English seashore with foaming waves curling around his bare feet, Kyle radiated joy and his green-eyed gaze sparkled. He wore swim trunks, and his gold Celtic amulet encircled his bare neck. Whenever her daydreams drifted toward Mark, she suffered conflicted pangs of guilt, like she had cheated on Kyle. "I'm sorry," she whispered out loud. *I was going to die, and I needed someone.* But like the scent of white jasmine in late winter promised spring's arrival, Mark continued to permeate her imagination.

Buzzing from multiple espressos, Tess spent the afternoon on the couch scouring the news on her laptop. Determined to understand Riku's warning about the security landscape changing overnight, she checked for headlines in Eastern Europe. Deep into articles on Belarusian and Russian terrorist cells, she was scribbling notes when the doorbell rang.

"Be right there," she called out. Clad in plaid pajama pants and her favorite rock concert sweatshirt, she teetered through her foyer on crutches, noting her stabbing leg pain had dissipated. She opened the front door with one hand.

"Hi, Tess."

A familiar, accented voice greeted her through heavy sheets of rain. The drizzle had transitioned to a downpour, and the wind blew raindrops inside, wet against her skin. She glimpsed a shock of dark blond hair and recognized Mark's blue-eyed gaze. "Mark?" To her surprise, her gauzy memories matched the svelte man standing on her doorstep. "Come in." She softened her smile to reflect her delight and gratitude.

"Great to see you again." Mark shook the rain off his navy wool coat and stepped inside.

His smile exuded warm energy, and his bruises had faded a couple of shades. Opening his arms to hug her, he paused a millisecond as if vetting whether she intended to hug him back. Without thinking, she wound her arms around his back and embraced him tightly. Her crutches fell into the foyer, and she laughed, trying to untangle them. "Weren't you in New York?" Flustered, Tess tried to regain her composure.

"Change of plans." He leaned back to study her face and touched the thin line of sutures melding the broken skin over her cheekbone. "The surgeon did an excellent job, and those stitches shouldn't scar."

"I'm relieved." An awkward flush spread across her cheeks, and she took him in from head to toe. Choice moments of the forest liaison replayed in her mind, and her body tingled with attraction from one magnetic pole to the other.

He leaned over to pick up her crutches and handed them back. "I'm glad you're able to keep mobile. Keeping the blood flowing in your legs is important."

"Always the doctor. How'd you find me, anyhow?" To her knowledge, her address wasn't listed anywhere, and his lopsided smile hinted at mischief.

"I called Kingsley Tech in London and spoke with Tilly Baxter. I wanted to send you a get-well gift and needed your address."

"My admin is a traitor." Feigning admonition, she crossed her arms and grimaced. "Clearly, I need to speak with her."

Mark shuffled backward with both hands up in the air. "Hang on there. In Tilly's defense, she refused to share any of your information until she verified my credentials and even cleared it with David first."

"I'm glad you persisted. Somehow, I didn't get your number before you checked out of the hospital." Tess placed her hands on her hips and gave him a questioning look.

"After what we've been through, sending flowers seemed inadequate, so I decided to visit you, instead."

"You drove all the way to Seattle to say hello?" His unexpected appearance on her doorstep delighted her, but after overcoming her surprise, she wondered what motivated his visit.

"I figured you'd want this back." From his pocket, he produced the red-handled pocketknife they'd used to escape the barn. "I sanitized it."

"My lucky charm for travel. Thank you." His answer, while sweet, still didn't address her question, and she resolved to figure out his intentions later. She touched the knife's smooth steel before setting it on the dining table and led him into the living room, where the fireplace glowed with crackling, orange flames. "Come, have a seat. I'll take your coat."

"Thanks. You've got a stunning view." Mark crossed the room and stopped at the wall of floor-to-ceiling windows.

Outside, the boats lining Lake Union bobbed up and down in the heavy wind. She admired his broad shoulders from behind, and heat flushed her cheeks as her gaze drifted south to his hips.

"I've always loved the water, and this reminds me of the fjords near Bergen." He rotated to face her and smiled.

"The lake is stunning, even on stormy days. Since moving from London, I've barely spent any time here, but I enjoy it when I do." She sank onto her overstuffed suede couch and put her foot onto an oversized pillow.

He sat next to her and leaned forward to elevate her ankle higher on the pillow. "How are you recovering?"

Hypersensitive to his presence, she sensed his every move and suppressed the urge to run her hands over his muscular body.

"My ribs need a few weeks to mend, but my punctured lung is healing without surgery, which is a big win."

"I'm happy to see you, but what really inspired your trip? It's a long way and an international border crossing." She had expected he'd be eager to fly home.

He steepled his fingertips in front of his mouth. "Well, I didn't make it to New York. I was too sick to fly, so I rested longer in Vancouver. Also, I needed to meet George Bouchard from Timberline Ventures before he returned to Toronto. Seattle was nearby, so I reserved a hotel and drove south after my meeting."

"George Bouchard. I didn't manage to meet with him before everything happened." She'd nearly forgotten why she traveled to Cedarcliff in the first place—to secure venture capital for Kingsley Tech.

Mark took a deep breath. "I resigned my medical advisor position on Timberline's board, and I needed to tell Bouchard in person."

"Wow, big decision. Though given what happened, Bouchard could hardly blame you." Rapt with attention, she watched as he sported an ironic smile and shook his head.

"No, not so big. I'm not a corporate guy, and I won't miss it. I belong in an operating room, not a boardroom."

"So, what's next?"

He displayed his left hand, its deep purple scars garish in the bright daylight. "Healing my hand. I need intensive therapy to return to work and start doing surgery again, and that's what I want most."

Tess offered him an encouraging smile and gave his shoulder an affectionate squeeze. The simple gesture quickened her pulse, and a familiar warmth spread across her pelvis, despite her best effort to concentrate on their conversation.

"First though, I'd like to know why this attack happened, so I can move past it. In Crimea where I injured my hand, it was a war zone, where you willingly accept the risk of omnipresent danger. Processing Cedarcliff is harder because the attack was so unexpected. Seriously, no one expects a terrorist attack in Canada."

"True." Hesitant to voice her uncertainty, Tess glanced out the window toward the lake. "I'm afraid we might not get closure anytime soon."

"Have the police updated you?" Mark leaned forward and rested his elbows on his legs.

"No, nothing's resolved. Yuri and Dmitry haven't been found, and the police believe David is in danger." The anxiety lodged in Tess's throat tightened, and she couldn't rein in her worry before meeting his expectant gaze. The fact that her captors still roamed free sucked away her optimism.

"So, uh, you're not mad at David? I mean, you took quite a hit for him." Bouncing one of his knees, he rubbed the back of his neck.

"How could I blame him for this? No, I was unlucky." She shook her head, all while noticing his nervousness. Conscious of his leg mere inches away, she found herself distracted by the heat radiating from his body.

"Well, I'm lucky you were there. We made an excellent team."

He leaned over to squeeze her hand, and a part of her melted. His expression was open and earnest, hiding nothing.

"Indeed." She reflected upon their first

conversations and how well they worked together under pressure. Also, he reawakened a long-dormant, precious part of her, but she didn't know how or if to tell him.

"Survival's worth celebrating. In honor of living, I'd like to take you to dinner. What do you say?" He rubbed his hands together.

"Wonderful idea, but I'm not quite mobile yet." She met his alluring gaze and smiled with excitement and regret.

"No worries. What if I pick up dinner? I don't cook, but I'm excellent at ordering takeout."

"I'd love to have dinner with you, but I need a shower first." The playful sparkle in his gaze made her breath catch. Sensual pangs crackled inside her, incongruous with the faded flannel pajama pants and concert sweatshirt she wore.

"Take your time. I'll head out and pick up dinner. Any suggestions?"

"How about Thai, Seattle's comfort food? Thai Heaven down the hill is great."

"Perfect. See you soon." Mark headed out the front door and back into the rain.

After flicking off the fireplace, Tess climbed upstairs to freshen up. Standing naked in her shower, she relaxed as the steaming water warmed her bruised body. Her heart raced with excitement in anticipation of his return, making her giddy as a twenty-year-old going on a first date.

An hour later, darkness had set over the Seattle skyline when Mark returned, carrying a bottle of syrah and a bag towering with steaming boxes of Thai food. The scent of spicy curry and lemongrass permeated the air.

Tess carried plates from the kitchen to the dining room and found Mark studying the collage of Kyle's pictures that adorned her fireplace mantel. She regretted leaving a shrine celebrating her past in such a prominent place but figured he kept a similar display of his lost family. "Dinner smells wonderful. Thanks for picking it up." Tess clicked the stereo remote and selected jazz before sitting at the table.

"The boats on the waterfront here remind me of sailing as a young boy. Someday, I'm going to get my own sailboat." Mark gazed at the lights flickering on Lake Union before taking a seat.

Opening a box of Pad Thai, she spooned out a serving and offered a warm smile. "Ah, so you're a sailor. You'll feel right at home in Seattle. Many Scandinavians settled here, and you can buy *lutefisk* in Ballard, a couple of miles away."

"*Ja, lutefisk.*" Mark laughed as he corrected her pronunciation, and the mood in the room took a humorous turn. "People say St. Patrick invented it in Ireland to poison Viking raiders, but he wasn't alive when the Vikings attacked Ireland. Besides, *lutefisk* makes Vikings even stronger."

"Lye-soaked fish? Must be an acquired taste." Finding his cheerful enthusiasm contagious, she couldn't resist grinning while enjoying another bite of the spicy coconut curry dish. "How'd you end up in the US?"

Mark refilled their wine glasses with syrah. "I grew up with my parents and Ingrid, my sister, in the house our family has owned for generations in Bergen. I wanted to be a surgeon but opted to train in the US instead of Norway. After med school, I did my surgical residency in Washington, D.C."

"Do you feel homesick?" Tess leaned forward in the plush dining chair, grazing her fingertips over its brushed texture.

"Always. Bergen's home and my family are there. I'll live there again someday, but not yet. America needs trauma surgeons more than Norway ever will." He bit into a fresh spring roll before wiping his hands with a napkin.

"Why is that?" Tess asked.

"Because Americans can't stop shooting each other. More kids here have been killed by gunshot wounds in the last twenty years than among police and military in the line of duty combined." He shook his head and closed his eyes for a moment. "I cannot understand this, but I aim to save as many people as possible."

Tess covered her face with her hands and groaned. "It's awful, and it's a shame we're safer outside the US. Well, most days, anyhow. Canada should have been safe."

He winced and rubbed his chest as if he'd been hit. "Right. Most days. Sorry to be so dark. You said your family relocated often."

"We lived in Boston until my father joined the State Department when I was five. Then, we lived all over—Bangkok, Cairo, Bogotá, London, and Bern— but I returned to America for college." She savored another sip of wine. The syrah emanated a smoky, blackberry bouquet and tasted luscious. "I'd planned to stay in London and even applied for British citizenship, but Kyle died. Kingsley Tech plans to build an engineering team in Seattle next year, if we secure enough venture capital. I thought creating a new home base might help me move on. No memories here for me, unlike London."

"Life takes unpredictable turns. Meeting you was a surprise." He took another sip of his wine and winked.

"Are there any other kind?" Unsure of what to say, she could only form an awkward smile.

"What is it?"

She drummed her fingertips on the tabletop, then leaned back in her chair. "We've experienced trauma together, but don't know much else about each other. We're doing everything out of sequence."

"Life isn't always linear, so we're filling in what we didn't know before. Besides, it's the first time I met a woman while being held hostage, and I vote the usual dating rules don't apply." Ever calm, Mark folded his hands in his lap.

"Dating?" The word sparked her attention, and her curiosity beat out caution. "I'm happy to see you, but I'm a little unsettled." She tucked a curl behind her ear.

"You don't need to be nervous with me. We have a lot in common."

His steady gaze unnerved her, and she marveled at his placid self-assurance after what they'd endured. Curious, she aimed a side-glance in his direction. "How?"

"We've both lived international lives in unstable countries and lost our partners along the way. And now, we've survived a kidnapping together, which isn't usual."

She couldn't help but laugh. "True, though the kidnapping better be a one-time thing because I can't endure another one." Serious again, she sneaked a glimpse at her photos of Kyle on the fireplace mantel. "You understand Cedarcliff and what loss means."

"It's no surprise we found physical comfort in each other, given we were trying to survive." His gaze sparkled, and he smiled over the rim of his glass.

"Are you flirting, Dr. Nygaard?" Taking notice, she pushed her usual defenses away and allowed herself to enjoy the moment.

"Will it land me in trouble?" Tilting his head, he offered her a wink paired with a crooked smile.

"I hope so. You're not shy, are you?" Not to be outdone, she tilted her chin and flashed what she hoped was an alluring smile.

He shrugged. "Not often. But for a long, long time, I believed recovering after Maya died was impossible."

"How long did it take you to feel ready to begin again?"

"Until about, well, sometime yesterday." His expression warmed into a smile.

Without hesitation, she returned the smile, impressed by his bold move of visiting her unannounced. Refreshed by his directness, she appreciated his earnestness and complete lack of presumptuousness. She hadn't dated since Kyle died, and attraction propelled her forward before caution could surface. "Why did you come to find me? I'm curious."

"The truth?"

"Yes, please." While she suspected he was teasing her, his voice also contained a fleeting hint of vulnerability she wanted to understand.

"You had grit. I was impressed by your bravery."

"No, not bravery. I'm not brave at all, just

stubborn. I took stupid, insane risks at Cedarcliff." Shaking her head, she demurred.

"Those stupid risks saved my life, and I'm grateful for your courage." Mark raised his wine glass.

She toasted him over the empty boxes of Phad Thai and basil eggplant before downshifting into lighter topics of schools, cities, and travel. As the evening flew by, the conversation flowed easily, as if she'd known him for months rather than a few days. "May I offer you a glass of scotch? I promise it'll be better than Farmer Campbell's whiskey." Tess turned on the gas fireplace in the living room, then limped toward the kitchen.

"I love an aged scotch after dinner."

"Lucky for you, I have a special bottle of scotch somewhere, but I need help finding it." She pointed to the moving boxes stacked on the dark wood floor next to the pantry.

"Glad to help." He followed her into the kitchen and sorted through the neat stacks of boxes against the wall. "You moved in recently?"

"September. I've been too busy traveling to unpack." While mostly accurate, the reality proved more complex. Perpetual globetrotting for work offered a convenient excuse she could use to avoid restarting her life alone. Like a dandelion blowing in the breeze, she was always flying from meeting to meeting, rarely landing long enough to grow roots.

Mark extracted a couple of boxes from the pile and selected one from the bottom row. "Success—*booze and bar stuff.*" Knife in hand, he sliced the cardboard top and opened the box. "Here we go. Crystal glasses and a fifteen-year-old scotch."

"Perfect. Thanks for the assist." Tess selected two glasses, opened the aged scotch, and poured them a drink before handing the glasses to Mark to carry to the living room. Once seated on the couch, Tess accepted a glass and toasted him. "Cheers to surviving."

"*Skål*." Mark lifted his crystal glass in her direction and took a drink.

"What an insane week." Savoring a long sip of the aged, peaty scotch, Tess adjusted her leg and tossed a woolen throw blanket over it.

"The kidnapping and the hospital, yes, crazy. But the part with us wasn't. It might have been the sanest thing I've done in quite a while." He set his glass down on the cherry coffee table.

"You should know I don't sleep with near-strangers in the woods very often." Tess studied his hands, the left with its purple, jagged scar, and the right, steady and perfect.

"I'd hope not. Only after escaping mortal danger, right?"

"Only then." Tess laughed again, then lowered her gaze, feeling sheepish. "Will you forgive me for seducing you in the woods? I'm a bit embarrassed."

"Don't be. We needed each other. In fact, I hope…" His voice drifted off, leaving his sentence unfinished as his fingertips grazed her cheek.

Mesmerized by his sapphire gaze, she longed to kiss him again. Suspended in a dreamy haze, she draped a hand over his shoulder to confirm he wasn't a painkiller-induced hallucination built on fantasy. His body radiated heat under her fingertips, and her head trilled with energy.

He raised a hand to her face, then met her mouth

with a slow, tender kiss.

The tip of his tongue tasted like whiskey with hints of leather and candied almonds. The faint scent of sandalwood from his golden skin and the salt of his lips stoked her desire. Impatient to discard inhibitions of her past, she exiled boring words like *careful* and *slow*, leaving an urgent *now.* "Stay with me tonight," she whispered and caressed his shoulder.

"Even if no one is chasing us?"

"Especially because no one is chasing us." She closed her eyes as Mark's fingertips grazed the delicate skin below her neck and teased her with gentle touches and soft kisses.

Mark answered with a long kiss and scooped her up from the couch into his arms, careful not to jostle her ankle. She wound her arms tight around his shoulders, and they crossed her living room to ascend the staircase one step at a time. In her bedroom, Mark laid her on top of the queen-size sleigh bed, covered in damask linens. With one hand, she eased his cashmere sweater over his head and tossed it on a chair.

"I'm so happy to see you again." Mark proceeded to shower her skin with kisses. Grasping her face between his hands, he kissed her mouth while caressing her cheek, then slowly unbuttoned her blouse, stopping to kiss each newly exposed inch of skin. After the last button, he unhooked her lace bra and stroked her back in soft, circular motions.

"I'm glad you're here." Between kisses, she aligned her body against his, lingering over every touch, free from danger.

"*Min kjære*," he breathed before kissing her throat and moving southward down her torso with a soft, slow line of kisses. He kissed her again and touched her cheek. "May I?"

Breathless, Tess nodded and removed his T-shirt with gentle tugs but hesitated upon seeing the canvas of bruises covering his chest. Purple-and-black splotches discolored his skin. "Your bruises…"

"Just kiss me."

"I don't want anyone to hurt you again." An impulsive need to protect him from harm overtook her. Reunited, the warm skin of their torsos merged in perfect symmetry. Any danger haunting Tess ebbed away, replaced by desire. She admired his muscular shoulders and long legs, golden against her alabaster skin. She wrapped one leg around his hip to draw him near, and as they pulled closer, her senses sparked like spreading wildfire.

Once together, she savored every sensation, exhilarated by seeing him again. Later, nestled against his chest in the satisfied afterglow, she marveled how a day that started so lonely could finish this way. Burrowed under the down duvet, she listened to the steady stream of raindrops pelting the roof.

"The Seattle rain is soothing." Mark pulled the duvet to their chins. "Though I'm glad we're inside."

"That's for sure. I still can't believe you're here." Seeing Mark was the last thing she'd expected, and the surprise visit compounded the evening's surreal mood.

"Spontaneous decision, obviously." He wound an arm around her.

"Which part? Coming to Seattle or ending up in bed?" she teased.

"Yes." Dissolving into laughter, he kissed the top of her head.

Entwined with Mark, she was drifting toward sleep when images of Yuri and Dmitry appeared, unwelcome intruders in her mind. Knowing they still roamed the earth free, she stared at the ceiling with growing uneasiness. Although she felt safe in Mark's arms, nothing could assuage her worry that danger lurked around the next corner.

Somewhere out there, a reckoning awaited her, and she didn't know how long a reprieve she'd have before she'd need to fight again.

Chapter Ten

The Morning After

Heavy rain drenched Seattle through the night. Stirring in her bed, Tess rolled over, and the alarm clock on the bedside table read 3:37 a.m. Pleasant memories of the afterglow from hours earlier enveloped her. After snuggling under the covers, she was almost asleep again when Mark's voice startled her.

Beside her, he was tossing and turning, back and forth. "*Ikke skyt meg.* Don't shoot me. *Vær så snill å ikke skade henne*. Please don't hurt her." Alternating between groaning and speaking Norwegian in short bursts, his shouts shattered the bedroom's tranquility. He thrashed his arms in every direction, hitting blindly.

"Mark, wake up." She scooted away, switched on the bedside lamp, and tugged on his bare shoulder.

No response.

Sweat dripped from his forehead, and he appeared glazed over and trance-like. Alarmed, she shook him harder.

Mark jumped with a start, flipped over to his knees, and tackled her to the mattress.

With her shoulders pinned down and the wind knocked out of her chest, she couldn't move. Panicking, she kicked with her good leg to dislodge him from on top of her, but to no avail. "Mark, stop it. You're in

Seattle, and you're having a nightmare." She raised her voice.

Looking down, he leapt off her at once and retreated. "My God, I'm so sorry. Sorry."

"What just happened?" Shaken, she stepped out of the bed, slipped on her bathrobe, and tied it closed with a secure knot while studying him warily. Bruises painted his lower torso like charcoal storm clouds. Sweat rolled down his flushed cheeks, and his eyes watered.

Squinting, he scanned her bedroom walls several times while his hands grasped at the bedsheets. Once his breath stopped hitching, he raised a hand and swiped at his damp forehead, then stared at his toes. "I've had a little trouble sleeping lately." Mumbling, he angled his body toward the wall and slouched against a pillow.

"Understatement of the year." She didn't buy it.

"I hope I didn't hurt you."

Feeling exposed, Tess circled her arms around her knees to alleviate her discomfort. "Remember how we agreed to be honest with each other, whether the truth was good, bad, or ugly? I'm no stranger to sleeping pills, and I couldn't wake you up or shake you out of the nightmare. Talk to me." Aiming to strike an assertive but kind tone, she calmed her voice. The tears welling in his eyes revealed a profound, deep sadness she recognized, having experienced it herself. His gold-toned cheeks flushed scarlet, and he slumped his shoulders as if defeated. Ruddy splotches dotted his skin.

After a long silence, he exhaled. "Since Cedarcliff, my sleep has been disturbed—lots of night terrors and sleepwalking. The stress of getting my hand shattered in Ukraine combined with the kidnapping at Cedarcliff pushed me too far."

"What do you mean, *too far*?" Paranoia gripped her like a vise, and her breath grew shallow. Since Cedarcliff, her sense of time had morphed, randomly stretching and shrinking, but in reality, only one week had passed since they met. Nothing in her life was normal anymore, and she questioned her instincts, second-guessing whether she'd misjudged his character and misplaced her trust.

Mark blinked and took a deep breath. "After the explosion at my hospital last spring, I developed post-traumatic stress disorder. A psychiatrist in New York, a specialist in combat trauma, treated me with Eye Movement Desensitization and Reprocessing therapy, medication, and the works. I recovered, but Cedarcliff sent me backward." His voice trailed off, and he rubbed at one temple.

"I don't understand. During the gunmen's attack at Cedarcliff, you were the calmest person in the room. How can it be harder for you now, given that we're safe?" She considered the term PTSD from multiple angles and spun it around in her head. The morning of their forest trek, when he'd shifted from relative calm to rage in seconds, came to mind. His volatility had disturbed her, and the night terror amplified her unease. She wrestled over how to soothe his pain yet protect herself.

Mark lifted his scarred left hand to his mouth. "Every night, I wake up, and I'm back lying on the damn barn floor with Sergey's gun in my face. Over and over again."

"I'm sorry. Reliving the violence must be hell." The choices she made to survive Cedarcliff flooded back, and she shuddered as goose bumps erupted on her skin. Since coming home, she hadn't dared reflect upon the attack, preferring to banish the memories and deny what had happened. Besides, focusing on her physical injuries was more productive than reliving how she got them. She inhaled to ground herself in the present. "Mark, we suffered a *terrorist attack*. Everyone will be sympathetic to what you've gone through."

"Look, I'm the one who heals people and saves lives, not the other way around, so don't pity me. You've already suffered enough."

"You're too hard on yourself. Are you still getting help?" Tess climbed onto the opposite side of the bed and tucked her terrycloth robe around her legs.

"While in the Vancouver hospital, I called my psychiatrist, who recommended I restart medication and avoid being alone. You understand Cedarcliff, which helps."

Uncertain what to say, she stalled and took a long sip from the water bottle on her nightstand. The cumulative volume of tragedies Mark must have witnessed as a surgeon was staggering. To then endure two terror attacks himself would be devastating. "You've healed countless people but the series of traumas you've faced…I can't even imagine."

"Several doctors quit our Ukraine hospital team because of PTSD, but I swore I'd never be one of the weak ones." His voice shook, and his right hand formed a fist.

"Christ, you were attacked by terrorists—*twice*. Bad luck? Terrible luck, but not weakness."

"I'm an excellent surgeon and can't afford to lose my career because of my hand or mental state. Maya and Nils are dead; without my work, I'd have nothing left. Unacceptable." He leaned his head back and stared at the ceiling.

Tess placed a hand on his shoulder. "You'll recover, but you need time. I haven't begun to process what happened in Canada, and I was a wreck even before then."

Mark lifted a single eyebrow and cocked his head. "Are you kidding? You, a wreck? My God, you were fearless and a total badass in Canada. You didn't shy away from anything."

The gap between his perception and the reality of her reckless week before the attack flabbergasted her. "The day before Cedarcliff, I was drowning in grief and a total mess. Hours before I flew to Canada, I spent the night at a dodgy London punk club, guzzling vodka tonics like water on a scorching summer day."

"You're joking, right?" He lifted a single eyebrow.

"Which part? The club or the vodka? Both are true."

"Wow, well, punk clubs are *hot.*" Wearing a sly grin, he rested his hand on hers. "But tell me about the vodka. Sounds like a lot of pain."

"The anniversary of Kyle's death nearly crushed me, and I needed to numb my loneliness and forget everything. I was coming unglued, like nothing mattered." She averted her gaze, embarrassed about her Torque misadventure. "Twelve hours later, I arrived at Cedarcliff."

"Sometimes grief demands so much that your sanity requires you escape it, even if only for a few hours. Believe me, I know." His brow furrowed.

"You understand." Relieved not to feel alone, she appreciated being seen. Platitudes of sympathy from friends and strangers helped, but he understood at a personal level what others couldn't imagine.

Eager to shift the conversation, she repositioned her legs to be more comfortable. "Do you live alone in New York?"

"Yes, but after my hand heals and I can work again, I might move. I don't know." He darted a glance out the window. "In Ukraine, the medical team lived together like a family, and we processed the rough times together. New York's lively, but I haven't found a niche there. First, though, I need to get my head together."

"I can relate." While determined to avoid judgment, she couldn't deny his erratic behavior unnerved her. To be fair, she'd avoided dealing with any of the Cedarcliff trauma herself. Denial's sweet relief demanded nothing of her, so she mentally packed away the disturbing memories, boxed them to process later, and scheduled them for the calendar block labeled *never.* If her approach blew up at an inconvenient time, so be it. Rubbing Mark's shoulder, she chose compassion over doubt and took a chance. "Stay with me for a couple of days."

"That's very kind, but I don't want to trouble you. I'll sleep downstairs." He moved to stand, and the blanket dropped to the floor.

"Maybe I don't want to be alone, either. Stay, and we'll sort things out tomorrow." She reached for his unscarred hand and stroked his fingers. Pinpointing her feelings proved impossible. The passion they shared tantalized her, but the backdrop of his distress made her pause. Her desire, loneliness, and curiosity tangled into a ball of confusing emotions she couldn't unravel.

"Thanks, but no. You need sleep to heal, and I won't risk hurting you if I suffer another night terror." He grabbed his clothes from the floor and headed downstairs.

Stung, Tess crawled under the covers. Grief had squeezed her heart like a vise all year, and the sexual relief they'd shared comforted and healed her. However imperfect their respective states of mind, desire outweighed wariness, and she was too spent to discern whether getting involved was wise or foolish.

Exhausted but wired, she craved the release of oblivion and popped a double dose of oxycodone capsules. With luck, tomorrow she'd know what to do next, because right now, she had no clue.

After hours of rain, faint sunlight filtered through her bedroom's curtains and roused Tess from her painkiller-laced sleep. Fragments of a conversation lodged in her ear, and she pieced together Mark was in the kitchen, speaking to a woman. Curious, she slipped out of her bed's warm cocoon to investigate and lunged to pick up her crutches before skulking to the top of the second-floor landing.

Through the staircase spindles, she spotted Mark leaning against the fridge and holding his phone with an arm extended, taking a video call. The screen was too far away to see the caller. Pressing herself against the hallway corner out of sight, she strained to hear a few sentences.

"I trust you, so I don't understand why you want me to be miserable. I feel like you're punishing me when I haven't done anything wrong." Mark pushed a hand through his tousled hair.

"That's because I don't think you're being honest with me, or yourself, about what's going on. You haven't convinced me you'll change."

Hearing the woman's dropped *r*'s and long, drawn-out vowels, Tess pegged the caller as a native New Yorker. Did Mark have a girlfriend? Passion prevailed over reason last night, and she hadn't even thought to ask if he was seeing someone. Jealous feelings arose, and she failed to banish them and erase her lingering doubts.

"But I've changed everything. I've quit my job, so I can't be a workaholic anymore, and I'll have more free time. I can't give anything more." He shifted his weight from one foot to the other and stretched his neck. "I've got to go. I'll call you later, and I'll be back in a couple of days so we can talk about this in person. Bye."

Careful not to make a sound, she slinked back to the bathroom to process what she'd heard. Once there, she signaled she was awake by making more noise than necessary while washing her hands. Unable to resist their magnetic attraction, she admittedly let herself get swept away last night. Before Cedarcliff, Mark had a life in New York. Between their chemistry, his PTSD, and this suspicious phone call, she fought a wave of jealous nausea. Defenses firmly back in place, she resolved to maintain more distance and tightened her robe before heading downstairs.

In the dining room, Mark was reading *The New York Times* like nothing unusual had transpired a few hours earlier, let alone five minutes ago. His golden features projected a portrait of calm, and nothing seemed awry.

"I'm glad you got back to sleep. Would you like some coffee? I just brewed a pot." He stood, pulled out a chair, and gestured for her to sit.

"Yes, please." Tess shuffled to the table and eased herself into the chair. "How are you feeling this morning?"

Mark went to the kitchen and returned moments later with a steaming cup of coffee. "Better, thanks, but I'm embarrassed and sorry about disturbing you last night."

"No one could blame you for needing recovery time, Mark. I can't face thinking about Cedarcliff." Aiming to connect through their shared experience, she heightened the empathy in her voice.

"You can't avoid it forever."

"Watch me." In truth, sometimes bravado was the only thing keeping her afloat. A vision of Sergey crossed her mind, and she dismissed it. Eager for a change of scenery and fresh air, she devised a plan. "Fall sunshine in Seattle deserves celebration, and I need to get out of the house. I'm taking you to Ballard, our Scandinavian neighborhood. Game?" A quest for lye-soaked fish sounded like a death wish, not a delicacy, but keeping the mood light today seemed wise. To her relief, Mark rewarded the suggestion with a satisfied smile.

"Great, but you're taking oxy, so you can't drive. I've got a rental car, so I can drive us."

"I'll get dressed, and we'll head out." As she dressed, she figured a casual brunch would prove an enjoyable distraction from topics she wished to avoid, like Cedarcliff or PTSD.

Minutes later, Tess helped Mark navigate to the waterfront neighborhood northwest of Lake Union and suggested a small Scandinavian deli on bustling Market Street. They parked close to the Ballard Locks, where ships crossed from Seattle's sprawling lakes into Puget Sound's seawater. Seagulls squawked above them in the salty, brisk air, scavenging for food. The deli exuded minimalist Scandinavian design, as exhibited by the polished white counters and modern, angled chairs. Natural light beamed through the oversized windows.

A vast glass display offered a tidy assortment of unfamiliar but tasty-looking dishes. Tess peered at the options, unable to choose. "Hmm. I recognize the salmon, but I'm not sure about the rest."

"*Ja.* Here we have the *koldtbord*, what you call smorgasbord, along with *gravlax* with dill." Rubbing his hands, Mark surveyed the menu items offered. He shuffled to the second display case and pointed to entrées. "The white fish is boiled cod, served with roasted beets, and the round balls are *kumla*, potato dumplings. What would you like?"

"I'll try anything except *that*." Unable to identify the species, she pointed to an animal head on a plate surrounded by vegetables. While not a vegetarian, she couldn't imagine eating the decapitated head of…well, anything.

"Excellent—you're adventurous." He leaned close. "I wouldn't touch the *smalahov*, boiled sheep's head, either." Smiling, he ordered two *koldtbords*, a beet salad, and *kumla*. "Ah, they have Bergen's best aquavit here. I'm impressed. Let's order a couple of shots."

"Count me in." Seeing his renewed exuberance,

she relaxed and teased him about his enormous appetite. A table by the window opened, and she waited for him to sit before digging into her platter.

"*Skål.*" Mark toasted her with a glass of aquavit.

Confounded by her inability to resist him even the slightest bit, she reciprocated his toast with a generous sip. Hopefully, the aquavit would mute any lingering doubts about his phone conversation. Magnetically drawn to Mark's chiseled features, intelligence, humor, and compassion, she sensed the electricity crackling between them. Meanwhile, she sampled another slice of *gravlax,* and to her surprise, found the savory *koldtbord* meats and cheeses scrumptious. "The dill tastes delicious."

"This is like being home for me. Thank you." After devouring his first *koldtbord*, Mark tucked into a second platter.

"My pleasure. You must miss Norway." A pang of guilt about taking time away from work struck her, but she ignored it. Work could wait because right now, she felt her heart opening in ways she hadn't imagined possible one week ago.

"Always. My heart belongs to Bergen, and I miss *kumla*. And the aquavit." He raised his glass and leaned closer.

"Have you considered staying in Bergen while you're recovering?" Spending time in his favorite place might comfort him and speed his recovery. Her question must have struck gold because a dreamy quality filled his gaze. Whatever he was thinking, he seemed far away from the café.

"Bergen would be great. And now I'm free to go wherever I want." He swirled the remaining aquavit in his glass, coating the sides of the glass with clear liquor. The corners of his mouth tilted into a smile.

"What about New York? It's such an exciting city, and it must be great for dating." Somehow, she needed to squelch the insidious doubts bothering her. Attempting to catch Mark in a lie without being obvious, she projected nonchalance despite her not-so-innocent question.

"Maybe for some." A frown crossed his face.

What did that mean? Unable to interpret his response with any accuracy, she opted to let it go. "Tell me about Bergen. It sounds comforting to have a solid home base where you can return."

"I can't imagine life any other way. I am Bergensk before I am Norwegian." He beamed, and a grin sprang across his face as he circled the rim of the aquavit glass with a finger. "Although I've been in America for many years, growing up in Bergen shaped me and remains a huge part of my identity. How about you?"

"My family moved so much we didn't have one home base. To this day, I still don't." Whenever a yearning for permanent roots struck, she ran faster and traveled more to resist growing them. Having avoided building a life anywhere, she bought the Seattle condo as a practical necessity in anticipation of Kingsley Tech extending its territory into America. Another hearty sip of the aquavit burned her throat, and the alcohol hit her bloodstream fast, resulting in a strong buzz.

"Careful. Aquavit will make you invincible."

"Given how beat up I feel this week, I could use some invincibility." She set down her glass and picked a cucumber slice from the platter.

"You're stronger than you realize."

"I appreciate your flattery." Reassured to see the mischievous sparkle back in Mark's gaze after last night's strange episode, she unwound a bit. In the early afternoon sunshine, his night terror seemed a one-time blip and unlikely to reoccur. Sitting in this chic deli, he radiated only ease. Maybe he spoke the truth, and no mystery girlfriend waited in New York, pining for him.

"How about I indulge you with another shot? In Bergen, we make our aquavit from fermented caraway and dill seeds, then store it in sherry casks. And here's the best part." He leaned forward and winked. "We send those casks on a sea journey around the world to mature—a six-month vacation."

"Not bad. Speaking of time off, I could use a sunny beach holiday." A long holiday with lots of sex would be a welcome break from the past year and she envisioned lounging on an island.

"I agree. Let's skip forest hiking and head for the tropics."

"Perfect." While she'd planned to keep her defenses, she found their chemistry melting her resolve and soon forgot her intentions. The goal of the brunch was to distract him with something happy, but the change of scenery suited her too by crowding out images she'd rather forget.

After lunch, she and Mark strolled a couple of blocks along the Ballard Locks and enjoyed the parade of boat traffic as it crossed the narrow canal in single file. Cool breezes rippled across the water, and the sun emerged at frequent intervals, creating warm patches on the ground. Fiery orange and yellow leaves lined the sidewalk and contrasted with the deep-blue sky. Despite the gorgeous day, she sagged onto her crutches as her energy flagged. "I love it out here, but I'm afraid my ankle is swelling again."

"Let's get you home and ice it. Here, take a seat, and I'll drive the car around and pick you up." Mark steered her to an open park bench with one hand on her lower back.

"Thank you." Increasing pain overtook her desire to remain in the rare fall sunshine. Grateful to get off her feet, she soaked up the day's cheeriness and stored it away for the coming winter. With the sun heating her back, she could ignore her doubts and appreciate the moment. Almost.

****

Once back home, Tess limped to the couch and allowed Mark to help her settle in. With her leg elevated on a suede-covered pillow, she hoped the pain would subside and not distract from the evening ahead. Outside her window, banks of clouds lowered over Lake Union, obscuring the earlier sunlight and dimming the living room's light.

"Let's take a look at your wound." Mark flipped on a bronze floor lamp and removed her surgical boot. Raising his phone's flashlight, he examined the incision site, and his eyebrows knit together as he frowned at the puffy ankle. "No signs of infection, but lots of swelling. Let's apply ice, get you a dose of anti-inflammatories, and recheck it in a couple of hours."

"For the record, I hate being an invalid." Relieved to be off her feet, she sank into the oversized cushions, grabbed a warm, fuzzy blanket, and tossed it over her legs just as the doorbell rang.

"Don't get up—I'll answer it." Mark hopped from the couch and strode across the room to open the front door.

A uniformed mail carrier stood outside her door, holding a large envelope in his hands. "International overnight delivery for Ms. Bennett. I need a signature, please."

Mark signed a form, thanked the mail carrier, then carried the envelope and receipt to the couch. He studied the front and back of the envelope before handing it over. "You think it's safe to open and not booby-trapped or something?"

Tess checked the return address. "Yes, it's from Molly MacTavish, Kyle's mother, and I recognize the handwriting." Leaning over, she picked up her pocketknife from the coffee table and sliced open the envelope to find a note from Molly tucked inside.

> *Dear Tess,*
>
> *Martin and I prayed for your speedy release and were relieved to learn you are home safe. You are in our prayers every day.*
>
> *Our bank called, requesting we empty our safe deposit box before they discontinue the program, so I couldn't avoid it any longer. You've reminded me to do it since Kyle's funeral, but I couldn't face it. The bank log said he visited it the week before he died.*
>
> *When we opened the box, I found this envelope addressed to you. I sent it overnight straight away, and I ken you'd be verra interested to see it.*
>
> *We miss you and hope you are well. It has been a sad year, and every day has been dreich since Kyle died. The sun shines dimly without our beloved bairn, and we miss him and you.*
>
> *All our love,*

Molly and Martin MacTavish

Thinking back, she remembered Kyle mentioning visiting the family safe deposit box before he died. At the time, she assumed he had intended to retrieve his grandmother's platinum band for their upcoming wedding and never connected the errand to anything else.

Tess placed Molly's letter on the coffee table, and the words inscribed on the big manila envelope leapt from the paper. *Confidential: For Tess Bennett in the event of my death, Kyle.* Tess traced his familiar, scrawling handwriting with a fingertip and flipped the envelope over to the sealed flap. An old-fashioned red wax seal secured it, decorated with the initials *KAM*. While known primarily for his futuristic savvy, Kyle possessed an unexpected flair for colorful historical details.

Although desperate to read Kyle's letter, she didn't want to open it in front of Mark. The day Kyle died she had been leading a meeting in Paris when the call came. The police told her Kyle had been killed, and she relived the moment her world shattered. The shocking abruptness of his death and being robbed of a chance to say goodbye made the grief even harder to endure. If nothing else, his final message might offer closure to help her heal. "Please excuse me for a few minutes. I'll be upstairs."

"Of course. Take your time. I'll be here reading if you need me." He picked up a copy of *The New York Times* and stretched his legs out on the couch.

Tess trudged up the stairs one by one with her booted foot feeling heavier than a tree trunk. Weary from the climb, she plopped onto the bed and sighed.

The unopened envelope floated on her damask duvet, and Kyle's flourished signature beckoned. Putting such a personal note in his family's safe deposit box didn't make sense and fueled her anxiety about what his final message might reveal.

The ominous statement on the envelope's front, *In the event of my death, Kyle*, struck her as formal, even paranoid, for a healthy thirty-six-year-old with a clear understanding of risk. Curiosity won out, and she sliced open the envelope, leaving the red wax seal intact. A diminutive brass key tumbled out and landed in her palm, along with a small leaf of paper. With his letter pressed against her chest, she granted herself a minute to work up the courage to read it.

> *Dear Tessa,*
>
> *If you're reading this, you must not have received any other messages I sent. I'm in danger, and my life's at risk.*
>
> *I've left you the only copy of this key. Protect it and tell no one. You'll need it to collect a vitally important package I've left in London. I can't risk leaving the address, but I trust your memory. Go to the restaurant where we had our third date. From the front door, turn right and head straight for one kilometer. Search for dragons. Look right. The name includes an indirect reference related to my favorite song. Inside, you'll find a box under your name. Use this key.*
>
> *No matter what happens to me, be strong, be brave, and go as soon as possible. I love you.*
>
> *Kyle*

Tess clasped the brass key and felt she'd somehow

reconnected to Kyle beyond the grave. What the hell did he mean? She placed the key back into the envelope, more confused than ever. Not grieving, not crying, but disturbed. Danger? Kyle was a straight-arrow guy. If he faced a threat, he wasn't seeking it himself. Was he depressed or suicidal, and she'd missed all the signs? No, impossible. They were both happy then, each of them glowing in anticipation of the wedding. True, Kyle had been more stressed than usual and was buried in a work project at the time, but nothing alarming. Rereading his words, she wanted to race to London to find the box now. No other choice made sense.

Downstairs, her satellite phone rang, but she ignored it. After a brief pause, the ringing persisted, stopped after four rings, then restarted. Footsteps sounded on the staircase, followed by a soft knock at the door.

Mark appeared, carrying her phone, and placed it in her hand. "I apologize for interrupting, but someone called three times in a row."

The screen display read *Declan O'Leary, VP Engineering*. Everything at work she wanted to forget rushed back with harsh intensity. The momentary peace in the sunshine today disappeared like crystal water slipping through her hands into a cesspool of muck. Raising her head, Tess squinted at her phone and made a guttural groan. Declan's call history indicated something serious was wrong, and dread filled her veins. Holding her breath, she pressed her colleague's name on the screen and gestured for Mark to sit.

"Tess, it's a total shitstorm here."

Declan's raw Irish brogue hit her before she could

say hello, and the strained edge to his voice set off alarm bells. The bedside clock read four o'clock, which meant it was already midnight in Greenwich Mean Time. *Not good.* "What's going on?"

"The police say the terrorists are planning a strike on Kingsley Tech in London. And Kavita's scheming trouble."

Adrenaline pumped through her bloodstream, and the back of her neck burned with prickly heat. Hyperalert, she clenched her jaw, and her back tightened like a metal rod. "Not going to happen. What did the police find?"

"They intercepted deep web chatter, a Belarusian terror cell planning an attack against a software company in London abbreviated KT. We're running scared."

"What did the police advise?" Random data points swirled inside her head.

Declan groaned. "They told me to keep calm and not panic. Yeah, right, fucking useless. No word on whether they intend a physical attack or cyberattack. To be safe, we sent everyone home and cleared the office."

"What else?" Overwhelmed with concern, she shut her eyes and prayed he had a plan.

"Someone called David and threatened him. The police searched his home in Mayfair and found hidden cameras recording his family. He freaked out and sent Penelope and Nigel to stay with his parents in the country."

Shit. "What a nightmare. What are you doing next?" Attempting to stay calm, she drummed her fingers in a repetitive pattern while her insides contorted into panicked knots.

"David wants a tech review after our network tests are complete, noon tomorrow."

She bolted upright. "I need to be there. What's Kavita scheming?"

"Ah, crap. She's lobbying David to take over your job."

Bitch. Containing her anger without exploding consumed every ounce of restraint she could muster. "Screw that. I'll get there as soon as I can. Text me where the tech review will be held, but don't tell David or Kavita I'm coming."

"You got it. We need you, but David's too damn polite to bother you. Luckily, I'm a rude arsehole unafraid to pick up a phone."

"Stay strong and keep me updated." Excessive politeness was never one of Declan's gifts, and despite herself, the corners of her lips formed a weary half-smile. The combined impact of Kyle's letter and Declan's news smacked her like a physical blow. Enduring another crisis days after her life's most terrifying experience might break her for good, and she hurled her phone to the ground. "Goddamn it!"

"Hey, you'll break that fancy phone if you throw it again. What happened?" Quiet until now, Mark placed a hand on her arm.

"I need to fly to London. *Now*." Her reserves dipped below zero, depleted beyond recovery, but this crisis at Kingsley required the entire leadership team to join forces and fight.

"Absolutely not. You must wait a week before flying." Mark narrowed his gaze.

"A *week*? Are you serious?" Glaring, she staggered to stand. Stymied by Mark, who stood with elbows extended wide from his body and chest thrust out, she wanted to throw her arms in the air and swear at the heavens. "This can't wait."

"At least three more days." Not budging, he stood with his arms crossed like a defensive shield.

"I don't need my damn leg to run a company." She straightened her body like a taut, live electrical wire at high voltage.

"Don't be reckless. You just had emergency surgery and are at a high risk of developing compartment syndrome. I won't allow it."

Astonished, she took a second to absorb his comment before erupting. "*Allow?* You don't own me. Whose side are you on?" Her voice carried a razor-sharp edge.

"The side wanting to keep you alive." Mark stepped closer, towering over her.

"If David becomes incapacitated for any reason, I'm legally responsible for Kingsley Tech. Me."

"Christ, Tess, *you're* incapacitated. You can barely stand."

"I'm catching the next flight to Heathrow." Compulsion drove her like a bullet train speeding in the wrong direction—*run, run, run.*

"Fine. Ignore my medical advice and do whatever you want." He turned away.

"People are counting on me." Stung by his sarcasm, she pressed a hand to her temple, where involuntary spasms inside her head announced a headache's arrival. Judging from Mark's rigid back and locked jaw, he couldn't contain his frustration, either.

Hell-bent on catching the next flight, she grabbed Kyle's envelope from the bedside table and zipped it into a secure pocket deep in her laptop bag. The quick move avoided any need to confess the other task driving her race to leave, but the exertion made her overheat. She yanked off her sweater to counter the dizzy wave of wooziness washing over her. In a flurry of motion, she marched to the closet, emptied the still-packed suitcase from Cedarcliff, and stuffed it with fresh business clothes.

"Tess." Mark slid his hands under her arms, lifted her up, and swung her around in one move. "Stop, now. Back in the truck, I promised always to give you the truth, so here it is. If the terrorists have planned another attack, you can't prevent it, and you also can't bring anyone back from the dead."

Visions of Kyle and Riku reignited her grief. "I know." She dropped her voice to a whisper. "That's why I can't let anyone else die."

Feet apart, she and Mark stood locked in a silent, intense battle of wills. Seconds passed, and a pressure-filled dam of emotion burst inside her chest and exposed her vulnerability. Stepping closer to Mark, she gingerly wrapped her arms around his chest and listened for the thud of his heartbeat.

He pulled her closer and stroked her hair. "I'll admit it. I care about you, and I can't just stand here and let you risk your life again."

Her heart dropped like a rock into a deep lake because every choice meant risking something. Trapped with no good options, she resorted to primal instinct, which was to run. "I need to go to London, so I guess this is goodbye for now." Looking up to meet his gaze, she winced and regretted her words.

Mark dropped his jaw open, then closed it before

shaking his head. "Fine. I'm going home." He backed away and headed downstairs.

His anger and disappointment sliced through her, and instantly, she realized no amount of oxycodone would soothe the pain of watching him leave.

Chapter Eleven

Kingsley Tech in Crisis

Tess landed at London's Heathrow Airport in the late morning and stopped at the airline's executive club to freshen up with a hot shower in a private bathroom. The shower gel's scent, a fiery mix of ginger and pink peppercorn, washed away a few layers of her post-flight haze and awakened her for the tech review meeting. However, her leg ached fiercely, despite her following all of Mark's in-flight medical precautions, which he dispensed via a terse text message. Given her pain outweighed her hunger, she skipped breakfast, popped two oxycodone tablets, and chased them with a double shot of espresso.

A metallic ping announced a new text from Declan.
—Tech Review @ Ivy House, Noon. Red Dining Room, second floor.—

Outside, she hailed a cab and paid the driver extra to hurry. The throngs of Londoners and tourists grew thicker as the taxi neared the city's center and approached Dean Street in Soho. Packed with countless theatres, cafes, and edgy art galleries, the borough pulsed with activity. Crutches in hand, she slung her leather laptop bag over one shoulder and bristled at the irony of crashing an exec meeting she typically led. Finally, the cab pulled up outside Ivy House, one of

Westminster's oldest brick townhouses and now a thriving club for well-heeled executives with ample expense accounts. In the lobby, the club's elevator sported an *Out of Service* sign. Cursing, she lumbered up the narrow wooden stairs. Sweat broke out on her torso from the effort while caffeine and oxycodone churned in her otherwise empty stomach. Agitated voices floated out into the hallway, and she burst through the door.

David and Kavita sat arguing at the oval mahogany table, littered with laptops, schematic diagrams, and empty coffee cups but stopped the second she entered.

"Jesus, Joseph, and Mary." Declan burst out and jumped to his feet, almost knocking her off her crutches before hugging her.

Dark shadows under his eyes revealed his weariness, and wisps of sweaty black hair stuck to his forehead. He'd grown a full beard in the past week, and today, his style tilted more toward timber logger than British tech executive. His welcoming smile faded as he registered her cheekbone's stitches, still sealed with transparent surgical tape, along with the bruises and scratches which still crisscrossed her face, neck, and hands.

"Christ, lass. They beat you to a pulp." He lifted a hand to cover his mouth.

"I'm fine. Couldn't stay away, so let's get going." Today, denial was her superpower, and nothing would stop her. After leaning her crutches against the oak-paneled wainscoting, she settled into a mahogany chair by the window across from David.

"Dear God, Tess. You're not well. You should be resting at home." Arms hanging loose at his sides,

David stared and shook his head.

The blood drained from his face and his trademark wavy red hair curled in an untamed mess. A once-crisp, French-cuffed dress shirt had wilted on his frame, marred with sweat stains, suggesting he'd worked straight through the past few days. Worry lined his forehead, and his expression shifted from stunned to apologetic. Visibly distraught, he studied her wounds and flinched as if they were his own.

"I understand Kingsley Tech might be attacked, and we don't have time to waste. What's the latest police update?"

"We can no longer return to the office. The Metropolitan Police are investigating which Belarusian or Russian criminal gangs have encryption expertise and which might have the financial backing to stage an attack. No leads yet." David took a long sip of water before continuing. "The police ripped out the hidden cameras the criminals had planted in my house, but they're worried I might be abducted, so they assigned bobbies to escort me everywhere. A couple of plainclothes officers are downstairs."

"I'm afraid we're all at risk." No one wanted to hear the truth, but Tess spoke it anyhow. Tension filled the room, and she spied Kavita tapping her slender, stilettoed foot on the carpet and fiddling with the shirt cuff poking out of her designer blazer. Beside her, Declan clicked his ballpoint pen like a nervous tic and squinted at his laptop, as if he could coax better answers out of the machine by staring it down.

"Another bloody thing to worry about. Feckin' hot in here." Declan wrested off his black wool sweater and rolled up the sleeves of his red plaid flannel shirt. He wiped his palms on his ripped jeans.

Kavita sat straighter and looked around the table. "Gents, let's get on with it and talk operations. David's mystery caller claimed they'd breached us months ago and had *most* of our Firefly source code. Declan, we ran your diagnostic tests on our network three times, but they showed no entry point or suspicious activity, even going back two years. The live servers also passed, and our network perimeter is secure."

Declan grunted and slammed his pen on the table before resting his head in his hands. "Shite. Zero evidence of a breach. What are we missing?"

Kavita cast him a scowl. "Declan, mate, I'm giving you positive news. We're clean—"

Tess's frustration bubbled up and overflowed. "Nothing? Do you think these guys were bluffing us? When they threatened to kill me, they demanded *all* the source code for Firefly and Rapadon. Firefly was our internal code name, not something public. How'd they find it?"

"Kyle held multiple patents, so the phrase might have been included in the patent documentation." Rubbing his temples, David frowned.

"Or it slipped out in a media interview. Kyle did a lot of trade press after the patents were announced." Kavita tapped her stilettos on the carpet.

"Please." Tess shot her a sour look. "Kyle wouldn't have spilled an internal code name in an interview."

"My developers are code reviewing Kyle's final build of Firefly before he, um, well, passed. After his death, we merged Firefly into a new code tree, Firestorm. Either way, if they've breached our source code, Kyle's encryption algorithms are at risk." Declan shifted in his chair.

"Another theory is we've got a mole, an engineer who downloaded a debug build of Firefly and gave it to someone outside." Tess studied each of her colleagues for any signs of guilt or recognition.

Head bowed, David stood and paced back and forth in front of the room's fireplace. Suddenly he stopped and looked up. "What if one of our engineers was blackmailed?"

"Might explain it, but there'd be a download history. My team triple-checked our server records and found no such evidence." Kavita propped her elbows on the table.

"No developer of mine would dare leak code and risk losing their security clearance. Full stop." Declan bit at a fingernail, then rubbed the back of his neck.

David stopped pacing, and his expression softened into a faint smile. "With Kyle's gifts, I'd like to think he structured his encryption algorithms to be unhackable."

Declan rotated in his chair. "Come on, nothing's unhackable. People swore the Titanic was unsinkable and look how that turned out. We all know Kyle was a genius, but he was also human, so his code must have vulnerabilities somewhere."

"Sure, but even if they got his code, breaking those algorithms would take ages. Without inside help, it would be impossible." David flicked a scone crumb off the table.

"If someone was cracking smart enough to hack Kyle's code, our enemy must have super badass hackers on their payroll. God knows if I could summon Kyle from the dead, I sure as hell would." Declan pressed his palms together and glanced up.

Tess tightened her jaw, and her vision tunneled as a flash of Kyle's black sedan tumbling over a cliff appeared in her head. *Icy water, then nothing.* Usually, the image struck her with raw grief, but today, her temper spiked from a low-grade simmer to a boil. Unable to endure the team's bickering any longer, she grabbed a small vase from the table and hurled it against the wall, shattering it.

David turned toward her, and his frown spread into a tight, grim line.

"Stop it. All of you. No one wants Kyle back more than me, but he's gone, and you're missing the point." Impatient with her colleagues, she spoke without restraint.

"And the point is what?" Declan was on his feet again.

"Getting our source code alone won't help the terrorists hack banks. Without the individual encryption key to a specific financial institution, they can't breach a paper bag." Her words spilled out in a rush.

Kavita closed her laptop. "But, if you mastered our encryption algorithm, you could generate the actual root key for a client, start a zero-day event, and drain millions of bank accounts in minutes without a trace."

For a brief, strange moment, Tess wanted to hug Kavita. "*Exactly.* What if they used Firefly to replace existing encryption root keys and create new ones for the banks they wanted to hack? Sure, that'd be easier than stealing the existing root key, but they'd need to plant adversarial actors inside the banks and grant them administrative permissions."

Declan scoffed and crossed his arms over his broad

chest. "Not bloody possible, and besides, an inside scheme would require a huge conspiracy with immense resources and multiple actors."

Across the room, David started pacing again.

Tess judged the wrinkles at his temples had deepened several degrees since last week. His throat reddened, a telltale sign his pesky blood pressure was rising, and he wore a tight grimace.

"The police said these Russian and Belarusian crime syndicates are sophisticated. Many possess the financial backing to execute complex heists, but I doubt our own customers would be at risk." David leaned against the wall and rubbed his temple.

"Riku mentioned something odd to me." At the mention of Riku's name, the group fell silent. The comment about crime syndicates jogged her memory, and she strained to recall Riku's words before the lights were cut. "He said the threat was worse than the heightened threat level in Eastern Europe, and we hold the keys to not just one castle but hundreds. David, he wanted the three of us to meet somewhere secure this week." The ache in her leg became more persistent, and sourness turned her stomach. Her boss studied her intently from his perch near the fireplace.

"What else did Riku say?" he asked in a low voice.

"The shooting started then." She willed herself not to visualize Cedarcliff as her queasiness grew unpleasant. The conference room froze, as if all the oxygen had disappeared, and the executives remained motionless like wax figures.

"Isn't the credible threat bloody obvious? It's the bad guys who shot up the blasted party." Declan slammed a hand on the table, knocking over a half-filled cup of coffee.

Offended but not surprised by Declan's aggravating quip, Tess stopped herself from picking a fight. Human Resources gave up attempting to modulate Declan's profanity long ago. While renowned in the industry, Declan's technical expertise far outshone his professional decorum. Squirming in her blazer, she wished the room were cooler. Mouth dry as sawdust, she thirsted for water.

"Seriously, Declan." Kavita shot him a glare.

"Christ, O'Leary. Have some respect. We're talking about Riku." David stood frowning, hands on his hips.

"Riku was killed in front of me before he answered my question. Either our attackers are the same group he suspected, or we're facing multiple, even potentially unrelated threats." Tess clipped her words and folded her hands on the table.

"We're all upset, and Tess, I can't imagine what you've suffered." With one hand stuck at his temple, David stood behind a dining chair, and red splotches crept up his neck above his shirt collar.

Something about his discomfort suggested guilt, but she shrugged it off and wiped beads of sweat from her forehead. "The reality is our company could implode overnight if Firefly is in enemy hands. Any European bank using our software could have a huge, gaping hole in their networks and be draining money in systematic micro-withdrawals every second."

"Don't forget we're all in danger." Kavita shifted her arms.

The white bandages on Kavita's arms, souvenirs of Cedarcliff's attack, reminded Tess she wasn't the only one who had suffered at the hands of Yuri and his gunmen. Another piece of the puzzle clicked in her mind. "I get it now…Riku meant we're the key maker *and* the locksmith. The terrorists want our code because they know we can unlock *all* the banks."

"We hold many individual encryption keys, the easiest access point, and the source code, which they could reverse engineer to replace the existing keys and recreate new ones. Either way, they use us to siphon the money away." David wrote several notes in his notebook.

"And everything we've worked for disappears. Bye-bye, stock options." Kavita frowned and slumped lower in her chair.

"If Kingsley Tech fails, the banks fail, and we lose our jobs. Worse, we might not survive. These men aren't afraid to kill or torture to get what they want." After sharing the worst-case scenario, Tess paused. The mood in the conference room had visibly plummeted. Her scalp tingled like it was covered with live electrodes, and her stomach reeled. She swallowed hard and considered running to the bathroom.

"So, we're screwed." Groaning, Declan pressed his hands against his head.

The crisp white bandages under Kavita's shirt cuff distracted Tess again, drawing her attention like a magnet. Glancing at her colleague's face, she swayed, and the scene before her blurred, like a charcoal portrait with all the outlines erased. Her vision filled with spots, and the room spun like a carnival thrill ride before fading to black.

She slipped out of her seat and fell to the floor, unconscious.

Sometime later, Tess woke flat on her back on a carpet with her feet propped on a chair. People swarmed around her, and she detected motion in broken glimpses. Covered in sweat and with her heart pounding, she couldn't identify the room. Worried, upside-down faces appeared, and the blurry faces shifted to reveal David and Declan.

"Tess, can you hear us?" David was asking. "Kavita called for a doctor."

Not steady enough to move, she remained on the floor, and her head felt like a pile of bricks. Slowly, she sat up and accepted a glass of ice water from Declan, which she sipped in rapid swallows, grateful for the liquid sliding down her parched throat. The room still spun, though its velocity slowed.

A cacophony of voices in the hallway grew louder, and the club's head server opened the door. "Dr. Miriam Patel has arrived," he announced.

The doctor, a petite Indian woman wearing a polished but simple navy dress paired with low-heeled pumps, rushed to Tess and opened her leather medical bag. Pulling out a stethoscope and blood pressure cuff, she got to work.

With a thermometer stuck in her mouth and a cuff squeezing her arm like a boa constrictor, Tess mumbled and attempted to summarize her recent surgery and medications.

Dr. Patel thrust her hands on her hips and rocked backward and forward on her low-heeled pumps. She made *tsk-tsk* sounds while unwrapping the orthopedic boot to check for swelling. "You're telling me you had emergency surgery days ago, got on a long-haul flight, then came straight to this meeting? Didn't your doctor warn you against flying so soon after surgery? Dangerous."

"Yes, I was warned. What do I do now?" Chagrined and more than a little embarrassed, Tess wished she'd followed Mark's advice and stayed home in Seattle. Already regretting the risky, impulsive decision to travel, she accepted the rebuke without protest.

Dr. Patel assisted in moving Tess from the floor up to a chair, then smoothed a strand of her short, bobbed hair behind one ear and adjusted horn-rimmed glasses. "No work, period. Your blood pressure has fallen quite low, you have extreme dehydration, and worse, your leg wound is swelling. No fever, but you must rest, rehydrate, and stay off your foot for the next forty-eight hours. Ice it every two hours. No exceptions. Please look after yourself, Ms. Bennett." She handed Tess a business card. "Call if your symptoms come back."

"Yes, ma'am. Thank you." Reprimanded, Tess acknowledged the instructions and watched as Dr. Patel exited, clicking her sensible pumps on the wood floor and still *tsk-tsking* disapproval.

Kavita and Declan had left the room during Dr. Patel's visit, and only David remained. He shut the door and scooted his chair closer. "Tess, you're not well, and it's affecting your judgment, which you proved in spades by coming here in the first place. You need to recover."

Lancinating pain burned down her leg, but she dodged explaining the extent of her discomfort. "I'll be fine. Just a little jet lagged."

"Stop bullshitting me. I need you at top form, not throwing glassware and collapsing in meetings. We will cover the business until you're back."

David rarely swore, and he'd never looked so stern. "Kavita wants my job." Glaring, she spoke through barred teeth.

"She has *always* wanted your job, but you're irreplaceable, Bennett. However, you're coming off the rails, full stop." Wrinkles bridged the expanse of his forehead, and he studied her at length. "What the hell happened to you at Cedarcliff?" he asked in a quiet voice.

"Our captors were violent, and I got pretty beaten up." Knowing she lacked the emotional fortitude to recount the ordeal, she declined to say more. The Canadian police's decision to keep the investigation's details private shielded her from having to rehash disturbing events or address triggering questions, which she appreciated.

"Sending you to Cedarcliff was my fault, and I take full responsibility. You suffered on my account, and I want to apologize."

The remorse in his voice and his stricken look consoled her, even though she didn't consider him at fault. "Look, I traveled because we had venture capital at stake, so it's not like you sent me on a suicide mission."

His features contorted as if she slapped him.

"I feel like a complete ass. You suffered because of me, and I should have been the hostage, not you, and not Dr. Nygaard. You didn't deserve this, and I am so very sorry."

"David, no one deserved it." A surge of resentment made her throat tighten, and the injustice of the attack hit her all over again. "Why did the kidnappers want you anyhow? Ransom? Given your Silicon Valley days, I figured you'd be a prime target." He belonged to the lucky club of overnight millionaires minted in the heady early days of the Internet, amassing an untold fortune he'd leveraged to start Kingsley Tech.

He opened his hands wide. "Server access. I can access our source code fast. If they only wanted money, Riku would've been a more lucrative target."

"Yuri, the head gunman, said their motive was money, and we think the gunmen were all Belarusian. Don't know the name of the terror group or who they worked for, but they're under pressure to hack something and need our code to do it."

Voices in the hallway grew louder, and someone knocked on the door. "David, everything all right?"

"Give us a minute, please." David shouted at the door, then lowered his voice. "All criminals want money, but it could be for drug trafficking, revolutions, or anything. According to the police briefing yesterday, organized crime cells are proliferating like mad across Belarus. Many are small copycat groups, but others are dangerous rogue threats."

"Riku's first rule of security—never trust Russia or Russia's friends."

"Riku. How bloody awful. I miss him." David's Oxbridge accent wavered, and he dropped his chin to his chest and wiped his eyes.

Uneasy about processing more grief, she shifted in her chair. A lump formed in her throat, and she dug her fingernails into one palm to ward off tears. "I held his hand until he died."

"Christ, the loss is unfathomable. And I've got bigger problems than Kyle's code floating around."

Visions of Yuri and Dmitry unsettled her, and a familiar chill spread through her body. "The two gunmen are still on the run."

"I've been working with Chief Inspector Michael Adams with the Metropolitan Police, and the Mounties are working nonstop in Vancouver, too." David's expression remained fixed.

"Nothing's resolved, then." Goose bumps spread over her skin. Despite their confident assurances that they'd find the gunmen, the RCMP officers hadn't updated her. No news meant bad news. Dead set on avenging the gunmen's violence, she clenched her jaw tight.

"All we can do is stay vigilant and secure our network perimeter. We'll be safe."

She wanted to throttle him. "Know this, David: you are *not* safe. Not here, not anywhere. These men could take you out in an instant." Imagining danger didn't equate with suffering violence firsthand, and she understood primal fear in a visceral way he couldn't.

"Don't be paranoid. The police will protect me, and I'll be fine." He swiped his hands together.

Given their enemies were still running free, she scoffed at David's blind faith. "Look, you can pretend everything's buttoned up, but it's not. If I'd waited to be rescued, I'd be dead. Protect yourself."

As he exhaled, David slumped his shoulders and tilted his head. "No one questions your dedication, Tess, but you're too stubborn to do the right thing. I'm placing you on medical leave, effective immediately."

An order, not a request, and David seldom gave orders. Staring at him, she saw compassion and guilt playing tug-of-war in his expression, with each struggling for dominance. Heat coursed through her body, and her cheeks burned. "What? The *right thing*? For God's sake, I'm not twelve. I'll make my own health care decisions."

"No, I know you. You'd never give up on your own accord. My driver is parked outside—he'll take you to your hotel."

"You're making a huge mistake. You've never needed me more." Rising to stand, she almost folded over from dizziness. His refusal to admit the magnitude of the looming threat infuriated her. Before reaching the door, she whipped around. "Once you wake the hell up and realize how much danger you're in, you'll need my help—if it isn't too late." Before he could reply, she slammed the door and passed Declan and Kavita in the hallway without a word.

Declan followed her and grabbed her shoulder. "What happened in there?"

Too angry to speak, Tess swept his hand away and didn't turn back. The club's elevator was still broken, and she tackled the staircase on crutches, one cumbersome step at a time. Effectively exiled, she retreated and slipped into the black chauffeured sedan outside to head for Westminster.

As the car pulled away from the curb, she doubled her resolve to find the truth, no matter how high the stakes, even if she had to do it alone.

Chapter Twelve

An Old Friend

After checking into her usual hotel in Westminster, a small suite with a view of the River Thames, Tess sank onto a damask-striped slipper chair and took stock. Floating in a purgatorial void, without work or activity for distraction, she decided a round of self-care was her best course of action. Room service delivered a chicken sandwich, tomato soup, a giant bottle of mineral water, and an ice bag for her leg. Watching the boats float down the river, she devoured the lunch and swallowed another oxycodone capsule with water.

A long shower helped to shake off the calamitous meeting. While drying her hair, she fixated on her laptop bag, where Kyle's manila envelope peeked out from the top pocket. Upset about Mark leaving and the failed tech review, she hadn't formed a plan to search for the mysterious package. Kyle's letter symbolized a virtual resurrection of his soul, alive again for a few precious moments. What message had he left behind, and why did it require such secrecy?

Restless and curious, she slipped into fresh clothes and folded the letter with the brass key into her trench coat pocket. While grabbing her crutches, she staggered, dizziness overtaking her, and plopped onto the nearest chair with a groan. "Crap."

Forced to ask for help, she debated calling Declan or her admin, Tilly, but rejected both ideas. Per policy, the entire executive staff would receive notification of her leave status. With any luck, her friend Sophie might be in London and not on assignment outside the UK. A quick scan of her phone contacts turned up *Sophie Reed,* and she texted.

—Need you. Meet outside my Westminster hotel?—
Seconds later, a response appeared.
—Lamest proof of life ever. Give me 20 minutes.—

Sophie, a powder keg of ever-shifting and conflicting moods, had been her best friend since they were girls. Tess grinned, her spirits lifting. Perhaps Sophie could expedite finding Kyle's package.

The hallway's navy-blue carpet's interlocking gold pattern undulated and rippled with her vision. Unsteady, she anchored her feet on the floor and crossed the lobby with painstaking steps out to the hotel's garden, where an empty wooden bench surrounded by autumn flowers welcomed her. After several minutes, footsteps approached, and she grasped the bench's iron-black armrest to wobble to a stand.

A smooth, manicured hand slapped her unwounded cheek.

"What the hell?" Tess lifted a hand to touch her stinging skin, more gobsmacked than hurt. Sophie towered over her, wearing alligator stiletto heels, and decked out in a sleek black suit topped with a loden trench coat. Stunning as ever, Sophie's tousled black hair and wind-swept bangs highlighted her sable-colored eyes. She wore dusty rose blush that complemented her olive skin and angular cheekbones.

"Goddamn you, Bennett."

"All right. I apologize for missing our weekend in Paris. Foolish me, thinking being kidnapped was a legit excuse." Unprepared for an argument, Tess struck an indignant tone, then braced herself for the diatribe she suspected was coming.

"I risked my cover a hundred ways to text you a warning to stay away from Canada, and what do you do? You fly right into it. For fuck's sake, girlfriend. Were you on drugs?" Legs planted wide, Sophie tilted her chin high and made sweeping arm gestures.

"Of course not. Though I was tempted for a brief, stupid moment at Torque." Tess took a couple steps backward while massaging her stinging cheek. "I never received any text, or I wouldn't have gone. You realize I was taken hostage by terrorists, right?"

"Right, and almost got yourself killed, goddamn it." Sophie's stiletto pumps clicked in a frenetic rhythm on the cobblestone walkway. "We made a pact to never die, and here you are, beaten to a pulp. Did you learn nothing from our dads growing up?"

Tess tensed her body and glared with equal passion. "Dad taught me how to fight to survive when there's no escape, and I did."

"Remember the family security briefing at the Swiss embassy when we were fourteen? You sat right next to me. Security rule number one: *avoid trouble*." Sophie's tone softened several decibels, and she folded her arms.

Despite over two decades of friendship, Tess could never predict Sophie's mood, but at least her friend's belligerence had downshifted to wounded annoyance. Fragments of a long afternoon surfaced from deep in Tess's memory, and she recalled the pungent smell of bleach-mopped floors in a stark Swiss conference room. Embassy administrators outlined endless security and emergency protocols for families of State Department officers. "Sure, I'm a diplomatic security brat, but I'm not telepathic. Stop acting like I should've predicted the attack."

"They could've killed you." Voice cracking, Sophie swept her into a hug.

She buried her nose in Sophie's pashmina scarf and inhaled the exotic scent of jasmine with top notes of tuberose. The last dose of oxycodone kicked in, and her head buzzed with pleasant warmth. Her crutches slipped and threw off her balance, but she gripped Sophie's arm and couldn't suppress a tipsy smile. "I missed you."

"Now I know you're high." Sophie offered a broad smile.

"No. Well, maybe. Just pain meds for my leg surgery. And if it makes you feel any better, I wasn't alone in captivity." Scrambling to redeem her actions seemed unjust, given Sophie rarely faced any consequences for her tempestuous behavior.

"Ah, the hot Norwegian doctor, right? Great pictures of him in the international news a few days ago. Damn. If I were still sleeping with men, I'd go for him."

The painkiller dulled Tess's inhibitions, and despite her usual discretion, she beamed with a knowing smile.

"Bennett, you're blushing. Did you…" Sophie stepped closer.

"Don't pry." She groaned, annoyed her secret slipped out. Figuring the saucy smile on Sophie's lips signaled a shift from antagonism to amusement, Tess relaxed her shoulders.

"You slept with him, didn't you?" Sophie erupted in laughter and landed a faux punch on her arm. "Oh, my Gawd, it's about time. Kyle was amazing, and may his dear soul rest in peace, but you need to start living again. So, how was the doctor?"

The tension between them disappeared like a burst soap bubble. Tess let out a long, pleasurable sigh. "Incredible. Life-affirming. He visited me in Seattle after I got home from the hospital."

"How brilliant—an empirically hot, smart guy. One-night shag or something more?"

"More, I hope. Mark's kind, selfless, and witty. A surgeon." She allowed her thoughts to drift to Mark and yearned to see him again. Then she remembered their argument over her London trip and frowned.

"So, what's the problem?" Sophie's dark brows knitted together.

"I'm the problem. I screwed up and raced back to London against his medical advice and scared him away." Regret joined the narcotic buzz pulsing through her veins, and her forehead creased. Hiding anything from Sophie never worked. "Look, I didn't call you away from international diplomacy to analyze my quite-limited sex life. Kyle left me a message, and I need help."

At the mention of Kyle, Sophie's smile disappeared, and she placed a hand on Tess's arm. "Tell me what you need."

Numb from the bracing air, Tess stuffed a hand in her pocket and touched the cold brass key and the letter's smooth edges to ground herself. "I'm on a mission, and we need a taxi for Hotel George now."

"Afternoon tea? How lovely." Sophie clapped her hands together.

"Not today, my dearie. Kyle left me a treasure hunt, starting with an unexpected stroll down memory lane. Much as I love a tasty scone spread with clotted cream and topped with jam, I need help staying vertical."

"You hopeless American, you spread the jam before the cream. I'm in, and let's go." Sophie raised a manicured hand to hail a taxi.

A black cab screeched to a stop at the curb.

"Lovely to see you're still stopping traffic, Ms. Reed." As the cab sped toward Trafalgar Square to the corner of the Strand, Tess summarized the Cedarcliff attack, the current threat against Kingsley Tech, and Kyle's last request.

Sophie whistled and shook her head. "You're in deep, Bennett."

"Kyle worried he was in danger a few weeks before his car accident. He left me clues, and the trail starts here." She spotted the historic hotel outside the window and signaled the taxi driver, a sixty-something man with white hair tucked under a navy wool hat. "Driver, stop here, please."

Bright spotlights shone upon the iconic green letters *G-E-O-R-G-E,* highlighting the hotel entrance like a theatre marquee. The taxi left them in front of the renowned landmark hotel, famous for its Georgian architecture, luxurious accommodations, and gourmet dining.

"If we're not having tea, what are we doing?" Sophie asked.

"Kyle's puzzle starts with our third date. We fell in love here." She gazed up at the façade of the building, admiring the hotel's entrance as memories of her past with Kyle came alive.

"Back then, how'd you know Kyle was the one?"

"One moment, he gazed at me, and everything around us fell away. All I could see was our future and the journey we'd have together." The heady blend of nostalgia laced with narcotics made her yearn for the past. Kyle had given her a joyful smile on the balmy summer evening in question, and his green-eyed gaze had gleamed with affection. Something unspoken and ethereal passed between them, and the moment crystallized in her memory.

"The grief must tear you to pieces," Sophie said in a low voice and shoved her hands in her pockets.

"Every day." Pictures of Kyle flashed in Tess's mind, flying past like a slide show running too fast, but at unexpected intervals, images of Mark appeared, too. The juxtaposition of the two men unsettled her, and to avoid crumbling, she focused on the tourists clustered outside the taxi stand at Charing Cross.

"Where to?"

"Next, the treasure hunt continues with a one-kilometer walk, if I can make it that far." She turned away from the hotel and gestured toward the bustling thoroughfare of the Strand. Exhaust fumes laced the air, and she coughed. "How's your *art gallery*?"

"You rescued me from a boring afternoon. Ugh. I was stuck near Parliament, getting lectured about budget regulations by some bureaucratic gasbag. Hours of administrivia before I fly out tomorrow to, um, an undisclosed location." Sophie winked and steered Tess around two dogs yelping and barking on the sidewalk.

"I know the drill—be safe and *avoid trouble.*" Tess used air quotes intended to goad her friend. "Don't lecture me about being safe, little Miss Pot calling the kettle black. You can't reveal which intelligence agency you work for, let alone what your real job is."

"Touché." Sophie returned the smirk.

"Not only that, but any sexy women you meet will be quite disappointed to learn you're not an actual London art dealer. You're scattering broken hearts everywhere."

"True. A known peril of being an international woman of mystery."

She and Sophie stopped at the next crosswalk to wait for the traffic light to change. Tourists queued in front of a booth piled high with stacks of London T-shirts and thong underwear emblazoned *Mind the Gap.* A kiosk beside them sold Cornish pasties, and the smell of buttery pastry and meat sparked her hunger. The streetlight transitioned to green.

"You know, you could still enter the service—CIA, NSA, the State Department, any of them. You'd be a shoo-in, given your cybersecurity network and family connections." Sophie raised her voice over the cacophony of honking horns and passing trucks.

"I can't even think about another job. Kingsley Tech is in crisis, and I'm David's number two. Since I became vice president, I've been too busy to breathe most days."

"Whatever, you workaholic. You never breathed before your promotion, either. I'm saying doors would swing wide open, should you want a change."

Tess stopped abruptly on the sidewalk and stared.

191

"Are you serious? Risk ending up like my dad, shot in the line of duty, and bleeding out on a highway in Colombia? Reduced from leading the diplomatic security circuit to a sorry painkiller addict? No, thank you. Corporate life's not perfect, but it's safer."

Sophie stopped and leaned forward until only inches separated their faces. "Is it? Your *safe* corporate job almost got you killed in Canada. Have you contacted your dad?"

"Don't start with me. You know we're not in contact." Sophie's retort cut deep through her, like jagged glass shards, and heat infused her cheeks. Talking to her father would only increase her stress level, and she had too many crises to handle already.

"Call him, Bennett. He's your dad, and you almost died."

"No."

"All I'm saying is you can't shut him out forever. It's awfully rich of you to reject him, given you're the one high on pain meds. Right. Bloody. Now." Sophie scowled and bent to pick up an empty soda can from the sidewalk and crushed it in her fist. "Damn litterers."

"Bugger off and help me find this clue, all right?" The last thing Tess wanted was a family reunion.

"Fine."

"Let's focus here, shall we? Kingsley Tech is under siege, and I need to find out what Kyle was hiding." In a silent détente, she resumed the search. Double-decker buses clogged the street while throngs of businesspeople and tourists crowded the sidewalks. Tess speculated what the brass key might open. A mailbox? A flat? Proceeding down the Strand, past the Royal Courts of Justice and the Tea Museum, the

Strand merged into Fleet Street, the banking district. Her phone beeped to indicate she'd traveled one kilometer, and she stopped on the sidewalk, making a three-hundred-sixty-degree turn to scan the nearby buildings and forcing Londoners to scatter.

"Kyle said to watch for dragons." She tipped her head skyward and lifted a hand to shade her eyes from the filtered afternoon sunlight. The Temple Bar Monument honoring Queen Victoria stood in a traffic circle, like a royal island in the center of the street. With a satisfied smile, she pointed upward. A fearsome, roaring dragon crowned the top of the memorial. "We're getting warmer."

"Well done. Next clue?" Sophie checked both ways before crossing the street.

"An indirect reference to Kyle's favorite song, 'In a Big Country' by the Big Country band."

"How retro. Guess '80s music is back. Kyle had a kooky sense of humor."

"Shush, you." Tess clasped the brass key like a beacon guiding her to Kyle. She scanned building names, attempting to connect them to the song. "So many buildings everywhere, and it could be any of these."

"You can do this. Use free association. Go." Sophie patted her back.

A flow of words coursed through her thoughts. "Country, keys, dragons, queens, royalty, riches, Fleet Street, banks."

"Splendid. Keep going." Sophie cheered her and waved a hand in a signal to continue.

"The band is from Scotland." Riffs of Scottish bagpipes echoed in her mind, and she hummed the song's chorus under her breath. One building with striking architecture and the words *MacMillan and Co.* were etched across the ground floor windows. No connection. Stepping closer, she read the door sign, *Royal Bank of Scotland*, and broke into a grin. "This is it. Help me up these steps, Soph."

After climbing the steps adorning the building's façade and opening a spotless glass door, she and Sophie boarded the elevator for the bank's entrance on the second floor.

Minutes later, an older woman dressed in a prim tweed pantsuit appeared behind the service desk. "May I help you, miss?"

"I need to access a box under the name Tess Bennett." Her pulse accelerated.

The clerk scanned her American passport, picked up a written visitor log, and gestured for her to sign it. "Your box is B-313. You have the key?"

Tess extracted the brass key and presented it in her sweaty palm. Red indentations outlining its shape remained visible on her skin.

"Follow me." The woman swiped a card key reader to unlock the connecting door and traversed a long hallway before arriving in front of a vast metal vault.

With Sophie looking over her shoulder, Tess waited while the clerk entered a ten-digit code on a digital keypad, and a green light beeped. The air-sealed vault door opened with a sucking sound, revealing walls lined with identical metal boxes stretching from waist height to the ceiling.

"I'll unlock the outer box and place the container in a private viewing room outside the vault." The clerk gestured at a tiny, windowless room and placed the container on a small table. "Here you go."

Excitement and dread simmered in Tess's stomach. Body tense, she held her breath and inserted the key into the polished metal lock. It was a perfect fit. Rotating the key one turn popped the lid open a crack, allowing her to peek inside. The sole contents were an envelope addressed with her name and a transparent plastic case.

Her heart thudded against her rib cage while the room shrank around her. The viewing room was smaller than the barn stall where she'd been imprisoned, making her anxious. She opened her coat and fanned it for more air before turning to Sophie. "I can't do it. I need to get out of this tiny room."

"Since when did you become claustrophobic?" Sophie squinted and tilted her head to one side.

"Last week—not keen on confined spaces right now." Surprised the drab, innocuous room could inspire such panic, she wiped her damp forehead and slid the envelope into her coat.

Sophie relocked the empty box and hit the call button to summon the clerk. "All these puzzles led to one envelope. Do you think Kyle is hiding something illegal?" she asked as they hurried toward the bank's exit and headed back to the street.

"No way. Kyle's squeaky clean, and breaking the law is against his nature." Between jet lag, fatigue, and pain, Tess's reserves had run out, and she needed to recharge before facing Kyle's last message. "Let's taxi back to the hotel." She bit her lip, growing more uneasy about what the message's contents would reveal.

After arriving in Westminster and getting settled at the hotel, Tess set Kyle's envelope on the polished walnut coffee table. Immobilized, she sat staring at it like a ticking bomb.

"Are you going to open it or what?" Sophie paced beside her, waiting.

"Kyle feels alive now, and after I read this, he'll be dead again. No more letters from him, ever." Any satisfaction she'd won from solving the puzzle vanished and gave way to dread.

"I get it. You need privacy, so I'll hang in the lobby. Text me if you need me." Sophie picked up the room card key and slipped out.

"Thanks." Distracted, Tess murmured without looking up. With her pocketknife, she slit open the envelope inch by inch to avoid ripping it. She prayed for closure and held the letter with her fingertips.

Dear Tessa,
My life is in danger, and I might be killed.
Last week, an emerging terror cell from Belarus called Malinavy Molat—*Crimson Hammer—approached me and demanded the encryption code I wrote at Kingsley, but I refused. The group threatened to kill you this week if I didn't hand over my code or if I called the police. They're tracking my location and phone calls, and I can't disappear without endangering you. Don't trust anyone at Kingsley Tech. Crimson Hammer could blackmail our employees.*

I gave Crimson Hammer code for Firefly 1.0, but not THE code. I added safeguards to prevent them from breaking my encryption algorithms. If they break them, they'll access all our financial customers' networks, and the European banking system will collapse overnight.

Crimson Hammer is new but hell-bent on hacking multinational banks. They're well-funded and have assassins on their payroll. If I die unexpectedly, it won't be an accident. Tell my parents I loved them, and don't fret. I spent my last few years loving you, and if my time's done, I was blessed to have you.

You are my one in seven billion, and I love you. Tessa, you're strong, a survivor in every sense. If I die, please promise to find a worthy partner who loves you and can accompany you on the rest of your life's adventure.

Love always,
Kyle

She stopped reading. Torn between grief, rage, and love, she sensed her pulse pounding. How was it possible to feel comforted but ripped apart at the same time? Holding her breath, she flipped to the letter's second page, where a small USB drive in a transparent plastic case was attached.

CRITICAL

Do NOT open this USB drive on any computer or network. Protect it.

Take this USB drive to the Raven. No one else. You can trust him.

Call +1-555-416-1746. When the Raven finds you, he'll ask a cryptic question. The answer is: The Druid has fallen. He'll know what to do.

If I don't survive and this plan fails, find Declan, but first, confirm he hasn't been compromised and swear him to secrecy. Good luck, Tessa. I have faith in you.

Love,
Kyle

The realization hit Tess like a wrecking ball, and bile crept up her throat as a guttural wail escaped her lips. *They killed him.* She trailed her fingers over the smooth fibers of the paper, connecting to Kyle in whatever posthumous form he had assumed. She reread the date: November 4. His car accident happened a week later, on November 11, Remembrance Day in the UK. Kyle had been working at a feverish pace the week of the car accident, but no alarm bells rang to signal something had been awry. He often had bursts of energy and wrote code for days, even forgetting to eat or sleep while listening to Pink Floyd or Nirvana on his headphones. But no more.

The letter slipped from her hands and spiraled like dead leaves long past their season of supple green. The renewed grief crushed her, but no tears fell. The papers spilled to the floor, and she sat numb for a minute before texting Sophie.

—Please come now.—

The pieces fell into place: Kyle, Riku, the attack, and the kidnapping. Rage broke through her initial shock, and she couldn't keep her hands from shaking uncontrollably. Overwhelmed, she swung between wanting to sob and smashing something heavy against the wall.

A knock on the door sounded, and Sophie appeared in the doorway, her eyebrows knit together. "What is it?"

"They killed him." She handed Sophie the first page of the letter by way of explanation and sat in stony silence.

"Shit, Bennett." Sophie scanned Kyle's note, and her frown deepened each second. She raised her fingertips to her mouth and shook her head in a slow, broad sweep. "Oh, honey."

Hands ice-cold and shaking, Tess considered her next steps, which sputtered out in broken fragments. "The police need to reopen Kyle's case as a murder. I must avenge his death, whatever it takes. We have to stop Crimson Hammer, and David and Declan need to know. I've got to find this hacker, the Raven, now." Tess bounded from her chair but tripped and stumbled forward.

Sophie caught her before she face-planted.

"Whoa. Hold tight, Bennett. You're not going anywhere tonight."

Flustered, Tess brushed Sophie's hands away and choked back tears. She wanted to call Declan, one of Kyle's best friends, but stopped and cursed. *Don't trust anyone at Kingsley.* Still fuming at David for banishing her, she wouldn't stoop to call Kavita, either. "Any of my colleagues could have been blackmailed, so I can't trust anyone."

"Tess. You honestly didn't receive my warning about Canada?" Sophie's mood shifted like a dark storm cloud blocking the sun.

Tess displayed her empty hands, palms up. "Nope. I got nothing. Why? What happened?"

"Sorry, I can't say. I know things and people who know more things."

"Fine." Tess acquiesced without a fight, too bewildered to protest Sophie's need for confidentiality.

"Dark web chatter last Friday flagged western Canada as an unusual but potential terrorist target, and some intel discovered in Japan checked out. You flew straight to British Columbia hours later, like a moth into a flame."

"Damn it. I told you I didn't get your text." Something Riku mentioned at Cedarcliff lingered in Tess's memory, but whatever he said, she couldn't quite remember now.

"Let me check your text messages." Sophie held out a hand and gestured at Tess's phone.

With a shrug, Tess surrendered it.

"I texted you last Friday before the attack. Hey, what's this?" She highlighted a text time-stamped the day of the attack from Unknown Caller, Cyprus, and inside, a long stream of garbage characters.

"Just unreadable spam." Often overwhelmed with texts, Tess rarely read them all.

"No, this text was my warning. Damn it, between translation and encryption, it got screwed up. Goddamn technology." Sophie grimaced at the phone with an eye roll.

"Maybe David was briefed since he was supposed to lead the summit? He summoned me to attend in his place last minute."

Mouth gaping open, Sophie stared. "What? You're telling me your boss bailed and sent you in his place the day of a terror attack in a country that never has them? How remarkably interesting."

"You're not suggesting David sold me out, are you? Don't be ridiculous." Tess snapped and clenched her fist, almost frightened by the murderous intent filling Sophie's gaze.

"I don't believe in coincidences, and neither should you."

Annoyed at the accusatory finger Sophie pointed in her direction, Tess lashed out. "Don't you dare insinuate David sent me to die! We've worked together for ten years, and he'd never betray me."

"You sure? Whether you meant to or not, you risked your life for him. Next time, I hope you make a different choice." Sophie paced the room, cracking her knuckles.

"We are not talking about this, period." Unwilling to consider David a potential villain, Tess aimed an icy glare at Sophie. "Quit harassing me. Escaping required a high price, and I had to do awful things."

"Self-defense?"

Tess couldn't stop her lip from quivering and pressed her palms onto her thighs, not wanting to break down. Since the gruesome night in the barn, she'd replayed the fight countless times but never found any alternative to killing Sergey. Although her confession to Sophie was heavily veiled, it offered her a dose of much-needed relief.

Sophie squeezed her hand tight, and empathy filled her gaze.

"Since Cedarcliff, I've been so scared I considered getting a gun again. I want to defend myself." Tess looked up. "I can't stand being vulnerable."

"Sure, I get it, but first, this is the UK—no guns allowed. Second, you're a great shot, but you're even better with a sword. Have you considered that?"

"You're not helping." Overcome by the need to release her guilt, Tess gripped Sophie's hand harder and stifled the urge to cry. She grabbed a water bottle and gulped half of it as a distraction, hoping to wash away feelings she couldn't outrun.

"You're gonna need something stronger than water, Bennett. You were damn brave, but civilians aren't trained to handle *lethal complications*. You made the right call, so don't waste time second-guessing yourself." Sophie opened the minibar refrigerator, extracted two bottles of vodka and tonic, mixed them together, and offered Tess the highball glass. "You're running on empty and need comfort food. I've got to go now, but I'm ordering you room service, and don't try to stop me."

A few minutes after Sophie left, a hotel waiter delivered a cheeseburger and salty fries. She nibbled at the meal, pausing to lick the salt off her fingertips. A bath sounded comforting, so she headed for the bathroom, ran the hot water, and dumped a heaping scoop of lavender salts into the white porcelain tub. With a deep sigh, she sank into the steaming water up to her chin. However, Kyle's words flashed like a neon sign in her brain. A lump filled her throat, followed by a dry sob. The emotional levee she'd built since Cedarcliff burst, and her tears splashed into the fragrant bathwater and disappeared. The reason the new age self-care nonsense she tried last year had failed to ameliorate her loss became apparent. Soothing wind chimes, aromatherapy, and candles were all pointless.

She needed anger—and justice.

Taking stock, she couldn't resurrect Kyle or trust her colleagues. Sophie was traveling to an undisclosed location for at least a week. As Mark had warned, traveling too soon proved a stupid choice. Outside her window, the city lights appeared like stars, and one by one, they wove a glowing blanket of light above the River Thames. Toweling herself off, her skin freshly scented with lavender, she debated how to mobilize and engage her contacts. Several people popped up as possibilities, but only one name motivated her enough to pick up the phone and dial.

Her call transferred to voice mail, and she waited for the electronic beep. "Mark, it's Tess, and I want to apologize. Flying to London was a mistake, and I need your help. Please call me." All at once, she felt overwhelmed with loneliness. If Mark didn't call her back, she'd have to face this crisis alone…a prospect too grim to bear.

Chapter Thirteen

Chasing Leads

After a fitful night's sleep, Tess woke to find London had shifted into action for the day. Late autumn sunshine poured through the gauzy curtain sheers lining the hotel room's windows. Grogginess gave way to anxiousness, and she checked to see if Mark had called, but he hadn't. *Damn it.* She dragged herself out of bed, still feeling the sharp pang of disappointment.

Next, she searched her phone contacts for Inspector Archie Willis, the police detective who investigated Kyle's accident last year. Typing quickly, she texted him regarding her new evidence and requested to meet at once. His immediate reply, which suggested a time slot in one hour, bolstered her hopes for progress. Three cups of strong coffee later, she ignored Dr. Patel's advice about resting and hailed a cab to the Metropolitan Police Station at New Scotland Yard in Westminster.

When Willis met her in the lobby, he projected an aura of command, just like she remembered from Kyle's accident investigation. Stout but not yet portly, his erect posture added inches to his otherwise diminutive height, and his immaculate, black leather oxfords reflected the light. Weathered, deep wrinkles documented his decades of police service, and he wore his grayish-blond hair in a no-fuss crew cut. He greeted her with a nod, surveyed her top to bottom, and his gaze lingered over her orthopedic boot.

She shook his hand and struggled to manage a half-hearted smile.

"Morning, Ms. Bennett. Ye just can't stay out of trouble, can ye? Come upstairs, and we'll get this sorted." He gestured toward the elevator.

Tess followed him to his private office on the second floor, where the smell of day-old coffee lingered in the air. Tess took the guest chair next to his desk, exactly where she sat one year ago, and grasped the metal armrests. An odd déjà vu overcame her, and she felt doomed to restart the grief cycle, instead of coming full circle to complete it.

On the wall behind Willis, rows of framed commendations praised his service for countless investigations—everything from transit strikes and common thievery to citations for bravery during the 2005 London bus bombings. A twenty-year service award commemorating his dedication to the people of London stood on his bookshelf. Reminders of his achievements strengthened her confidence in his ability to solve this case.

He took a seat and pointed at her injured leg. "I'm sorry ye suffered harm during the Cedarcliff mess. Ye might disagree, but I'd say ye were damn lucky. Kidnapped hostages rarely escape, and those who don't usually come home in a box."

"I'm grateful to have survived." Weary from the previous night's catharsis, Tess attempted to remain unemotional.

"I read the Mounties' report, the *full* report, and ye

showed extraordinary bravery, especially for a civilian." Willis clutched his pen and studied her. "Highly unusual."

"Thank you. I'm hoping the remaining two gunmen are behind bars. Have any arrests been made?" She assumed the police were closing in on her attackers but simply hadn't notified her.

Willis pressed his lips together and exhaled. "Our counterterrorism team is working the Cedarcliff case and cooperating with the Mounties. It pains me to tell ye this, but we have no solid leads to identify the attackers."

"Excuse me?" Floored at the investigation's lack of progress, she nearly choked, and her mood spiked from calm to livid in two seconds.

"Terror attacks are unheard of in British Columbia, and no group has claimed responsibility. Witness interviews on the scene didn't reveal any clues about the group's affiliation either." Willis tapped a black pen on his desktop.

"That's it? Nothing?" She slammed a fist on Willis's desk and growled. "Look, *I* am your lead. Go find *Malinavy Molat*, which means Crimson Hammer in English. They're a Belarusian terrorist group, Russian sympathizers, with assassins and hackers on their payroll."

"You're serious, Ms. Bennett?" Frowning, Willis pushed away from his desk and laced his hands over his chest. As he jiggled a knee, a spring in the wheeled office chair squeaked.

"Very." Not surprised by his reaction, she stood her ground, nonplussed and confident she held the truth.

He swept aside the empty coffee cups littering his

desk, whipped out a spiral notebook, and opened it to a blank page. "I'm listening, Ms. Bennett. But frankly, wild speculation won't help us track the suspects, so ye'd better have solid evidence. Tell me more."

"Fine." Tess recounted what she had learned since Cedarcliff and how Kingsley Tech planned its defense against imminent attack while Willis raced to scribble names, dates, and connections. Summarizing all the technical details and key points from her captivity, she constructed a clear outline of all the players and their motives. Willis's initial rejection of her claim shifted as she shared more information.

His first pen ran out of ink, and he grabbed another one from his drawer. "Okay. Explain how this relates to Kyle and how ye pieced it together. As ye know, we ruled his death a single-car accident and closed his case in January."

"Crimson Hammer assassinated Kyle, and you need to reopen his case now."

"I see. Let's review Kyle's case file." Willis stopped writing and swiveled to face his computer screen. "Automobile accident, fatality, dated November 11, Kyle MacTavish of Westminster, London." He scrolled through the record and frowned. "Wait a second. Something's wrong here."

"What is it?" Before Kyle's death, Tess considered car crashes a tragedy. A terrible, cruel turn of fate, but one lacking blame or deliberate intent. In comparison, Kyle's brutal end, executed by criminals, added seeking justice to the weighty grief she already carried. Determined to keep any tears at bay, she popped a mint into her mouth, hoping to avoid dwelling too long on the crash.

"Someone's tampered with his case file. The record now lists the investigator as Inspector John Doe. Ridiculous. I certified the official final report for Kyle's case, but my supporting files are gone. The case verdict displays as Reckless Driving Under the Influence, Opiates." Willis scowled at his computer.

She slumped as if someone had kicked her in the gut. "Opiates? What total rubbish."

"Agreed. Kyle's toxicology report tested clean. No alcohol, drugs, or garbage like that." He drummed his fingers on the desk. "One possibility is the suspects forced his car off the road. However, when we retrieved his car from the bay, only crashed metal remained, and we couldn't prove foul play. No witnesses either."

"What would anyone have to gain by hacking Kyle's record?" Changing the record seemed pointless, given the original data was ruled an accident, a designation less likely to incriminate someone.

Fuming, Willis reviewed the record. "Someone's slandering Kyle's character and deleting evidence to cover their tracks, in case anyone asks questions like ye are today." He gestured toward her. "After the life insurance claims settle, we close the case, and it's rare for us to revisit the record. Someone expected questions would arise and altered this record in advance."

"What date did the record change?"

"October 28, three weeks ago. The date can't be a coincidence." Willis wrote the date in his notebook and tapped a pen against his weathered wooden desk.

"Why?"

Willis stopped writing and glanced up from his notes. "Because I don't believe in them."

"Right." *Another non-believer in coincidences.*

"Do you have daily backups in the cloud or a database archive from the same day and week? Any digital trail, or unusual network activity, could surface leads. Can you retrieve change reports to check which records changed that day?"

"I'll call IT and request our backups right away." Willis jotted more notes into his notebook.

Tess gripped the chair's armrests. "A police database breach is unwelcome news any way you slice it. Who do you think changed Kyle's record, someone inside the squad or an outside hacker? And for what motive?"

"I'll tell ye, if someone on the inside did this, heads would roll. Either way, somebody's lying, and I'm reopening the investigation." On his keyboard, he typed several words before continuing. "Back to Cedarcliff for a moment. Can ye supply more substantive evidence to identify the terrorist group?"

"Kyle wrote this the week before they killed him. The Cedarcliff shooters were Belarusian." The first page of Kyle's letter peeked out of her leather bag, and the paper crackled in her hand as she handed it to Willis. A flicker of doubt bothered her, and she left the second page and USB drive in the bag to keep the Raven's information private.

Willis picked up a pair of black-framed reading glasses from his desk and scanned the letter. A couple of minutes later, he whistled and shook his head. "Yer absolutely sure Kyle wrote this?"

Judging from Willis's rigid, straight posture and severe expression, she figured Kyle's letter offered the requisite evidence to move the investigation forward. "Positive. Only Kyle called me Tessa, and it's his turn

209

of speech and signature."

"May I photocopy this?"

She nodded her assent. The copy machine on Willis's desk made a soft whirring sound as it swallowed the letter and released it out the other side. She picked up the original and slid it back into her leather bag. "So, what happens next?"

"SCD7, our Serious and Organised Crime Command, must see this evidence to connect the dots between Kyle's death and Cedarcliff." He leaned back in his chair and regarded her over his glasses. "Quite a twist ye've thrown me, Ms. Bennett, and this could be the big break we need. That is, if I can substantiate yer lead against evidence collected from both crime scenes."

She scooted forward in her chair. "Remember, keeping Kyle's secret about his code is critical. He said I can't trust anyone at Kingsley."

"Correct. For yer safety, I strongly advise ye to keep quiet while we investigate these leads. If Crimson Hammer managed to blackmail Kyle, an upstanding citizen, they could blackmail anyone at Kingsley, easily." Willis lowered his voice. "The truth is, once ye threaten a person's family or their kids, they'll do anything to protect them. *Anything.*"

"Understood." Ice filled her veins. David had a wife, son, and a baby due in the spring, but she had no one. For years, she and David had collaborated to grow the business and rarely butted heads. If he knew an attack loomed at Cedarcliff and sent her to save himself…she couldn't finish the thought. The mere idea David could sell her out chilled her to the core. However, if he acted under duress, it could explain his eagerness to put her on medical leave, away from the investigation. She wrestled with the startling possibility David had deceived her and tightened a fist. *Who could she trust?*

"Will ye be in London all of this week?" Willis asked with a hand poised over his notepad.

She tore herself away from her anxious thoughts. "Mostly, but I might spend a couple of days in the country to clear my head." Omitting any mention of the Raven, she needed to scheme how to find him, given her limited physical mobility.

"Right. I'll call yer mobile as soon as we know more. Thanks for reaching out, and meanwhile, don't take unnecessary risks." Willis bid her goodbye and picked up his phone.

The bright midday sun blinded her when she stepped outside Old Scotland Yard to hail a cab. The smell of recent rain soothed her lungs, and she contemplated the open puzzles which remained. Whether it was a rogue hacker or insider mole who had compromised the Metropolitan Police's digital fortress, the net effect was the same—trusting the police could backfire. She clutched her bag close, glad she withheld instructions to contact the Raven in case the police proved untrustworthy. Sophie was unreachable during fieldwork, and while she trusted Kyle, he was dead.

Yet again, she found herself alone and lonely.

Back in Westminster, she regrouped in the hotel room, unsure what to do next. She refused to sit around doing nothing while the company fell under siege, and her attackers, Yuri and Dmitry, roamed free. While she regretted ignoring Mark's advice not to travel, she pushed harder to placate her sense of duty. As her uncertainties fell away, she saw the only acceptable path forward. She needed to go rogue.

First, she brewed a cup of coffee and fired up her laptop, determined to gain a foothold on understanding Crimson Hammer and Russian and Belarusian hacking capabilities. After reviewing countless articles about Belarus, she conceded hunger outweighed her concentration and ordered room service for lunch.

After accepting the food delivery, she downed the dill-infused chicken sandwich and snacked on potato crisps, pausing between bites to lick the salt from her fingertips. Mark still hadn't called back. Slumped in her chair, she ripped open the bagged chocolate chip cookie on the tray and ate it.

Restless, she wandered over to her leather bag and removed Kyle's letter and USB drive. Rereading his words, she recommitted to avenging his death. What disturbed her most was Kyle's warning that *any* of her colleagues could be blackmailed, a concern Willis reinforced. She disliked paranoia, but her situation required a hefty dose to stay alive. The only other person she could trust was the Raven, a total stranger.

She grabbed her phone and dialed Kyle's number for the Raven. The line beeped once, disconnected, then fell silent. While waiting for a callback, she immersed herself in studying Belarusian security methodologies. Reading article after article, she sucked on chocolate-covered mints, letting each one melt.

Hours later, her mobile buzzed, and the screen read *Private Caller*. Expecting the Raven, she answered at once, heart pounding.

"Tess, Mark here. You called." Airport noise sounded in the background.

Thrown off guard by the business-like tone of his voice, she shifted her thoughts from work. "Yes, I'm glad you called. I'm in London, and well, I collapsed yesterday, and David ordered me to take medical leave."

"Can't say I'm surprised." The sound of a jet taking off overpowered his voice.

Even if she was wrong, she interpreted his attitude as neutral and not accusatory. "I made a mistake." The line remained silent, and as each uncomfortable second passed, she wondered just how mad he was.

"Glad you listened to somebody, even if I couldn't convince you. Anything else?"

His tone remained impassive, and she couldn't hear over the noisy airport sounds. Worried this moment could decide whether she'd ever see him again, she opted for transparency. "There's no one here I can trust, and I need help. I'm stuck in London for the next few days, but I want to see you again. Where are you?"

"JFK. I needed to visit a couple of people here before flying to Bergen."

"Oh, right." Did *people* include his mysterious female caller? Ugh, best not to speculate. On cue, she felt like a swarm of butterflies filled her stomach.

"My plans are flexible, and I change planes in London. If it's urgent, I could arrange a stopover."

"Yes, please come. Can you?" She tightened her grip on the phone and held her breath. After yesterday's grim discovery, she leapt to accept his offer and regained hope when everything had seemed lost.

"My flight's boarding now. Text me your hotel info, and I'll arrive late evening, London time. See you later."

"Thanks. Bye." Marveling how thirty seconds changed her outlook, she unclenched her jaw and sank into an overstuffed chair. She texted him the hotel address and wished him a safe flight before calling the hotel concierge to add his name to her room reservation. Inside, she couldn't stop her nerves from fluttering. Considering their strained goodbye, she held no expectations about how their meeting would go, but the promise of seeing him tantalized her imagination and reduced the weight on her shoulders.

She popped an oxycodone capsule, climbed onto the bed, and researched recent computer virus outbreaks in Belarus until she drifted to sleep. After sunset, her mobile rang, jarring her awake, and she bolted upright in the darkness. Patting around the tousled blankets to find the phone, she glimpsed the screen: *Private Caller*. Mark must have landed in London.

"Hello?" She tried to sound awake.

"You called a phone number today." The robotic male voice sounded computer-generated.

"Yes." Caught off guard, she shifted, and the half-melted ice bag on her ankle slid off the bed and spilled ice cubes and water all over the carpet.

"What's your name?"

"Tess Bennett." Attention rapt, she worried what she'd learn next and braced her back against the headboard.

"What news do you have for me?" the voice continued.

The cryptic phrase in Kyle's letter sprang to memory at once, but she hesitated, lest verbalizing the words wrought more catastrophe. "The Druid has fallen."

"You'll be given instructions." The call disconnected.

"Wait. Come back. Are you there?" Silence. Hoping to reach the unidentified number, she punched the redial button but found it blocked. *Damn it.* Whoever this Raven character was, he guarded his privacy like a fortress.

Jittering a foot against the floor, she checked the crystal clock on the bedside table every few minutes as Mark's arrival drew closer. Vacillating over what to wear, she wriggled into a snug cashmere sweater but changed her mind and chose a silky, sky-blue blouse. Unable to guess Mark's intentions, she readjusted the blouse and surveyed the mirror. If he wasn't interested, he wouldn't have returned her message, so his willingness to stop in London offered some solace. Still, each minute stretched like an eternity, and she grew antsy.

A knock at the door sounded. Digging into her bag, Tess grabbed a perfume and spritzed her neck with a jasmine scent. She slid onto her crutches and checked the door's peephole to confirm Mark stood on the other side. After a deep, calming breath, she opened the door. "Hi. Come in."

Mark held a large paper takeaway bag smelling of curry. He stepped inside the suite and pecked her on the cheek. "Hi there. You're vertical—good sign."

"Yes, better than yesterday." The hint of sandalwood cologne in the air weakened her knees. Unsure if the platonic kiss signaled he intended to keep her at a distance, she projected a positive, but guarded, mood.

"Are you hungry? I didn't eat on the flight, so I

picked up takeaway near Charing Cross. Curry acceptable?" With an eyebrow arched, he rubbed his jaw and pulled back slightly.

"Always. I haven't eaten, either." As she looked him over, something struck her as missing. "Hey, don't you have a suitcase or coat?"

"Oh. I left them in my room, a few doors away." Mark placed the steaming bag on the small dining table, and the smell of tandoori filled the room.

"You reserved a room here? But…" Leaving the sentence unfinished, she absorbed a sting of rejection and straightened her posture. Just like before, she was still intoxicated by Mark's sapphire gaze. However, given how distant he seemed, she considered whether something had changed in New York and remembered his female mystery caller.

"Since we left things at loose ends in Seattle and you're under such pressure, I didn't want to assume I'd be your guest. Why don't we eat and talk about it?"

"Sure. Thanks for picking up dinner." With some effort, she remained composed enough to hide her annoyance. Her personal universe was blowing up but he seemed utterly unrattled. Mind racing, she recalled she was the one who got angry first in Seattle and resolved not to overreact.

Seated at the suite's table, she and Mark downed the curry takeaway without any conversation. She debated making small talk about cardamom and turmeric to break the awkward silence but couldn't muster the words. *Calm down.*

After finishing his chicken *tikka masala*, Mark pushed his plate away and wiped his hands with a napkin. "I'd like to check your leg and ensure your healing is on track. Tell me again what happened yesterday."

Tess recounted the incident from her patchy memory, and heat filled her cheeks. "I've iced it several times today and tried to rest."

"I'm not surprised you got sick. Sit on the couch, and I'll examine the wound." He inspected her leg carefully and shone his phone's light on the surgical incision from every direction while rotating the ankle in slow circles. He checked her pulse, felt her forehead, and palpated the lymph nodes on either side of her neck. "Still taking the oxycodone and staying hydrated?"

"Yes. I learned my lesson and should've been more careful." While confident the exam was comprehensive, she found its purely clinical nature disappointing. Even so, she struggled to contain the steamy desires his presence inspired. "I didn't mean to act rashly in Seattle, and I'm afraid I scared you away. Forgive me."

He slipped her foot back into the oversized boot and tightened the noisy hook and loop straps. A corner of his mouth lifted in a half-smile as he got to his feet. "I'm glad you called, although I don't know where we stand."

True words—Tess had no idea where they stood, either. Seeing the spark in his gaze again, she relaxed, and the tension in her throat released. She'd intended to hold back, but excitement prevailed. "I'm so relieved to see you. How'd your trip to New York go?"

"Fine. Boring appointments." He shrugged one shoulder and massaged his scarred hand.

She waited for him to say more, but whatever tedium he suffered in New York, he elected not to elaborate. "After Cedarcliff, I imagine seeing familiar faces would offer comfort."

"No, just physical therapist appointments for my hand, not much else." Mark took a seat next to the small couch.

Watching his response, she debated whether he omitted anything critical, or if he spoke the truth and wasn't hiding any salacious activities. Unable to read his expression, she deliberated over his vague word choice.

"How's London?" He leaned forward with his hands on his knees.

"Pretty terrible." Since reading Kyle's letter, she'd tried to beat back her fear and grief with little success and couldn't stop her lower lip from wavering. "Kingsley Tech is under imminent attack, and I've been ousted on medical leave. I'm chasing a lead Kyle left behind and tracking down a hacker." Tired from recounting the details, she dropped her shoulders and exhaled.

Listening intently, Mark sloped his head to one side and fixed his gaze in her direction. "Did something else happen?"

She swiped away a few tears and straightened her back. "The worst news is Kyle's death was no accident. Crimson Hammer killed him. I met with Inspector Willis at the Metropolitan Police to reopen the investigation of his death."

"I'm so sorry, Tess." He sat beside her on the couch and wound his arm around her shoulders. Stroking the back of her head, he smoothed her hair and gave her a tight squeeze. "That's a whole different kind of grief."

"They killed Kyle and Riku, and they almost got us, too. They're planning an attack on Kingsley Tech, and I don't know if we can stop it." With her lips clamped tight, she trembled and thought the mountain of obstacles would overwhelm her.

"You can't fight them tonight."

Mark's warm baritone soothed her, but she bounced between renewed grief over Kyle and uncertainty about Mark's intentions. Flummoxed by conflicting emotions and torn between the past and the future, she flailed against the uncertain present. "Grieving Kyle is complicated given you and I are involved, or whatever we are."

"Life's messy, *min kjære*. We control very few things in life, and grief isn't one of them. I'll help see you through this." He wiped a tear from her cheek and squeezed her hand. After mining his jacket pocket, he extracted a white envelope. "Someone delivered this letter when I was checking in, so I offered to hand-deliver it."

Holding the envelope at arm's length, Tess recoiled in case it held radioactive waste or something equally toxic.

"Aren't you going to open it?" Brow furrowed, he waited.

"The last time I opened an envelope, I got my heart broken." Pursing her lips, she picked up her pocketknife and sliced the envelope open to find a plain white note card.

57.4764525, -4.1002073.
MacTavish
Tomorrow, 15:00

Mark peeked over her shoulder at the card and

whistled. "Random numbers. What do they mean?"

Excited to have a tangible clue to pursue, she kicked into high gear. "It's a meeting invitation and a puzzle to solve."

"Everything's a puzzle for you techies. Why can't you meet at a coffee shop like normal people?"

Mark's tease coaxed out a smile, and she fetched her laptop from the coffee table. "Because that would be boring. The numbers aren't random—they could be passwords, passcodes, or two-factor authentication. No, not those. A location. A street or landmark. Coordinates."

Under Mark's watchful eye, she flew her fingers over the keyboard, clacking away to test different combinations. "Got it. These are GPS coordinates using digital degrees. The first is latitude, and the second is longitude."

"Great, but where is it?" He pulled up a chair and sat.

"A GPS converter will tell us." After selecting an app, she entered the digital coordinates into a box on the screen and hit the search button. Tapping her foot, she waited as the image downloaded on her laptop.

"A big empty field. Strange." Mark's eyebrows rose in a high arch.

"Coordinates can be any place on earth; we're lucky it's not in the ocean."

"*Ja,* but we could be on the Titanic now, enjoying a water view."

"Sure, if you enjoy midnight iceberg swimming." Despite the dire situation, Tess laughed before returning to the map. "Double-checking. Still an empty field. Enlarging. Oh, my." Fixated on the screen, she dropped her hands from the keyboard.

"Good 'oh, my,' or bad 'oh, my'?" Mark cracked open a bottle of mineral water and took a long drink.

"Not any field. A battlefield." Tess caught her breath and peered intently at the image. "Culloden Battlefield."

"Doesn't sound familiar."

"The coordinates place the battlefield outside of Inverness, Scotland. I see a monument in the field next to a large visitor center. Here, look." She pointed to a tall, cylindrical structure built of large, square stones.

"Before getting too excited, are you sure this isn't a trap?" Mark rolled his shoulders in small circles and stretched out his legs.

A waft of sandalwood caught her attention, but she kept her amorous urges at bay. "Kyle trusted this contact, and he would never endanger me. His last request was for me to deliver this disk to the Raven, and I must honor it."

"*Who*?" Mark demanded, raising a single eyebrow.

"The Raven."

"Come on. Real people don't speak this way." He gestured with both hands open, and the corner of his mouth twitched.

"Welcome to the underworld, Doctor. Hackers are often enigmatic. For safety, I told Inspector Willis I'd be out of town a day or two. David shut me out, and the only way I can fight Crimson Hammer is to chase this hacker and find out what he knows."

"How about we ask the police to follow up, instead? They live for this stuff." Mark rubbed his palms together.

"Given Kyle's altered police report, we can't trust

the police. Besides, I doubt the Raven likes cops very much. Will you come with me?" A phone rang somewhere in the next room.

Mark studied her a long time before answering. "Yes, but I have conditions."

"Which are?" Tess shot him a curious glance.

"First, you agree to follow my medical advice and protect yourself. Second, notify the detective we're both traveling to Scotland should anything go wrong. Fair?" He extended a hand.

She shook it. "Deal. I'll book us on tomorrow's first flight to Inverness." While accustomed to traveling solo worldwide at a whim, she couldn't argue his position was unreasonable. And, given her rash flight to London against medical advice, she both literally and metaphorically lacked a healthy leg upon which to stand.

Mark opened his mouth, then closed it without speaking.

She knew he'd protest and held up a palm. "Before you tell me we can't fly because of my leg, an hour's flight is less stressful on my body than a nine-hour car trip. Besides, we don't have time to waste."

"Only if you promise you'll rest before meeting the vulture, hawk, or whatever bird of prey awaits us. You techies." Mark gave her an eye roll.

"The Raven, and we'll face him together. At least, I hope you will." Relieved to hear his easygoing humor, she savored the light moment of happiness, knowing stressful, dangerous work remained ahead.

"I was afraid you'd ask. People tell me Scotland is god-awful this time of year." He stood with his hands stuffed in his pockets.

"True, but we'll have each other." She cast a sideways glance to see if the wisecrack amused him, and his broad smile gave her hope. Building on the camaraderie, she invented a reason for him to stay longer and not disappear to his room. "I've got lots of difficult things to manage, and I'm grateful you're here. Care for a scotch? The hotel staff keeps the rooms here stocked to the brim." She gestured at the minibar tucked underneath a polished wood cabinet.

"Uh, sure. That would be nice." He sat on the couch.

At this point, she was so grateful he didn't dash out of the room that the tension in her shoulders released several notches. She opened the minibar, poured scotch into two crystal glasses, and handed him one before settling beside him on the love seat.

"*Skål.*" He lifted his drink and clinked her glass. "To our safe travel."

"Cheers." She took a slow sip, allowing the scotch to trickle over her lips and into her mouth. The smoky peat flavor emboldened her, and she ventured into trickier territory. "By the way, you didn't need to reserve a separate room."

"Yes, I did. I had a complete meltdown the last time I slept next to you, and I'm too embarrassed to risk repeating it."

"Don't be. You don't have to avoid me." Warmth radiated from his body, and she couldn't ignore the sensual stirrings deep inside her. She placed a hand on his arm.

"I have another reason."

Fearing rejection, she tensed her spine, and sweat coated the back of her neck. A handsome man like

Mark could easily have a love interest in New York, if not several. Or, what if he had contracted a sexually transmitted disease? She cataloged potential complications, none of which were positive. Lungs tight in her chest, she feigned calmness. "Could you please explain?"

"You're not over Kyle, and grief takes time. Sometimes, a lot of time. If we sleep together every time we meet, I'll like you even more." He clasped his hands over his lap.

"That sounds like a win to me. Can't find any downside for either of us." Tess cracked a flirtatious smile. Swirling the scotch in her glass, she traced the rim before licking the amber liquor off a finger. Having him so close enticed her, and she lacked the restraint to ignore temptation.

"No downside?" He let out a groan. "Tess, terrorists are chasing you as we speak. Losing Maya nearly killed me, and I can't handle losing someone again. You're beautiful but risky."

Outside the hotel window, city lights glowed across the Thames. Right now, enveloped in a bubble of safety, Tess didn't care if danger lurked. Undecided on how to refute his mixed message, she set her glass on the coffee table. "Fair enough. A grieving woman targeted by terrorists isn't the greatest romantic catch. However, to be clear, I plan to survive." Suddenly restless, she rose from the sofa, as if movement alone could shield her from disappointment.

Mark stood to join her.

Rotating to face him, she met his intense gaze but couldn't interpret his expression. She glided a hand over his shoulders before running her fingertips down his chest. Closing her eyes, she encircled his waist and outlined the inverted triangle of his muscular back. Melding her chest against him, she trailed her fingers against his shirt, and the resulting body heat between them made her head tingle.

"I can't resist you," he whispered before seeking her mouth. Groaning under his breath, he stripped off his shirt and wrapped his arms around her, rocking his body gently against hers.

Tasting echoes of peaty scotch along with salt, she parted her lips as the silky tip of his tongue found hers. When his hip brushed against hers, she melted with desire, and warmth spread throughout her body. She tore off her blouse, leaving her black silk bra smooth against his bare chest.

Once the spark uniting them ignited, stopping became impossible. She slid her hands to caress his bruised torso and kissed him hungrily, her breath rising as desire took hold. Slipping off her bra, she pressed her bare chest against his skin. Happily, she forgot the world outside and lost herself in pleasure. She lowered a hand below his waist. "I want—"

"Take all of me." Breathless, he lifted her off the ground and navigated them toward the suite's bedroom. Once inside, he swooped her onto the perfectly made bed. After landing a line of kisses down her bare torso, he moved up and kissed her, long and slow.

A soft, golden light emanated from the bedside lamp. Each brush of his lips offered a delicate gift of what she needed—a fresh infusion of life. As if awakening from a long winter's hibernation, she quickly thawed and longed for more. She rolled onto one side and slid close beside him. As his golden stubble brushed against her cheeks, she trailed one hand down his bare back, appreciating the well-defined, rippled muscles. Breathless, she relished the sight of him and grew hungry with want.

Tess's mobile rang, and she groaned. "No-o-o!" Ignoring the phone, she kissed him again. "Whatever it is can wait ten minutes."

"Only ten minutes? I'd prefer at least an hour." Mark gave a soft chuckle.

The ringing stopped for a moment but restarted. "Call marked urgent," a computerized voice announced.

"Crap. I'm sorry." Tess rolled away and grabbed the phone from the bedside table. The screen read *Declan O'Leary*. Something was seriously wrong. She pressed the phone to her ear and heard Declan's breath hitching in sporadic bursts. "What happened?"

"I need your help. David's gone—kidnapped."

Chapter Fourteen

Vanished

Declan's announcement officially dashed the romantic mood. Tess lurched upright and turned up the bedside light and shivered, as if she'd plunged deep into an icy lake. The smoldering sensual energy she and Mark had built up evaporated. Dread replaced desire, and she felt her chest tighten with anxious, shallow breaths. Like a horror movie on replay, she was transported back to the barn and reliving her fatal fight with Sergey. Ghoulish images of him unleashing sadistic revenge upon Mark flashed through her thoughts, and she battled queasiness.

"Tess, you there? Can you hear me?" Declan stammered.

She hadn't realized she'd gone silent. Snapping herself back to the present, she detected the frantic edge to his tone and prayed he was wrong. With closed eyes, she clutched the phone tight and braced herself. "I'm here. Tell me what's going on."

"David didn't come home after leaving Ivy House tonight. Penelope called the police, and they can't find him." His words poured out in a rush.

"What the hell happened? Didn't he have police protection?" She needn't have asked the question. *Crimson Hammer happened, that's what.*

"Police did a crap job. For feck's sake, it's a total cock-up."

Declan, who could swear worse than the saltiest sailors, added a long string of expletives. As curse words reverberated in her ear, she grasped for any evidence that could make the news less awful. "Could they trace his mobile signal?"

"No. How do you vanish from fucking central London without a bloody trace?" Declan grumbled and grunted. "Christ."

Declan's anxiety was contagious, and Tess sensed prickly heat spreading over her body as a fresh dose of adrenaline pumped through her bloodstream. Hands shaking, she smashed a fist into the damask duvet as a deluge of panicked thoughts nearly overtook her. The emergency demanded she set a course forward and navigate this new storm.

Mark squeezed her clenched hand and placed a blanket around her bare shoulders.

"Hang tight—here's what we're going to do. I'm taking myself off medical leave immediately and will serve as CEO in David's absence. Declan, I nominate you as acting corporate vice president. Call Kavita and tell her she will head up both Development and Operations."

"Done. Thank you."

Relieved to hear Declan's voice more solid, she regained her footing and continued. "Good. I'll send out comms to the company, then activate our emergency continuity of business plan. Let's meet at seven o'clock tomorrow morning at Capers, the café by the Westminster Tube station."

"Deal. Kavita, too?"

For some inexplicable reason, her gut said *no,* and she hesitated while trying to invent a rational excuse why. Failing to come up with one, she obeyed her intuition and figured Declan was too stressed to protest. "No. We'll get David back. Stay strong." She signed off and felt her heartbeat thudding against her chest walls. "Goddamn it!" Hurling her phone against the wall, she left a gash under a framed picture of London's Green Park.

"So, David's gone now, too?" Hair tousled and bare-chested, Mark sat up in bed and swiftly yanked the bedsheets to his waist.

"Kidnapped." Tess rose from the bed and balanced on her good leg, keeping weight off her orthopedic boot-clad foot. Memories of Cedarcliff's violence rushed back like a raging flood that could sweep her away and crush her under the water's weight. And now, David was next.

"You're in shock. What can I do to help you?" Mark met her gaze and touched her arm. "I'm here for you."

"Thanks. When will this goddamned disaster end?" After a couple of deep breaths, she pressed a hand to one temple and corralled her chaotic thoughts long enough to form a short mental list. "Okay. I'd like you to meet Declan with me at seven o'clock, then you and I will fly to Inverness. Meanwhile, I must lead Kingsley Tech through this crisis and pray David survives this. Christ."

"Anything you need." Mark hopped out of bed and picked up his jeans from the floor and pulled them on. Opening the closet, he pulled out a fluffy white bathrobe, which he wrapped around her before landing a kiss on her mouth.

She kissed him back and let out an exasperated sigh. "Declan's timing couldn't be worse."

"Agreed, but I'll try not to give him a hard time at breakfast. While you work, I'll take a cold, bracing shower and come pick you up at six thirty."

"Thanks for being here. I could use a couple of days without a crisis." At this point, she could hardly remember normal life.

"Me, too. You'll get through this, though, and I'm only two doors to the right if you need me earlier." He flashed a smile and left, closing the door behind him.

She dove into work, hoping the mental effort would prevent the painful memories of Cedarcliff from resurfacing. Becoming acting CEO due to a terrorist kidnapping offered no sense of accomplishment, just impending doom. Fear for David's well-being triggered the memory of Yuri's interrogation, and she tasted bile in her throat. *Please, no torture.*

Rejecting negativity, she tackled her to-do list. First, she notified their legal group about the emergency and activated the executive succession plan. Next, she carefully crafted a sober, but reassuring, e-mail for Kingsley Tech's entire staff and outlined the situation as vaguely as possible to avoid creating panic. After sending the e-mail, she wrote instructions for Declan and Kavita to manage press inquiries and anything else that might arise during the next twenty-four hours.

When Mark knocked on the door at six thirty, she'd face-planted on her laptop keyboard, fast asleep. At his second round of knocking, she hoisted herself from the chair, shuffled to the door, and let him in. "It's morning already?"

"Afraid so. I prescribe coffee." He held out a tall caffe latte and stepped into the room.

Judging from the dark circles under Mark's eyes, she figured he hadn't slept much, either. "Thanks. I'd mainline caffeine shots if I could. Give me two minutes to shower, and we'll go." Tess gulped down half the cup to usher away her residual haze. Dropping the robe on the floor, she headed into the bathroom. True to her word, she appeared in a thick white towel minutes later, slipped into black stretch pants and an ivory sweater, and shoved her uninjured foot into a sleek, black-suede boot. "Ready. But first, a couple of precautions."

"Such as?" Stretching his neck from side to side, Mark rubbed at the stubble on his chin.

"We can't mention Crimson Hammer or the Raven. At least, not yet. Crimson Hammer could be blackmailing Declan and Kavita, and Willis insisted I withhold that information. I *might* be able to trust Declan, but we tell no one for now."

"Understood. Let's go."

The sun had lifted over the horizon by the time she and Mark arrived at the Capers Café. Right away, she spotted Declan sitting alone in the corner, facing an oversized carafe of coffee. Making her way toward his table, she noted his untamed black hair and the reddish skin around his eyes. "Morning, Declan. I'd like to introduce Dr. Mark Nygaard, my fellow hostage in Canada. He's familiar with the group who I believe kidnapped David."

"Hey, Tess." Declan stood to shake Mark's hand and whistled. "Welcome, mate. Have a seat. You're unlucky to have ended up in this bloody mess. Nasty bruises you've got there."

"Good to meet you, and I'm sorry to hear David's missing. And you're right—Canada was way more action-packed than expected." Before sitting, Mark pulled out a chair for Tess.

Settling in, Tess reached for the coffee pot. "Let's drink this while it's hot." She poured each of them a cup and watched as Declan sized up Mark, like a football player scoping the opposing team.

Declan poured three packs of sugar into his coffee before directing his attention toward Mark. "Kavita said you were braver than hell at Cedarcliff."

"Ah, well, she must have been referring to Tess. She saved my life." Mark rested his hands on the table and smiled in her direction.

Declan gave her a mock salute. "I don't doubt it. She keeps her head straight in a crisis way better than I could."

"Goodness knows, I try." Eyebrows raised, she forced a grim nod, amazed at their faith in her. *I'm not brave. I'm reckless.* In the past week, she'd taken numerous life-threatening risks and only survived by sheer luck. "Any police update since we talked, Declan?"

Eyelids lowered, he swung his head in a *no* and frowned. "I called again on the way here, and no news. Your e-mail this morning will keep our teams from bloody freaking out and tame the gossip mill. Thank goodness, the second we learned of the imminent threat, we closed the head office, even before David disappeared."

"Bleak times, but we'll stay strong and get through this." Focused on staying logical, she stuffed her emotions deep and avoided visualizing David. "How much time do we have?"

"Midnight tomorrow." Declan slumped his shoulders and hung his head.

"Not much time. Ransom?" Mind racing, she hoped the Inverness trip would be quick because the clock was already ticking.

"Yep. The kidnappers want Firefly and Rapadon, but whatever the hell Rapadon is, it's not ours." Declan brushed a palm over his sweaty forehead.

Still surveying the lay of the land since the ill-fated tech review, Tess pressed on, hoping to unearth some positive news. "What's happened in Ops during the last twenty-four hours?"

"Shite. Nothing, which is bizarre. A subset of Kyle's code is out there, but we don't know how it slipped out." Glancing down, Declan dumped another packet of sugar into his coffee.

"Any unusual network activity?" Keeping her voice neutral, she hated lying, especially since she knew precisely who released the code and why. She leaned toward trusting Declan but resolved not to disclose any of Kyle's information until she found the Raven.

"None. Zip. Zilch. Last night, Operations worked to harden our network perimeter, and they're running diagnostic tests continually. If anyone even considers breathing near our servers, alarm bells will ring loud enough to wake the dead."

"That's reassuring." The coffee scalded the roof of her mouth, and she winced. Tess snuck a glance at Mark, who was paying close attention to Declan's every word. "Any sign of a mole inside the development team?"

"Not a chance, mate. Our engineers are rock solid, and nobody's off brooding or launching Molotov cocktails." Declan stirred his coffee, then clinked the spoon against the ceramic saucer.

"Good." *Could David have succumbed to blackmail?* What if he faked his kidnapping to safely wait out the crisis? Unlikely—David was no coward. Besides, getting kidnapped could confirm David hadn't sent her to perish at Cedarcliff. Only one possibility on their executive team remained but she loathed asking. "What about Kavita?"

Declan dropped his jaw and stared. "You're fucking kidding, right?"

His red cheeks and disgusted expression left no doubt she'd insulted him, but she sidestepped starting an argument. "These terrorists are violent and often use blackmail. Any one of us could be compromised. After David, you, and me, Kavita's next in line."

"Jesus, I can't believe you'd doubt her for a moment. She was injured at Cedarcliff, too, remember?" He leaned forward and growled. "What the hell happened to you in Canada? Did you blow a gasket or something?"

Gritting her teeth, she flicked her gaze upward and formed a fist under the table. "You're the one who told me she aimed to steal my job. Tell me why." Try as she might, she was losing her patience.

"Kavita showed up with a thirty-sixty-ninety-day executive plan on how to run your VP office. Super detailed, like she'd been scheming a long time. Given the chaotic circumstances, she was quite prepared."

"God, does she ever stop?" Tess gulped down more coffee. Having stoked Declan's ire, she chose her response carefully to avoid setting him off. "To be clear, I respect Kavita's work and dedication. However, have you noticed anything unusual about her the last couple of weeks?"

"Other than she survived a terror attack and got her arms sliced up? No. Without fail, she delivers like clockwork. What are you playing at? Suddenly, you don't trust anyone. When did you become so effing paranoid?" He backed away with raised hands.

"After terrorists gunned down Riku right next to me." She mustered every ounce of restraint to resist hurling something at a wall.

"Shite." Elbows propped, Declan rested his head in his hands and groaned.

No one spoke.

Mark squeezed her hand under the table, and his phone buzzed and lit up on the café table.

In her peripheral vision, she spotted the sender's photo filling the screen and glimpsed a red-headed woman, early thirties, with supermodel cheekbones and perfect makeup. *Elena Rabinowitz.*

—Great to connect yesterday. Video call tonight?—

Mark punched a button to stop the buzzing.

Although annoyed, she projected calm and exhaled, determined to avoid assuming anything about Mark's love life in New York. "Let's move on. Declan, I've sent you and Kavita everything you need to deal with the press today. Any questions?"

"Why aren't you dealing with the press yourself?" Declan shifted his knees, and the café table wobbled.

"I'll be gone the next twenty-four hours. Mark and I are tracking a lead to help save David. You and Kavita need to cover today." A stack of buttered rye toast filled the air with a savory aroma, and she devoured a slice to silence her growling stomach.

"What kind of lead?" Arms crossed, Declan jutted out his jaw and squinted.

"I can't discuss it, but I should learn more later today." As her discomfort grew, Tess curved away from the table. Declan's expression exuded suspicion, and she wanted to leave before getting caught in a lie.

Declan rose to his feet, and the back of his chair knocked against the wall. "You're David's number two, and the first thing you do as acting CEO is to skip town with a guy you just met and refuse to tell me what's going on? I trust you and David more than my own crazy family, and you're shutting me out now?"

"Sit down and lower your voice." Tess shot Declan a warning glance. "Don't test me. Not today."

"Hey, you two. Stop." Mark made a time-out signal with his hands. "You're under tremendous pressure, but your team will need you to model calm, not panic. Everyone wants David back."

After counting to three in her head, Tess wondered how scandalous it would be to order a vodka tonic so early in the morning. She let out a sharp exhale and turned to Declan. "I understand David's suffering, because Mark and I endured it ourselves. I won't sugarcoat it—his life is at risk, and this lead is my best shot at getting him home alive." Kyle's words kept echoing in her mind: *Don't trust anyone at Kingsley.* "Mark, we need to get going. Declan, feel free to call if you need anything." Aware of Declan's narrowed, piercing gaze tracking her, Tess feigned nonchalance and reached for her bag. Although she had committed a lie of omission rather than a falsehood, she was a terrible liar and knew it.

After a speedy exit from the café, she and Mark stopped at the hotel to pick up their suitcases and hail a cab. The morning rush had begun, and London's streets filled with commuters. Noticing Mark's perplexed expression, she reached over to squeeze his hand. "Hey, what's on your mind?"

"Why didn't you tell Declan about Kyle's letter? It does seem like you're shutting him out." Mark rolled down the cab window, and cold air flowed through the back seat.

"Easy. Declan's stressed, and telling him terrorists murdered his best friend won't make it any easier to manage David's kidnapping. The truth will gut him like it gutted me." She swiped away a stray tear.

Mark grasped her hand. "I see, but you've got to tell him soon. He knows you're holding something back." He leaned his head against the headrest and stared at the cab's ceiling.

"I will. You can't trick Declan, but you can rely upon his loyalty, or at least I've always thought so. He's whip-smart and can memorize vast amounts of data by osmosis, but sometimes, he lacks filters." To block the frosty morning air, she wound her cashmere scarf higher on her neck.

The cab hit a speed bump, and Mark turned to face her. "Despite Declan's lack of filters, I doubt he'd work against you. Did you decide whether you can trust him or not?"

"I believe in Declan, but Kyle said not to trust *anyone* at Kingsley." She tapped out a message on her phone. "Okay, I sent Willis our travel plans and asked him to call if there's any update on David's whereabouts. We could use good news."

As she and Mark boarded the flight to Inverness, she wished the disaster would end more than anything. Instead, she was trapped on an out-of-control carousel, spinning faster and faster. Too late to jump off, she had to hang on tight with all her might to not fall off the wild ride and crash. Luck saved her life several times last week, but that luck could also disappear without warning.

A shiver crept up her spine as she peered out the window at the baggage handlers loading the plane. No one beats death 100 percent of the time. *No one.*

Chapter Fifteen

Truth-Seeking

A couple of hours later, Tess and Mark landed at the Inverness airport in Scotland. The gray, gloomy skies did nothing to assuage her unease about the challenges ahead, and she shivered in her trench coat while waiting for Mark to pick up a rental car.

A small, black German sedan pulled up to the curb and parked. Mark hopped out and opened the passenger door. "Searching the Scottish Highlands for a hacker on the run is the last thing I expected to do this week."

"You and me both. Hope you're ready for an adventure." She tried to sound upbeat, but the mixture of exhaustion and worry had deflated her spirits.

Clutching the steering wheel, Mark exited the airport parking lot and flew over a speed bump before landing hard and merging onto the roadway. "Shout if I veer to the right. Why the British decided to drive on the left is beyond me."

"Embrace the unexpected but watch for those speed bumps." Tess tightened her seat belt and consulted her phone to confirm they were headed in the right direction. "Glad you're driving instead of me. First time in Scotland?"

"Yes, though Bergen's across the North Sea to the northeast. When Norwegians travel, we prefer warm, cozy places with actual sunlight, rather than dismal northern countries."

"Sadly, our hacker doesn't live in a tropical resort with white-sand beaches. This Raven guy better have useful information. I've got nothing else." She drummed her fingers on the dashboard.

"You realize if David's in danger, you're not safe either, right?" Mark trained his focus on the twisting road ahead.

She hadn't. Bracing against a sudden swirl of nausea, she rolled down the passenger window and tilted her head to gulp the fresh air. Wrinkling her brows, she avoided considering the risks. "Thinking of David suffering at the hands of Yuri and Dmitry makes me sick. None of this should have happened." The car passed through a wooded section with bare trees and piles of brown, yellow, and orange leaves. She touched his arm. "Hey, how are you feeling lately? You seem calmer."

"My meds kicked in, which helps. No night terrors last night, just bizarre dreams. I'm managing it." He sprayed the windshield with cleaner, and the wipers slapped back and forth.

"You'll tell me if I can help you, right?" Whether he'd accept her help was another thing entirely.

"I'm good. I conquered this before, and I'll do it again." He peered ahead at the stark, rolling hills. "The other docs in Ukraine called me Dr. Calm, and I intend to earn my nickname back."

"All I'm saying is, you don't have to do it alone." She wanted to be supportive without being pushy, but an edge of defensiveness had crept into his voice.

With the hint of a smile, he offered a slight nod and

kept driving.

The text message he received earlier from the stunning redhead bothered her, though she tried not to obsess about it. Nothing he'd shared suggested a lingering love interest in New York, but still, she feared getting her heart trampled. Grilling him about his texts was a nonstarter, and she loathed appearing vulnerable or acting like an insecure high schooler. Chiding herself for worrying, she resolved to stop ruminating.

The road forked, and Mark took the exit on the right. A few blocks up the street, a riverfront hotel appeared. "Destination reached. That's one win for the day."

"This looks like a medieval castle out of a fairy tale. Not at all my usual, generic business-travel hotel." The Gothic Revival architecture and manicured grounds sparked her imagination, and she pictured a different reality, one without terrorists and a ransom deadline.

"As long as we're not camping, I'm happy. Perhaps we'll hear mysterious hounds baying on the moors." Mark switched lanes, and the river came into view.

"How can you keep a sense of humor while slogging through a nightmare?" Wearing a wry smile, she discreetly admired the curve of his shoulder and fantasized about a weekend getaway filled with romantic dinners, breakfast in bed, and lots of sex.

"Humor keeps me sane when reality's too grim to bear." Mark eased the sedan into the hotel's parking lot and chose a spot near the entrance. "I didn't expect taking leave from my last mission to be this dangerous. On the plus side, it freed me up to chase hackers with a beautiful executive." He gave her a quick wink.

Laughing, she savored his compliment and wished the dire situation would disappear. "I'm flattered, but I feel guilty for dragging you into this. The Raven's my best lead. My *only* lead."

"I'm kidding, Tess. Mostly." He squeezed her right knee and pocketed the car keys. "I've got your back, but I'll inject gallows humor where I can." After helping her out of the car, Mark popped open the trunk and extracted their bags.

Tess visited the lobby to check in, then rejoined Mark to walk to their room. The suite offered a gorgeous view of the River Ness, which wound in snakelike curves past the hotel's lush grounds. The room's design channeled traditional Scottish interiors and was composed of dark, wood-paneled walls, a canopy bed frame with thick, spiral wood posts, textured drapes, and a muted plaid carpet. The only nod to modernity was the gas fireplace filling the room's corner. An embroidered canvas on the wall depicted a kilted bagpiper and a banner entitled *Welcome to the Highlands.*

Setting the luggage down, Mark pointed at a mahogany side table. Three crystal decanters perched next to two highball glasses, an ice bucket, and tongs. "Phew. Whiskey, gin, and sherry. At least, we're well-stocked with alcohol."

"Another win." Stomach growling, she remembered skipping breakfast. "However, if we're day drinking, I need lunch first. Let's go find a pub nearby."

Outside, she and Mark followed a rugged cobblestone path to the main street and selected a neighborhood pub emblazoned *The Highland Arms.*

Flower baskets stuffed with autumn mums hung from ornate iron hooks and adorned the building's exterior. Inside, booths shaped like church pews lined the windows, and small wooden tables filled the center of the room.

Minutes later, after they'd settled in at a window booth and ordered lunch, she couldn't stop her anxiety from rising. Biting her lip, she jiggled a leg under the wooden table. "What if finding this hacker doesn't help me save David? Kyle said the Raven's trustworthy, but what if he's wrong?"

An aproned server appeared and served them huge baskets towering with fish and chips and two pints of dark ale. He set leaky bottles of malt vinegar and ketchup on the table and returned to the kitchen.

"We can hope, but we can't know." Mark dug into the battered cod filets and wolfed one down before pouring vinegar onto his chips.

After eating a handful of chips, she took a long sip of ale. "If Crimson Hammer intercepted my call, we're headed straight into a trap, and I don't want either of us getting hurt on my account."

Outside, a few locals passed by, strolling along the stone sidewalk.

Mark stopped eating his cod filet and stared out the leaded glass windows. After wiping his mouth with a napkin, he set his hands on the table and exhaled. "Tess."

His serious tone caught her attention, and she shot him a curious glance while picking up another chip from the steaming basket on the timeworn wooden table.

"Your caution is wise. I'm relieved you're not

being *uforsvarlig,* reckless, and you respect the fact you almost died." He rested his hands on his lap.

"How could I forget we nearly died in that barn? Sergey threatened to slice my throat open." Tess balked, raising her voice several decibels louder before noticing several pub patrons peeking over their tables with wide-eyed stares. Baffled by Mark's sad expression, she couldn't figure out what she was missing.

Frowning, he pressed a hand to his mouth and fixated on the table before raising his gaze. "No, Tess, your leg. Your puncture wounds were so deep that compartment syndrome posed a life-threatening risk after surgery. You could've faced amputation, renal failure, or death." He traced the rim of the ale glass with a finger. "I've treated soldiers with less-severe injuries than yours who had amputations or died. You…you almost didn't make it."

The air in her lungs disappeared, and she gasped. "What the hell are you talking about? I don't remember any of this."

"You were unconscious. I fought with your surgeon over the best protocol to use, and because he agreed to use a method I developed in the field, you avoided amputation." Mark rubbed his cheekbones with his fingertips.

Upon hearing the gruesome revelation, she recoiled, and her lower lip quivered. Unable to speak, she couldn't believe she blocked out such a pivotal event. The top of her head tingled, and everything seemed surreal. Hideous images flashed through her mind, and what remained of her fish and chips lost all appeal. After taking an ample drink of her Irish malt ale, she straightened her spine and grounded her feet on the pub's sticky wooden floor to anchor herself. "The doctors said I suffered a severe injury."

"Very. You blocked out what your doctors told you—too much trauma to process after the kidnapping. Patients often experience memory loss after accidents. The point is, you're not immortal."

As his words sank in, she stared at the tower of alcohol bottles that filled the bar and reflected a kaleidoscope of color in the wall's mirror. Polished pint glasses lined the counter. *He saved my life.* She experienced wild emotions exploding inside her like powder kegs, ranging from disgust, horror, and guilt to more tolerable feelings like gratitude and relief. Humbled by the realization, she gained new clarity. "You worried I might die, which is why you were furious about me flying to London."

Mark met her gaze point-blank. "My mission is to save lives. When it comes to surgery, I rarely make mistakes. Patients who ignore my advice and risk dying for pointless reasons, like refusing basic precautions to avoid amputation, piss me off."

As her brain processed the severity of what she survived, she wanted to kick herself for the stupid recklessness. Now she understood why Dr. Patel in London rebuked her so harshly. "I had no idea, and I can't remember big blocks of time at the hospital. You must've thought I was crazy." She lowered her head and felt her cheeks burn.

"Not crazy but traumatized, which is quite different." Mark sipped his beer and leaned away from the table. "If I haven't been clear, Tess, I want you alive with both of your sexy legs intact. Please be careful."

Tess couldn't ignore the leg under discussion, which throbbed uncomfortably inside her plastic boot. Lack of sleep depleted her reserves. Catching a glimpse of her reflection in the pub mirror, she saw red splotches covering her cheeks. The mood at the table dive-bombed, and she wanted to leave. "Let's go. Before we travel to Culloden, I need to clear my head."

She didn't speak on the walk back to the hotel. Once back in the room, she retrieved her laptop and iced her leg. Unable to shift gears, she failed to coax her thoughts away from the grisly revelation. Meanwhile, the clock measuring the remainder of David's life continued its countdown. Pressure squeezed her from all sides, like a vise growing tighter every minute.

"We've got thirty minutes until we leave. You need some time alone, so I'll go for a walk while you're icing." Mark stretched his arms above his head and grabbed his phone from the bedside table.

"Okay, but no running. Remember, you're still injured, too." Grateful for some regrouping time, she didn't like being the only one chastised to be careful.

"No worries. My ribs need at least a month more to heal. Back soon." He planted a kiss on the top of her head and left.

Alone, she swallowed half an oxycodone dose to beat back her pain but not dull her senses. Whatever challenges the Raven presented, she wanted to be sharp to face them. Over three hundred e-mails had piled up in her inbox on her laptop. Lacking the concentration to focus, she admired the River Ness, instead. The fresh air and open sky beckoned her toward freedom, far away from this mess. Seeking escape, she daydreamed about swimming in a warm, tropical sea alongside Mark and drinking fruity cocktails garnished with paper umbrellas.

An annoying buzz from her mobile interrupted her respite. *Declan.* After taking a couple of deep breaths, she gathered her patience before answering, "Hello?"

"Tess, are you alone?"

Sensing the taut urgency in his voice, she dreaded more bad news. "Yes. Have the police found David?"

"No. What the hell were you thinking? We need to talk."

Certain he was fuming, she heard the indignation dripping from his voice. Not eager to rehash the morning's awkward café discussion, Tess winced and suppressed a groan. "Fine."

"Why are you shutting me out?"

"I'm not. I'm searching for answers to find David, and I'll know more by morning." She straightened her posture and braced against his resentment.

"You're hiding a hell of a lot more than you're letting on."

Stung by the accusation in his voice, she couldn't tell whether he was more hurt than angry and chose her words carefully. "I don't have any answers yet."

"Come on. Kyle and I were friends for fifteen years, and you're such a crap liar. I trust you and David and can't figure out what changed. And, you don't get a monopoly on missing Kyle. I miss him, too. Every single, bloody day."

"I know." Knowing she'd cry if she spoke about Kyle, she steered him in another direction. "Look, Kingsley Tech is under siege. We can't predict what form this attack will take, but the hackers could blackmail anyone to get what they want."

"Fuck, I'm not compromised. Since Cedarcliff, I've worked nonstop. When you were kidnapped, we never hesitated, and we had your back. Do you have mine?"

With laser-like precision, Declan's provocation hit its mark, and she took the guilt square in her gut like a physical blow. Consumed by her own trauma at Cedarcliff, she hadn't contemplated much about her colleagues' struggles. "Of course, I've got your back. I'm chasing a lead to help us rescue David unharmed, and I'm prepared to risk whatever it takes."

"Just don't be all American about it and rush in with guns blazing. Though you might survive that, too."

"Not without lots of damage." Staring at her injured leg, Tess shivered and studied her fingers, glad to see all five digits intact. Never mind the emotional damage, which was worse. "These bastards are fond of torture, and we have zero guarantee we'll rescue David alive. The less you know, the safer you'll be."

"Christ, you take me for a snitch, but I'd never spill a secret. Yet, you trust this doctor you've known for, what, a whole week now? Why?" Declan grunted.

Snap. "Because Mark almost died for me. They broke his ribs and punctured his lung, but he still risked taking a bullet in the face so I could escape." This time, she didn't filter her response.

"Shite." Declan whistled under his breath.

"Your loyalty isn't on trial here. This is my best shot to help David before the ransom deadline, but this also involves Kyle." With Declan cooling his heels a bit, she released her shoulders.

"Kyle? How?"

Declan's voice grew quieter and less accusatory, and she exhaled. "He left behind a puzzle only I can solve, but I've got to hurry. The answer could help us save David."

"Wait, where are you? Are you safe?"

She held her breath while deciding how much to reveal. "I'm in Scotland with Mark. I'll phone you the second we arrive in London." Eager to get off the phone, she closed her eyes.

"Take every precaution, okay? Don't be an effing hero."

"I promise." After the smackdown from Mark and another from Declan, she felt every ounce of her mortality and vulnerability. *Great.*

"You damn well better call, Bennett, or I'll send a search party the feckin' size of Gibraltar north to find you."

"Stay strong, Declan. Bye." Tess flopped on the bed and groaned out loud. Deep down, she trusted Declan, but what if she was wrong? She couldn't afford a single mistake.

A few minutes later, Mark returned from his stroll. "The wind coming off the River Ness is bone-chilling. How're you doing? Ready to go?"

"Give me a minute. Declan phoned, pissed I didn't disclose everything at breakfast today. If he can cool his heels overnight, I'll have useful information to share."

"Understandable." He glanced at his stainless-steel watch. "We'd better leave for Culloden. What's your plan?"

"I'm assuming we meet someone and give them the USB drive. This morning, I uploaded pictures of the letters to the cloud for safekeeping." Tess slipped the slim plastic case into a leather satchel before grabbing her crutches.

"I'll be ready in a moment." Mark left his mobile phone next to the whiskey carafe and headed into the bathroom, closing the door behind him.

Noticing his phone light up, Tess strolled over and checked the screen, which displayed the last caller's photo. Elena Rabinowitz again, with her perfect red tresses and radiant complexion.

—*Call time: twenty-three minutes.*—

She clenched her stomach and scowled to release her frustration before Mark returned. *None of my business.* Ignoring her growing uneasiness, she pulled on a trench coat and gloves, smoothed her hair, and resolved not to act grumpy.

Mark reappeared, drying his hands with a white towel and smelling like lemony soap. "Shall we?"

"Let's get this done." Tess geared up to tackle another round. Imagining the Raven's appearance, she envisioned an overweight, bald, loner guy with a penchant for illegal firearms. An empty ache filled her chest, and she wanted to text Sophie and vent about everything.

The road to Culloden meandered through gentle hills for several miles east of Inverness. Menacing, dark clouds blocked direct sunlight, reducing visibility to about one hundred yards. Mark lifted the windshield visor and leaned forward to assess the sky. "Looks like nature's funeral outside."

"Perfect." Irritated, Tess tried to judge whether his mood changed after his Elena phone call, but his peaceful demeanor revealed nothing amiss. *Dr. Calm, indeed.*

Mark exited onto the A9 motorway, which joined Culloden Road, then entered the car park by the battlefield's visitor center. He hopped out, circled the car to open Tess's door, and extracted the crutches from the back seat. "I'll grab us a map."

Tess buttoned her trench coat against the whipping wind and crossed the lot to read a historical marker about the battle. They'd arrived at the 1746 site of Scotland's Jacobite Rising, a vast, flat field with few trees. Clusters of heather and small shrubs grew near the short, well-tended grass, but the overall effect was haunting. Aside from a tall memorial cairn that towered in the distance, the immense field was empty and barren.

Mark returned, carrying a glossy, colorful tourist map. "Here's a brochure about the Culloden Walk and information describing the battle's history."

"We're meeting the Raven on the final resting place for 1,500 Highlanders. It's spooky how many men died here." Tess shielded her face with an arm as another gusty wind cut across the open land.

"War *is* death. Don't dwell on it for long, because the darkness can destroy you." He leaned over and touched her cheek.

"At least, we'll see anyone approaching on the moor, so they can't ambush us." Channeling her father, Tess scanned the field in all directions and committed the few landmarks to memory. "The message referenced MacTavish, Kyle's last name, but I don't understand the connection."

"Was he a big war history buff?" Mark opened a gate to the pathway.

"Not particularly. Kyle's family never mentioned

Culloden or talked much about their Highlander ancestors. Let's check out the memorial cairn."

She and Mark traversed the gravel path of Culloden Walk, which was empty of visitors. When the twenty-foot-tall stone monument came into view, she read the inscription at its base. *"The graves of the gallant Highlanders who fought for Scotland and Prince Charlie are marked by the names of their clans.* Let's check all the stones."

Clusters of stones marked the walking trail, and each one documented a family's battle losses. Clan Fraser. Clans MacGillivray, MacLean, and MacLachlan. Clan Campbell. Clan Cameron. A small ancient stone covered with green moss read *Mixed Clans*, designating a mass grave. A long stretch passed without any markers before a collection of newer engraved stones appeared built into the path.

Several yards ahead, Mark stood bent over, examining the path. "Hey, I found something."

Tess ambled over the uneven ground and joined him to study the engraved text on the marker: *In Remembrance of Our Fallen, Clan MacTavish*. "This must be it, but it's past three o'clock, and no one's here."

"Well, we couldn't be easier to find, given the gale winds scared away all the tourists." Mark fastened the top button of his coat and turned up the collar.

The sky darkened by shades of gray toward the charcoal tones of night. Total darkness would descend over the moor in minutes, and the gravesite grew more macabre the longer the wait stretched. No one approached. Fifteen minutes passed, along with Tess's patience. "An empty cemetery's safe, right? This better not be a trap." The howling wind kicked up again, chilling her exposed skin. She wrapped another layer of cashmere scarf around her head as wind barreled across the open field. More fog rolled across the moor, so thick she couldn't see her feet.

"Someone's over there." Mark gestured toward a dark shadow emerging from the fog.

Shivering from the chafing wind, Tess stood close by his side, waiting to determine whether the figure was headed their way. A man dressed in solid black advanced. Thin verging on gaunt, he wore jeans, a woolen coat, and a knitted beanie. His white skin, smooth as polished alabaster, contrasted with his dyed-black hair and deep-set brown eyes. On his neck, the outline of a black raven stood out against his pale skin.

As the man approached, he inspected them from head to toe and turned to her first. "Tess Bennett."

"Yes." She had an odd, preternatural sense he could read her thoughts. Although his tone wasn't hostile, it wasn't warm, either. Raindrops plastered her cheeks, and a roll of thunder boomed in the distance.

"Who are you?" The man pointed at Mark.

"Dr. Mark Nygaard. I was taken hostage with Tess at Cedarcliff." Feet wide and arms crossed, he stood tall and straight.

"I am the Raven." He bowed his head and clasped his hands. "The Druid's death was a tragedy, and I'm sorry for your loss, Tess."

"The Druid? You mean Kyle MacTavish?" She didn't understand but spotted a flicker of recognition in the man's somber expression.

"The Druid is well-known, but only by his hacker handle." The Raven folded his arms and stood motionless.

"Well-known by whom?" Mark shoved his fists deep into his pockets and cocked his head toward the man in black.

"The dark web, of course." The Raven gave no further explanation.

"Right." Confused but unwilling to admit it, she turned to the Raven. "Kyle died one year ago. Two days ago, I received a letter he wrote the week before he died with directions to contact you. He instructed me to deliver an important USB drive and said you'd know what to do."

"You have the drive with you?" Scrunching his eyebrows together, the Raven perked up.

"Yes." Unnerved, she felt as if this strange man could see through her.

"I need you both to come with me, and we'll drive to a safe place where I can study it." He gestured at the parking lot in the distance.

Mark stepped in front of Tess and raised a hand. "Wait a second. How do we know we can trust you?"

"Because you can. I'm unarmed, and you're welcome to check." The Raven held his arms out to his sides.

Mark proceeded to search the wiry man and found nothing but a car key on a black, braided leather key chain. "No ID?"

"No. For all legal purposes, I don't exist." He adjusted his beanie, then crossed his arms. "Now, I must confirm neither of you carried a weapon here. I despise guns."

"Fine, but don't get fresh with me." Tess exchanged a glance with Mark. She stood rigid as a flagpole as the Raven frisked her. When his fingers accidentally brushed against hers, she noticed his skin was smooth like a woman's and oddly softer than hers.

Next, the Raven patted Mark down and then searched his jacket pockets. Lifting each of Mark's pant legs, he checked the tops of the socks before finishing and clapping his palms together. "Now that's done, follow me to my car, and we'll drive about fifteen kilometers to my cottage. You may leave any time you want, and I don't mean any harm."

Although she felt uneasy, she remembered Kyle's letter and took a leap of faith. *The Raven might have the key to saving David's life.* Sensing Mark's hesitation, she offered him an encouraging nod. "We're ready."

Tess and Mark followed the Raven to the parking lot and walked to a tiny, black hatchback shaped like an egg and polished to a flawless shine. Once Mark was seated in the back, she settled into the front seat. A moment of panic set in, and she clutched the door handle. Every safety article she'd ever read warned against riding with strangers. Maybe the Raven was safe, but what if he drove them to people who weren't? She offered a last-minute prayer to Kyle in the afterlife. *This Raven guy better be trustworthy because if he's not, I'm in serious trouble.*

The Raven piled into the driver's seat and backed out of the parking lot. In seconds, the little car was speeding away from Culloden and heading southeast into the hills.

Whatever this afternoon held, she and Mark couldn't turn back now.

Chapter Sixteen

In the Hacker's Lair

The claustrophobic interior of the Raven's hatchback grew thick with tension. Raindrops thwacked the windshield, and Tess marveled at the bizarre events leading to this moment—riding in a tiny car with a suspected Scottish hacker and speeding to a random, unknown destination. What if Kyle's letter was fake? No, she remained sure he had written it. Despite the precarious predicament, she sensed her curiosity growing until it outweighed her fear. She snuck a peak at Mark in the rearview mirror and hoped the confined space wasn't aggravating his PTSD, but his usual golden complexion had paled several shades.

The Raven exited the main highway and drove up a bumpy gravel road surrounded by woods. A mile up the road, an overgrown, unmarked trail appeared. Carefully, he centered the car on the narrow tracks, but the tires hit a patch of mud and spun, making squishy-squashy sounds until gaining traction. A weathered stone cottage appeared in the sparse remains of daylight. The sun had set at four o'clock, and darkness quickly advanced.

"We're here." The Raven switched the motor off and exited the car.

Mark squeezed out of the car and circled around

with the crutches to help Tess out of the vehicle. "Are you doing okay?"

Beyond the hacker's earshot, Tess placed a hand on Mark's arm and kept her voice low. "He's unarmed, remember? He doesn't seem like the torture type. You know, the kind of guy hoarding a stash of unsterilized surgical instruments."

"Now *that* would terrify me." Grumbling, Mark guided her to the front steps of the cottage.

"Wait, I almost forgot." The Raven bounded down the steps, walked to the car, whipped out a handkerchief, and wiped down every car handle she or Mark had touched.

Standing agape, she tried to interpret the Raven's unusual cleanliness. Was the Raven a clean freak, or did he suffer from obsessive-compulsive disorder?

He glanced in her direction. "I'm removing the fingerprints for your protection." Pocketing the cloth, he traipsed back up the stone steps.

She and Mark followed the Raven to the cottage's front door. A generator and a hefty satellite dish sat tucked behind a wooden fence, shielded by thick shrubs that disguised their incongruous appearance next to the historic architecture.

The Raven punched in a code on a sleek digital keypad. The keypad snapped open and revealed a digital fingerprint reader. He placed his index finger on the reader, and the door lock beeped once and unlocked.

"Tight security you have here." Intrigued, she examined the discreet black box. The modernity of the device clashed with the weather-aged wooden door.

"I can't afford to take chances. Please come in."

She stepped inside with Mark just behind her. The foyer opened to a sparse, tasteful living room with a mahogany leather couch resting on a plaid, wool rug woven in muted navy, greens, and reds. A leather club lounger graced the opposite corner, paired with a carved wooden side table covered with paperback novels. The stone fireplace appeared functional, and an oil painting depicting the Battle of Culloden hung above the mantel. A collection of ornate, pewter, Scottish quaich bowls formed a straight line in ascending order of size. A large, sturdy basket stood nearby, filled with tidy bundles of kindling.

"Please have a seat while I check the house. I need to confirm no one's been here or planted bugs so we can speak freely. And I'll scan both your mobile phones, too."

Mark's eyebrows rose, and he jabbed her arm with his elbow.

The Raven took their phones and ran a handheld scanner over each one before returning them. "You're clear. No bugs. I'll be right back." He disappeared down a hallway toward the back of the cottage.

"This place is immaculate. I've never seen a bachelor flat so tidy." Tess spoke in a low, quiet voice and gave Mark a nudge.

"Have you seen many bachelor flats?"

Although amused, she didn't respond to his quip. To the left, the kitchen sported gleaming counters and a spotless floor. The dining room, however, held a massive desk and an explosion of electronic spaghetti. Trails of countless cables lined the floorboards along the wall and connected with a dizzying array of computers. Green lights flashed in a constant rhythm on multiple surge protectors and the eerie, artificial glow contrasted with the living room's welcoming golden hues.

"What an amazing sword." She drew her breath. A highly polished broadsword was displayed on the wall next to the fireplace, designed with a unique steel cage basket encircling the hilt. Wide hooks held the gleaming weapon horizontal. A spotlight above targeted light onto the blade, which bounced off the steel. "Wow, a double-edged blade with a basket cage around the hilt. How unusual…is it eighteenth-century?" Eager for a closer look, she approached the display, taking care not to touch the blade.

"How do you know about swords, Tess?" The Raven leaned back on his heels and cocked his head to watch her.

She detected a more-welcoming tone in the Raven's voice and wondered how much, if anything, Kyle had told him about her. "When my father was stationed in Switzerland, I studied fencing for three years in high school. My instructor also taught me the history of swords. My dad insisted I learn several forms of self-defense, but fencing's the one I enjoyed most."

The Raven strolled over to the sword. "This original weapon dates from the 1740s, and at the time, Highlanders and Jacobites preferred it. The basket protected the soldier's hand from being injured in the throes of battle."

"Smart." Mark shoved his scarred hand into his jeans pocket.

Seeing regret in Mark's expression, she stepped close and placed a hand on his back.

"Would you both like a cup of tea? I have biscuits,

too." The Raven gestured at the kitchen.

"Yes, thank you." Forty-five minutes of gusting wind on Culloden Moor had chilled Tess to the core. "Mark?"

"Yes, thanks." He sat on the leather couch, leaned into the deep backrest, and stretched his legs.

"One moment. I'll go heat up a kettle." The Raven disappeared into the kitchen.

Tess rested her crutches against the wall and sank onto the couch beside Mark. She teased him with a playful jab on the shoulder. "See? No unsterilized surgical instruments, only biscuits. Who would've guessed?"

The Raven returned, carrying a round, leather bar tray with three cups of black tea, small pitchers of milk and sugar, and a plate stacked with shortbread biscuits. He handed each of them a cup of tea, then folded his smooth hands in a prim cross. "Right. Now we're settled, I insist on the following rules. Whatever we discuss tonight, we guarantee to keep it confidential. I will keep everything you tell me in strict confidence, and I expect the same of what I share. Do you both agree?"

Tess nodded without hesitation.

"Yes." Mark reached over and selected a few shortbread biscuits.

"Good. May I please see the USB drive?"

Reluctant to release it, Tess stalled. "First, you need context about Kingsley Tech and the attack at Cedarcliff."

The Raven folded his arms and leaned forward. "Crimson Hammer kidnapped David, and you've got fewer than twenty-four hours to hand over Firefly and

Rapadon before they kill him. Let's not waste time."

Taken off guard by the Raven's omniscience, Tess faltered. "Correct. And Kyle's car accident—"

"No, not an accident. Murder. Goddamn senseless loss for the Druid to die at thirty-six." The Raven bit his lip, and his chin wavered. "The answers are on the USB drive. May we begin there, so I can ascertain who and what we're dealing with?"

"I see you're well-briefed." An indignant sound escaped Tess's throat. Incensed this stranger uncovered these details and had even pinpointed her hotel room number in London, she grew wary. As she considered what other personal information he might possess, she tightened her body from head to toe. Without another word, she reached into her bag and handed the Raven the USB drive.

"Thank you. Can you please verify no one has touched or altered this drive or put it in any computer?"

"The package was locked inside an airtight bank safe deposit box for the last year. Kyle's mother, Molly MacTavish, sent it to me in Seattle via international post, and I've carried it with me since. Never opened the case."

"Let's see." He strode over to the bank of computers and looked up. "I apologize. I work alone and don't have guest chairs."

With Mark by her side, Tess scanned the Raven's patchwork of monitor screens with no idea what to expect.

First, the Raven ran several diagnostic checks and virus scans on the USB drive before searching all the directories for specific file extensions. "Huh." He paused to type short notes in a separate window on one of his monitors. While several directories loaded, he opened one group of files. "Kyle left a lot of source code on this disk, which I expected. I need the gestalt of what's on the drive to judge where to dig deeper. I've found Firefly v1.0, but not Rapadon, the other code Crimson Hammer wants."

"Rapadon doesn't exist. David and Declan spent days searching for it, but Kyle never mentioned it to me." Tess polished off a couple of biscuits.

"You're right. Rapadon isn't a password, either." The Raven tapped his fingertips on the desk.

Gears shifted in Tess's mind, and she visualized the letters rearranging. She grabbed a blank sheet of paper and a pen from the desk. With growing eagerness, she scanned the screen and scribbled several words in different sequences until one combination clicked. Beaming, she tapped the paper. "I understand Kyle's message. Rapadon isn't a code or a project. It's a strategy, in the form of an anagram: Pandora."

"I don't follow. How does it relate to this code?" The Raven raised his head and squinted at the monitor.

"Think of mythology. Pandora's Box, when opened, unleashes all sorts of evil but leaves one thing in the box—hope." Studying the Raven's screen, she continued. "Kyle's clue is that the hackers demanded the anagram of Pandora, not Pandora itself. The code sends a silent signal, so when the Firefly code executes, it sends *Rapadon*, flagging the user as unauthorized. To deflect the attempted breach, the code must unleash destructive actions to punish the intruder."

The Raven leaned back in his chair and scanned several open screens on his monitor, murmuring to himself until he burst out laughing. "Tess, you're brilliant."

"What is it?" Mark held a teacup close to his chest.

Chuckling, the Raven slapped his knee and grinned. He beckoned them to come closer with a forefinger and pointed to one screen. "Pandora's box is classic Druid. Glad you solved the riddle, Tess. Kyle tricked the terrorists and sent an instruction to me in puzzle form. Like you said, the metaphorical box, when opened, unleashes the motherload of all computer viruses. He's asking me to create a virus to defeat the hackers. He'd have done it himself but ran out of time."

"Sure. But stealing the source code won't help the terrorists hack the banks. They need the encryption *root key* for any specific institution to unlock Firefly." Tess pushed a curl behind her ear.

"Right, the secret key to the kingdom, which is tricky to get. They need specific bank names to identify it." Processing screens of code from Kyle's disk in rapid succession, he highlighted several lines with a cursor. "Weird. The chumps asked for the wrong thing. Code, not key."

Mark reached out and pointed at the text the Raven had selected. "Code and key have similar meanings, and they might have lost the nuance when translating Russian to English. Code is *kod*, a similar word, but key is *klyuch*. The terrorists heard a familiar word and demanded *code*."

"Astute observation, Mark. You know Russian?" The Raven arched his eyebrows.

"I worked as a surgeon in Crimea, and many patients spoke Russian and Ukrainian."

"Plenty of unrest there. Damn shame what happened in Crimea." The Raven turned back to his monitors.

Tess concentrated on the various puzzle pieces and imagined them reassembling and clicking into the proper place. "They dealt us a red herring. Crimson Hammer hunted Kyle because they believed Rapadon *was* the encryption key. They can't break into the banks without it, so they wanted to kidnap David to get it."

"Let's search the code and figure out what they'd see." The Raven pored through several code-filled screens. "I found it here. This tiny subroutine reads like an innocuous performance improvement, but the algorithm triggers the Rapadon message if someone unauthorized tries to access it. Then, it requires the Rapadon *code* to continue. Our hackers are stuck, and Kyle tricked them."

"But how does it help us save David? If Crimson Hammer can't steal money from the banks, they'll kill David and come after Tess and Declan. How do we stop the cycle?" Mark rubbed his chin while peering at the monitor.

"With my help, which is why Kyle requested you contact me. Crimson Hammer is Belarusian, but dark web chatter suggests they're tight with Russia." The Raven scanned his multiple screens, frowning. "I'll investigate Kyle's other files."

As they worked to unpeel layer after layer of the puzzle, she felt her head tingling and plopped on the leather couch next to Mark. "No shortage of conspiracies in Russia, of course, but their end game could be anything."

The Raven typed at warp speed, and his computer screens updated. He stopped, paused at one straightforward text file, and flipped back and forth between two similar files. "Oh no." He groaned and spun his chair around to face them. With his piercing eyes wide open, he shook his head and contorted his face. "I'm sorry, but you guys are in serious deep shit."

Chapter Seventeen

Trouble in the Highlands

Standing before the Raven's computers, Tess fought the panic raging throughout her body—heart pounding, nerves spasming, and palms sweating. Everything else dropped away, and the past week's events culminated in this pivotal moment. Finally, she would learn the truth, or, at least, she hoped so. She exchanged a worried gaze with Mark, who was biting his lip and jiggling one knee. "What did you find, Raven?"

Mark moved closer and placed a hand on her back.

The Raven took a deep breath and pressed his palms onto his knees. "Most hackers instigate digital crime, instead of wreaking physical violence, but I'm sorry to say, you two were quite unlucky."

Given her current run of bad luck, she struggled to imagine things getting much worse. Watching the Raven, she snapped her reflexes to attention and braced herself to absorb the bad news. Behind him, the fireplace crackled with sparks and burning logs. She grabbed Mark's hand with an iron grip. "Who is it, and what do they want?"

"*Malinavy Molat*—Crimson Hammer in English."

"But Kyle already knew Crimson Hammer was behind this." Tess furrowed her brow and concentrated.

"Right, but the reason why is important. After Belarus declared its independence in 1990, the country became a democracy but in name only. Corruption runs rampant, human rights abuses persist, and no free press exists. Alexander Lukashenko held multiple presidential terms, but many questioned whether he's the legitimate winner." He paused to inhale before continuing.

"Uncertainty breeds opportunity for the underworld, and Crimson Hammer is an emerging terror group with two branches. One which hacks banks for its initial funding, and a second branch, which performs terror for hire, aiming to score money to grow their ranks and gain power."

"What's their ultimate objective?" *Something terrible, obviously.* The quagmire in which she found herself already appeared bottomless.

"Hard to say. Crimson Hammer's hackers infiltrate banks. The first, most critical step is to set up systemic micro-withdrawals, and then to leverage shell companies often based in London. After they pay off their minions and build surplus cash, they can lead terror strikes around the globe." The Raven shifted in his chair. "I suspect they eliminated Kyle because he knew too much. Hiding their organization became more important than stealing his code. At least, for awhile."

Crimson Hammer killed Kyle so they could kill even more people. Sickened by the endless cycle of carnage, she clutched her stomach as if she had been stabbed. "What changed?"

"Based on Kyle's files, he predicted Crimson Hammer planned to hack European banks to fund their activities. Terrorism as a *service*. Disgusting butchers."

Scowling, the Raven spat the last words.

Mark leaned a shoulder against the wall next to the Raven. "Most terror groups unite around a political or religious agenda. What does this group want—to rejoin Russia?" He lifted his scarred hand in the air. "I've lived through separatist violence."

The Raven stared at Mark's purple scars and shook his head. "Sadly, the medical teams caught in the crossfire often suffer for their kindness." His gaze clouded over. "Kyle ran out of time before solving it, but Crimson Hammer aimed to hire out their services under the table, to countries and leaders with one thing in common—their dislike of the US."

A moment with Riku at Cedarcliff echoed in Tess's memory. He warned politics mattered more now, and not every attack could be fought with code. The potential threats hit her like a deluge, and she grew cold, although the fireplace rustled with sparks and the sound of burning logs breaking apart. "Russia, North Korea, China, Iran…the list is long."

"Way too long." Mark rubbed the back of his neck.

The Raven interlaced his fingers together and leaned his elbows on his chair. "Anonymity fuels small terror cells because it gives them power. Flying under the radar, they avoid association with any government or entity, and no one takes responsibility. Cracking plan for them, but a shame they've targeted the Yanks in their crosshairs. Sorry, Tess."

Disturbing scenarios surfaced in Tess's thoughts, and she calculated the impacts. "Belarus is next to Russia, so it's a convenient sell."

"Impossible to say, lass, but I agree." He tented his fingers over his keyboard.

"They're keen to hack banks, but what's next, and how do we stop it? And who tipped off Riku about the looming attack in Eastern Europe?" She pondered what other intel Riku might have possessed but how he acquired it mystified her.

"Yamashita knew exactly what was going on." The Raven's scowl deepened, and he puckered his lips.

Since the attack, she'd lost several reliable constants in her life, but her respect for Riku remained ingrained. The Raven's disapproval was unmistakable, and defensively, she shifted her hands to her hips. "Are you implying Riku acted in opposition to the US?"

"Not at all. Yamashita kept many secrets, but selling out the Yanks wasn't one of them. I can't say more." The Raven pressed his fingertips against his temple.

"At Cedarcliff, Riku spoke of a new threat and wanted to strategize with David and me after the summit." Tess prodded, hoping to draw more information from him.

"I don't doubt it." The Raven folded his hands and placed them on his lap before swiveling back to his computer.

Apparently, no further information was forthcoming. Tess wondered how many secrets died with Riku and what other allegiances he had held.

Pacing back and forth along the living room window, Mark stopped. "Raven, you're telling us we endured this hell for a terror cell wanting to harm the US?"

"And wouldn't Crimson Hammer target US banks next?" Hour by hour, all the anchors she trusted were vanishing. Truth and lies dissolved together like salt in the ocean.

Pivoting in his leather desk chair, the Raven shrugged. "No US bank uses Kingsley Tech's encryption yet, so I doubt it. Instead, think beyond banks, like power grid control or isolated, random terror attacks."

"Great." The conspiracy's scope overwhelmed her, and she ground a foot into the carpet. "Since they didn't steal Kyle's code, how'd they fund their activities this past year?"

"Any shady oligarch in an adversarial country with loads of cash could fund them, but I suspect Russia. Or, it could be Crimson Hammer's funding ran out, and they attacked Cedarcliff to get money fast. They'd kidnap David and extort the encryption root key to breach European banks faster."

She tensed her body, and a wave of anger washed over her. "So, Mark and I crashed right into the mess. Kyle and Riku died for this, and David could be next." Deep scowl lines etched her forehead.

"Yes, I'm afraid so." He clasped his alabaster hands in his lap and looked down.

Fury boiled inside her bloodstream, and she felt her heart thumping against her chest like a ticking bomb. Lost in her pain, she let out an agonized groan.

"Tess?" Mark extended a hand and touched her shoulder.

She shrugged his hand away. "I need a minute." Making a beeline for the outside porch, she exited and let the door slam behind her.

Outside the Raven's cottage, she shivered as the full horror of her predicament cracked open. Constants like black and white muddled into dull gray, but glimmers of clarity formed as she breathed in the frosty air. The Raven revealed a far-fetched world, but every puzzle piece clicked, and she wouldn't rest until she rescued David and preserved Kyle's code. She resolved to protect his legacy and would not tolerate terrorists exploiting Kyle's work to fund violence.

No stars shone above, and the night offered nothing but a shroud of darkness. As the ransom deadline crept closer every minute, she needed a plan—now. Trapped in this dark underworld, fact and fiction blurred together. She vowed to fight, and whatever it took, she'd protect Mark from further danger.

The cottage's front door opened, and Mark appeared. He pressed his hand firmly against the small of her back. "Hey. Are you okay?"

"No. This is all insane." Pulling at her hair, she howled a response between a shout and hysteria.

"Never a dull moment in the Highlands. Who knew taking leave from Ukraine would be so dangerous?" Mark rubbed her shoulders. "Uh, that was a joke. I know this is a disaster."

"You got that right." She stared at the dark sky, torn over how to respond. If danger befell him, she alone would own the guilt. The only way to guarantee his safety was to keep him far, far away from Crimson Hammer. "Mark. You should be safe with your family in Bergen, not fighting a terrorist cell."

He released a long sigh. "I can't lie. Getting kidnapped sucked. But don't forget, I want Yuri and Dmitry locked up, too. I need my nightmares to stop."

She stood close with her body against his side, generating a line of heat. Grateful for the darkness, she conjured words she didn't wish to speak. "We should

271

let the police handle this, and you should fly to Bergen in the morning." Silence hung heavy in the freezing air, and when he didn't respond, she wondered if he heard.

"Nice try."

"What do you mean?" Puzzled, she faced him.

Without speaking, he maneuvered her against his chest and wound his arms around her.

Taken by surprise, she tilted her face, and his mouth caught hers with a passion-fueled kiss. At that moment, she thirsted for him with a desire she couldn't imagine would ever be sated. Feeling alive and vibrant in the wintry air, she pressed her body taut against his. She unfastened the top few buttons of his coat and skated her fingertips across the base of his neck. Knowing time didn't allow for any romantic interlude, she ignored the wild ripples pulsing through her pelvis. Pausing her roaming hands, she slowed her choppy, uneven breath. "You didn't answer my question."

"You fought off an armed terrorist with your bare hands to save my life, Tess."

"That's not an answer. Anyone would've done the same." She curved away from his chest.

"Wrong. Most people would've had the common sense to run like hell, but not you." Chuckling, he touched her cheek. "Under your beautiful exterior, you're a fighter. No matter what danger you face, you never shy away for a second or flee. You fight and somehow survive."

How could he so easily articulate qualities she possessed when she couldn't understand them herself? Despite the military training her father passed down and her family urging her to pursue a career with the State Department, she not only flatly refused but rebelliously chose a corporate life. Years later, even Sophie recruited her at regular intervals. Unable to decipher her jumbled thoughts, she faced him. "What are you trying to tell me?"

"You're polite to offer me a convenient escape and dump this on the police. But be honest. You won't let David die or see your company destroyed without a fight, even if it means risking your life."

"Look, this is my vendetta, and I refuse to let you endanger yourself any further." The icy edge of the Highlands wind promised frost overnight, and she rubbed her arms while her teeth chattered. "More people will die, and I can't risk you being one of them."

He lifted her chin to meet his gaze. "When casualties flood a field hospital, you must make impossible choices. You triage. You treat the patients you can save first, then save as many lives as possible. Concentrate. If you triaged this crisis, how would you break it down?"

The fog lifted as she cleared her thoughts and identified the conflicting priorities. "Save David's life before the ransom deadline. Protect you from danger. Seek justice for Kyle and Riku's deaths. End this ordeal and make the truth known." Opening her eyes, she found Mark beaming.

"Stay in motion, and never doubt your strength." He kissed the top of her head and wound an arm around her shoulder. "You're shivering. Shall we go inside?"

The fresh clarity offered relief but fell short of solving her multiple dilemmas. "Fine, but promise me this, Mark Nygaard. You will not risk your life, and you will fly to Bergen tomorrow, far away from this mess."

"We'll talk later." He held the cottage door open

and gestured. "After you, *min kjære*."

Standing by the stone hearth, she rubbed her hands over the crackling fire, relishing the cottage's warm air. Kindling branches broke with satisfying snaps, and wood smoke permeated the air.

"You two all right? I've got some dinner." The Raven pointed to the coffee table, set with three dinner plates and glasses.

"I needed a break." Welcome warmth from the fire restored blood flow to Tess's tingling, chilled feet, but she craved more heat. "Raven, do you have any whiskey? I could use a not-so-wee dram."

A broad smile spread across the Raven's face. "Lass, I'm a Highlander. Ye might as well ask the sky if it has air. Back in a flash." A few seconds later, he emerged from the kitchen, carrying a tray of steaming cheese pizza in one hand and a giant bottle of scotch whiskey in the other and set them on the coffee table. "Help yourself. Best not to be hungry while tackling epic challenges. We'll plan how you two can escape this."

"Thank you." Grateful for the hot pizza, she smiled at his hospitality. The man who seemed so strange and imposing a couple hours ago was proving a helpful ally. "I'm curious how you met Kyle."

The Raven poured himself a whiskey before settling in his leather chair. "Imperial College, London, though I graduated a couple of years ahead. Kyle's talents were formidable from day one, though he preferred ethical hacking over anything even hinting at impropriety. Years later, he led an encryption chat room on the dark web. After I cracked his code-breaking challenge in the chat, he befriended me. In time, I deciphered the identity of the mysterious Druid: Kyle from Imperial."

"Did he contact you a year ago, before he died?"

"No, but dark web chatter suggested he stumbled into something nefarious. When he disappeared online, I suspected the worst."

With the help of twelve-year-old scotch whiskey, she recognized the fleeting nature of these hours. Tonight might be her only chance to learn about Kyle's last days. "You risked a lot to help us, especially given the deadly enemies we're fighting. Why?"

The Raven topped off his whiskey before answering. "Two reasons. I owed Kyle a debt of honor. Years ago, when I was young and reckless, I promised something I couldn't deliver. An informant in Afghanistan ratted me out, and I faced a slow, brutal death if caught. I got desperate. Kyle helped me crack a security code which saved fifteen US service members from an ambush in Kabul."

Mark whistled. "So, Kyle saved your life and fifteen others? That's amazing."

"Saving those soldiers was great, but I was sentenced to three years in prison for computer crime because I refused to reveal my colleagues' identities, including Kyle's. Prison's wretched, but it's worse than hell for gay men like me. After I served my time, I disappeared and went dark."

Reeling, Tess swore her heart skipped several beats as she unpacked the implications of the Raven's tale. During all those years with Kyle, she never suspected the risks he'd taken and how easily he could've landed in prison. *Her Kyle.* She felt duped.

"And the other reason?" Mark swallowed another

sip of whiskey.

"Kyle's like extended family. Our family's clans fought next to each other in the 1746 Battle of Culloden. Enough of our men survived to carry on the clan." Fingering the rim of his whiskey glass, the Raven beamed.

"What?" She widened her gaze. "His family never mentioned any ancestors so far back in history."

"We kept it a secret so no one could ever link us. One day, Kyle quoted: *Our blood is still our fathers', and ours the valour of their hearts.* I recognized it from the memorial. Jacobite politics aside, the Highlanders fought at Culloden to protest the English effort to erase our culture, like banning the Gaelic language and prohibiting all our traditions, like tartans." His features darkened.

Mark leaned forward with his elbows on his knees. "There's a huge gulf between Culloden and computer hacking. What's the connection?"

"Kyle and I made a pact to protect innocent people from tyrannical governments and discrimination like the Highlanders experienced. Kyle preferred to play defense with encryption technology. After prison, I stayed underground and played offense. I unleashed my anger on the worst criminals—terror groups perpetrating ethnic cleansing, known enemies of democracy—and cut off their funding."

"All those years, Kyle helped organize these attacks?" Tess gripped the edge of the leather couch until her knuckles drained white and caught the Raven's conspiratorial smile.

"Lass, Kyle masterminded our first mission. After September 11, while the war on terror raged, he wanted to fight terrorism with computers. At first, he ensured our attacks destroyed only enemy assets and left other infrastructure untouched. Later, he undertook more aggressive cyberattacks and riskier missions with me."

"Risks like Crimson Hammer." The whiskey wasn't calming her nerves fast enough, and she quickly poured another dram.

"Exactly." The Raven frowned and set his glass on the mahogany table. "Kyle left a tremendous, albeit secret, charitable legacy. After diverting terrorist money to offshore accounts, we invested the proceeds and made anonymous donations to humanitarian charities worldwide."

"A modern-day, digital Robin Hood." Mark flashed a lopsided smile. "How much money have you redirected since you started?"

The Raven leaned back in the lounger and crossed one foot over his knee. "One point three billion in US dollars, as of last week."

Eyes wide open, Mark sucked in a breath. "*Billion?* Incredible. I'm impressed."

"Doubt the authorities would agree, mate, but I find the poetic justice quite satisfying." The Raven splayed his fingers flat on his chest and sighed. "Nothing tops the sweet, sweet reward of bankrupting evildoers."

Too overwhelmed to speak, Tess tumbled down the rabbit hole into the strange, post-apocalyptic cyber world. The fall terminated abruptly, ending in a metaphorical thud. No mad hatters or tea parties, but instead, a shadowy landscape of hackers, terrorists, and money launderers. Without the Raven's loyalty, Kyle might have spent three years in prison, instead of innovating the security software industry's future. Any degree of insanity seemed feasible to Tess, including her growing belief in the Raven's bizarre tale and the violent web which ensnared them. What other secrets had Kyle withheld? How far into the darkness did he travel? Silence fell over the group.

Mark spoke up from the couch. "Raven, you've carried an enormous burden, but I'll never reveal your secret."

"Thank you. After so many years, I'm relieved to tell someone, but my survival depends upon remaining in the shadows."

Tess tore herself away from her thoughts. "I swear on my life." Rejoining the discussion, she was still processing multiple revelations simultaneously. The huge whiskey bottle beckoned, and she poured another glass, swallowing a hearty sip to steady herself. *Everyone has secrets. Everyone.* She admired Kyle's humanitarian ambitions but resented him for deceiving her for years. Kyle had lived a double life, yet this stranger had known about his duplicity all along. Now, a year after Kyle's death, she faced a mountain of unexpected doubts.

From the couch, Mark stretched forward and touched her on the shoulder. "Are you holding up all right?"

"I appreciate Kyle's noble intentions, but his mission got him killed." She remained troubled by the flurry of questions raised tonight, but despite the Raven's hair-raising tale, she believed he spoke the truth. Kyle had abhorred violence and insisted upon integrity without exception. His seeming telepathic ability to predict hacker behavior no longer mystified her, but she fought ambivalence over how he'd honed his talents.

"Kyle made a huge sacrifice, and that's hard to accept." Mark reached for the whiskey bottle.

"A sacrifice I must avenge." She stared at the Raven's plaid carpet until it blurred into crisscrossing lines of color, then raised her head.

Wiping his hands clean, the Raven fetched a laptop from the massive desk and sat across from them. "Let's get on with it."

Tess rose and stepped closer to the desk. "We have less than twenty-four hours to save David's life, so here's the plan. We invent a catastrophic virus that unleashes, undetectable, during the download. At the ransom handoff, we pretend to hand over Kyle's source code and make them think it's the Rapadon key. Raven, got anything in your arsenal I can use tomorrow?"

Tapping his fingers together, he nodded. "I built a couple of options for emergencies that will destroy their network in minutes. Recovery will take them weeks to months, which gives law enforcement loads of time to find and prosecute them. Pure digital combat. No violence."

"Perfect." Back straightened, she focused on logistics. "Talk me through this so I can coach Declan on what he needs to do with it. Don't leave anything out."

"The code package I built requires updating, which I'll do tonight. After I finish, I'll give you a data drive with what appears to be the Rapadon sequence but weaponized. Hand it off to Crimson Hammer, and you're done."

The plan was great, except for one huge, gaping

hole. "Wait. They'll retaliate and fight back, and I don't want to play whack-a-mole." Frustration burned in her throat.

"Find out which bank they want, along with who and what generated the root key. Ask Declan to track it down. You must identify their target before you can protect it, and when you find the specific number, think hard about how you'll use it," the Raven cautioned.

"How long do you need?" She had hours, not days, and every minute counted.

"Overnight. I'll meet you tomorrow morning with the updated virus. Kyle said you can trust Declan, but please don't reveal my identity or how you acquired this. I must stay dark."

"Agreed." She still fretted over a nagging question. "Why didn't Kyle trust David? I mean, he's the one we're risking our lives to save."

The Raven shrugged. "No idea. He never expressed concerns about David."

What if Kyle meant she could trust Declan, instead of implicating she *shouldn't* believe anyone else? Too many details clamored for her attention now, so she made a mental note to revisit them later. "It's rather late to guess what Kyle intended, and we need to charge forward."

"I'll be with you the whole time." Mark squeezed her hand.

She opened her mouth to say he couldn't be there because he'd be flying to Bergen but opted to delay that discussion until they returned to the hotel. "All right, we've got a strategy. Let's do it." Relieved to have a plan in place, she breathed a little easier. "Whenever Kyle faced an all-nighter, he'd say it was a brilliant night to code. May the coding gods be with you tonight, Raven." Rubbing his hands together, he grinned with the eagerness of a child entering an amusement park.

"Lucky for me, they often accompany me. I'll drive you back now so I can begin. Mark, could you please give us a moment?"

"Sure, no worries." Mark got to his feet and slipped on his coat. Stepping outside, he closed the door quietly behind him.

Leaning with one hand against the door frame, the Raven began. "You're having doubts about Kyle."

Reluctant to admit her doubts, she folded her lips together while forming a diplomatic response. "No matter how much we love someone, we're never privy to all of a person's secrets."

"True, but don't waste a single moment doubting Kyle. I swear on my clan's grave, he loved you beyond measure." The Raven held a hand over his heart.

Surprised by his show of emotion, Tess lowered her guard and listened.

The Raven clasped his hands. "Anything he kept hidden, he did so to protect your life. At great risk to himself, he prevented many terrorist attacks and saved countless people. Even if he couldn't tell you everything, I hope you'll remember him as a hero."

She appreciated the Raven's compassion and welled with tears as she recalled Kyle strolling on the beach years ago, filled with life, promise, and joy, as well as the indefatigable desire to protect the innocent. She grasped for a new form of calm rooted in acceptance. "A hero whose charitable deeds shall remain secret, forever."

"But never forgotten."

She left the cottage armed with some hard-won peace assuaging her grief, but also with an urgent compulsion to avenge Kyle's death. Uncertain how she'd retaliate, the one thing she knew for sure was the hour of truth drew near, and she was ready to fight.

Chapter Eighteen

Late Nights

Arriving back at their Inverness hotel after midnight, Tess tossed her coat into a chair and sank onto the bed. Depleted after so many blindsiding revelations, she pointed to the mahogany wood table graced with three crystal carafes of liquor. "What a welcome sight after this trying day. Nightcap?"

"Yes." Mark pulled off his socks and shoes, then shuffled over to the drink table. He poured two glasses of whiskey and handed her one.

In the guest room next door, a child wailed about not wanting to go to sleep.

She exchanged an annoyed glance with Mark and switched on the radio next to the bed, hoping a Beethoven symphony might drown out the commotion.

After Mark downed one shot, he got up and poured another. With slumped shoulders, he frowned. "I own my decision to follow you on this adventure, but the Raven's story floored me. Wow."

"The Raven threw us a crazy twist, but I can't begin to unpack it while the clock's ticking for David. We'll pick up the USB drive from the Raven, fly back to London, and prepare Declan for the handoff."

Mark padded over to the room's window, which overlooked the snake-like curves of the River Ness, dim under the night sky. Standing rod-straight, he set his whiskey glass on the windowsill and stared at the water. He stretched his arms and cracked his back.

She crossed the room and slid an arm under the back of his T-shirt, her palm warm against his bare skin. The room grew quiet, and she sensed an anxious lump rising in her throat. The wall radiator clanked on with a rumble. "What is it?"

Shoulders hunched and head bowed over the windowsill, he hesitated before turning to face her. "I don't want to say this."

"Then I will. We're in a scary, unthinkable situation. Winston Churchill said if you're going through hell, keep going. I must keep going, but you don't have to." She could no longer avoid telling him he needed to go to Bergen. Despite how much she desired him, she refused to risk exposing him to more danger.

He picked up his whiskey glass but set it down without taking a drink. "What do you mean?"

"You need to take the first flight to Norway tomorrow. Fighting Crimson Hammer to save David is my problem, not yours. I won't let you risk your life over this." Standing tall, she projected authority into her voice, and paused mid-breath to await his response.

"The police need to run the ransom meeting, but they should minimize Declan's role, and you should avoid the handoff. Don't go." In the room's dim light, he stepped away from the window and leaned a shoulder against one of the bedposts.

"I can't let Declan face this alone. He's determined but also an anxious mess when it comes to confrontation." Feet glued to the floor, she wavered, feeling like the day's heaviness might topple her.

"True, but that isn't the point. I'm not taking some safe off-ramp to Bergen. Whether you like it or not, I'm staying with you until this crisis is over." Mark leaned his head back and blew out a noisy breath. "The reality is you're not done grieving Kyle, and I can't compete with a ghost. At least, not tonight."

Forced to face an uncomfortable observation she wished to deny, she weathered the wave of disappointment. Protecting Mark's safety was critical, but confronting her conflicted grief was beyond her capacity now. "Damn it, it's not a competition. Kyle's dead, and he's not coming back. You think I don't realize that?" She couldn't contain her frustration. The radiator in the hotel room clanked, and the stuffy, stale air became stifling.

"I'm sorry. I shouldn't have said that. Look, you can't rush your grief, Tess. Doesn't work. You learned a lot tonight and need to process it." Mark raised a hand to his chin and met her gaze. "Take the time you need."

"I don't understand what you want from me." She crossed her arms. While appreciating his compassion, she sensed an invisible wall of tension separating them and couldn't break through the barrier. One second, she longed to kiss every inch of his body and master its peaks and valleys. Then, moments later, she missed Kyle with such intensity her heart ached.

"We should get some sleep." He gave her a quick hug and stepped away.

"You're right." Blinking, she stood vexed by a hundred conflicting feelings. Too exhausted to continue, she knew each minute dragged them closer to the ransom deadline. Relieved the noise from the neighboring room quieted, she turned off the radio and changed into a T-shirt. Once in bed, she laid flat, grateful Mark was beside her, even though mere proximity didn't offer the specific comfort she desired. Surrendering to fatigue, she lowered her eyelids and inhaled his sandalwood scent as tonic for her turmoil.

Hours later, deep in the night, a child's scream shattered the elegant inn's peaceful silence.

Mark bolted upright and his breaths came in shallow, rapid gasps. He flicked on a light and shook the bed as he leapt to his feet.

"What's going on?" Wide-awake from the harsh light and motion, Tess spied him pulling on his jeans and a T-shirt.

"Incoming wounded. We've got casualties." He headed for the door.

Alarmed, Tess stumbled to her feet. She slipped on a hotel bathrobe and grabbed the room key on her way out the door to find him. Wobbling on her crutches, she stepped into the empty hallway and checked both ways when she heard the child cry again, with lungs at full strength. Following the sound of the hysterical cries to the guest room around the corner, she saw Mark barefoot, knocking on the door.

A bedraggled man in his thirties wearing red-plaid pajamas appeared at the door and squinted at Mark.

"A boy screamed—is he injured? I'm a doctor." Mark's words flowed in a rush, and he peered around each side of the man.

The boy's father glared at Mark and backed several inches away from the door. "Our son had a nightmare, and we apologize for disturbing you."

"You're certain he's all right? He's hysterical. I

can take him to my hospital." Mark stepped forward.

Tess hurried to Mark's side and noted the anxious lines creasing his forehead. Peeking into the room, she spotted a young boy in shark pajamas clutching a fuzzy teddy bear while sucking his thumb. The boy's mother made soothing *shush* sounds and rubbed his head, trying to comfort him. Nothing appeared awry.

"Hospital? No, thank you." The man stepped backwards. "I assure you our son will be fine. Good night." Without further conversation, the man turned and closed the door.

Tess watched as Mark's expression grew baffled, and he traced the numbers on the door with his fingertips, as if trying to commit them to memory. Realizing Mark was in a trance and might not recognize her, she exercised care not to startle him. "Mark, everything's fine. Let's go back to bed now." She placed a hand on his bare arm and gently steered him through the empty hallway with slow, deliberate steps.

He nodded but checked over his shoulder twice before rounding the corner.

She noticed him staring at his scarred left hand like a problem needing a solution and his skin had paled from its usual golden glow. Once back in their room, she touched his forehead and found it damp and clammy. She guided him to the bed and handed him a bottle of water from the minibar. "Drink this."

After draining the bottle, he squinted at his hands, then scanned each wall of the room. "This isn't the hospital, is it?"

She shook her head. "What's going on? Whatever you need, Mark, I'm here for you." Aching from seeing his misery, she softly pressed a palm to his cheek.

"What has unsettled you? A nightmare?"

"Shit. Not a nightmare. A memory. An awful one." He gasped and lifted a fist to cover his mouth.

"Sit here, and let's talk it through." She patted the bed with a hand and wrapped a blanket around his shoulders. Several pieces clicked together in Tess's mind, and she caressed his shoulder. "The boy crying tonight triggered you."

"Oh, God. I remember the hospital attack." A sob escaped him, and he bent forward over his knees. "I couldn't save the boy." He shoved his face into his trembling hands, and tears flowed down his cheeks.

She wrapped an arm around his shoulders and cradled him tight against her chest. With one hand, she massaged his back with slow, gentle strokes, hoping to whisk away his distress. She smoothed his ruffled blond hair and spoke soothingly. "*Shh*. You're safe here, so let it all out. I've got you."

He rubbed his fingertips in circles against his forehead. "Seven-year-old boy hit by a land mine. I'd just scrubbed in to save his arm from amputation. When the shelling started, the walls collapsed, and a hundred shards of white-hot burning glass stabbed my hand. Couldn't breathe. The acrid air scorched my nose, and grit and rubble filled my mouth, like eating sand. The shockwave blasted the boy from the table, and a metal beam fell, crushing his torso."

"I'm so sorry." As she listened to Mark's account, she held her own tears back and grasped his uninjured hand.

"My surgical team screamed at me to evacuate, but I crawled through the debris to dig the boy out. When I reached him, part of his rib cage had caved in, and I started compressions to resuscitate him. Couldn't revive him. Everything went black, and I woke up on a medivac chopper. He was my patient, in my O.R., and I failed him. I couldn't protect my wife and son from dying, and I couldn't save this boy, either." He stared at the wall and clenched his hands.

"Mark. You did everything you could, given you were injured, too. Trauma takes time to heal. You can't blame yourself."

"I'm fine during the day, but after dark, these night terrors torment me. I keep waking up lost. My therapist insists remembering the hospital attack is a major step in my recovery. So, I suppose this is progress. Painful progress." He stood and stretched both arms over his head, then paced around the room, pausing to inspect the cheery *Welcome to the Highlands* needlepoint hanging on the wall next to the door. Staring at the box-beamed ceiling, he moaned. "Christ, I'm in Scotland."

"Yes, but we're safe, and it's a lovely hotel. Besides, they promised us scones in the morning." Hot, fresh-baked pastries might not assuage his pain, but she couldn't think of anything else uplifting.

"Breakfast. Now there's a reason to live." Part laughing but part groaning, he came back to bed and drifted off a few minutes later.

Although a glimmer of Mark's usual spirit returned, Tess worried about the seriousness of his lapses. The last thing she expected from Cedarcliff was the prospect of a relationship. She recognized her growing feelings for Mark but feared making herself vulnerable. *What if she lost him, too?*

****

Morning arrived, along with the unwelcome reality

289

Tess dreaded. The sun struggled to pierce through the clouds and light the boggy moor during their drive to Culloden. The car filled with the buttery scent of fresh-baked scones from the hotel's coffee bar, the homey smell incongruous with the lethal risks she was contemplating. They sat gazing out over the deserted battlefield when the Raven drove up in his tiny black hatchback, rolled down his window, and gestured to them.

"Follow me to the cottage." Attesting to his sleep deprivation, dark circles lined the Raven's red-rimmed, bloodshot eyes.

Mark signaled okay with his upraised thumb from the rental car and exited the parking lot to follow the Raven. Inside the car, they remained quiet, keeping pace with the Raven's hatchback along the twisting roads east of Inverness. Mark's phone screen lit and buzzed on the console separating their seats.

Out of the corner of one eye, she snuck a peek and groaned inwardly. The redhead again, Elena Rabinowitz. Ugh. Why did this woman ring Mark every day? She buried her annoyance and focused on what they needed to accomplish this morning. "Hey, your phone."

Oblivious to the ringing, he blinked several times. Glancing at his mobile, he hit *Decline* and continued driving. "Not safe to talk and drive."

The seed of doubt lingering in her mind sprouted another leaf. *Who was she?* As they approached the Raven's cottage, the skies opened and dumped rain along with punishing winds.

The moment they arrived, the Highlander helped Tess up the steps and ushered them to his warm living room.

Mark wandered to the fireplace, picked up a poker, and stoked the fire, which had reduced to embers overnight.

Inside the cottage, she glimpsed the oil painting of the Culloden Battle above the fireplace. Today, the battle scene sent new chills through her spine. The outcome of tonight's ransom handoff was anyone's guess, and she grew more unsettled every hour. She handed the Raven a pastry bag filled with scones. "We brought you breakfast."

"Ah, lovely. Thank you." The Raven clapped his hands together. "Long night, but I wrote the code you need."

"Great. This could save David's life or at least buy us time." The ball of tension inhabiting her shoulders lightened several degrees. The faint scent of wood smoke lingered in the room.

The Raven sipped from his yellow coffee cup, embellished with a happy face emoticon. "I hope the handoff goes without a hitch. Don't want anyone getting hurt."

The cup's smiley face reflected the opposite of her mood. "We can't risk your identity being discovered. I want you to remain safe." Not wishing to envision the dangers which could befall him, she didn't elaborate.

"My network is the new Resistance, and I accepted the risks long ago." He picked up the small plastic case with a red label from his desk and placed it in her palm. "Here."

"Talk me through this." The USB drive appeared innocuous, but she handled it like a bomb which could explode any moment. The destructive power contained within the featherweight case rattled her nerves.

"This is Kyle's original Firefly 1.0 code, a debug version containing developer comments and the Rapadon branch Kyle wrote, altered to unleash the virus I created." The Raven opened the pastry bag and selected a blueberry scone.

"Declan will insist on inspecting the code. Can he open this safely?" Tess studied the container.

"No. I created a second thumb drive with placeholder code he can review to learn how I structured the attack. However, the kill switch is enabled so it doesn't execute on his machine." He set the scone on the desk and handed her another USB drive, this one with a green label. "The red one goes to Crimson Hammer, and the green goes to Declan."

"Won't they want to confirm the program works before releasing David? How will they validate the code's legit?" Mark gestured at the drives.

"Couple of things. They won't discover the code is malicious for at least three hours, or maybe longer, depending on network conditions. The moment they open it, the virus spreads, and they'll be quietly under siege. You'll be far away before they notice."

"And the money?" She doubted Yuri and his gunmen would pardon a lack of payment.

"Easy. Don't pay it. The police need to plan for this, so David's not at risk." The Raven pinched the skin at his throat.

"But what if they kill him because we didn't pay the ransom?" Not paying the ransom introduced another serious risk she hadn't considered.

"If you expect a firestorm, you'd better secure the police's help in advance. No one can guarantee David's safety, and I don't deal with guns. Sorry." Fidgeting with his hands, the Raven avoided making eye contact.

"I'll give everything I've got tonight, but I want this to be over." As the reality of the risks sank in, she resented the impossible stakes.

"Chin up, lass. I have faith in you. You're fighting for justice, and your courage has saved you multiple times." The Raven took another sip of coffee. "Besides, Declan goes to the handoff, not you."

"Right—once you give Declan the drive, law enforcement will do the rest." Mark folded his arms and faced Tess.

"Wrong. I'm not leaving Declan alone, holding the bag. Period." Tess shot them both a warning glance.

Grimacing, Mark leapt to his feet. "You are *not* facing Crimson Hammer—"

"We'll talk later." Tess cut him off and sat fuming on the couch.

With a shadow of a smile on his lips, the Raven cocked his head to one side. "You two might not agree on everything, but you complement each other well. Protect the connection you have together. Such a precious gift is rare."

Indeed. Surprised by the comment, Tess jolted upright and glanced at Mark. Given how much uncertainty loomed, she appreciated the Raven's omniscient support but also felt her nascent feelings exposed. By second nature, she shielded her emotions, but the lifelong habit inhibited her from admitting her feelings, most of all to herself. Straightening her back, she refocused on the mission. "What happens next?"

"Text me tonight's time and location using the mobile number you used before, and I'll keep Crimson

Hammer's network activity under surveillance. They'll leave you and your company alone from now on." The Raven set his mug on the desk. "After tonight, you won't be able to contact me."

Nodding her understanding, she wished she could offer more than gratitude for his help. "Thank you for everything and for sharing your secret. Learning the truth helps, despite the questions it raises." The Raven had offered her an unexpected portal into Kyle's history. While she wished to learn more about Kyle's missions, no time remained. The portal to his secret life was shutting, and she'd never see the Raven again.

Mark stood to shake the Raven's hand and gave him a pat on the shoulder. "Thanks for helping us get through this. Stay safe and be well. Tess, I'll go start the car."

Left alone in the cottage with the Raven, she slipped on her coat and stood to leave.

The Raven leaned against the wood frame of his front door. "I wish you and Kingsley Tech luck. Kyle will live on in our memories and through our actions."

His wistful tone and sad expression touched her, but she detected other emotions lingering under the surface, like a revelation beyond her grasp. "You were quite fond of Kyle."

"The Druid proved to be a loyal friend, which is the best kind. A formidable online chess opponent, too, impossible to defeat." Smiling at the memory, the Raven's expression softened with vulnerability, uncovering a hidden layer of emotion.

For an ephemeral moment, she glimpsed subtle light in his expression and a quick lowering of his eyelids, revealing a longing far beyond intellectual kinship. When she recognized the romantic roots and intensity of his affection, she felt stunned. The Raven's unspoken yearning reflected a wish to travel a journey, one made impossible due to death and mismatched sexual orientation. Or did Kyle hold yet another secret? In the tangled space of their shared loss, she ventured to learn more. "Did you ever meet him in person?"

His face brightened a few shades, and color dotted his cheeks. "A couple of times. We played chess at a dodgy pub in Newcastle before I was sentenced to prison. Of course, our life paths would never intersect, not in that way, but I loved him." Melancholy crossed his gaze.

Her bloodstream surged several degrees warmer. She absorbed his unexpected admission in an instant, surprised neither jealousy nor shock overtook her. "He was my one in seven billion, and I swear to you, I'll find justice for him."

"Lots of danger awaits you, so stay tough, and never forget, you're a survivor." He reached out and patted her arm with a warm smile.

She bowed her head a moment before answering. "I will. Be safe, Raven."

"Kyle would approve, you know." He escorted her to the foyer and poised his hand on the polished iron doorknob.

"Sorry?" She stopped in her tracks to face him.

"Mark. You don't realize it yet, but he'll never fail you. Best of luck to ye, lass."

Tess swallowed as a thousand thoughts swirled through her mind like a windstorm. Aside from chasing Crimson Hammer and saving David's life, a larger question loomed. If she survived tonight, she might have a future, and any future she imagined included Mark. But love meant risking her heart again, which scared her even more than fighting Crimson Hammer.

When she said goodbye, she memorized the Raven's enigmatic face, regretting their paths would not cross in the future.

Outside, Mark waited in the car and hopped out to open her door.

With care, she descended the stone steps in the drenching rain and slid into the passenger seat. The sedan's engine purred, and sleet slapped against the windshield as the wipers whizzed back and forth at breakneck speed. She slipped a hand into her trench coat pocket to confirm the two USB thumb drives were there.

Mark drove down the rough, potholed road with his hands tight on the wheel. "He's not the burly criminal I expected, and we're lucky he wanted to help us. He's insightful."

"Very." Vertebra by vertebra, she relaxed her back against the heated leather seat, grateful for the safety the car offered from the elements. Unsure what conclusions to draw from the Raven's observations, she filled her lungs and stretched her legs, garnering her strength for the next phase of their journey. Gray fog threatened to swallow the puddle-laden moor of Culloden's battlefield in its entirety, obscuring it from sight.

Mulling over the Raven's closing words, she placed a hand on Mark's left knee. "Thank you for being with me now."

In return, Mark squeezed her hand and smiled.

His   warmth   soothed   her   and   eased   the

awkwardness of last night's events, but his scarred hand underscored how much danger they faced ahead, with no promise of safety.

On the flight back to London, she felt unnerved as her apprehension about the ransom handoff escalated. Despite the early hour, she swallowed two vodka tonics in quick succession to ward off her unease.

In the airplane seat beside her, Mark napped, and when his hand draped open across her lap, she interwove their fingers together. The multiple Elena phone calls irritated her. Years had passed since she experienced jealousy like this. Gazing at Mark's chiseled cheekbones and the sensuous curve of his shoulder, one thing became clear. She had no desire to share him with the mysterious redhead, or anyone else.

The vodka tingled in her throat and tangled her thoughts, and the mild buzz helped numb her anxiety. Recent memories of Mark's bare skin against hers juxtaposed with visions of Kyle so vividly, she swore he had returned from the afterlife, alive again. But every time, the images vanished, shrinking from the edges before they curled inward like a burning photograph dissolving into ash.

Staring out the window, she contemplated the impermanence of everything. She worried for David's life and Declan's safety at the handoff and realized nothing guaranteed her survival, or Mark's. Shivering, she prayed the day didn't end in more death.

Chapter Nineteen

Scheming in the Crypt

As the plane made its final descent into London, Tess tensed, her blood pressure spiking in parallel measure with her dread. Kyle and Riku were gone. And now, with David kidnapped, everyone was in danger from Crimson Hammer. Somehow, she must find an end to this chaos, but how? The walls of the plane shrank around her, trapping her, and she wanted to bust out into the open air. The crush of tonight's deadline weighed on her shoulders like an anvil that could flatten her at any moment. The second the plane's wheels touched the tarmac, she texted Declan.

—*Just landed @ London City.*—

—*You safe, or should I summon the cavalry?*—

—*Let's sync up, fast. Where?*—

—*In 30 minutes @ The Crypt Café, Trafalgar Square.*—

—*Crypt, like tomb?*—

—*Right. Hell's broken loose. Shattered, need help.*—

—*On our way. Bring a clean laptop.*—

—*I always do.*—

Outside the airport, she pocketed her phone and popped more painkillers while waiting for Mark to hail a cab. The taxi ride passed like a blur. Unhindered by traffic, the cab sped west, passed through Canary Wharf, then approached Trafalgar Square, where it stopped amidst the bustle of tourists outside St. Martins-in-the-Fields Church. She followed Mark down a paved path to the café, which was hidden on a side street and burrowed under an old church crypt.

Toting their bags on his shoulder, Mark approached the entrance, wearing a crooked smile. "Next time you plan a techie meeting, please no creepy places filled with dead bodies. Shed your Goth darkness and come into the light. Reality is twisted enough."

"In Declan's defense, this *is* a café." Concerned by Declan's choice of the somber setting, she feared this crisis could throw him into a pit of anxiety so deep he'd never climb out. "At least you can't say travel with me is boring."

"Never." Mark held the door open.

Across the empty crypt, Declan sat half-hidden under a brick arch far from the cashier's station where a lone barista perched and texted on her phone. He raised an arm and pointed at the three coffee cups which stood in a neat line on the table.

Tess waved as she approached and eased herself into a chair across from Declan. Glimpsing an engraved inscription on the ground, she realized the entire floor beneath them consisted of rows of tombs and shivered. "How're you holding up?"

Declan bent over the table and shook hands with Mark. "Dandy. This cock-up has left me like a barmy nutter rolling around in rubbish. I'm destined for the loony bin. You?"

"Splendid. Couldn't be better." She met him with an equal dose of sarcasm and noted his bloodshot eyes and pale cheeks. "So, why are we in a crypt?"

"I've been wondering that myself." Mark shifted in his chair and scanned the room.

"I figure I'll be dead soon enough, so I'm previewing real estate for the afterlife." Declan rubbed his eyes and yawned. "Pick a coffee and let's get on with it."

Noting three empty sugar packs beside his mug, she peered into Declan's cup. "Judging from your triple-shot macchiato, you're gonna crash hard."

"Nope, I'm wired." Jaw clenched tight, he whipped out a silver flask from his coat pocket and dumped a liberal shot of Irish whiskey into his coffee.

Shocked to see him day drinking, she grabbed Declan's wrist. "Since when did you start carrying a flask?" Recalling her recent infusion of vodka tonics on the plane, she silenced herself, deciding it best not to cast stones when living in a glass house.

"Since two o'clock this morning, when the guy holding David hostage rang me. Goes by the moniker The Hornet." Declan held a sugar packet and propelled it across the table with a fingertip.

About to take a sip, Mark set his caffe latte down. "The *what*?"

"The Hornet. They want Rapadon, but the wankers can't grok possessing the code itself won't help. Weird. They need the encryption root key for specific banks to access them. I asked which bank they want. No answer. Either they're trapping us, or the arseholes are woefully misinformed." Declan propped an elbow on the table and leaned his chin in one hand.

She perceived something ominous lurking nearby, ready to surface. Growing apprehensive, she felt her pulse pounding in her forehead. "What else?"

Declan shook his head and covered his face with his hands.

Mark shot her a questioning glance.

"Tell me." At close range, she detected prominent dark shadows buffering the puffy bags under Declan's eyes when he lifted his head and twisted his mouth as if he tasted something foul. "What happened?"

"They're torturing David. The police couldn't trace the call, so they got jack all. No leads, and we only have until midnight." Declan stared at the table and fingered his coffee cup.

"Goddamn monsters." Tasting bile creeping up her throat, she resisted the nightmarish gore hijacking her imagination. Despite the cool stone walls lining the crypt's interior, she unbuttoned her jacket and wiped away the sudden film of sweat from the back of her neck. Seeing the misery darkening Declan's expression, she also feared the worst.

"He might not survive." Declan slouched in his chair with his arms limp by his side. Tilting his head, he gazed at the crypt's ceiling, then made the sign of the cross.

"I know." She attempted to eradicate the gruesome images flashing in her mind and stay present. Lips shut in a tight line, she held herself together, barely.

"This is hard, you two, but don't waste energy catastrophizing the worst possible scenario. We have time to save David." Mark leaned forward and alternated his gaze between Declan and Tess.

Tess took a deep breath and focused her thoughts. "Declan, I need to swear you to secrecy about what I'm going to tell you."

"You have my word." Declan pressed a palm to his heart.

"I traveled to Scotland because Kyle needed me to go. Two days ago, I received a letter he wrote the week he died. I'm afraid I have brutal news." She steeled herself before continuing. "A terror group named Crimson Hammer murdered Kyle. Inspector Willis and I figured out Kyle's accident report was hacked at Met Police headquarters." Holding her breath, she winced watching Declan's expression waver between grief and fury. Like a watercolor painting that'd been ruined by rain, his face paled to a gritty white.

Declan gripped the side of the table to steady himself, then suddenly slammed a fist on the café table. "Christ. Goddamn bastards. To think some brute killed him on purpose. *Fuck*."

"The truth broke me, too." She placed a hand on top of his. "Now, I need to share important information, but I cannot tell you how or where I acquired it."

"Anything to dig us out of this hellhole." Declan waved a hand.

"Rapadon exists, but not how you think." She cast a quick glance at Mark, who was managing to stay out of the fray.

"Not possible. I reviewed every goddamn line of code our company has ever written, like five fucking times." Arms crossed, Declan scowled.

"You couldn't find it because it was a riddle, not a coding problem. Rapadon is an anagram of Pandora. Kyle wanted to punish Crimson Hammer for hacking Firefly, the metaphorical Pandora's Box. He made them think Rapadon is a key, and they're attacking Kingsley Tech because they can't crack it."

"Bloody hell. I was so fixated on the code I couldn't see other possibilities." Groaning, Declan pushed a palm against his forehead. "Who found the algorithm?"

Without answering, she pressed her lips tight together.

"You can't tell me. What else?" Declan pushed up his sleeves.

"We'll give them Firefly with a fake branch named Rapadon, which will unleash a virus and destroy their network." Folding her hands on the table, she caught Declan eyeing her like a raging criminal.

"Where the hell did you find this?" He narrowed his gaze, first at her, then Mark.

"Don't ask me." Tess pressed a hand against her temple.

"Did you steal this from the dark web? Who are you working with?"

"Damn it, O'Leary. I've been kidnapped, beaten, shot at, and I'm going to end this tonight." Hands clenched, she resisted lashing out and gritted her teeth instead.

"What if they retaliate? Are you working something illegal, with a competing terrorist cell?" Declan demanded.

"Are you *kidding*? I'm way beyond giving a shit about what's legal. Crimson Hammer are *terrorists*, and they're torturing David." She wanted to scream. "They won't call the bloody police to complain about being hacked."

"Fine, screw the law. But what if they strike back at us or Kingsley Tech? Have you considered the risks?" Declan raised an eyebrow.

"If their network is toast, they can't fight back." She glared and leaned away from the table, eyeing him carefully. An involuntary spasm appeared to ripple through his body.

"What about the ransom?" He gawked while his chin shook almost imperceptibly.

"We don't pay it. The police advised against paying because acquiescence breeds more terrorism." Tess leaned back and went silent.

"You'll need to coordinate with the police, though, so they're prepared to handle the terrorist's response to not getting the cash," Mark said. "Frankly, I don't think any of us should go anywhere near this handoff."

She dug into her pocket, then displayed the two USB drives in her palm. "Declan, the red one is for tonight's handoff. Don't open it, period. The green one is yours and includes a sample of the virus structure you can load onto a clean machine to learn what the program will do. The kill switch is activated so it doesn't destroy your box."

Declan retrieved a second laptop from his backpack and powered it on. After taking a swig of his spiked triple espresso, he inserted the drive and began reading.

Tess flattened her palms on the table and chewed her lip, waiting as he reviewed the files.

"These algorithms are crazy. Cracking unbelievable. Firefly is there, but with a new dimension layered on top. It's elegant, the way Kyle coded, but its execution is malevolent." Declan scanned screenfuls of code, one after the other. "Kyle's programming talent was legendary, but this is absolute genius. Wicked, but genius." He dropped his hands, and wrinkles spread across his forehead. "Tess, this code's not just dangerous. It's a weapon. Who wrote it?"

"I can't reveal their identity." Tess teetered on the tightrope between revealing enough to satisfy Declan, while keeping the Raven's role secret.

"This is the type of deep web stuff rogue governments harbor. Where the hell did you go in Scotland?" Declan burst out and gripped the table.

"I can't say more." Refusing to incriminate the Raven, Tess remained firm in her resolve.

"Crap. What's next?" Jutting out his jaw, Declan tapped the tabletop repeatedly.

"Take the red drive to the handoff. It'll save David." She folded her hands in her lap.

Mark positioned himself between Tess and Declan. "Correction. Give the red drive to the police, who will run the handoff. Not you."

Leaning his chair back against the crypt's wall, Declan appeared deep in concentration but formed a devilish smile. "What you've shown me is incredible, but I can improve it."

"Bring it, O'Leary. These bastards killed Kyle, so don't hold back. Go nuclear." Relieved Declan was getting onboard with the plan, Tess exhaled.

"Obliterating their network is fantastic, but it doesn't catch the perpetrators. Cut off the monster's head, and the damn thing grows another." He tapped a finger against his temple.

"What's your plan, Declan?" Mark drained the rest of his coffee with one swallow and set the cup down.

"We need the geographical location of every hacker, so we can send the crooks to prison."

"Great, but how?" Tess breathed easier as Declan

perked up with more energy and his weary expression lightened.

"I'll add an algorithm to the virus which sends the IP address and GPS coordinates of every computer on their network straight to the British authorities. The silent signal details their allegiance to Crimson Hammer." Declan downed the rest of his coffee. "We anonymously gift the police this gold mine of data, and they can prosecute these wankers right into the clink."

"Brilliant. You'll catch them in the act." Mark gave him a broad grin.

"O'Leary, you surprise me. Fantastic plan—do it." For the first time all day, Tess smiled.

"Any way we can screw these maggots. Thanks for the virus. Without it ready to go, we'd be hosed." He crossed his arms and shook out his legs. "But we've got other problems."

She slumped her shoulders, realizing what she almost forgot. "Damn it. The encryption root key. We must determine which bank they want to match with the proper access code. Without it, they can't proceed."

"Which means you both remain in danger. Not acceptable." Mark rested his elbows on the table.

"A year ago, we deployed our software suite with the last version of Firefly for several of our corporate banking clients. Given what the police found, those banks are probable targets for money laundering." Declan's voice had calmed.

"We need those bank names and any ties they have with Belarus or Russia. Check everything in Eastern Europe." Tess jotted a note on a napkin.

"I'll search now." Declan focused back on his screen.

"We also have a window of time to escape to safety. The virus this unleashes will be undetectable for at least three hours." She appreciated the Raven's work built in a safety window.

"Yeah, whatever. The last thing I'm gonna to do is wait and find out." He scowled over his laptop. "Okay, we've got three possibilities: Polski Bank Federalny and Pierwszy Narodowy Bank, two of Poland's largest banks, and Sverbank, Russia's largest one. No deployments in Belarus, but I'll investigate these three and examine your mystery disk."

"What are the police teams planning?" Mark turned to Declan.

"They're supervising the handoff tonight, but I don't have specifics yet. We damn well better find David alive."

"How many hours left?" Many details remained ambiguous, which bothered Tess. Nothing about the coming police operation felt buttoned up.

"Not enough. Midnight. I'll study this code until I receive the police's instructions." Declan continued typing on his laptop.

"Let's divide and conquer. Ask Kavita to help you from the network side. Mark and I will visit Archie Willis, the detective who's working Kyle's case, and figure out his plan for tonight." Still bothered by yesterday's argument with Declan, she aimed to smooth things over. "One more thing. I apologize for not telling you about Kyle sooner, but I couldn't hit you with crappy news the same day David disappeared."

After removing the flash drive and pocketing it, Declan closed the laptop and slid it into his backpack. "I understand. Can't say I wasn't pissed, but I forgive

307

you. I'm gutted, but you found the answer to save David's life, and now we can seek revenge for Kyle, too."

"Let's hope we find it. Keep us posted." She stood and gave his arm an encouraging squeeze. "You can do this."

Declan pecked her cheek, then leaned over to shake hands with Mark. "Thanks, mates. We need all the luck we can get."

Trafalgar Square bustled with tourists who ogled at the huge stone lions and milled about the plaza in front of the National Gallery. Pigeons scattered over the two matching fountains, and gray clouds filled the sky. A constant stream of cars, trucks, and London black cabs passed by the square with honking horns and puffs of exhaust.

Avoiding the crowd, she and Mark trekked several blocks down Whitehall's grand boulevard toward the Metropolitan Police building near Great Scotland Yard. Minutes later, after a perfunctory greeting and introductions, she was sitting in Inspector Willis's office in his now-familiar guest chair positioned closest to his desk. This time, however, she had Mark by her side, which offered welcome support she'd lacked on her solo visits.

"All right, let's get straight to the update." Inspector Willis took a seat at his desk and grabbed a pen and black, spiral notebook.

"Super. Tell me who hacked Kyle's records and why." Glad not to waste time with pleasantries, Tess crossed her arms and shifted in her chair.

"I'm afraid we haven't identified who hacked our system yet, but our IT department managed to restore a backup of the original accident report and evidence files." Willis grimaced, and the corners of his mouth tilted downward.

"Did you find any clues or a place to start searching?" Mark scooted forward in his chair.

Willis rose and started pacing across the office. "Yes and no. IT investigated which accounts were connected to our network when the record changed and who altered it. They found one account called *00-General*, which doesn't identify anyone. By default, the database tags the logged-in user who created the record, but the intruder was savvy enough to change the username."

"Does the evidence point to someone inside?" Tess couldn't decide which was worse—a corrupt police officer or a hacker brilliant enough to breach the London Police's firewall. Neither option boded well.

"Inconclusive. An intruder who gained system access could've invented a generic-looking name and avoided triggering any red flags." Willis continued pacing.

"The impenetrable Met Police vault was hacked, and you have no suspects? Seriously?" Tess tilted her chin high and spread her elbows wide. She sensed hot anger coursing through her body.

Willis stopped moving and pursed his lips. "Not yet, but it's an important clue. I synced up with Chief Inspector Adams, who worked with David while ye were kidnapped. I understand ye both suffered quite an ordeal." He gestured at Mark with a nod and an open palm.

"Well, I'm afraid the ordeal's not over yet." Mark narrowed his gaze and rested his scarred hand on one knee.

"We need to understand tonight's plan. The kidnappers demanded Declan O'Leary meet them at midnight. How will you keep him safe?" Tess didn't mince words as she sensed her hackles rising.

"Adams is on point, and the team's tactics depend on whether the location is urban or an unpopulated setting. The meeting place hasn't been communicated yet." Willis clenched a black pen.

"Right, which means it must be near London. Who are you sending?" Tess kept pushing to gain some confidence the police had a solid plan.

"Standard procedure is we send an emergency response team, along with a backup squad. According to our Serious and Organised Crime Command, Crimson Hammer poses the highest-level threat, and we'll take every precaution. Based on the Cedarcliff attack, we're aware of their capabilities, weapons, and tactics." Willis wiped a bead of sweat from his forehead.

"But how will you protect Declan from harm? I'm not clear on that." Mark cast a glance in Tess's direction.

Given Willis failed to provide any assurance the preparations were airtight, Tess appreciated Mark's request for specific details.

"Our tactical teams are trained with extensive protocols, which they adapt for any scenario. We've got the meeting time, which gives us the distinct advantage of being able to prepare for any attack."

"What about David Kingsley? Declan's delivering the code in exchange for his life." Tess chewed at the inside of her lip to beat back her escalating worry.

"We hope they follow through. Until then, we're searching for David day and night. We just haven't had any luck."

"*Hope*? That's it? You better come up with a damn better strategy right now." Something inside Tess blew. "You realize David could die tonight, Inspector Willis?"

Releasing a noisy exhale, Willis took a seat. "Ms. Bennett. We will do everything possible to bring him home safely, so just sit tight. Stay away from the crime scene and don't endanger yourselves. I insist ye remain somewhere safe in these final hours." He jutted his jaw out.

"Fine, but what else?" Deeply dissatisfied, she tried to throttle down her worry by obtaining more data.

"MPS hired Chief Inspector Adams a few months ago, based on stellar commendations from his Liverpool post. He built a solid track record by leading several high-profile counterterrorism initiatives. He'll keep tonight's situation under control." Willis stood and escorted them back downstairs. "If ye have any concerns, call my mobile."

Dismissed and disgruntled, she and Mark returned to the hotel in Westminster. Once settled in their room, Tess kicked off her shoes and sat at a small table. "Something's off about this, and I don't like it."

"Agreed. The police plan is vague, at best. Yes, they're preparing a team to travel, but what then?" Mark joined her at the table. "Perhaps it's like when hospitals get notified of incoming wounded. We can prep our staff, but we can't diagnose the patients without examining them firsthand."

"The police received notice and time to build a

robust strategy. They should've made more progress. Declan will need lots of reassurance to keep his head together tonight. I'd better call and see how he's faring." She fumbled for her phone and dialed.

"O'Leary here. You calling to give me last rites?" The phone line crackled with static.

"Stop it. You're not dying on my watch." She grumbled and slid off her jacket. "We met with Inspector Willis, who confirmed Chief Inspector Adams is leading the operation, but no location yet. Has Crimson Hammer contacted you?"

"No."

Declan's voice sounded forlorn and empty. Realizing how much stress she'd thrown his way, Tess felt guilty. Revealing Kyle's murder and then asking him to hand off a virus to terrorists was like dropping a live grenade into his hands. With David kidnapped, and her own absence from work, Declan had shouldered countless crises and needed help. An idea popped into her head. "Willis told us to stay home, but you shouldn't face this alone. What if we drove with you to the meeting place for moral support?"

Although Mark dropped his jaw and stared, he didn't interrupt.

Silence filled the line for several seconds. "That's insanely stupid. Your leg's a mess, and Mark's injured, too. I appreciate your offer, truly I do, but forget it." Declan's voice trailed off.

"No. I'll see this nightmare through to the end. Maybe there will be a staging area or someplace where we can wait." When he didn't reply, she continued. "You're exhausted and in shock. Multiple people have died or suffered—Kyle, Riku, David, Mark, and Kavita,

312

too. Willis said Adams is sending two teams to the handoff to protect you tonight. You still there?" She heard heavy breaths, like hyperventilating.

"Tess, I can't do this. I want to save David, but I'm terrified I'll die." Declan's voice quavered.

Given Declan's tall, husky frame, she suspected he'd won more than his fair share of schoolyard fights as a lad. However, tonight posed untold danger. No childhood fistfight could ever prepare him for the menace of Crimson Hammer. She considered how best to fortify his confidence. "The police's job is to keep people alive and eliminate risk. They'll brief you and dress you in a bulletproof vest for extra protection, but they'll have to deal with Crimson Hammer. I can't imagine they'd dare let you enter the target zone, period."

"Hmm, still not reassuring." Declan grunted, then groaned several seconds. "Got anything better?"

"My offer stands. We'll drive with you to the meeting area and wait somewhere safe. What's Kavita working on?" She steered him toward technical details, which she knew would focus his nervous energy.

"She's got two teams lined up and ready should anything threaten Kingsley Tech's networks or our customers tonight. We didn't mention the handoff to the staff. Figured people would freak out."

"Smart choice. Let us at least travel with you, Declan." She ambled to the loveseat, sat next to Mark, and pressed a hand onto his knee.

"If you insist."

"Can you pick us up from our hotel in Westminster after they give you the location?" she asked.

"Sure. I'll call you when I know. It's not like I can

313

think of anything else."

"We'll survive this together." While hoping to reassure him, she needed to convince herself, as well.

"You'd better not be wrong." Declan signed off.

After downing a quick dinner at a pub around the corner, she and Mark returned to the hotel to prepare for the evening. She sprawled on the bed and sank deep into the pile of overstuffed pillows and the massive duvet, relishing a break before the night commenced.

Mark joined her on the bed. "So, *min kjære*, I'm relieved we're not going to the front line, but how should we prepare?"

The fierce desire to protect him from harm topped her priority list. At this point, anything else was a bonus. "I don't want you taking any unnecessary risks, so you're staying in the car, safe. If you weren't so stubborn, I'd prefer to leave you here."

"I'm *dedicated* and need closure, too, because I won't sleep the night through until every terrorist has been caught. If I keep sleepwalking in strange hotels, I'll get myself arrested."

"Excellent point." She gestured toward the bottle of whiskey they picked up near the Embankment Tube station on the way to dinner. "Pack booze. If things go south, I'll need liquid courage."

"Can't argue with your reasoning. What else?" Mark smiled and shoved the bottle of whiskey into a jacket pocket.

"We'll be outside for a long time, so warm coats, mobile phones charged, backup battery, and water. My lucky pocketknife." She considered what else to bring.

"How about you put your feet up, and I'll gather everything?"

She kissed him and stroked his cheek, happy to see his bruises from captivity were fading. The awkwardness from the morning disappeared, and she felt back in sync. "I'm grateful you're here with me. Mark, I…" She stopped, unable to translate her confused feelings into words.

"What is it?" Mark draped a hand over her shoulder.

Suddenly self-conscious and too nervous to form a coherent sentence, she struggled to find the right words. Fear, doubt, hope, and desire wove together, resisting any logical order. She set her shoulders straight. "You took a huge risk coming to London and Scotland to help me. Why?" At once, she detected tenderness softening his gaze, and his blue eyes darkened with intensity. A thin veil of color flushed his cheekbones.

"Well, I wanted answers about the attack."

"But you're injured, too, and we've only known each other a couple of weeks. Why would you risk so much? You didn't need to do any of this." Why he'd risk anything after Cedarcliff was beyond her.

"Tess, you must stop thinking so much. Give your left brain a break." The corners of his lips lifted into a smile, and he released a quiet exhale.

"What do you mean?" Confused, she couldn't grasp his insinuation, which hinted at a mischievous secret.

"The truth is you were the main reason."

She hadn't expected that.

"Sometimes you don't need loads of data to make smart decisions and choose the right path. You can be spontaneous, trust your instincts, and follow your intuition."

"Sure, but I still don't follow." She noticed he kept his gaze trained on her.

"I'm saying you're intelligent, brave, daring, and determined as hell. You fight, and if you fall, you pick yourself up and never stop protecting the people you love. We work well together and balance each other. I haven't read your résumé or met your parents, and I didn't know your full name before I kissed you. And none of those things matter."

"Why not?" She was missing something, but what?

"Because you and I being together this week healed each of us more than either of us ever could have expected. We're a strong match, and you know it, too. You're just too afraid to admit it out loud."

Caught utterly off guard, she took a shallow breath and attempted to slow her thoughts. How could he already know what she barely had started to grasp? However unexpectedly, she was healing and still feared exposing the shattered part of her heart she'd locked away after Kyle died. "Am I so transparent?"

"Not at all. You can bury your pain deep, but you can't hide it from me. I'm a healer, and I understand how grief crushes a person. Opening your heart after a loss is terrifying."

"I'm not afraid. I'm so grateful you joined me." She sensed herself thawing around the edges, enough to lower her defenses slightly. "I can't imagine you not being here now, but for all I know, you could be involved with someone else." The second she mentioned it, she wished she hadn't.

"Obviously, I'm not." Keeping his gaze steady, he opened then closed his mouth before rubbing the back of his neck. "Why would you suggest such a thing?"

"I'll sound like an idiot if I ask this." Noticing the wounded surprise in his voice, she pulled at her sweater's collar.

"Can't be worse than dying. Try me." He sat upright, hands on his knees.

She took a deep breath, hoping not to humiliate herself. "A woman, Elena something-owitz, calls you every day." Despite the woman's full name burning itself in her memory the second she spotted it, she refrained from saying it to avoid appearing like an obsessive stalker.

"Dr. Elena Rabinowitz is my psychiatrist, an incredible doctor. After I called her in distress from Vancouver, she insisted on daily check-ins. Her parents were Holocaust survivors, and now she treats veterans with combat PTSD."

"Your doctor is the stunning redhead?" She didn't believe it.

Perplexed, Mark's forehead wrinkled, but a second later, he burst out laughing. "No, the redhead is my doctor's admin, Kelly, who sets up our video calls. Elena's seventy and too arthritic to type."

Embarrassment flushed her cheeks with burning heat, too fast for her to hide them. Mortified but unable to retract her admission, she wanted to crawl under the table. "I'm sorry. I had no right to act jealous."

The corners of his lips curled upward. "Don't be. I'm flattered you cared. Don't worry about labels. Our time together means whatever we decide. Waking up next to you, I'm happy and drawn to you. What more could I want?"

Butterflies clustered in Tess's stomach and fluttered in all directions like pre-performance jitters, but a thousand times worse. Still entranced, she rested her fingertips on his chest and returned his gaze. With one finger, she traced his cheek along the edge of his jaw, running it down his neck to the smooth arc of muscle beneath his collarbone. With her heart quaking, she tilted his chin and invited his gaze. "I-I want you and need you. I just do."

"And that's all you need to know." Mark wrapped her into his arms and squeezed her tight.

Damn it, he was right. For one year, she'd avoided feeling anything and obliterated her emotions by whatever means necessary. Stymied by grief since Kyle's death, she'd concluded she'd never find love again and kept her heart under lock and key, like a destroyed fortress. A steadfast, loyal soldier, she remained behind and alone to guard the sacred rubble and prove her allegiance to a slain king. Rebuilding her life required more courage than mourning its wreckage, and the magnetic attraction she shared with Mark propelled her forward. She relaxed onto his chest but couldn't ignore the impending danger. "We don't have much time."

"I know." Mark sighed and gave her hip a firm squeeze. "Any chance you'd…?"

"No, not now." Studying his expression, she smiled demurely.

"Oh." Lips downturned, he ran a hand through his hair, leaving the top tousled.

Still smiling, Tess shook her head. "You're irresistible and I want you, *madly*. But I want our next time together to be when we're not traumatized or about to die, like tonight. No crises. No emergency phone calls. I want hours, *days*, to enjoy you, without interruption." Delighted to see him beaming, she caressed his chest. "Quite possibly longer."

"Did you just express some feelings, Ms. Bennett? Because those sounded a lot like feelings. Actual emotions."

"You caught me. I want us to go out and have a proper, romantic date." Blushing, she felt exposed but decided it was okay. Love required risk, but without love, little else mattered.

"I can do that. Let's survive tonight and plan a real date. Although not too proper, I hope." Mark grinned with a wink.

"That I can promise." Basking in his sparkling blue-eyed gaze, she returned the grin. Glowing, she cherished the moment, glad she'd risked opening her heart despite how scary it felt.

Her mobile phone buzzed. *Declan.* Jolted back to the present, she tightened her jaw and refocused her energy. She feared something would go wrong tonight. Deadly wrong.

Chapter Twenty

Live by the Sword

Tess answered Declan's call right away. "Hi, we're at the hotel. Yes, we're almost ready to go." She nodded at Mark and read out the hotel's address in Westminster. "So, where's the showdown tonight?" Tess balanced the phone on her shoulder and grabbed a notepad and pen from the suite's desk.

Declan exhaled loudly. "Richmond Park, the telescope at King Henry's Mound. I called Adams to alert him. He said they'll be prepared and waiting for us. I'll pick you up at eleven o'clock, then we need thirty minutes of travel time."

To her relief, Declan's voice held steady, despite the dire risks of the upcoming confrontation. "We'll be outside. Drive safe." Remembering the Raven had asked to monitor the electronic handoff from afar, Tess texted him the time and place before pocketing her phone.

Mark pulled a couple of water bottles from the minibar and rushed to gather their coats and shoes before tossing a jacket and a scarf in her direction.

After leaving the room, she followed Mark outside and sat in the hotel's garden to wait for Declan. Shivering in the chilly air, she paused a moment to admire the serene haven of autumn flowers. The garden's surreal beauty offered a fleeting but welcome respite from the evening's grim undertaking. The growing connection she felt with Mark made tonight's mission even more dismal in comparison.

Ten minutes later, Declan motored up to the hotel driveway's entrance in a large, black British jeep and screeched to a stop. He popped out of the jeep wearing jeans and a black leather jacket. "Hi, mates. Ready for our demise?" Grimacing, he walked around to open the rear passenger door.

"Excellent. No shortage of optimism, I see. How're you holding up?" She hoped his anxiety hadn't transformed into reckless self-defeat.

"Let's just say I'm not buying any green bananas this week. I'll expire before they do."

"See, you've still got a sense of humor." Tess gave him a friendly swat on the back. "That's the spirit."

"Looks like a great night to thwart terrorists." Mark closed Tess's door and took the front passenger seat.

A loud snicker escaped Declan, and he whacked the steering wheel. "Mate, get real. I'm an engineer nerd with a desk job, not an effing warrior."

"Hey, I'm no soldier either, but I'm a medical geek who lived in a war zone for three years. Your brain needs oxygen to function, and slow, deep breathing will help—trust me. Use your adrenaline to sharpen your focus," Mark spoke in a soothing voice and patted Declan on the shoulder.

"Dear God, let this nightmare end. I've got money riding on Manchester United for Saturday's playoff with Chelsea." Declan groaned and clutched his steering wheel with white knuckles as he merged into traffic.

"You'll be alive to collect, though I would've bet on Chelsea." Mark adjusted his seat belt.

"No way. They're a bunch of pansies, and you'd be better off betting on a plate of crumpets." Declan guffawed as he changed lanes.

After sharing a laugh, the men chatted about soccer for a few minutes, a welcome distraction for them all.

Sitting alone in the back seat, Tess avoided imagining terrible outcomes, but gory images flooded her thoughts anyhow. The idea David was suffering violence right now disturbed her, and she clenched the armrest as a nauseous wave rolled through her. Bouncing her knee to offload her agitation, she focused on holding herself together. "I'm worried for David." The second she spoke out loud, she regretted it. No one needed reminding about how vanishingly slight his chance of survival was.

Everyone remained silent for the rest of the trip. After leaving London and heading southwest on the A3 motorway, Declan exited north on Queen's Road to search for Richmond Park. A signpost directed drivers to use an alternate parking lot.

"Shite, the main entrance closed at 1630. I can park here but will need to cross through these goddamned woods and find the bloody meetup inside the park." Declan groaned and cursed a long string of expletives.

In the front seat, Mark glanced at his watch. "Strange. It's 2330 already. Shouldn't we see police cars everywhere? This park is empty."

"Agreed. You sure this is the right place, Declan?" The situation didn't make sense, and she couldn't shake her doubts.

"The instructions were clear, but I'll call the police

again." He whipped out his mobile and dialed. "Voice mail. Shite. Yes, this is Declan O'Leary. I'm in Richmond Park, and the damn place is empty. Where's your team, Adams? Call me ASAP."

Each second took too long to pass, and Tess grew restless. After unfastening her seat belt, she rotated in all directions to survey the surrounding park area. Nothing but trees and empty parking spaces. "What if the police arrived but hid to avoid tipping off the kidnappers? Or what if they scared Crimson Hammer away already?"

"But why the hell doesn't Adams answer? Let's give him a few more minutes before I go into the woods." Declan drummed noisily on the bottom of the steering wheel.

The panic in Declan's voice had escalated by several magnitudes, and she hoped his worry wasn't contagious. To untangle her thoughts, Tess forced herself to count backward from twenty in four different languages—anything to prevent anxiety from chipping away at her strength. Ten more minutes passed.

2340. Like a nervous tic, Declan patted the USB memory stick in his shirt pocket, but no signs of life appeared in the park.

"Should we abandon this, Declan? You can't just charge in there without police protection. Too dangerous." Mark shifted in his seat to face Declan.

"Time's ticking, mate. Five more minutes. Can't let David down." Declan raised a hand to his mouth and chewed a fingernail.

Tess studied Declan's reflection in the rearview mirror. Sweat had erupted on his forehead, and his gaze darted back and forth. Three hundred more seconds drifted by at the pace of a glacial iceberg, and still nothing. The jeep's digital clock flipped to 2345.

Declan slammed his hands against the steering wheel. "Screw it. I'm not going to be a feckin' coward and let David die because the police aren't here to hold my hand. I'm going."

His sudden movement startled her, and she poked her head into the front seat. "Stop. You don't have to do this. We can turn back."

"Don't you understand? We're David's last hope. I can't be a wimpy-assed pansy and let him die." Declan clenched his fists against his forehead and groaned.

"I'll go with you and stay near the meeting place if you need help." Mark zipped up his coat and reached for the passenger door.

"Absolutely not." Tess scooted toward the door to get out. Mark's calm voice had been smooth and devoid of fear, like when Riku was shot. She grabbed his arm as panic raced through her. "You're injured and unarmed."

Mark turned to face her. "We'll be back soon, Tess. I promise. Lock up and stay safe. Let's go, Declan."

"No. Mark. We agreed we'd wait for the police." Given their earlier discussion, she couldn't believe he was risking everything. Speechless, she swerved between panic and fury.

Without a word, Declan tossed her his car keys. The men stepped out of the jeep, slamming the doors shut before she could protest further. She gasped as they trekked across the deserted parking lot and aimed toward the trailhead, about fifty feet away. Swearing, she clicked the doors locked and scanned for oncoming police car lights from all directions. The pitch-black sky smothered the park like a blanket, and nothing interrupted the darkness but one dim park light flickering by the trailhead.

She whipped out her mobile. Fingers flying, she punched in 9-9-9 to reach the British Telecom operator and request police help. She drummed her fingers and waited for the call to be transferred.

"Police Emergency Team," the dispatcher announced. "What is your emergency?"

"Send a crisis response team to the telescope at King Henry's Mound at Richmond Park now. Alert Inspector Willis, Chief Inspector Adams, and your counterterrorism unit at Met Police. We've got a hostage exchange going wrong, so please hurry."

The dispatcher recorded her information and responded a police squad was on the way.

Her adrenaline kicked in, and she gritted her teeth. A surge of hyperactivity followed, and she experienced the overwhelming urge to sprint somewhere, anywhere, faster than the wind. If it weren't such a stupid idea, she'd run into the dark woods alone. Her mobile rang again, and Willis's name appeared on her screen. Breathless, she answered. "I'm here."

"Got your 9-9-9. Are ye somewhere safe?" he spoke in short, staccato bursts.

Like a scene from a horror movie, dark, secluded woods framed the solitary black jeep. She then recalled promising Willis she'd stay safe and remain at the hotel. *Whoops.* "Uh, no. We traveled with Declan to the meeting location at Richmond Park."

Willis let out a long groan. "Ye must be kidding me. Ye did what?"

"Look, Adams told Declan his crisis team would lead this handoff, but no one's here. What the hell? We've got fewer than fifteen minutes before Crimson Hammer kills David Kingsley, so Mark and Declan just left for the handoff point without the police. Damn it, we can't let David die."

"Shite. The handoff is an ambush!" Willis exploded. "They need to steer clear *now*."

"W-what?" Tess could barely speak.

"Headquarters canceled our entire operation with no explanation an hour ago. Adams disappeared, and now, no one can find him. Someone either took him out, or he sabotaged the meeting. Take cover somewhere safe while I call for help."

The call disconnected, and she blinked, unsettled by the eerie silence inside the jeep. The digital clock radiated 2352 in neon-green. Pounding her uninjured foot in a frenzy on the floorboards, she cursed and redialed Declan. No answer. "Damn it, come on. Pick up." She texted both men and left a voice-mail with Mark. Still, no response. *Please, let them all survive.*

Seconds later, her mobile buzzed. A new text marked *Unknown Caller* appeared with the country code for Turkey. *Strange.* She clicked it.

—*You're in danger. Get far away from the car. NOW.*—

Goose bumps erupted over her entire body. She scanned the dark again, expecting to see stalkers closing in. Growing frantic, she wondered if this was a sick ploy to trick her into leaving her safehold. She hesitated to abandon the locked jeep, which offered protection and escape. Since she couldn't reach Mark or Declan by phone, she realized her only option to warn the men was to enter the woods. "Goddamn it." She punched her fist into the back of the seat. Grabbing the whiskey Mark brought, she unscrewed the cap and gulped a double shot of liquid courage before slipping Declan's keys into her pocket and hobbling out of the jeep. She slammed the door with more force than necessary and hurried away in an awkward gallop with her crutches.

2354. Halfway across the parking lot, her phone rang, and Kavita's photo flashed on her screen. She answered.

"Bad news. Two Polish banks encrypted with Firefly have been breached. Millions of Polish zloty in micro-withdrawals are disappearing every second. They're hemorrhaging cash." Kavita spoke lightning-fast.

"Crap. Get those banks under network lockdown ASAP. We're in trouble. Declan's been set up. Keep trying to contact him. Tell him to run from the handoff but not to return to his car."

"What? You mean he's—"

"Don't think. Just make it happen. I need to find Declan and Mark." She clicked to end the call and charged forward, aiming for the trailhead. Breathing hard, she felt the frosty air sting her lungs, and the whiskey's heat filled her bloodstream. The Culloden quote Kyle shared with the Raven jolted her with its full impact, searing itself deep in her bones so she wouldn't forget. *Our blood is still our fathers', and ours the valour of their hearts.* Summoning her father's bravery, she kept moving.

A massive explosion sounded. Crashing metal and glass accompanied the deafening boom, and the blast knocked her to the ground with her crutches and covered her with debris. Lying flat on the pine-needle-lined trail, she peeked through her fingers. A blinding fire lit up the park's skyline, and the resulting smoke plume floated upward thirty yards high. Declan's jeep had blown apart, reduced to a twisted metal skeleton engulfed in flames. Melted, amorphous chunks of debris released steam and smoke as they burned in the parking lot.

Acrid soot burned the inside of her nose. Desperate for air, she gasped, but inhaled smoke instead, which sent her coughing, face down on the ground. She swept her hands across the earth around her body and touched decomposing leaves mixed with hot ash. She rolled onto her back to catch her breath before attempting to get up. Who found the intel about the explosion and warned her? A mere sixty seconds saved her from being vaporized like the jeep.

Pushing to a stand, she stumbled at first until regaining her balance. Hands freezing, she slipped on her gloves and scanned the lot to see if the explosion drew anyone out of the trees. No one. With no shelter or police in sight, she steeled her courage and limped into the woods alone. She slogged through the darkness at a laborious pace and passed the trailhead, maneuvering over the uneven ground.

Three deer with full antlers crossed the trail and spooked her. After the scare, she used her phone like a flashlight, checking every few yards to confirm the path ahead remained clear. Her crutches hindered her speed, but she stepped with her healthy leg in tandem and managed an awkward gallop while ignoring her pain.

In her urgent exit, she had left the car with a

trajectory but no plan. *Foolish.* If she encountered Crimson Hammer, she carried nothing to defend herself. The silent forest remained undisturbed by sirens, thwarting her hopes for a quick rescue. How long could it take for a damn police car to arrive? Flights to the moon took less time.

While darkness made navigation difficult, she was thankful the woods offered ample cover. Dressed in her black trench coat, she blended into the night and avoided making noise. The path's bushes grew thick, and her visibility extended to about three yards. An owl hooted above in the trees, reminding her of the forest she and Mark trekked in British Columbia. Luck might permit them to survive twice. Still no response from Mark or Declan.

1156. Four minutes left. She suspected another wild deer when a shadow passed several yards before her. An icy wind whistled through the treetops, and leaves rustled underneath her feet. She swore and soldiered on, propelling her body forward in wide arcs. *Please let me find them before it's too late.* A small, open clearing appeared along with a signpost pointing uphill toward King Henry's Mound.

Steeling her energy, she was accelerating up the steep hill when a set of arms snatched her from behind, locked around her torso, and knocked her off her feet. The point of a knife grazed her neck. The smell of cigarettes and beets hit her nose, and a bare, rough hand covered her mouth. The earthy taste of dirt and unfamiliar sweat made her gag.

"We meet again, Ms. Bennett. You can't hide from me because I will always find you." A wheezing Slavic voice growled.

Yuri. She screamed, but his hand muffled the sound to a barely audible rasp.

"Scream again, and I slit your throat." The gunman's grip around her torso tightened.

The steel tip of the knife chilled her neck, and she felt her hands freeze despite her gloves. Straining to coax her limbs into motion, she floundered, livid with herself for entering the woods unprepared. If the universe's spiritual accounting required a zero balance, a life for a life, she still wouldn't trade hers in payment for Sergey's. The gunman's weight threw her off center, and she struggled to stay upright. "What do you want?"

"Nothing but your silence. The dead cannot speak," Yuri grumbled.

The knife remained sharp against her neck.

Yes, they can. She smirked in the darkness, remembering Kyle's letter, and reckoned the dead had more to say than most people. "What's so important? Why do you hate the US so much?"

"Because I do whatever Russia wants. We need your Rapadon code to bypass bank security and steal the cash." Yuri hissed, still restraining her torso.

"So, you're working with Russia." Unable to escape his grasp, she needed to keep him talking.

"You techies think you're so smart. Russia's the first stop. The Hornet, Kostenko, routes the hacking and dirty work through Belarus," Yuri snapped and tightened his grip.

Well, that answers one question, but where the hell were the police? Worse, if she couldn't trust Willis and he was dirty, too, her chance of rescue, as well as Mark's and Declan's, dropped to zero. Scheming her next move, she emptied her mind of panic and concentrated. Pissed off to face Yuri again, she fought to extricate herself to no avail. Body tensing, she sensed the blade's pressure against her throat increasing.

Out of nowhere, her father's commanding voice reverberated through her head. *First, survive.*

In a flash of clarity, she realized nothing mattered but stalling Yuri long enough to stay alive. "Let me go." Her request met only a cruel laugh from Yuri.

"Stupid girl, you and the doctor are trouble. You killed Alexi and that pig, Sergey, though the *svoloch* deserved it." He coughed and spat on the ground.

Desperate to preserve her equilibrium, she rejected visions of pitchforks and braced herself to keep him at bay. *Breathe and delay, breathe and delay.* Self-preservation prevailed, and she howled. "Let. Me. Go."

"Quiet. No more." He repositioned the knife in his other hand.

"Stop, help!" She felt his iron grip around her neck tighten, but his hand, an immovable vise strangling her, muffled her shout. Her head tingled from lack of oxygen. Knowing few seconds remained before she passed out, she bashed at his knees with her metal crutches. In the brawl, she felt his blade nick the side of her neck, breaking open the skin. Warm blood dripped down her chest, and the nerve endings of the cut stung like electrical shocks.

Footsteps raced on the path behind where she stood, followed by the sound of a dull, metallic bump.

Yuri grunted.

He tumbled on top of her, knocking her flat.

The knife flew out of his hand into a pile of deer berry bushes.

His mass crushed her, deflating her lungs of air in one burst. Trapped, she couldn't move and squished her face against the frosty ground.

"Lass, give me your hand," a Scottish Highlander accent hollered.

Not believing her ears, she strained to lift her head toward the voice. Dumbstruck, she extended her hand.

Dressed in black, the Raven stood above her, brandishing the imposing broadsword from his cottage. With difficulty, he wriggled and tugged to extract her from under Yuri.

The inert form groaned in response to movement.

When her torso cleared the gunman's, she scrambled on her hands and knees over the dirt, and the Highlander yanked her up.

"Hurry. I just knocked him out enough so you could run away. He'll wake up soon."

She rebalanced herself and stared at Yuri. Other than a whack on the head, he appeared uninjured.

Moaning, Yuri opened his eyes and gawked at the Highlander, who kept his Jacobite sword pointed at the gunman. "Raven," he wheezed, gasping for air. "Still fighting for justice? You should've fought with us for more money."

The Raven stood with his sword pointed at Yuri's throat. "I'd never stoop so low to fight with you insurgents."

"Kostenko would've paid you loads of cash. You and the Druid could've joined Crimson Hammer and gotten rich." Yuri clutched his head, moaning.

"Kyle?" She dropped her mouth open, seized by a sense of paralysis. Kyle couldn't possibly have considered such an arrangement. The mere thought repulsed her.

"The Druid would've never harmed Britain or America. He valued honor and integrity and despised you disgusting rodents." The Raven flicked the tip of his sword under Yuri's chin.

"You fucking boy scouts and your ideals. No one gives a shit about the truth. The powerful invent whatever truth they want you to believe." Yuri snarled, with his hands flat on the ground by his sides.

"Give me your sword." The anger simmering under the surface of her grief boiled over and overflowed. She erupted with raw rage and yanked the Raven's weapon from his hand, startling him. Stepping forward in an attack stance, she whipped the blade tip around in a perfect, smooth arc under Yuri's chin. She rested its point square on his carotid artery, giving the double-edged blade another firm push to clarify her intentions. "Did you hurt Kyle?"

"I'm a killer. I kill many people." Jutting his chin, Yuri sneered and chuckled.

"In the name of God, did you kill Kyle MacTavish?" Tess roared, her throat burning. After a year spent trying to obliterate her grief, she cut loose its fiery twin—revenge. She felt her fury detonate like glass shards escaping her body from the inside out, piercing her in bloody stabs. *Stab, explode, release.*

Pinpointing her sword tip against Yuri's upper throat, she pressed as hard as she dared without puncturing his skin. "By God, you'd better tell me now. Did you murder him?" With the sword tight in her steady right hand, she tracked his gaze as it moved up the straight line of the blade to the hilt.

"Your boyfriend? I ran his car off the cliff by the

bridge. He crashed into the water. Yes, I killed him." Yuri laughed and patted the ground, grasping for his knife but unable to reach it.

Tess breathed in uneven gasps as her body shook, and the sword wavered in her hand as revenge pulsated through her blood. She needed more air. Stabilizing her grip, she kept the sword tip tight against Yuri's neck, unable to control the rage coursing through her body. One thrust of the shining blade could slit his throat and end this forever. "You. Fucking. Murderer. I will crush you."

On the ground, Yuri lay paralyzed, not speaking, with his attention focused on the sword in her hand.

She seethed with grief, fresh and raw as the day Kyle's beautiful spirit was yanked from the earth. Nothing else existed but avenging his murder and seeking justice for all the people Yuri killed. She compressed the sword tip harder against his neck and prepared to strike.

"Lass, ye don't want to live with killing a man. Death is forever."

The Raven's gentle brogue broke through the invisible perimeter encircling her battle with Yuri. Holding her breath, she fixated on the gunman's prone body, and her hand wavered.

"I'm sorry. I believe in God, but I've done terrible things," Yuri whispered in a scratchy rasp.

Yuri's beady eyes bored into her, and he grasped his necklace, a steel crucifix, like an offering. With slow, jerking motions, he made the sign of the cross over his heart. "God have mercy on me, the sinner. Forgive me. In the name of the Father, and of the Son, and of the Holy Spirit, have mercy. Thy will is done."

"What?" she burst out, keeping her sword steady at his neck.

"So now you pray? You rodent," the Raven replied.

Yuri's jaw gnashed back and forth, chewing something. He swallowed twice, and his face twisted before his eyelids drooped closed.

"What did you do?" Not understanding, she stared at the gunman. She would not be cheated of this moment. Lowering her sword a few inches, she ducked forward, grasped his collar, and jerked his head off the ground.

"What I should have done years ago." Yuri's eyelids fluttered, and he gasped once.

"What the hell?" She stared at his limp form, flat on the trail. His body seized several seconds before relaxing like a flag unfurling in the breeze. His chalk-white hands opened, and all movement stopped. Stunned, she looked at the Raven.

"Damn coward killed himself. Cyanide. The worst bullies are always the weakest inside." With a gloved hand, the Raven reclaimed his broadsword and slid the blade into the leather scabbard attached to his belt.

Staring at Yuri's corpse, Tess felt a peculiar emptiness. Although she was freed from fear, she was robbed of legal justice. Yuri would never face judgment, suffer, or rot in prison for his crimes.

The Raven touched her arm. "Surviving takes the most courage of all, but you're brave. A fighter. Farewell, Tess. Stay safe." Silently, the Highlander disappeared into the night, and the soft ground of the forest absorbed his footsteps.

Chapter Twenty-One

Voices in the Trees

Left alone with Yuri's body, Tess desperately wanted to leave, but she opted to confirm he was dead and hadn't somehow faked his demise. She bent over to search his neck for a pulse. *Nothing.* Next, she studied his face, now a ghastly gray, and committed the moment to memory. With this proof, she hoped to exterminate him from her thoughts forever and willed away the images of what he'd done to Kyle. The fear haunting her since Cedarcliff gently fell away, like debris washed aside by a heavy rain shower.

She needed to find Mark and Declan but wanted to protect the Raven's anonymity. Recounting the past few minutes, she checked the ground and found no evidence which could incriminate him. She'd worn gloves, which meant she hadn't left fingerprints on the sword, should the Raven need to abandon it in the forest for some reason. Her mobile vibrated in her pocket. Panting from trekking over the uneven ground, she stopped to withdraw an arm from one of her crutches, lifted the phone to one ear, and answered.

"Inspector Willis here. We're on Queen's Road, approaching Richmond Park. Any update?"

"I'm nearing the Mound trailhead. Slow going." Not ready to reveal Yuri's demise, she skirted the truth.

"I haven't found Mark or Declan, but there's been no gunfire either."

"Let's keep things peaceful, and we'll arrive shortly." Willis signed off.

Glad he didn't waste time chastising her for being in the woods, she rotated in a circle, divining which direction would lead toward the main trail. She managed a steady gallop over the gravelly ground and strained to hear police sirens. The fork of the path branched, and she veered left. After trekking down one route, she hit a thicket of trees that obstructed the way and was lost again. "Damn it."

She checked her watch. Four minutes past midnight. Huffing and grumbling, she hiked back to where the trail split. Inexplicably, she grew uneasy and felt a premonitory sense she was no longer alone. Across the fork in the trail, several yards away, she heard a clunky, dragging noise and froze.

Someone stumbled and crashed through the bushes and foliage like a drunk.

She cupped a hand against her ear to listen. The rustling stopped, followed by a blunt thud on the ground, heaviness landing on leaves. First, she heard a groan, then a pained howl. She flashed back to the barn when Mark wailed from Sergey's punches and sensed her lungs tightening. Could Declan be in the trees? Grateful for the cover of darkness, she aimed to remain silent and hidden. But what if it was Mark? Afraid of falling into a trap, she ventured a tentative step forward.

"Help me," a male voice groaned. "Please."

She flinched. The man's refined English voice, a clear tenor, projected suffering veiled by politeness. The Oxbridge accent echoed with familiarity but was so

337

hoarse she couldn't identify it, despite a rising glint of hope. Betting the man wasn't an enemy, she couldn't desert someone injured. "Who are you? Reveal yourself." She kept her voice low and hushed.

"I'd recognize your American accent anywhere, Tess."

"David. Thank God. Where are you?" She spun to find his location, her spirits skyrocketing.

"A few meters behind the trail fork, next to the huge tree," David spoke in a labored rasp.

"Let me get you out." She switched on her mobile's flashlight, having forgotten to use it since the encounter with Yuri. Shining the light across the trees in a broad sweep, she detected a figure curled against the base of a gigantic oak tree. Using her crutches to swat foliage away, she stepped toward him through pockets in the bushes. "Almost there."

Two steps more. She trudged through the thick undergrowth to reach David and angled the flashlight to avoid blinding him. Knowing he'd been tortured, she sucked in a breath to work up the nerve to assess his wounds. Coated in blood, sweat, and dirt, he appeared ill, with a red-stained rag wrapped around one hand. "My God, what have they done?" She covered her mouth.

"Some sadistic arse named Yuri tortured me. Cut off my finger with a dirty knife. It's gone, but it hurts like hell." David's voice cracked as he presented his left hand, and the rag dropped. A dirt-covered, bloody gauze bandage twisted around the gory wound, covering most of it.

Choking down the bile rising in her throat, she contorted at the nasty taste. Her second worst fear had materialized—they had maimed David.

She slid off her right glove and felt his forehead, which was burning hot. "You have a fever. How long ago did this happen?"

"Two days ago. God Almighty, the torture almost killed me."

"You need a hospital. Police are coming, and I'll fetch an ambulance. You're safe now." Whether help arrived in time to stop further violence, she couldn't say. She squeezed his shoulder and bit her lip, trying not to visualize Yuri abusing him. She stuffed the glove back in her pocket and straightened to scan the thick trees around them. "This nightmare stops tonight."

David grabbed her arm with his good hand. "Wait. They blackmailed me, and, well, I had to make sacrifices."

"What kind of sacrifices?" She tensed as new, foreboding chills crept up her spine.

"Ah, shit." David's voice quavered like he might cry. "When they tortured me, I gave away the root encryption keys to two of our customers. Polish banks."

"Yes, those banks got breached, and they're losing cash by the minute." Her brow furrowed. Based on Kavita's call, the timing didn't make sense. "How'd you access those numbers while kidnapped? How'd you figure out what they were after?"

"I received a security alert about heightened activity in Eastern Europe right before the Cedarcliff attack. Riku warned me about new dark web chatter indicating Poland might be targeted."

"*Before* the attack? How the hell did Riku find out?" Her blood pressure surged, and she reconsidered whether David had betrayed her. Had he withheld critical information?

David sighed. "Turns out Riku had tight contacts with the American C.I.A. They're investigating bank fraud in Eastern Europe and the Middle East, in areas where Americans hold significant assets. Agents from Latvia as far south as Turkey and Cyprus." David stopped and cleared his raspy throat. "The day Cedarcliff was attacked, chatter suggested a massive financial breach loomed in Poland. That's why Riku wanted to meet with us."

She attempted to access the information tucked away deep in her memory but couldn't. "Fine, but how'd you decide to copy the root keys?"

"Our meeting in London. As you said, breaching a bank network depends on accessing the encryption root key. After you left Ivy House, I researched our Eastern European customer banks with London locations. Found two Polish banks, then extracted their root keys to a portable drive I kept with me. A bargaining chip if I needed it."

"Thank goodness you had the foresight to take them." She would've done the same thing had she been in his position. "But your kidnapping—how did it happen?"

"Chief Inspector Adams was my police escort that afternoon, but instead of driving me home, he handcuffed me inside the car, then dumped me off at a shipping container east of London, where two Belarusian gunmen tortured me. Adams spoke perfect Russian and had us fooled all along."

"Adams is a traitor." She shook her head and prayed Willis wasn't dirty, too. He'd said he was sending help, but what if he was manipulating her to serve Adams?

"I couldn't produce Rapadon, so they cut off my finger, then threatened to kill Penelope and little Nigel." David's voice wavered again. "I traded the keys to the banks to save their lives and my own."

"Christ, no one can blame you. Kyle made the same trade-off last year to keep me alive, and Crimson Hammer killed him."

"Oh, dear God." David dropped his mouth open and shook his head before clenching his eyes shut and releasing a shaky breath. "The car crash wasn't an accident?"

"No—long story. Kavita's teams are working to stop the breach. We need to get you to a hospital. Can you stand?" She helped him to his feet.

Groaning, he crumpled back to the ground. "Can't move, sorry."

"Stay here. I'll be back with help soon." She hustled out of the foliage and charged toward the hill demarcating King Henry's Mound. Despite her aching leg, she surged past all sensible limits and barreled down the path.

Finally, the wail of a police siren cut through the air, followed seconds later by an entire squad of blaring horns.

She'd never been so glad to hear a siren. Wiping the sweat from her forehead, she kept scrambling through the woods. A couple of minutes later, she spotted Declan's familiar silhouette racing down the steep trail and saw anger painted across his face as he passed under a lone, lit lamppost near the trailhead.

"Why the hell aren't you in the car?" He shook her shoulders with both hands.

"I found David. He's alive but needs an ambulance."

"Thank God, he's alive. A guy toting an assault rifle showed up and whipped out a laptop. I gave him the red drive I modified, which he uploaded via satellite data link." He paused to take a breath. "Something exploded, not sure where. When sirens came, the bloke ran away." He stepped closer. "You're covered in smoke and dirt. What happened?"

"Your jeep blew up a few yards away from me in the parking lot. Lots of debris." Though the car bomb exploded less than an hour ago, so much transpired that it felt like months ago.

"My jeep's gone?" He dropped open his mouth, then squinted. "Hey, your neck is bleeding."

She pressed her bare hand to her neck and stared at the fresh blood coating her fingers, wondering if she'd end up with another scar inflicted by Yuri. "One of the terrorists caught me, but I got away."

Declan offered her a crooked smile of awe. "Shite, Bennett. You're a badass. But we gotta run—the arsehole's still out here."

She grabbed his sleeve. "But where's Mark?"

"I can't find him now." Declan stared at the ground.

"Goddamn it, he shouldn't have come out here." Tess fumed and dug a fingernail into one palm to fight her growing worry. "Look. Adams played you, then canceled the operation and disappeared. He left you to be killed."

"You mean that bastard let me walk into this shitstorm alone? Fucking traitor." Breathing hard, Declan slammed his foot into a pile of sticks, scattering them far and wide.

The cacophony of sirens transformed into a caravan of swirling lights arriving at Richmond Park. The park's west side formed a blinding white wall that lit up the woods a couple hundred yards away. Pounding footsteps thundered, heading for the light.

Tess waved a hand above her head. "Police, over here," she yelled.

Two SCO19 Metropolitan Police Service officers were the first to spring around the corner and discover her and Declan.

She held her empty hands in the air to prove she was unarmed. "I'm Tess Bennett, and this is Declan O'Leary. David Kingsley's alive but needs an ambulance." She described where to find him. "They tortured him."

Declan grabbed his gut and threw up on the dirt trail.

"We'll help you out of here." One of the officers signaled to the group of armed police awaiting orders by the clearing.

The other officer paged an ambulance. With guns drawn, the men split into two groups and disappeared down the trail.

Seconds later, an armed backup team arrived, led by Inspector Willis. "Glad ye stayed safe. What can ye tell me?" Deep lines stretched across his forehead, and he adopted a wide stance.

Pulse racing, she updated him but omitted one detail—Yuri's death. Despite seeing the gunman's corpse, her fear didn't evaporate at once, as she expected. "Mark's missing, and we must find him."

Willis frowned and relayed the information to the

response teams via radio.

In the nearby clearing, a bank of blinding lights flicked on. Raising a hand to shield her eyes from the intense wall of light, she searched for Mark in the gathering crowd of officers but couldn't find him.

A different radio channel beeped, and Willis adjusted his earpiece and pushed the mouthpiece toward his face. "What do ye have?" His eyebrows knit together in a frown. "No sign of a struggle? Nothing? Yes, we need a second ambulance here. I'll send EMTs."

Overhearing his conversation, Tess tensed her body as her apprehension rose. *Please let Mark be safe.*

Willis clicked off his radio and turned toward Tess. His mouth formed a tight, flat line and revealed no emotion. "Yuri Petrov is dead."

"Are you sure?" A bit of shock and denial delayed her relief from sinking in, and she resisted trusting her newfound safety.

"Yes, but we're not sure why. No bleeding or obvious trauma." He rocked back and forth on his heels. "My officers assumed a heart attack, given he reeks like a chimney and carried three packs of smokes. But our senior officer smelled bitter almonds around the suspect's mouth, consistent with cyanide poisoning. We think this terrorist group trained with Russia's KGB or FSB, depending on their age. Suicide capsules were common in their field survival kits."

"Suicide." Although she witnessed Yuri's death, hearing the police declare it official comforted her. She slipped her thoughts back to Cedarcliff when Yuri cracked her cheek open. His death offered relief but failed to erase her scar, a permanent reminder of his brutality. "He almost killed me tonight with a knife, but I got away."

"Ye were bloody lucky to have survived the brute. Yuri Petrov was notorious for torture, and few people survive an encounter with him once, let alone twice."

Tess hadn't stopped long enough to realize how fortunate she'd been to dodge death again, and Willis's observation made her pause. With Yuri gone, safety became attainable again, and she offered a prayer of gratitude to the universe. An icy wind whipped through the trees and chilled her to the bone, and the one person she wanted most was missing. "Willis, who's searching for Mark?"

An altercation erupted nearby. Men's angry shouts blared several yards away, near the clearing.

She exchanged a worried glance with Declan.

Willis held up his palm to signal her to wait. He addressed a group of officers waiting at his side to investigate. His radio beeped, and he excused himself to answer it. "What? Please repeat. Who? Hostage?" Grimacing, he lowered one hand to his gun. "Yes, damn it. I copy."

Glowering, he bolted toward one of the uniformed officers awaiting orders. "Ye got a negotiator with ye, Thomas?"

"Yes, sir." The officer nodded.

"Send him down there, now," Willis boomed.

"Wait. Who's the hostage?" Tess tightened her body like a brittle stick, and she grabbed Willis's arm.

"The situation is fluid and could change any minute." Avoiding eye contact, he pressed his temples and fingered his radio as his shoulders sagged.

Balking at his attempt to airbrush the mess, she

threw her crutches to the ground and yanked Willis's jacket to pull his face closer. "Goddamn it, don't give me vague bullshit. Who is it?"

He met her stare. "The remaining gunman has taken Dr. Nygaard hostage."

Tess froze. She heard the words but refused to accept them, as if denial held the power to change the truth. Registering Willis's dismal expression, a silent scream rose in her throat. *No, not Mark. Please, not again.*

Chapter Twenty-Two

Truth

Standing in the park clearing with the Metropolitan Police officers, Tess felt her heart tumble off a mile-high cliff into free-fall. As the grave reality struck her with full force, she winced as a surge of adrenaline hit the top of her skull with the force of an ice pick. "Take me to Mark. Now."

"No. Whatever goes down, good or bad, I promise it won't help ye to watch it." Willis stood solid, unmoving in his boots.

Tess gritted her teeth, fearing she'd burst into a fireball of fury. "I'm not going to stand here and do nothing. You cannot let Mark die. I can't lose him."

"No one is letting him die. We've got a crisis negotiator and ten armed, expert officers protecting him. A peaceful resolution is our top priority." A vein in Willis's forehead throbbed and bulged.

His response exuded confidence but provided zero information. The platitude was probably a handy quote police officers memorized and used when pressed for details they didn't wish to share. "I won't stay here." Tess folded her arms and glared.

"The teams are trained to defuse situations like this. Like I said, restoring safety is our top priority."

Willis's attempt to talk her down from the ledge

fell flat. "I don't give a shit about your priorities. Do you understand how much Mark has suffered?" She lashed out, unable to control her anger a second longer.

Over the radio, officers shouted for Willis to join them right away.

Willis stepped closer and bent forward, near her face. "Listen. I will get him back. Stay here." He raced to join the group, which sped down the trail, dirt flying behind them.

Abandoned, she turned to Declan and stared after the running officers.

"Bollocks, what a fucking cock-up," Declan spat out.

"Take me to Mark. I can't let him go through this alone." She looked up, silently pleading he'd help.

Hesitating, he angled his head and regarded her before sighing. "We shouldn't do this, but I'll help you."

Before either of them could move, shouting erupted, closer than the commotion from a few moments ago.

"Everybody, clear out. Give the men space to move," someone with a bullhorn called. The pounding herd of footsteps reversed direction and started halfway back up the hill.

Declan assisted her amble down the trail, and the sound of footsteps helped her chart the path. She trod over pine needles and traversed two hairpin turns leading to a second clearing. Despite her determination to find Mark, she nearly buckled from the fatigue weighing down her legs. Lactic acid burned in her quads, and her healing leg ached from plodding across the woods.

Two voices rose above the whistling wind, and Declan gestured to their left.

She followed close behind and crouched next to him by a collection of trees tucked out of view.

In the clearing, Dmitry positioned Mark in front of him like a shield and gripped a cocked handgun in his other hand.

Motionless as a statue, Mark stood, his face glistening with sweat.

She raised a fist to her mouth so she wouldn't cry out. A lump lodged in her throat, and her heart pounded against her chest like a wrecking ball swinging against a brick wall.

A lone figure dressed in a black tactical vest and wearing a helmet stepped in front of the armed officers, about four yards from the two men. The man opened his bare hands wide and gestured in Dmitry's direction.

Glancing back and forth, the gunman kept his right index finger hovering near the handgun's trigger and hyperventilated.

A pack of officers with an arsenal of rifles closed around the men, forming a semi-circle.

The hostage negotiator, a slight man with graying hair, stepped forward. "I'm Malcolm Turner. We all want a positive outcome tonight, so everyone goes home safe. Dmitry, would you like to go home?"

The gunman didn't respond.

"I want to understand what's going on. What's on your mind tonight?" Malcolm forged ahead.

Still, no response.

"I want to help you, Dmitry, and I'm not a police officer. I'm someone who cares, and I'm here to listen to what you want to say."

Dmitry scanned both directions. "I borrowed money from Yuri to bribe Russians not to burn my family's house down. But I can't pay it back."

Malcolm nodded. "I understand. You owe Yuri money. It sounds like you don't want to harm anyone, Dmitry." He repeated the gunman's words, followed by empathic phrases, creating an intentional lulling effect designed to soothe.

"No. But I must pay money, or Yuri will kill me."

Tess groaned inside. Dmitry didn't know Yuri was dead. From her vantage point, she caught a couple of police officers in the group exchanging meaningful stares. Holding her breath, she winced as Mark's knees buckled slightly, but he recovered before falling.

"I understand you're worried about paying him back. Where's your family?" Malcolm's smooth bass purred with calm reassurance.

"They're dead. Militants invaded our village and killed my father and brother in front of me."

"I'm so sorry for your loss. I want to understand what you want. What are your plans tonight?" Malcolm kept his voice even, at a steady volume and tone.

"I can't go to prison. I'm trapped. What should I do?" Bending his elbow, Dmitry pulled his weapon back.

"We all want peace—no one hurt or injured. I think you want peace, too, Dmitry. I'm sorry you suffered hard things."

"No more talking." The gunman's voice wavered.

Declan nudged her and pointed to the crowd of police gathering below. Two officers from the back row fanned out to opposite sides, away from the center group. Several uniformed men tightened their grips on their weapons. A tingling lightness buzzed in her head, coaxing her to concentrate.

"I understand. I want to listen to what you need to say and have a conversation. I'm here to help you. Can we agree no one gets hurt tonight? Please," Malcolm continued.

"No." Devoid of expression, Dmitry's demeanor revealed no emotion.

Mark flinched under Dmitry's grip.

Her heart skipped a beat. She held her breath and watched as more police officers fanned out.

The assault team shifted into a new formation, guns cocked and ready.

Dmitry hyperventilated, gasping for air in the throes of a full-on panic attack.

Unable to tear her gaze away, Tess spotted Mark focusing on an armed officer several inches shorter than the others, standing in the front row.

The officer made a subtle hand movement in Mark's direction.

Despite having both arms immobilized, Mark gestured at the ground with one hand while bending his head forward a few degrees and mouthing something. Keeping his gaze locked on the officer, he dropped his chin, pointed one finger toward the ground, and then glanced back up with raised eyebrows and lifted shoulders.

The officer nodded once.

"I want to listen to what you want to say so I can understand. I'm here to help you." Malcolm's smooth, velvety voice continued in a soothing tone.

"Stop. No more," Dmitry shouted, aiming his handgun at the police officers.

Mark dove to the ground in a split second, covering his head with his hands when he hit the dirt, then rolled away.

Meanwhile, gunfire crackled. Two gunshots sounded a millisecond apart, and chaos and shouting ensued while sirens wailed. Dmitry was down.

Halfway down the hill, Tess tracked Mark's movements amidst confusion and a mash of officers blocking sections of the path.

Up ahead, Mark crawled on his chest, using his feet to propel his body toward a thicket of trees at the trail's edge, which could provide cover.

She sped toward Mark as fast as her legs and crutches would allow.

Yards ahead of her, two police officers reached Mark first and lifted him from the ground. "Dr. Nygaard, are you hurt?"

"I'm not injured. I'm okay," Mark murmured in a shaky voice.

"Lots of shrapnel flying. Are you sure you weren't hit?" one of the officers asked.

The other officer scanned Mark for any bleeding.

"No, I'm fine, but if you have casualties, I'm a surgeon and can help." Mark swayed on his feet and nearly fell.

"No wounded. The suspect is deceased. One officer took a bullet in his body armor, but he'll go home with nothing but a nasty bruise and a whopper of a story. You're safe, and we're getting you out of here."

As Tess approached, Mark spotted her.

He stumbled over and collapsed onto her shoulder, half gasping and half laughing.

"Thank God you're safe." She beamed and cried

simultaneously, dropping her crutches to cradle his head with her shaking hands.

He relaxed his shoulders against hers, almost limp. "I want you by my side always."

His warm baritone soothed her with sweet relief. She gripped him tight in an embrace she hoped would never end. "Good, because I'm not letting you go ever again." Captivated by his sapphire eyes and the chiseled curves of his cheekbones, she was barely aware of the relieved tears streaming down her cheeks. Breathing in his sandalwood and cedar scent, she kissed him hard, and his salty stubble bristled against her chin.

The police officers who lifted Mark guided her and Mark back to the Mound, where Declan and Inspector Willis hovered near the park entrance.

Several officers clustered near David, who remained flat on a gurney.

She wanted to check on David before EMTs loaded him into the waiting ambulance. An EMT had inserted an IV to administer fluids and painkillers while assessing his injuries. To her relief, the paramedics had covered David's wound. Bright lights shone everywhere. She leaned over him. "David, how are you doing?"

"I'm alive, which makes me one lucky bloke." Pale and sweaty, David attempted to sound cheery, but his scratchy voice cracked.

"Very lucky, indeed." She wanted to be encouraging but wished he'd been lucky enough not to end up maimed. "Both terrorists were killed, and you're safe. David, I'd like you to meet Dr. Mark Nygaard."

Mark greeted David with a smile. "Nice to meet you. I see the EMTs checked you out, but I'm a trauma surgeon and can examine your hand if you wish."

David nodded and held up his hand. The gauze covering dropped away to reveal the ragged, bloody stump where his finger used to be. "Please. The bastards cut it off."

Quickly, she focused on the trees beyond the clearing to avoid the gory view. She clenched her fists to brace against the stomach-churning reminder of what David had endured. The fact she nearly experienced the same maiming was not lost upon her, and she offered another prayer of gratitude to the universe.

Mark borrowed a flashlight from a police officer and examined David's wound from all angles. "I suspect you've got an infection, given your high fever, but you'll get intravenous antibiotics started tonight. Any chance you still have the finger?"

"No, lost it two days ago."

Mark exhaled and creases lined his forehead. "I'm sorry for your injury, but the promising news is with hand therapy and a prosthetic, you'll retain much of your hand's function."

"Look, I'm just grateful I survived the torture. I'm alive, and my son will still have a father. Nothing else matters." David raised a palm toward the sky.

"Excellent attitude. You're going to be fine." Mark smiled and patted David's shoulder.

"And don't worry about Kingsley Tech. Declan and I will work with Kavita to sort out the banks, and everything will work out fine." Despite her weariness, she wanted the business to survive, as well.

"Tess, I owe you my life several times over." David's voice grew wispy as the painkillers took effect. "You were right, and I should've heeded your warning."

"You're delirious. We'll see you at the hospital." She gave his arm a reassuring squeeze.

The EMTs lifted David's gurney into the waiting ambulance and drove away.

A group of SCO19 officers appeared from the mouth of the wooded trail. Behind them, they wheeled another stretcher loaded with a black body bag, zipped shut, and strapped to the top. *Yuri.* She felt a flood of relief and a clear conscience, free from fear and guilt. Guardian angels take strange forms, and she credited the Raven for coaxing her away from an irrevocable act of rage.

Mark gestured toward the gurney as it wheeled past them and nudged her.

"Yuri confessed to killing Kyle, then committed suicide with cyanide. He's gone." Yuri might have cheated her of the vindication she envisioned, but she achieved justice, and more importantly, she got Mark back alive.

One of the officers approached Willis and handed him a small medication bottle. "We found this prescription vial on the suspect's body."

After nodding his thanks, Willis put on his glasses and read the label, squinting.

"Mind if I see the bottle? Might give us another clue." Mark stepped closer to Willis.

"Please. No idea what this is." Willis acquiesced and handed him the vial.

Tilting the bottle into the light emanating from the rotating police searchlights, Mark studied the label. "Etoposide, a common chemotherapy drug for cancer."

A detail from their captivity jogged Tess's

memory. "While Yuri interrogated me, he was coughing and spitting up blood and mucous, and he wheezed a lot tonight, too."

"Hmm. Yuri could have had terminal lung cancer." Mark handed the vial back to Willis.

"If yer right, the bastard couldn't bear to face the long, painful death he earned. Coward."

Yuri could have easily killed her but didn't, and she couldn't explain why she survived. With Mark by her side, she stared as the EMTs wheeled Yuri's stretcher down the trail and exited the woods. When the gurney disappeared out of view, she snuggled under Mark's shoulder and relaxed, knowing all four gunmen from Cedarcliff were gone forever. She hoped the Raven had escaped the woods, both unseen and unscathed.

Inspector Willis marched over, shaking his head and grimacing. "Chief Inspector Michael Adams was dirty and played everyone at MPS. Mikhail Adamovich, his real identity, was born in Belarus to Russian parents who were both former KGB. They immigrated to England and raised him as an Englishman, and he hid his proficiency in Russian. Tess, if ye hadn't reopened Kyle's case, we wouldn't have discovered his betrayal. He's the mole who hacked Kyle's accident report."

"He's part of Crimson Hammer?" Tess tilted her head, grateful she'd followed her intuition not to fully trust the police.

"Adams blocked my IT investigation of Kyle's record breach, and a network log linked his log-in alias to 00-General."

"You think someone planted him in MPS to run this months ago?" Tess wondered how long ago the conspiracy started.

Willis nodded. "When he didn't show tonight, I sent detectives to search his flat in East Dulwich. No sign of him, but the officers found incriminating paperwork in his kitchen—big deposits from a Russian bank to a Swiss bank account in Adams's name. Someone important had been paying him off for months."

"Bastard's a traitor. Hope you catch him." Declan kicked at a pebble on the ground.

"We prosecute traitors to the full extent the law allows. He'll face prosecution and a lengthy prison term once we catch him. Ye can count on it." Willis set his jaw and planted his feet in a wide stance with his fists clenched.

"If Crimson Hammer directed Adams, maybe when you find him, you can dig for clues about where and how they're hacking. Stop them before they grow any bigger." Tess hoped for Adams's arrest and answers to all the open questions.

A corner of Willis's mouth twitched into a smile. "Odd. HQ just got flooded with e-mails from IP addresses located in Belarus, all identical. They claim the originating IP address belongs to hackers who are breaching banks to fund Crimson Hammer and should be prosecuted."

"Wow, what a lucky break." Tess exchanged a glance with Declan, who appeared nonchalant and more innocent than usual.

"More like a gift-wrapped present delivered on a silver platter. All the data we need to build an airtight case and prosecute the perpetrators. Damn lucky. Somebody did all our work for us. Brilliant." Willis turned to Declan. "Chap, I'm afraid yer jeep got destroyed tonight. A car bomb exploded right before we arrived. Ye folks will need a ride home tonight."

"Tess told me. Figures, given I paid the damn thing off last month. Shite." Declan groaned and exhaled.

Tess felt her lungs deflate. Someone had been tracking her location, watching out for her. Someone who had access to more intelligence data than she did. She suspected the Raven, for he could've spotted the culprit planting the car bomb in the parking lot. She hadn't yet processed the fact she was nearly vaporized in Declan's jeep and gripped Mark's arm to steady herself.

"With all the gunmen accounted for, I'll sleep better at night." Mark released his shoulders and stretched tall again.

Willis shifted his attention back to Tess. "Ms. Bennett, ye finally got justice for Kyle tonight, and I hope it brings ye peace." He had softened his tone.

"Yes, but the damn coward took the easy way out. I wanted Yuri to rot in prison for the rest of his life." Ambivalent, her feelings ricocheted between joy at surviving and anger at Yuri.

"Justice doesn't always arrive in the package we expect or want, but it's justice all the same. Ye both escaped with yer lives, and nothing beats that." Willis zipped up his coat. "Ye folks should go home and get some rest. We'll get a squad car to drive ye back to London."

Inside a trench coat pocket, her mobile buzzed, and she extracted it to check for text messages. The unknown phone number from Turkey appeared again.

—*Bennett, did you make it out? I broke a hundred*

rules to warn your sorry ass. Don't make me wait.—

Beaming, Tess wore a happy grin and texted back.

—Consider this proof of life. I owe you one. How'd you know?—

The phone buzzed one last time.

—Because I know people who know things. See you in Paris soon, and you better show 'cos you owe me, big time.—

Tess pocketed her phone and grabbed Mark's hand. "Let's go home. And if I recall, we've got a date to plan."

"There's no place I'd rather be, *min kjære.*" Mark pulled her into a long kiss.

Passionately returning his kiss, she relaxed into his arms and savored their reunion as well as the hard-earned safety they'd finally won.

The moment was nearly perfect, but she had one more promise to fulfill.

Chapter Twenty-Three

Sun in Wintertime

In the two weeks following the Richmond Park
incident, the brisk autumn transitioned to chilly winter.
Since then, Tess endured frenetic days dealing with the
police investigation, which required multiple
interviews, evidence, official statements, and countless
phone calls. Recounting her role in the events numerous
times for different agencies took an emotional toll.
After Inspector Willis declared they'd collected all the
needed testimony, she collapsed in gratitude, relieved to
never speak about it again.

Remedying the damage Crimson Hammer inflicted
upon Kingsley Tech's customer banks would take
longer. Ready for the challenge, Declan, Kavita, and
their teams did outstanding work to restore order to
their financial clients who suffered losses at the hands
of the hackers.

The first day Tess could take a break from work,
she booked a flight to Norway, and the heaviness
weighing her heart lightened. Before leaving the UK, at
dawn's first light, she boarded the morning train to
Sevenoaks, a small suburb outside of London, to
complete a private pilgrimage. At an open-air shop near
the rail station, she purchased a bundle of vibrant red
poppies, the traditional memorial flower for fallen

British soldiers, then hailed a cab to Greatness Park Cemetery on the outskirts of town. The taxi dropped her off at the Victorian-era chapel, perched at the center of the circle drive, which outlined the manicured grounds. Other than a lone gardener raking piles of leaves by the gated entrance, she stood alone in the sprawling memorial park, and no other visitors appeared.

On the pathway to visit Kyle's grave, Tess strolled through the Lawn of Remembrance, situated in a sunny spot next to an ancient oak tree crowned with enormous branches reaching toward the sky. In contrast to the weathered stones from a century ago, Kyle's one-year-old marble stone gleamed in the light, still shiny. Most World War I soldiers who had died in battle and were buried in this cemetery section were even younger than Kyle, who was thirty-six when Yuri killed him. So many young lives had been cut short decades too soon. Hands clasped, she offered a prayer for all those lost, then placed the bundle of poppies atop his grave. The red flowers burst with vibrancy against the stone's smooth gray-and-white surface. Wood smoke scented the air, and charcoal-colored tendrils curled from the chimneys of neighboring cottages outside the cemetery's fence.

"Kyle, it's me, Tess, and wherever you are, I hope you can hear me. I bought you red poppies, and I have so much to tell you." With one hand resting on his tombstone, she kneeled and spoke of her last year alone and the attack at Cedarcliff. Despite her intention to remain stoic, she cried a few tears but regained her composure and recounted the events at Richmond Park.

"In the end, the Raven stopped me from killing Yuri, but the gunman's cowardice drove him to suicide.

The world is safer without Yuri, and the Metropolitan Police Service is working with Interpol to prosecute the hackers. With the crisis over, I have peace again." Early winter light filtered across the horizon in dim slivers, and a gusty wind swept through the trees, coaxing the last few oak leaves away from the branches and onto the ground.

"The Raven shared your secret, and I'm proud of the lives you saved, serving justice with your talent. I wish I could have fought by your side, but I've got time to figure out how to keep your mission alive."

Back on her feet, Tess paced in a circle around Kyle's grave and surveyed the boxwood hedges, trimmed to perfect flat tops. Random bundles of flowers in various states of decay adorned the rows of graves. Awash in nostalgia, she cherished memories of his favorite song, Big Country's hit, "In a Big Country." The Scottish band's passionate anthem of survival, celebrated with bagpipe rifts and pounding drums, played in her head. "Every time the sun breaks through the clouds, like today, I'll remember you and what you fought for. This song draws your spirit close." In a clear, smooth voice, she sang the lyrics she remembered, about not trying to grow flowers in a desert and surviving to see the sun, even in wintertime.

Tess traced the carved letters of Kyle's name on the tombstone's face, resting a hand on the polished marble. The crisp winter morning marked the season's change but also the time for her to transition to the next phase of her own life. She debated how to share the last, most difficult thing but figured however the afterlife worked, no secrets remained.

She struggled against a lump in her throat. "In your

letter, you asked me to promise I'd find a worthy partner. Losing you gutted me, but while surviving the impossible, I found Mark and can move forward again."

After one last glance at Kyle's tombstone and the red poppies, she caught the glint of something shiny alongside the tombstone. Crouching, she removed her gloves and poked into the dewy foliage, touching something hard at the stone's edge. She snatched the grass aside and picked up the metal object, a round, silver medallion without a chain, which depicted an intricate rendering of a black raven perched on a tree branch. Under her fingers, a rough texture interrupted the smooth, metal surface, and she found a tiny engraving on the pendant's back: *Our blood is still our fathers', and ours the valour of their hearts.*

The Scot's words for the lost Highlanders, Kyle among them, resurfaced all the stages of grief she navigated last year. No doubt the scars from Kyle's death would mark her forever, but they'd heal and fade rather than define her. A newfound acceptance could grow from the wounds and offer her peace.

"Goodbye, Kyle." She placed the Raven's medallion on the tombstone. Her heart softened, then opened, bending to accept what eluded her until now. The morning clouds cleared for a fleeting moment, and smiling, she tilted her face up to the sky, the precious sun in wintertime, and another layer of her grief slipped away.

Chapter Twenty-Four

Winter's Light

The Norwegian winter had arrived early, and a light dusting of snow coated the ground when Tess landed in Bergen that afternoon. The second the plane doors opened, she grabbed her carry-on bag and rushed for the terminal exit. Buzzing with excitement, she hurried to the curb and spotted Mark's tousle of golden hair and sapphire gaze.

In a flash, he rushed over and spun her into a tight hug before kissing her.

He's real, and this is happening. She could hardly believe it.

"Welcome to Bergen, the best place on earth. And you're here with me." He lit up with a huge smile. "And look, no orthopedic boot! I'm glad to see you've healed."

"Yes, thankfully. I'm so happy to see you." Hearing his warm baritone whisked away the stress of the past weeks. She wiped away a couple of happy tears sliding down her cheek, then wound an arm around him. "I've missed you tons, and it feels like it's been forever."

"For me, too. Here, let's get in the car." After opening the passenger door, Mark stowed her suitcase in the trunk and slid into the driver's seat.

"It was two endless weeks of police interviews and client meetings." She settled in beside Mark, and her tension seeped away.

"Everything all right in London?" He started the engine and darted a glance her way.

"Controlled chaos. I'm still acting CEO, and repairing the breached banks took many all-nighters. Fortunately, David got released from the hospital yesterday."

"That's great." He stretched across the console and placed his hand on her leg. "Two weeks without you was a long time. No more work for you—our official first date begins *now*. We'll drive to Bryggen, stroll around the harbor, and enjoy my favorite view."

"Sounds perfect. Quite a spectacular setting for our first outing." Gazing out the window, Tess watched Bergen's lush landscape unfold. The flowing green valleys, fjords, and peninsula created a panorama of contrasts. "Are you happy to be home?"

"Thrilled. Speaking Bergensk, the Norwegian dialect I grew up with, and not spending mental energy on translation is refreshing. Christmas is coming, but best of all, you're here." Beaming, he relaxed his shoulders and broadened his smile.

"I hope you'll speak English until I can learn Norwegian, which might take a while." Leaning sideways, she glimpsed the warmth in his gaze as he nodded, which sent her pulse racing. The road leveled out in the approach to Bryggen, the city's harbor area. Beautiful, green vistas, some dusted with snow, stretched in every direction. Despite the frosty temperature, she opened the window just as the winds gusted and sprinkled fresh mist over her cheeks. Deeply inhaling, she relished the salty marine air in her lungs. "This is stunning—the mountains rise straight out of the sea."

"As a little boy, I believed the seven mountains were mythic warriors who surrounded the city to protect children from evil. I'd like to think they still do." Mark drove with one hand on the steering wheel.

Seeing his windblown hair and easy smile, she imagined him as a young boy, dreaming of mythological heroes and sledding in the snow. "The mountains must be mighty protectors because Bergen appears well-preserved. Can we see the view from higher up?"

"We'll park here, and I'll take you to the best place." He eased the sedan into a parking spot near the harbor's entrance.

The harbor's unmistakable smell of weathered wood, salt, and tar filled the brisk air. Colorful shops and cozy-looking cafés lined the cobblestone street which led to the waterfront. Although historic Bryggen attracted thousands of tourists yearly, the ancient harbor street was free from crowds today. Despite biting winds and thick clouds, she found the cold invigorating and the city welcoming. "Tell me more about growing up here."

"Ah. I'd visit this harbor every *Jonsok*, Midsummer's Eve, with my entire family. We'd eat ice cream, watch the boats, and play in the sunshine. When I feared I'd die in Canada, I dreamed of being here."

"Sounds like a perfect summer day. I can see why you love it." Tess surveyed several open-air booths lining the harbor as she and Mark strolled for several minutes.

Mark gestured to a small ticket booth. "Here we are—the *Fløibanen Funicular*, over one hundred years old. We'll take the tram to the top." He pointed at the cable cars forming a line along the mountain's face, then bought two tickets.

After boarding the cable car, she enjoyed the slow, chugging ride to the top of Mount Fløyen. She followed Mark as he disembarked at the summit, which offered a spacious viewing platform and an expansive vista. Sprawling green meadows nestled near the many fjords, and a safety ledge with a wide railing offered a panoramic view of the coast. With Mark standing behind her, she leaned against his chest, and pleasant warmth spread across her back. She reached behind to grasp his hand and interlaced their fingers, and all his fingertips squeezed hers with equal pressure. Surprised, she turned to face him. "Your left hand—you moved all your fingers!" A hint of pink flushed his golden cheeks.

"My hand therapy is progressing, and the motor control is returning, finally." He tilted the corners of his mouth upward.

"Will you be able to perform surgery?" Eager for happy news, she hoped for good luck.

"I'm cautiously optimistic. Yesterday, I sutured an orange and stitched perfect, straight lines. And my ribs are almost healed." Exhaling, he whistled softly. "No more sleepwalking or night terrors, either. I'll still check in with Dr. Rabinowitz weekly, but happily, I'm Dr. Calm again."

She turned and hugged him. "We have lots to celebrate." Clasping his hand, she strolled with him to the far edge of the platform to see the western view.

Mark's mobile phone buzzed. He scanned a new

text message, first blinking, then laughing. "You'll never believe this. Gordy, a fellow surgeon in Crimea, says our field hospital just received a huge, unexpected shipment of new equipment: a CT scanner, an MRI machine, and two ultrasound machines."

"Generous gift. Any word on who the donor is?" Despite her piqued curiosity, she suppressed a hopeful grin.

"I'll ask." He typed a reply, and the mobile buzzed again seconds later. "Gordy has no clue. The donor required complete anonymity as a condition of the donation. Strangely, though, the shipment included a case of vintage, fifteen-year-old Scotch." He formed a crooked, lopsided smile. "What do you make of that?"

"Nothing beats the kindness of a Scottish stranger." Elated by the serendipitous proof the Raven was alive and well, she released a sigh.

"Indeed." Mark raised the hood on his jacket and tightened his arms around her.

Leaning against Mark, Tess gazed at the mountain vista at the city's edge and inhaled the salty ocean air. Soaking up the landscape's outrageous beauty, she memorized the view of Mount Fløyen and watched the sun descend over the horizon as snowflakes appeared. A calm breeze shifted to a blustering wind. Shivering as darkness fell, she realized the nightmares of Kyle drowning in icy water, which plagued her for months, had finally disappeared.

"Let's take the tram back before it gets too windy. We're staying at the Bryggen Star, a gorgeous hotel with a harbor view. We'll spend a couple of days relaxing—no interruptions and lots of room service." He extended a hand, gesturing for her to walk before him.

"Perfect—I can't imagine a lovelier weekend." Impressed by his foresight and planning, she relished the prospect of cozy relaxation together. An hour later, she and Mark had checked in at the hotel and settled into their suite, which offered a panoramic view of the harbor and a small, but elegant, covered deck. The three-story historic exterior was built of traditional brick, but the interior featured modern furnishings and décor. The spacious room had a king bed with a rich, tufted headboard, an ebony dining table, and a suede couch paired with sizable armchairs.

Mark set their luggage in the corner and flicked on the room's fireplace before stepping over to the dining table. A large wooden tray held an ice bucket with a bottle of champagne and two crystal flutes. "It's not Farmer Campbell's whiskey, but may I offer you a glass?"

"I'd love one." Moistening her lips, she stroked Mark's back.

He cut the foil wrapper and removed the wire cage at the top with a decisive twist. With his thumbs on either side of the cork, he gently pushed and a soft hiss arose before the *pop.* A crackling fizz sounded, then subsided as he poured two glasses and handed her one.

"*Skål.* Here's to us surviving."

"*Skål.*" Attempting to repeat his pronunciation, she clinked his glass and found him grinning. The straw-gold liquid sparkled as the light shimmered through the glass. Effervescent bubbles swirled and spiraled before settling in a delicate layer of fizz. She savored the first sip, detecting citrus and ripe pear with a hint of buttery brioche. "Velvety and lovely."

Mark's cobalt gaze shone bright and glossy, and his lips formed a soft smile. Raising his hand, he skimmed his fingertips over her jawline. "You feel chilled."

"A little."

"Ah." He picked up the room's *Do Not Disturb* sign, slipped it around the outside handle, then locked their door. After picking up the champagne bottle, he nodded toward the bathroom. "Let's get you into a hot bath. Bring your champagne and follow me."

Happy to comply, she followed him down the hall. Tiled in white Carrara marble, the room held a large tub, a double-sink vanity in black onyx, and an array of luxury bath gels. Stacks of neatly rolled white towels filled a cubby under the sink.

Mark set their two glasses and the bottle on the counter, then turned the bath faucet on full blast.

Perusing the options, she selected a bath gel scented with neroli rose and poured it under the running water. A rush of bubbly foam appeared in the steaming water as the bathtub filled. On the counter, the champagne flutes emanated sparkling bubbles with a faint fizzing sound, and she savored a sip before giving Mark a flirty smile. Meeting his azure gaze, she drew him closer. Using both hands, she removed his sweater, then tackled the dress shirt underneath. After inhaling a whiff of his sandalwood and cedar fragrance, she worked each button faster until she reached the white T-shirt underneath and groaned. "How many layers are you wearing?"

Grinning, he emitted a peal of laughter. "It's December in Norway, but we have no bad weather if you wear enough clothing. And slow down, you overachiever—you're leaping ahead. Arms out, please."

Holding out both arms, she stifled her amusement as his subtle smile progressed to a mischievous grin. Trying to contain her eagerness, she relished his touch as he attentively removed her sweater, pants, and lingerie, pausing to caress her bare skin after each item slid to the floor. In contrast, she reciprocated by eagerly tugging off his remaining clothes until nothing separated them but steamy air. Admiring his blond stubble and sculpted torso, she inhaled deeply as a fleeting moment of shyness passed. "Well."

Mark took the bottle of champagne and filled his glass to the top, almost overflowing.

"Thirsty?"

"Very." He tilted the glass and drizzled a stream of champagne over her skin. Quickly, he leaned over and kissed away the glistening drops of sparkling wine.

The sensation brushed her skin like a delicate whisper. With her desire rising, she shifted closer and sought his mouth, parting his lips to taste the wine's citrus zing. She flushed with warmth like a fresh candle beginning a long, smoldering burn. Mesmerized, she cradled his face and committed every contour to memory. "I never want to stop kissing you."

"And I'll never be able to resist you. Ever." While tracing the edge of her jaw, he wound an arm firmly around her waist.

Even before he pressed his bare body against hers, she sensed the magnetism between them, buzzing like electricity. Melding together, she felt like he'd been designed for her. Without hesitation, he moved down her taut body and kneeled, his mouth exploring every inch. Lost in pleasure, she exhaled in thready breaths.

Struggling to form a rational thought, she noticed the scent of neroli rose had grown stronger and wondered why her feet were so wet. Hearing a splash, she opened her eyes and glanced up. "The tub's overflowing…turn off the water!"

Doubled over laughing, Mark leaned over the tub, shut off the faucet, and drained the excess water. "Better not flood the floor." He tossed down a couple of towels and mopped several puddles.

Still grinning, Tess eased into the steaming bath and splashed handfuls of water and bubbles over herself. Having never seen him naked in the light before, she caught her breath and admired his lithe, muscular frame from head to toe and all parts between. Especially *those* parts. "Come on in."

Stepping into the bath opposite her, Mark sat, then arranged his legs alongside hers. "Ah, just the two of us."

"Heaven." She trailed her fingers up his thigh and moved her legs between his before relaxing. Exhaling away the past year's struggles, she concluded the earth had returned to its proper axis after spinning far off its orbit. "Mark, the night we met, you told me we'd make it through everything. Turns out you were right, and you saved me from my grief. Thank you."

"The truth is, we saved each other. I wouldn't be alive without you." Mark grasped her hand from the water and kissed it. "Speaking of which—" He reached for his jeans on the floor and retrieved a small package wrapped in floral-patterned cloth. A smile lifted the corners of his mouth. "A gift to welcome you to Norway."

"More surprises?" She shook the water off her hands and offered a seductive smile. After removing the fabric wrapping, she opened a small, black-velvet case to find an intricate pendant on a delicate chain. "This is beautiful," she breathed, skimming her fingertips over the polished gold. A question formed on her lips.

"This is Freya's Viking shield to protect you from danger. Freya is the Norse goddess of sex, beauty, love, and death. You're my personal Freya, and wherever life takes us, remember to embrace your strength." Mark squeezed her hand.

"This is stunning. I love it." Feeling her heart might burst, she ran her fingers over the artistic engraving.

"Here, I'll help you." He gestured for her to turn.

Rotating, she put up her hair so he could fasten the chain. The weight of the warm gold shield rested on her chest, and she clasped it to her heart. "I will cherish you and this. Thank you." Touched by the gift's meaning, she appreciated how well he understood her. "I've been thinking about what happens next."

"Oh? Tonight?" He raised a playful eyebrow and splashed hot water over his arms. "Do tell."

"After tonight." She threw a handful of bubbles in his direction, eliciting a hearty laugh. Despite spending days strategizing how to build a relationship given their respective careers, she skipped any preamble. "London to Bergen is a short flight, and I could commute each week."

"True, but Norway's peaceful and doesn't need many trauma surgeons. I'd like to work in the US— more challenging cases and better jobs." Leaning his knees to one side, Mark cupped his hand and poured handfuls of hot, bubbly water over her shoulders.

"When David returns, odds are good we'll expand Kingsley Tech to the US, starting with Seattle." Slinking lower in the tub to seek heat, she detected a sparkle in his gaze.

"Hmm. I already researched Seattle hospitals, and there's a top-rated, level-one trauma center where I could seek a surgical post. I mean, if we wished to live closer together."

"Well, I've always wanted a Norwegian doctor—a brave, kind one who can survive anything—and here you are." Glowing, she felt her heart fill with an exhilarating mix of desire, gratitude, and admiration. "I don't care where as long as you're with me."

"So, we agree."

The water splashed as Mark pulled her through the island of floating bubbles and angled her chin to meet his kiss. Rising to stand, she motioned for him to join her. Lost in the moment with his body firm against hers, she enjoyed every breath, nibble, and touch until she couldn't wait another second. "Bed?"

"Yes!"

****

Much later in the evening, she nestled close to Mark on the bed, breathless. Twisted sheets and pillows were strewn across the floor as if a tornado of bed linens had stormed through the suite. After calming her breath, she wiped her forehead, pleasantly exhausted and never so satisfied. "You're unstoppable."

"I hope we can do this again later because I remembered some things I left out." He rolled onto his side and draped a sweaty arm around her shoulder.

"Let's not wait too long." Still aglow from his abridged version, she couldn't fathom what untold delights a complete, unabridged session might offer. She resolved to find out—soon.

"Given your encouragement, anything is possible." Chuckling, he stretched his legs and pulled her close. With a sigh, he stroked her hair and brushed wayward wisps from her cheek. "You carried so much pain when we met, but now you're glowing like sunlight and all peaceful."

"I found hope again." Reflecting upon her morning at Sevenoaks, she welcomed her newfound solace. The anxiety she'd battled since Cedarcliff had ceased, like a deafening noise gone silent.

Casting a glance out the window, Mark broke into a grin. He hopped out of bed and grabbed the two bathrobes hanging in the closet. After slipping into one, he handed the other to her. "Hey, Nordic treat. Come to the balcony."

After wrapping herself in the lavender-scented bathrobe, she followed him outside. The December sun had descended over the fjords hours ago, and frosty breezes gusted across the peninsula. A foghorn bellowed in the distance, and whitecaps surged and receded on the sprawling bay as waves pounded the harbor. Snowflakes fluttered in cascading spirals before melting on the cobblestone streets. The holiday lights wove a shimmering blanket of stars, infusing Bergen with festive cheer.

In that crystalline moment, she finally grasped the concept of home, which had always eluded her. Home wasn't a destination on a map; it meant being with the people she loved. She'd spent a lifetime driven by compulsive motion, all wings and no roots. The realization required she reset her internal compass to a new true north. The future beckoned, one with a happiness she would have found unimaginable several weeks ago. Content, she stroked Mark's cheek. "I crave you beyond reason, and I never want to stop."

"And I'll be with you, *min kjære*, every step." After kissing each of her fingertips, he tightened an arm around her shoulders and pointed high above the horizon. "Look at the sky."

As Tess tipped her head upward, she spotted expansive banners of northern lights in green, purple, and blue flowing through the atmosphere, filling the space between the sea and the boundless sky. Marveling at the kaleidoscope of colors, she felt thankful for the wild, spectral beauty of the lights but also the life she'd reclaimed. Anything *was* possible now…even starting over.

Together, they were home.

Acknowledgements

I'd like to offer my heartfelt thanks to everyone who contributed to my debut novel, *The Unexpected Hostage*.

First, I'm grateful for The Wild Rose Press and my editor extraordinaire, Leanne Morgena. Her incredible eye for detail and tireless efforts made my prose stronger. Kristian Norris, Les Tucker, Lisa Dawn MacDonald, Samantha Keating, and RJ Morris—your expertise was essential to launching! Thank you, Rhonda Penders, for welcoming me to the TWRP garden, and Frances Sevilla, for championing my story.

I'm especially thankful to my book coach, Joshua Marie Wilkinson, for his wisdom. Many authors offered me invaluable advice: Gerri Russell, Pam Bender, Susan Elia MacNeal, Damon Suede, Olivia Waite, Beth Slattery, and, in memoriam, Waverly Fitzgerald. Thanks also go to PNWA, RWA's Kiss of Death Chapter, and Hugo House.

While researching, I benefited from the expertise of Anthony Grieco, CISO, Cisco Systems; Svein Børge Hjorthaug, Microsoft Norway; Karin Huster, Doctors Without Borders; Sergeant Robert Knapton, Royal Canadian Mounted Police; Jonna Mendez, retired Chief of Disguise, US CIA; Kristi Cheldelin Zilbauer, US State Department; and Mike Quinn, former US Marine and CIA officer, who survived the 1983 Beirut Marine terrorist attack and inspired me to explore how people thrive after severe trauma.

Jessica Denhez, Darcey Blinn, Betsy Goldberg, Nancy Holst, Becky Kaplan Farone, Pam Policastri, Amy Taricco—Damsels, I love you! ARC readers, huge thanks. Thank you, Tim Taricco, for website design. Mom, Chris, Nancy, and Mo—thanks for everything.

Finally, Gus and Nik: your encouragement, support, and humor sustain me every day. I love you!

A word about the author…

Allison McKenzie has never shied away from adventure. She is at home skiing Canadian glaciers, exploring Scottish castles, and retrieving cultural artifacts from Rarotongan jungles as she is at her writing desk. After graduating *magna cum laude* from Wellesley College with honors in English literature and attending the University of Cambridge's International Art History Programme in England, she spent most of her career in the software industry.

Allison is the winner of the 2020 Pacific Northwest Writers Association Contest, and a Finalist for the 2021 Daphne du Maurier Award for Excellence in Mystery/Suspense, from the Kiss of Death Chapter of Romance Writers of America, for *The Unexpected Hostage*.

She currently lives in Seattle with her husband, daughter, and two rambunctious cats. She loves theatre, skiing, and Peloton biking to '80s New Wave music. *The Unexpected Hostage* is her first novel.

www.allisonmckenzie.net

Thank you for purchasing
this publication of The Wild Rose Press, Inc.

For questions or more information
contact us at
info@thewildrosepress.com.

The Wild Rose Press, Inc.
www.thewildrosepress.com